THE TERROR THAT WOULD NOT DIE

"We have learned where the American fighter planes are," Rauchman said and pointed to a thin blue line on the map. "We believe our base is beyond their combat range, but they could cause trouble when we begin our takeover."

Martin Bormann was silent. Then, after what seemed like an eternity, he spoke, his voice low and threatening. "Then they must be destroyed. Nothing must interfere with our plans. The Argentinians leave tomorrow and once our battle units are in position we can start our move."

The Nazi leader rose to his feet. "From the ashes of Germany, a new Reich will appear!" he cried. "Our phoenix is ready to fly!"

THE FINEST IN FICTION
FROM ZEBRA BOOKS!

HEART OF THE COUNTRY (2299, $4.50)
by Greg Matthews

Winner of the 26th annual WESTERN HERITAGE AWARD for Outstanding Novel of 1986! Critically acclaimed from coast to coast! A grand and glorious epic saga of the American West that *NEWSWEEK* Magazine called, "a stunning mesmerizing performance," by the bestselling author of THE FURTHER ADVENTURES OF HUCKLEBERRY FINN!

"A TRIUMPHANT AND CAPTIVATING NOVEL!"
— *KANSAS CITY STAR*

CARIBBEE (2400, $4.50)
by Thomas Hoover

From the author of THE MOGHUL! The flames of revolution erupt in 17th Century Barbados. A magnificent epic novel of bold adventure, political intrigue, and passionate romance, in the blockbuster tradition of James Clavell!

"ACTION-PACKED . . . A ROUSING READ"
— *PUBLISHERS WEEKLY*

MACAU (1940, $4.50)
by Daniel Carney

A breathtaking thriller of epic scope and power set against a background of Oriental squalor and splendor! A sweeping saga of passion, power, and betrayal in a dark and deadly Far Eastern breeding ground of racketeers, pimps, thieves and murderers!

"A RIP-ROARER"
— *LOS ANGELES TIMES*

Available wherever paperbacks are sold, or order direct from the Publisher. Send cover price plus 50¢ per copy for mailing and handling to Zebra Books, Dept. 2487, 475 Park Avenue South, New York, N.Y. 10016. Residents of New York, New Jersey and Pennsylvania must include sales tax. DO NOT SEND CASH.

A MISSION FOR EAGLES
JOHN-ALLEN PRICE

ZEBRA BOOKS
KENSINGTON PUBLISHING CORP.

ZEBRA BOOKS

are published by

Kensington Publishing Corp.
475 Park Avenue South
New York, NY 10016

Copyright © 1988 by John-Allen Price

All rights reserved. No part of this book may be reproduced in any form or by any means without the prior written consent of the Publisher, excepting brief quotes used in reviews.

First printing: October, 1988

Printed in the United States of America

Chapter One:
FLIGHT INTO AUSTRIA.
A FAMILY TRAGEDY.

May 1st, 1945

OFFICIAL ALLIED EXPEDITIONARY FORCES REPORT WARNING:
OPEN TRANSMISSION OF THIS DOCUMENT IS IN STRICT VIOLATION OF S.H.A.E.F.E. SECURITY PROCEDURES. VIOLATIONS WILL BE DEALT WITH SEVERELY.

As of April 30th, 1945 this is the tactical situation in Europe. British Second and Canadian First Armies continue their advance into occupied Holland and northern Germany. U.S. Ninth and First Armies have completed their encirclement of German forces in the Harz Mountains and are expanding their link-up with Russian Armies along the Elbe River. U.S. Third, Seventh and French First Armies are continuing their drives across Bavaria (southern Germany). Patton's Third Army has pushed as far east as the Czechoslovakian border and is entering the Austrian city of Linz. The U.S. Seventh and French First Armies have also advanced into Austria, going as far as Innsbruck and Salzburg.

It is expected that the Canadian First Army will finish the liberation of Holland, the British Second Army will make contact with the Russians near Hamburg and American Third and Seventh Armies will make contact with Soviet forces operating in Austria. The Russians have consolidated their hold on Vienna and are driving westward toward Linz.

END REPORT—5:45 a.m.

"Is this the message you're referring to?" Wing Commander Michael Woods asked, lifting a sheet of paper from the unmade bed. "Is this the one Van Hoff was talking about?"

"Yes, Commander," said the duty officer. "If it mentions Austria it has to be. He said his home was free at last and he had to leave. Since we have no ops to fly this morning, I couldn't think of a reason to stop him."

"You should've rung me, I'd have thought of something. This is nothing more than a general report on the military situation here. Though it does mention the liberation of Vienna by the Soviets and their drive west. That might well be his reason for leaving. Look, go to the radar shack and find out what direction Van Hoff is taking. I'm going to see Brandon and Kingston. I believe they should be having breakfast."

While the duty officer ran to get a jeep, Michael Noel Woods walked out of the officers' quarters and down the muddy road to the mess tent. His destination wasn't nearly as far as the airfield perimeter and this was the first time today he had been outside.

Usually, he would drive to the flight line and walk through the rows of parked aircraft. If the weather were good, he would be the first in the air, but not today. This time he awoke to find himself facing an emergency.

He walked as briskly as he could without breaking into a run. Woods knew if his pilots saw their wing commander running, they'd guess something was up and for the time being he wanted to keep this emergency a secret. At the mess tent's entrance, he stood for a moment and scanned the lines of tables. There weren't many officers getting breakfast this early in the morning and most of them weren't pilots. The few who were clustered in a small group, which Woods immediately joined.

"Michael, old chap," greeted Dennis Brandon, clearing a space for him at the table. "I see you just came back. We heard you go up but we didn't hear you land."

"No, I wasn't the one who took off. One of my squadron leaders is missing." Woods pulled from his pocket the report he had found on Van Hoff's bed and laid it down for the whole group to see.

"Well, you have most of your squadron leaders here," said Eric Kingston. "So by the process of elimination it has to be either the Count or Screwball."

"It's Van Hoff, isn't it?" asked Brandon, reading the report. "I don't think a Canadian would be too interested in the liberation of Austria. Not unless it involves shooting down some more German aeroplanes."

"He's returning home," said Woods. "After seven years Claus Van Hoff is going home. War or no war."

"Well, there certainly isn't much of a war to stop him," said Douglas Ward, the one other member of the group. "I haven't had a Jerry in me ruddy sights for over a month."

"How do you really know he's going home?" Brandon inquired. "This is only a general report. It doesn't say anything specific about Austria. Just that the Russians are pushing west of Vienna."

"It was good enough for Claus to leave," said Woods. "He's taken part of his kit with him and he had the flying duty officer give his Tempest full fuel and ammo loads. We should do the same if we're to catch him."

"Somehow, I had an idea you'd say that. Most other wing commanders would've sounded an alert and have sent an entire squadron after the poor bastard."

"That would certainly mean a general court-martial and I just don't have the heart to do it to Claus. He's saved all our tails at least once and we owe it to him. I only want us to go after him, we're not even going to take along our wing men. Dennis, you'll fly my wing and Doug, you'll fly Eric's. Change into your flying suits and meet me in the ready tent."

As Woods was already wearing his one-piece flight suit, he went straight to the rows of hardstands where his wing's mixed flock of Spitfires and Tempests were kept. He ordered the ground crews to arm and fuel his and other, selected fighters. At the squadron ready tent, Woods found himself on the phone as much as dressing for the mission. For someone who started out ahead of the pack, he ended up being the last to get his flying gear on.

"Michael, will you rush it?" said Brandon, impatiently. "The war will be over before we even take off."

"Just a sec, just a sec. I want to leave word for Jerry McCloud that he's in charge of the base."

"What? You're putting Screwball in command?" Kingston asked, a touch of incredulity in his voice.

"When we leave, he'll be the highest ranking flight officer at this base. I'd rather have him in charge than someone from the ground staff. And I need to find out where we'll meet the Americans and what radio frequency they're using."

"Oh God. Michael, you're full of surprises. Why on earth do you want to bring the Yanks along?"

"Because we stand a good chance of running into either an American or Russian fighter sweep over Austria. The Red Air Force, and the American Fifteenth Air Force aren't too familiar with the Tempest. Or did you forget what happened to Dennis's squadron last week? When they were jumped by those Yaks."

"They were Lavochkins," said Brandon. "I thought they were American Thunderbolts until I saw those bloody red stars on their sides. Which Yank unit will be joining us?"

"That Ninth Air Force group down the road. The one you and Van Hoff have been trading French cognac for fresh bacon. Just the group's CO and one of his best squadron leaders. They'll help us should we encounter any quick-to-fire-types. Mustangs with invasion stripes are very distinctive."

"I can hear the 'erks starting up our planes," Ward noted. "C'mon, Mike, let's push it along."

"Okay, that's the frequency? Fine, tell Colonel Reynolds that we'll contact him on it, good-bye." The telephone handset had barely landed on the cradle before Woods had his flight jacket in hand and was leaving the ready tent.

He lagged behind the others, having to both run and finish dressing at the same time. His and Brandon's Tempests were also farther away from the tent than the Spitfires. Their pre-taxiing checks were more complicated as well, which meant the smaller Spitfires had made it into the air by the time Woods and Brandon were turning onto the taxi strip.

They lined up their brutish, angular fighters on the base's main runway, did their last set of ground checks, and pushed their throttles to the firewall. Unlike the Spitfires, the Tempests emitted a flat, deafening howl as they hurtled off the mile-long strip of marston matting. They clawed for the altitude the two Spitfires were orbiting at, then all four broke to the south.

In little more than a minute's flying time, the British fighters were circling over a base very similar to their own. Only the fighters parked in the revetments were different; olive drab and silver Mustangs with very distinctive bands of black and white stripes around their wings. Two of the P-51s were belting down a runway; the sole activity at the otherwise quiet base. They lifted off smartly and circled their home to reach the level of the Royal Air Force fighters.

Like them, they carried external fuel tanks; no one was sure how long the mission would last or how far they would have to roam. The Mustangs slid in on Woods's left wing, making the formation a lopsided, irregular vee.

"How fortunate for us you're up so early, Colonel,"

said Woods. "Tell me, who's the friend you've brought along?"

"Major Tony Acerrio, one of my best squadron COs," Reynolds answered. "He's been in on things like this before. So you don't have to worry about him, he won't say anything to the authorities."

"Yeah but, Colonel, the only time I was ever involved in stunts like this was back in the states," said Acerrio, cutting in on the conversation. "Or in Hawaii before the war. Never in a theater of operations. No offense, Wing Commander, but this guy of yours must be crazy to run off."

"Not crazy, Major, merely out of touch with his country and his family for the last seven years," informed Woods. "Now if we can come about and head due east? And let's lower our cruising speed as we do so? We're dealing with three different types of aeroplanes here, each with its own range and best cruising speed. Your Mustangs have the best range, over two thousand miles, and the Spitfires have the shortest, around eight hundred. My Tempest has a range in between those two and the slowest cruise speed. Would two hundred and twenty miles an hour cause you any trouble with your aircraft?"

"Not unless we fly the whole mission at that speed," said Reynolds. "Then we'd have some trouble with fouled spark plugs. Otherwise, that'll be fine."

"All right, reset your throttles and mixture controls accordingly. We'll stay at this altitude for now. We're above small arms fire though we are low enough to make a good surface search. Standby for ninety degree port turn on my mark."

The mixed formation of fighters swung gently into

the sun and flew south by southeast, the last known course Claus Van Hoff had taken. At their reduced airspeed, they still covered ground rapidly. In five minutes they had left Belgian airspace and were flying over Germany.

Occupied Germany, territory conquered by American and French armies. Here they were still relatively safe, with little fear of drawing ground fire or encountering enemy aircraft. Below them passed bombed and devastated cities, rail lines shattered by air attacks, military bases strewn with wrecked planes, tanks and other weapons of a one-time war machine. Closer to the front lines were the convoys of supply trucks, artillery bases and staging areas of the Allied Armies. Armies on the edge of achieving the final victory they had battled so long for; beyond them was Indian territory. Areas still held by what was left of a crumbling Third Reich.

Now they could expect trouble. Almost at once they encountered other formations of aircraft. Larger and more uniform flights, waves of fighters and medium bombers, all of them Allied, all of them heading for targets inside what was still Nazi Germany. The tiny, irregular vee of fighters changed the structure of their formation, becoming more compact and able to fight should they encounter any Luftwaffe machines.

"All right, we'll do this just like our rhubarbs," said Woods. "Banjo One, you and your wing man will stick with me. Bishop Leader, Pawn Leader, form our top cover."

"Aye, skipper, the crow's nest it be," Ward remarked, answering before Kingston could. "And if I get so much as an Arado trainer in me sights, I'll blast her from the skies."

"Hey, Colonel, who the hell's flying that other Spit?" asked Acerrio. "Long John fucking Silver? He sounds like a goddamned pirate to me."

"His ancestors probably were," said Woods. "Doug Ward's an Aussie. He comes from Botany Bay in New South Wales. He likes to say it was settled by the worst criminals in the British Empire, including his family. I think the real reason why he talks that way is his fondness for Rafael Sabatini novels and pirates movies."

The two Spitfires broke away from the other fighters and climbed nearly a mile above them, their soft green undersides blending in with the sky, rendering them almost invisible. The Mustangs swung under the Tempests and took the positions formerly held by the Spitfires, with Acerrio switching from Reynold's left wing to his right.

"Okay, our top cover is set," said Reynolds. "What should we start looking for, Mike?"

"Another Tempest, with markings just like mine," Woods answered. "Either in the air or on the ground. As we draw closer to Vienna, we should pay particular attention to any airfield occupied by the Russians. It's my guess that Van Hoff's flown to one of them and obtained some form of transport to his family home. Unless the Russians have shot him down."

Over enemy territory, action did increase though it was mostly Allied action. Bombing runs and strafing attacks by the waves of aircraft seen earlier. Only occasionally could a line of tracers curving up from the ground or mid-air flak bursts be seen. Apart from dodging those which came too close, Woods ordered that there be no retaliation taken. There were enough prowling fighters on target-of-opportunity strikes to deal with those anti-aircraft guns which had been so foolish as to reveal their positions. A few times, American and Free French fighters approached the tiny group; convinced so small a unit had to be German. But Reynolds's profane shouting convinced them all that the odd assortment of planes were friendly.

Swiftly, the types of Allied aircraft encountered changed from basically American to predominantly Russian. Yak fighters and Ilyushin Shturmoviks roamed the countryside in loose, unorganized gaggles. They displayed none of the precision of the Free French or U.S. Army Air Forces and attacked virtually anything they saw; even villages where there was no enemy activity. Unable to communicate with the Russians, Woods's formation had to rely on the prominent D-Day stripes worn by the Mustangs to identify them all as friendly.

"Better pull in our top cover or some of these eager bastards might shoot them down," Reynolds warned.

"Understood, I'll bring them back," said Woods. "I think with this much Soviet activity, the Luftwaffe would be very foolish to put in an appearance. Pawn Lead, Bishop Lead, this is Checkmate Lead. It's time to return . . ."

The Spitfires dove on the pairs of Tempests and P-51s, rejoining the formation though not completely, staying a little behind and on top of the others. Minutes later the collection grew again as a flight of Yaks swung in beside Brandon. The Russians waved and grinned ludicrously at their allies; Brandon was forced to keep them entertained while the rest continued to search for Van Hoff's plane.

"Banjo One, take a look to our right," said Acerrio. "I think it's a city. Hey, Colonel, is that Vienna?"

"I believe it is. Banjo One to Checkmate Leader, we have Van Hoff's home town on our right wing. I think I see an airfield as well. Let's swing over and investigate it."

"Let's do as he says, Michael," added Brandon. "These Ivans appear ready to explode if we don't turn in the direction Colonel Reynolds wants us to."

"Very well, it's one we haven't examined yet anyway," said Woods. "I only hope your Bolshevik friends will understand why we won't be landing if we don't spy another Tempest."

The airfield Acerrio had spotted was on the northwest side of Vienna, on the bank of the Donau River. Unlike the previous Russian bases the formation had seen, this one was permanent, with buildings and asphalt runways, instead of a grass field with tents. It had obviously been used by the Germans and heavily attacked during their occupation. Most of the base's buildings were either destroyed or badly damaged and wrecked Luftwaffe planes lay scattered all over its grounds. Rows of Yak fighters, Il-2 Shturmoviks and the odd C-47 were crowded in among the wrecks. And no Tempest could be seen.

While the American and British fighters circled the base, the accompanying Yaks started waggling their wings again and even lowered their landing gear.

"My friends will be very upset if we don't land," said Brandon. "I think they'd shoot us down if we tried to leave."

"I think they would as well," Woods noted, glancing

at the four dark green fighters lined up beside his wing man. "What am I going to do? This isn't turning out the way I wanted it. If we land, we'll end up spending most of the day partying with those Bolsheviks. That, we can't afford."

"I know, there's a war we have to get back to," said Reynolds. "Maybe we can use this to our advantage. Maybe we've been searching the wrong way. If we land, perhaps we can get the Russians to do the search for us."

"All right, we'll try it. What the hell, we can only be court-martialed as well for abandoning our posts. Checkmate Leader to group, dump your undercarriage, we're going in."

The Yaks stopped rocking their wings when the landing gear cycled down on the Tempests and P-51Ds. They broke away and entered the circuit for the airfield. The Tempests and Mustangs followed the Russians closely, the Spitfires trailed a little farther behind. First, they had to lower their own landing gear.

The Russians landed in pairs, the group followed suit with Woods and Brandon touching down first. The Soviet personnel on the field cheered wildly as each set of British and American fighters taxied into the tarmac area. They surrounded the planes the moment they came to a halt, crowding them so much that Woods had to hurry his post-flight checks.

With a final, loud howl the Tempest's Napier Saber engine was shut down. The propeller hadn't even stopped ticking over when a burly, exuberant Russian in a khaki uniform stepped onto the fighter's wing and peered inside the cockpit. The moment Woods cracked open his canopy he was greeted as a 'comrade' and treated to a short, repetitious speech in Russian. Once his seat belt and shoulder harness were unlocked, the giant reached in and grabbed Woods by his shoulders, lifting him out of his seat like a small child.

He was given a bone-crushing hug and repeatedly kissed before being handed over to the crowd which swarmed around his plane. They carried him on their shoulders and Woods found he was shaking so many hands, he didn't have a chance to wave. The cheering grew to such a din that Woods could scarcely hear the Mustangs and Spitfires taxi in barely ten feet away. He did see Brandon, Reynolds and Acerrio get hauled out of their fighters in much the same way he had. The celebration would have gone on for hours if it weren't for the intervention of a Soviet officer wearing a flight suit.

"I am happy you came to land!" shouted the officer, so he could be heard above the din. "We have so much to talk about. Are you commander of this squadron?"

"No, in a sense we're all commanders," said Woods, being lowered to the ground. "Though I am in charge of this outfit."

"Why are you here, comrade? Are you on mission? Come, I'll give you fuel and bullets. We go on mission together, we kill many Germans."

Just then Colonel Reynolds arrived, carried on the shoulders of more ground personnel. Some fourteen years older than Woods, though of the same relative rank, he was not quite as lean and had the beginnings of what would in later years be called a craggy face. With a sharp order from the Soviet officer, the enlisted men that had brought him from his Mustang put him down.

"You, you are older," said the officer, turning to Reynolds. "Are you commander of this squadron?"

"No, Wing Commander Mike Woods here is in charge. I'm Colonel Jack Reynolds, U.S. Army Air Force. From the stars and red stripes on your shoulder boards, I'd say you're a lieutenant-colonel. And that medal on your chest means you're a hero of the Soviet Union."

"Correct, comrade!" The Russian beamed a smile that looked buffoonish. Reynolds had just won an instant friend. "I am Lieutenant-Colonel Victor Chubukov of the One-thirty-third Air Guards Regiment. I am happy to meet both of you. Come, I wish to meet your wing men. We go party, then we go fight. With so many guests, we will have a great party. Not like the Twenty-ninth Air Regiment, they only have one guest where we have six!"

"Wait a minute, did you say that another unit has a guest?" Woods inquired, pressing in close to Chubukov. "What kind of guest? A pilot like us? Did he fly a plane like mine?"

"I don't know. Why do you wish to know, is this important?"

"Yes, it's why we came. We're looking for a pilot who left my command. If we don't locate him, he could be charged with abandoning his post in time of war. He could be courtmartialed. Can you find out for us?"

"I think I can," said Chubukov. "If this is why you came, then yes. I will help you. Come, let's collect your friends. We go to base commissar's office. He will have radios that we can use."

Chubukov started shouting orders at the crowd swirling around him and his new friends; the response was immediate. The cheering died away and those pilots still being carried were put down. Whatever direction Chubukov moved in, the crowd parted, making way for him. He met with the Yak pilots who had landed with him and started explaining the reason why the other Allied fighters were at their base.

"How did you know his rank?" Woods asked. "In all my years in the Royal Air Force, I've scarcely run into any Soviets."

"I met quite a few when I was with the A.V.G. in China," Reynolds explained. "And last year, my group was one of the first to get the P-51. We escorted shuttle raids for the Eighth Air Force and you tend to see a lot of Russians in Russia."

"Michael, what's wrong with these people?" Brandon asked, pushing his way through the crowd. "They're acting like the bloody war is over and it isn't. Not yet anyway."

"Russians like to celebrate," said Reynolds, before Woods could answer. "You should've seen them when we landed at Piryatin after our first shuttle raid. And if you think this shindig is something, wait until you see what they do throw when the war does end."

"I hope we're not waiting around here for long," said Ward who, with Kingston, had just arrived. "Ruddy damn wogs, one of them pinched me cigarettes."

"What? Did they break any?" Acerrio inquired.

"How do I know if they broke any, mate? They took'em from me when they hauled me up on their shoulders."

"Commander Woods, Colonel Reynolds, please bring your squadron with me," said Chubukov, returning to his new friends. "We are going to base office. I have ordered for us a transport. Come, we go now."

The transport Chubukov had referred to was a captured German half-track; still in its Wehrmacht warpaint, though its swastikas had since been overpainted with large, red stars. It came clanking down the flight line, pausing for a few moments to pick up the pilots, then it veered to the right, heading past the hangars to the administrative area. Inside one of the less-damaged buildings, Woods and his group found themselves facing the chief political commissar of Chubukov's air regiment.

An argument broke out between them before all of Woods's group had filed into the commissar's office. Since the exchanges were entirely in Russian, the group had to rely on Reynolds and his limited knowledge of the language.

"Christ, this bastard may call all the way to Moscow to find out about us," he whispered to the others. "I think he thinks we're spies."

"Leave it to a politician to come up with that," said Kingston. "We should feel lucky we don't have this kind of command. It'd be like having Clement Attlee telling us what to do."

"You, Wing man Woods, come here," demanded the commissar, pointing to the officer he wanted.

"It's Wing Commander Woods," he corrected, stepping up to the desk. "Michael Noel Woods, of the Royal Air Force."

"You are South African, Mister Michael Woods. Two of your friends here are British, two are American and one is Australian. And you are all here to find another friend, who is Austrian. This is very international, it reminds me of the international nature of communism. Of the help allies must extend to each other. It is good that you came to us, the forces of the Soviet Union are always ready to help those of its Allies. I will find out where your missing friend is and give you transport. In the spirit of international cooperation that will see the defeat of the Nazi hordes."

The commissar picked up the handset to the field telephone which sat on his desk. Chubukov told the group that the call was being made to the base's radio office and they would relay the request to the Twenty-ninth Air Regiment. Several minutes and a string of Russian oaths later, the commissar had the information he'd been impatiently demanding.

"Your friend's name is Claus Van Hoff?" he asked of Woods. "Good, he did land at our forward airfield near Laaben, which is south of us. He left his fighter there and was driven north to an estate called Falkestaaten. The house is marked on our tactical maps, it's the regional headquarters for the Nazi Gestapo. Is that where you wish to go?"

"Yes, it is," said Woods. "I recognize the name. Falkestaaten was Van Hoff's home before the war. We all heard it'd been taken over by the Nazis but we didn't know it was being used by the Gestapo. Do they still hold it?"

"No, our victorious army captured it early this morning. If that is where you wish to go then you will. I will have transport ready for you. Lieutenant-Colonel Chubukov will go with you, he will see to your needs."

The commissar had a few words for Chubukov, in Russian, as the group left his office. He caught up to them in the building's front entrance and ran out ahead of them, flagging down a large sedan that was just pulling alongside the halftrack they had used earlier. Chubukov opened one of its rear doors and urged his friends to climb inside. The car's interior was far larger than a normal staff car in either British or American service. Even so, six pilots all wearing flight gear and parachutes easily filled it.

"This is the commissar's own personal transport," said Chubukov, climbing in next to the driver. "I was able to convince him to let us use it. In the spirit of international cooperation. We will have no trouble getting to the house of your friend. No one would dare to stop this car."

"Except for some Germans with a bazooka," said Acerrio. "I've seen tanks that were smaller than this thing. In my neighborhood, you had to be a Mafia boss to drive around in a car this big."

"Mafia? Tell me, is that political party in America?"

"You could say it is. They arrange things, they get things done, for a price. And they always set that."

"Are they like the communist party?"

"Yeah, but they got class."

"Then they are not like the communist party. The communist party of the Soviet Union has no class."

"Buddy, you just said a mouthful," Acerrio replied.

"All right, let's not become involved in politics," Woods advised. "We're jammed in here like peas in a pod and we have a long drive in front of us."

"No more than half an hour, comrade," said Chubukov. "Gestapo not far. We strafe them vonce, twice then the commissar tells us not to do it no more. Says army wants to capture it in one piece. Many secrets inside. Is this why your friend went to the house?"

"No, as I explained before, he went there because it's his family's home. None of us had any idea what the Germans were using it for. Our friend didn't even know your forces had captured it. He simply left after he'd received a report on how far our armies had advanced. He hasn't seen his home or his family for seven years. What are you out to discover, comrade? That we're on some sort of secret mission?"

"He probably is," said Reynolds. "While I never learned enough Russian to really speak it. I do know you were told to watch us and find out what we're really doing here. So much for international cooperation."

"Comrade, you misunderstand," replied Chubukov, still beaming a friendly smile. "I am here to see you don't have any troubles and find out how we can help you more. Your Russian is not so good as my English. Perhaps you would like to talk in Chinese? I speak Chinese, I served in the Ninth Air Army in the far east before here. I know you speak it. The words on your plane are Chinese."

"It's what my group in China was called. The Fei Weing, the Flying Tigers. I do know a little more Chinese than Russian but only enough to make sure that civilians realized I was American and wouldn't tear me apart after bailing out."

"Bailing out? You mean to parachute from plane? I

vonce parachute from plane in the far east. Whole command, whole squadron of Zeroes jump on me from sun . . ."

The ride did take little more than a half hour, though with Chubukov describing his exploits, it seemed a lot longer. Whatever check points the staff car came across, the guards at them immediately waved it through; it scarcely had to slow down. Away from the airfield, away from the river it sat beside, the vehicle entered a scenic range of low, forest-covered mountains, the Wienerwald. The Vienna Woods. Foothills to the Austrian Alps.

Here they were closer to the front lines. The echoes of small arms fire could occasionally be heard, as could the dull thuds of artillery shells. Most of the fighting was confined to the valleys, with Soviet forces holding the high ground and firing at the retreating Germans. Tanks were everywhere and all of them were Russian. Lines of T-34s clogged the roads and any clear ground they found. They made travel difficult for all other vehicles, except of course for the staff car. All its driver had to do was impatiently blare its horn and entire convoys would move out of its way. With this kind of response, Woods and his group had few problems reaching Van Hoff's home.

Falkestaaten appeared to be carved out of the very summit of one of the Wienerwald hills. There was only one road that led to it and, again, it was jammed with vehicles. This time however, there were no tanks but trucks and more than a few staff cars. The one Woods and his group were driving in added to a growing collection of such vehicles when it turned into the courtyard. As soon as it came to a stop, the soldiers in the courtyard were either coming to attention or opening the sedan's passenger's doors. They were visibly confused when out popped a half-dozen Allied pilots instead of the expected commissar and his entourage. Chubukov told the group to wait by the car then disappeared, charging into the house where he hoped to find an official he could talk to.

"I'm taking my parachute off, Colonel," said Acerrio. "I was like a goddamned sardine in there. I haven't felt claustrophobia like that since my last 'Fifty-one caught fire."

"We were all pretty cramped," said Woods. "It comes from wearing full flying outfits. You're quite right, Major, we should dispose of our parachutes. Eric, see if you can't open this car's boot. If it's a fraction of the size of the passenger compartment, we can stow all our parachutes in it."

Taken together they filled the staff car's trunk, though the driver was still able to shut its lid. Chubukov made a boisterous reappearance at the house's main entrance, urging his friends to come in.

"Comrades, I have found your mate!" he shouted. "He is here. He is meeting with officials, hurry."

Freed from the bulkiest of their flying gear, the pilots ran for the doors and stuck to Chubukov's tail.

"Christ, this is a fancy place," said Reynolds, as they moved through the home's luxurious interior. "What does Falkestaaten mean, Mike? State of the falcons?"

"Close, it means 'falcon estate'," Woods corrected. "Van Hoff told me his family was known for raising and training prize hunting falcons. He often said he left his home a falcon and became an eagle."

After the front foyer came a huge lobby with a double staircase that wound down from the second floor. Chubukov led the group up it, squeezing past soldiers who appeared more interested in looting the estate than merely occupying it. Even officers were joining in and anything made of brass, pewter or silver was hungrily snatched up. Scattered among the scavengers were a few people more interested in confiscating files and other papers than in carting away valuables.

On the second floor Chubukov became less sure of his directions and had to open several doors before finding the room he wanted. Woods and his group followed him in and were delighted to find it wasn't being ransacked like the rest of the estate. When the heavy door was closed behind them, the din was muted; apart from that the room was comparatively quiet. The only activity going on inside turned out to be a heated argument at the far end. It was here the group found Van Hoff.

His blue uniform immediately distinguished him from the Russians and their German prisoners. He was fairly short but slim and definitely had an aristocratic look about him. If he hadn't been wearing Royal Air Force colors, his blond hair and blue eyes would've put him in with the Germans he and the Russians were questioning.

"Squadron Leader Van Hoff!" Woods barked. "We would all like a few words with you. If you wish to retain your rank, you will oblige us, immediately."

"My friends. My friends, I didn't mean for you to become involved," said Van Hoff, breaking out of the argument and running to greet his fellow pilots. "Why did you come? And why did you bring the Americans along?"

"So other Americans wouldn't shoot us down. And we're here because you abandoned your command in time of war. It doesn't matter much whether fighting has all but ended or not. It could still put you before a court-martial board. We know why you're here and we understand but you must come back with us. If not, we'll be in trouble in addition to you. Have you learned anything about your family?"

"Nothing, these pigs have told me nothing that I want to know. They talk to me about the Geneva rules of war. They are more willing to talk to the Russians than to me."

"That's because you ain't got no muscle behind you," said Acerrio. "These comrade-types have a whole fucking army behind them. Even if most of 'em are busy robbing you blind. Have you seen what these goons are doing to your home?"

"I have and it's of no matter to me. Most of what they are taking was brought in by the Nazis. What I'm concerned about is the fate of my family. For seven years all I've heard is rumors and now I want the truth. One of those animals back there knows but he's hiding behind the Russians and the Geneva Convention."

"Officers of the Soviet Army do not allow Nazi butchers to hide behind them," Chubukov stated. "This is a mistake. Please to let me correct it for you. Come, show me which one of these butchers killed your family."

He took Van Hoff by the arm and towed him back to the room's opposite end, where the argument had resumed following Van Hoff's departure. The appearance of a Soviet Air Force officer halted the interrogation of the German prisoners once again. After he introduced himself, Chubukov asked if the commissars would respectfully turn over to him one of their prisoners for special questioning. The one Van Hoff had indicated.

Chubukov reached into the collection and pulled out one of the black-uniformed Germans. He dragged him away from the rest and stood him by the room's ornate picture windows. Quickly, Woods and his group circled around their prisoner, cutting him off from the outside; they wanted to make their interrogation as private as possible.

"Under the Geneva rules I am only to give you my name, rank and serial number," the German announced, as he looked carefully at the pilots surrounding him. "You, I will not even say that much to. You are a traitor to the Aryan race."

He meant Van Hoff, who reached for his neck before Brandon and Ward stopped him.

"Easy, mate. We'll let you tear his head off later," said Ward. "Let's find out about your family first."

"You, you are the oldest." The prisoner turned away from Van Hoff and faced Reynolds. "Are you their commander?"

"That's the second time today someone has asked me that," said Reynolds. "To answer your question, no I'm not. But if I was, I'd give you sixty seconds to tell us what we want before I stop being an officer and a gentleman."

"If he doesn't give us the lowdown on the Count's family, I say we slit his gut," Acerrio suggested. "We can always tell the Ruskies he committed hara-kiri."

"No, the Japs commit hara-kiri, not the Germans. This is Europe, Tony, remember? We're not in the Pacific anymore."

"You are joking," responded the German, nervously. "I don't have a knife. How could I kill myself?"

"Don't worry, I'll find one," said Acerrio.

"Who is commander here? One of you must command."

"I am," said Woods. "And you now have thirty seconds to reply to Squadron Leader Van Hoff's demands. If you don't, I'll hand Major Acerrio the knife he'll use on you. I happen to carry a Hitler Youth knife as a souvenir."

To prove his threat, Woods pulled from his belt a black handled, short-bladed knife with a single edge. Etched on the blade was the Hitler Youth motto *'Blut and Ehre'*; Blood and Honor. Woods slipped it to Acerrio who immediately placed its point on the prisoner's stomach.

"Wait a minute, wait a minute," said Reynolds. "I've a better idea. One not as messy. Tony, you remember that routine the Mafia had for shaking down people in your city?"

"Of course I do, Colonel. You don't think I'd forget something like that, would you?"

"Would you like to demonstrate it with our friend here?"

"Sure," Acerrio purred, handing back to Woods his souvenir. "Keep this on hand, will ya'? Open those windows behind us. Okay, Mister, you better reconsider what you just said, real quick."

The German put up a brief struggle as he was

pushed back to the windows. His resistance continued until Reynolds punched him in the stomach and he went limp.

"My friends, you do not wish to kill him?" asked Chubukov, who was looking as nervous as his prisoner. "Do you? How will I explain his death to the commissars?"

"Tell them we gave him a flying test and he didn't pass," said Reynolds. "We're not going to kill him, Colonel. We're just going to make him wish we would."

Kingston swung open two of the window's hinged panels, then the prisoner was set down on its sill. Acerrio belted the slouching figure in the nose and he sailed out of the room, only to snap to a halt as Reynolds and Acerrio grabbed his feet. The prisoner slammed hard against the house's exterior facade; causing him to cry out in pain and lose his skull emblazoned cap in the process.

"Mister, you had better start singing like a bird or learn how to fly like one!" Acerrio shouted. "I've had it up to my ass with you bastards. Some fucking master race you are! Start talking, Mister, start talking!"

"My stomach, I am going to be sick," warned the prisoner, the color draining from his face, even though he was upside down. "Bring me inside I tell you. I am going to be sick!"

"Then you'd better tell us what we want to hear. If you barf your cookies all over those troops below us, they'll probably shoot you. I know I would."

"All right! All right, I will tell you what you want. Please take me in, please!"

With a note of reluctance, Acerrio and Reynolds

hauled the prisoner back inside, though they did keep him balanced on the sill.

"Okay, you've got your chance," said Acerrio. "But if you jerk us around, I'll dangle you by your dick next!"

"I will tell. Let me get my wind," said the German and, after a few moments, he began to tell the story everyone wanted to hear. "The Van Hoff family was arrested on March thirteenth, 1938 and the estate was seized at that time. The family, your family, was separated and held in several 'institutions' in Vienna until 1940. At that time, they were moved across the border, to Germany proper. They were reunited and taken to our special internment camp outside of Munich."

"Oh my God, he means Dachau," Reynolds clarified. "Patton's army liberated it about a week ago."

"Your family has long since been turned to ashes," the prisoner added, just before Van Hoff jumped on him. While Woods and Chubukov tried to pull him off, there were others who wanted to see justice served.

"Michael, let 'im have the bastard," said Ward, grabbing hold of Woods. "I say he deserves it."

"Atta boy, Count. Tear his fucking head off," said Acerrio, squeezing into the middle of the battle as Reynolds was trying to yank him out of it.

Curses and epithets started to fly in English, German and Russian though few punches were thrown, and most of those were aimed at the Gestapo officer in the center. The fight became a tight ball of struggling figures. It moved away from the window and toward the center of the room. As it did so, those on the inside of the melee lost their balance, causing everyone involved to come crashing down. Out of it popped the

German, with Van Hoff still holding onto him.

Chubukov was the next to rise out of the heap and he was easily able to pry the much smaller Austrian off his prisoner. Then he started to slap him around as he dragged him back to the stunned commissars.

"Easy, Claus," said Woods, restraining Van Hoff. "I'm sure he and all the others will be given justice. The Russians might even shoot them all when they're done with them."

"I would like to be here to see that," Van Hoff replied. "Even if they weren't the ones responsible for the deaths of my family. It's their kind who are responsible."

"True enough, but if you really want the guilty party, you should go to Dachau," said Reynolds, helping Van Hoff and the others get back on their feet. "Patton probably captured all those butchers and will hold them for war crimes trials."

"Excuse me, Count but why was your family thrown in a concentration camp?" Acerrio asked. "I thought the Nazis only put Jews in 'em?"

"More than Jews were sent to those camps," said Van Hoff, taking a seat at a nearby table. "The mentally ill and political prisoners were also condemned to them. My father and older brother were members of the Christian Socialist Party and my father was even a member of parliament. I left home three days before the Nazis invaded my country and one day after they had, my entire family was arrested. My parents, my brother and sister, even my grandparents and other relatives. That much at least I knew was true. But for seven years after that, all I heard was rumor. Nothing could be substantiated until this minute."

"What he said might not be true," said Kingston. "The bastard might've been lying, Claus."

"Why on earth would he lie?" Woods asked. "Look at the beating he received. Do you think someone would've invited that on himself, if by saying the precise opposite he could've escaped it? No, the German told the truth."

"I so wanted to hand this back to my father." Van Hoff had by then removed from his flight vest a small, hinged box which he opened. Inside was an iron cross, complete with ceremonial ribbon. Van Hoff lifted the medal up by the ribbon and dangled it in front of his friends.

"Ah, Jeez, you RAF-guys always get the good souvenirs," said Acerrio, admiringly.

"This is no souvenir. My father won it in the First World War, when he was in the Austro-Hungarian Air Service. He gave it to me the day I left, for safekeeping. He was afraid the Nazis would take it from him if they came. I promised him then I would return this when the crisis was over and I kept it safe since that time. Neither of us guessed the 'crisis' would last so long and I would be the only survivor of my family."

"I remember a time or two when you didn't keep it so safe, mate," said Ward. "When you took that there cross on a few missions. The ones none of us thought we'd ever come back alive from?"

"That's because I didn't want anyone else to have this," Van Hoff explained, carefully returning the medal to its case. "I knew if I died, someone would eventually take it as a souvenir. This is part of my family and it always will be. If not with my father, then with me. And now, this is all I really have to remember him."

He snapped the box shut and returned it to his vest. Woods put his hand on Van Hoff's shoulder and started to speak, only to be cut off by Chubukov's return.

"Comrades, we must leave at once," he announced. "Your friend as well must come with us. Hurry, please."

"Why, what's wrong?" asked Reynolds. "Are your political superiors going to have us arrested?"

"No, my friend. They like you, they like the way you questioned the Nazi pig. They wish for you to question the rest. If we don't leave at vonce, we could be here for all of today. You, everyone, must leave. I want to leave too. I want to kill Germans, not question them. Please, we leave."

"All right, we're going," said Woods. "Claus, it's time for us to leave. I'm sorry. I'm sorry for everything that's happened. Your family, your home—but we simply must go or the situation for all of us will become much worse."

"I understand," Van Hoff replied, getting out of his seat. "I don't wish to stay here, either. There are too many memories for me and I want their stain washed from this place . . ."

He pointed at the Germans the commissars were interrogating and had started to raise his voice when Woods and Reynolds cut him off. They didn't want to attract any more attention to themselves. The group quietly backed out of the room and plunged into the raucous turmoil outside.

By now large items of furniture were being scavenged off the estate and the chairs, bureaus, sofas, even beds, clogged the stairs and the first floor to such a degree that Chubukov had to start pushing people out of the way. Things were a little better in the courtyard, at least they didn't have to fight to get to their cars.

"We'll go to your airfield first," Woods told Van Hoff. "Collect your aircraft and you fly to the base the rest of us landed at. We'll meet you there, see if we can't be refueled and perhaps we may fly a combat sortie with our Russian friends. It's the least we owe them. If we're lucky, we'll be back at our home field by noon and I hope no one beyond our group captain has found out about this."

"Yes, I understand, Michael. And again, I'm sorry for having involved you in this, but you know why I had to do it. At least I've discovered what became of my family, now I must track down those responsible for killing them. For the rest of you, the war will end in a few days. For me it will not end, not until those who murdered my family are given justice. This I promise and I will let nothing stop me."

Chapter Two:
DISCHARGE.
THE MISSION BEGINS.

To: Col. Jack E. Reynolds, U.S.A.A.F.
   Officer commanding, 319th Fighter Group,
   2nd A.T.A.F.
   Tempelhof Air Base, Germany.

You are cordially invited to a farewell party for Wing Commander Michael N. Woods, who is leaving the Royal Air Force to return to the wilds of South Africa, where he will abuse impalas and have his privates eaten off by lions. Festivities to send him to this colony of sexual perversion with animals and agonizing death shall begin promptly at 19:00 hours, or seven o'clock for those of us who will soon be returning to civilian life, on Sept. 10th. Said festivities will take place in the officers club at R.A.F. Gutersloh and will continue until all participants are either unconscious or under arrest by base security. You may bring any number of guests with you, provided they are all female, and additional supplies of spirits is encouraged.

From: Sqn. Ldr. Dennis Brandon, R.A.F.
　　　Gutersloh Air Base, Germany.
　　　9/5/47

"Good evening, Colonel and welcome. I see you've managed to bring along what we most needed," Brandon greeted, as Reynolds entered the club. He took from the arriving officer an armload of liquor bottles and carried them to the bar. "These are more valuable than fräuleins, we already have enough of those. So far, you're the only American who's appeared. What's happened to the other Yanks we invited?"

"Most of them are at a stag party," said Reynolds. "One of the forty-ninth's pilots is getting married next week. And stag parties are more fun than farewell parties. The others have been transferred or back in civilian life, which includes Major Acerrio. He got his discharge papers about six weeks ago. I may be the only American to show up."

Freed of his gifts, Reynolds picked up a drink from the bar and plunged into the party, where he was, for the time being at least, the only khaki uniform amongst a sea of blue.

"Reynolds, old chap, good to see you again," said Kingston, as he joined a circle of familiar faces. "It's been months since we last saw you. How've things been with the American forces of occupation?"

"On edge, for the last few days," Reynolds admitted. "Ever since that bomber of yours got shot

37

down."

"Yes, regrettable business. Bloody Ivans are becoming more untrustworthy by the week. We very nearly lost our guest of honor in that incident. He became lost in poor weather and his flight wandered dangerously close to Soviet lines."

"Really, how did you get back?" Reynolds turned to ask his question of Woods himself.

"Another Lincoln found us," he said. "From the same wing that lost the one we were looking for. It had a radio navigation compass and led us back to base. When we landed, we found that the pilot of the Lincoln was none other than Geoffrey Sinclair, commander of the bomb wing. He's here now, perhaps the sole bomber pilot in the whole lot."

"Well, mate, how's it been?" asked Ward, joining the circle with a round of fresh drinks for everyone. "I've heard you people are going to be wearing uniforms like ours soon."

"Yes, Congress has voted to make us a separate service," said Reynolds, beaming proudly. "The United States Air Force. The change should happen at the end of this month. We're busy getting new forms, insignia and painting USAF on all our planes, just like when we had to paint in those red bars on our markings back last January. And yes, we are getting blue uniforms. At least I'll be able to serve out my final months in a uniform and a service I always dreamed of having."

"You mean you're being discharged as well, mate?"

"No, unlike the rest of you, I'm retiring early. I just turned forty and all I'll be able to fly in the new

Air Force is a desk. So I'm taking an early retirement and joining my younger brother; he's set up an air service and has a job all ready for me. He should, I've invested enough money in his operation."

"Well it sounds like you got a ready career for yourself," said Ward. "Wish I had me a job all set. Here, mate, would you like t'have a fresh one?"

"No thanks, I'll just nurse this one along."

"Okay, suit yourself. I'm not going to let this one go to waste." Ward lifted the proffered glass and downed its contents in one long gulp.

"Jesus, you're drinking like this is your party too."

"Oh, but it is," said Woods. "Douglas is also leaving the Royal Air Force tomorrow. He claims he'd rather have his celebration in Australia though he does seem to be enjoying mine."

"Someone has to be the life of the party, mate. What with Screwball McCloud gone, this base is positively dull."

"That's right, I haven't seen him around either," Reynolds remarked. "Or that Austrian of yours, Van Hoff. You're losing all your top men; where have they gone?"

"They left the service as well," Woods explained. "Jerry McCloud was transferred back to the RCAF before he was discharged. Van Hoff left about two months after the fighting in Europe ended. He went back to his family's estate in Austria. Remember that little trip? And how we all were almost court-martialed for it? I think the RAF was glad to let him go."

"Boy, for a guy who had nothing to go back to, he sure left fast. What's he doing? Have you heard from him?"

"In the more than two years since he stepped out of the uniform, hardly anything. But we know he's been active in the hunt for war criminals. He helped the occupation forces in Austria find a few. He's been all over the continent, apparently some of his family's fortune survived the war."

"But we'll be finding out soon what the Count's been up to," Ward added. "He sent us a telegram a week ago asking if we could visit him after our discharges."

"Do you think you will?" asked Reynolds.

"Of course, mate. We each got a couple of weeks of back leave coming and I sure'd like to spend some of it on an Austrian vacation. Maybe Michael here might not. After all, he does have a little woman to get back to in South Africa."

"Oh that's right, I haven't seen your wife around here," said Reynolds, turning to face Woods. "I only saw her briefly, at your wedding a few months ago, I wasn't able to stay for the reception. In fact I don't see any wives here and I know Brandon and Kingston are married."

"They've been sent home," said Woods. "Eric's being transferred back to Britain and Dennis's wife is pregnant. In fact very pregnant and Dennis would prefer she have their first child in a British hospital in Great Britain."

"It's not that I don't trust the base hospital we have here," Brandon injected. "It's just that her parents and my parents would like to be there when the baby's born and I can't afford to bring them all here. I'll be there as well. I'll fly to England in a few days on leave and when I return, I will have Michael's job and rank."

"It seems like all of us are on the move," said Reynolds. "Or soon will be. Well, Mike, will you be going on an Austrian vacation or heading back to South Africa?"

"I think I can afford to make a side trip. I have nearly as far to go to reach South Africa as Ward does to reach Australia. My wife knows I'll be making side trips. Like your brother, I'm also interested in starting an air service. A photo mapping business to be exact and I want to look for some suitable aeroplanes. I might not find much in Austria but you never know . . ."

The party lasted far into the night, though its guest of honor decided to turn in at the relatively early time of three a.m. The following day Woods was one of the first people up. He had to if the other revellers were to awake and it would be a long drive from northern Germany to Vienna.

For the last time, his batman brought his personal car to his quarters. A vintage 1934 Mercedes, it had been his for two years, ever since his wing was stationed in Germany with the Second Allied Tactical Air Force. His uniforms and belongings were carefully packed away, as were Ward's and a small circle of friends came out to stand by the car.

"I've made sure that your tank was filled with petrol and here are some names you can use at American army bases in the south should you need more," said Brandon, after giving Woods his final, official, salute. "You'll find a map in the car with a clearly marked route on it. You should reach Falkestaaten by late afternoon. Give my best to Claus and write to us, Michael. I'd like to keep in touch, I don't know when we'll see each other again."

They hugged and shook hands and then it was Ward's turn to say good-bye. Woods slid into the driver's seat and started the engine; the moment Ward was inside he gunned it. The Mercedes lurched away from the assembled officers and took the circuitous route to the base's main gate. Woods and Ward drove past the flight line one last time, taking a long look at the fighters they had flown for almost three years. Then they left, receiving one more salute from the guards at the gate as they drove through it.

Once clear of the base, they turned south, taking a series of interconnected local roads and intact sections of the autobahn system. Some seventy miles later, they encountered their first checkpoint. One which marked the beginning of the French zone of occupation and the end of the British zone. Woods and Ward were asked to produce their discharge papers, travel permits but little else. After a perfunctory exam they were on their way, driving across central Germany without a stop until they reached the American occupation zone.

"Hey, mate, could you tell us where we can pull off the road and relieve ourselves?" Ward asked of one of the American sentries. "Me bladder's ready to burst."

"We'll take care of that when we reach Regensburg," said Woods. "Excuse me, Corporal but could you give us good directions to the Regensburg Army Base? A friend of ours told us we could buy some petrol there."

"Sure, I'll give you guys directions, it's not far. I'll also phone ahead and let them know you're coming. You guys are civilians now, remember? If they don't know who you are, they'll probably turn you away at the gate. It's a good idea to get gas before Austria, things in that country are bad. They have shortages and supply problems; it seems like the Russians are only good at fucking things up these days."

"You know, he's right, Mike," said Ward, after they had driven past the checkpoint. "We're forgetting that we're not in the military anymore. I've been out of it scarcely two hours and already I miss it."

"No, you don't really miss the Air Force," corrected Woods. "Not with all the complaining you've done. What you miss are aircraft. Being in the cockpit of a fighter or any kind of aeroplane for that matter. But you don't have to be in the Air Force to enjoy it. You know how far our countries have demobilized, there are thousands of surplus aircraft. There are fields full of them and you can have one for a few hundred pounds. That's how I'll start my photo mapping service. I'll buy a Spitfire or a Mosquito, perhaps one of each, and fly them back to South Africa."

"Maybe I'll try that. A recon Spit is such a sweet flying kite. I took one up a few times and she was truly maneuverable. With the weight of those cannons and machine guns gone, her controls were almost as light as a ruddy Tiger Moth's. It almost made me become a recon pilot, only I don't think I'd have felt too safe flying over Germany with no guns."

"Well those days and those fears are long since gone. Now, if we choose, we can fly for the fun of it. With the only worry being how can we make it profitable."

The stop at Regensburg lasted less than a half-hour for Woods and Ward, mostly because the army base had been warned to expect them. Refueled and relieved, they continued on through lower Bavaria; reaching the Austro-German border by noon. The checkpoint at Passau was manned by Russians and they demanded not only discharge papers and travel permits but passports, driver's licenses and car registration as well. The wait at the border ended up taking longer than the stop at Regensburg. Woods and Ward started to wonder if they would ever see their documents again when everything was returned and the toll bar was lifted.

Inside Austria, the roads were in poor condition and there were more mountains to either climb over or avoid. As best he could, Woods stuck to the winding course of the Donau River. Crossing from one side to the other whenever the road was blocked. The farther east they travelled the more familiar the terrain gradually became, though it was hard to recognize without columns of Russian tanks moving around it. In the forest near Vienna, the map Brandon had given his friends was no longer needed. To Woods and Ward even the trees along the side of the road were familiar.

"I remember this area," said Ward. "It hasn't changed much. Remember how we were all packed in that comrade's car?"

"Commissar, Douglas, Commissar," Woods corrected. "I can recall how cramped we all were and how one of our American friends, the Major, was ready to jump through the roof."

"Oh, you mean the guinea. Yeah, I remember him too. He sure had a fancy trick for interrogating that SS swine. Hey look, I think I can see Claus's home."

First, they had to drive through the front gate. It wasn't until they were almost inside the courtyard that they could clearly see Falkestaaten. Unlike the last time, the road approaching the estate and its courtyard were empty. The Soviet vehicles were long gone as were the soldiers who had pillaged it. Woods drew his Mercedes up to the estate's main doors; it looked more intact than previously but appeared empty. He tapped the horn a few times then shut the engine down. As he and Ward climbed out of the car the heavy doors cracked open and a black man in olive drab clothes appeared.

"Looks like Claus has hired himself some colored domestics," said Ward.

"Quiet, Doug," Woods ordered. "That's enough of that. Let's not start off on a bad foot here. Good afternoon, would Count Van Hoff happen to be in?"

"He is, Mister Woods, Mister Ward and he's been waiting for both of you," said the man. "And no, I'm not the butler, domestic or any other servant. My name is Jesse Clinton and you could say I'm the Count's assistant."

"Nice to meet you," said Woods, shaking Clinton's hand. "Though you're not wearing any insignia, I'd judge that you are or were in the American Army."

"Yeah, my tailor's the U.S. Government all right. I got out of the Army Air Force a couple of months ago. Until then I was with the Three-thirty-second Fighter Group, what the Army called an all-negro outfit. If you'll come with me, I'll take you to see the Count."

Clinton turned and walked back inside the estate with Woods and Ward in tow. The front hall and lobby were almost bare, as if the Russians had just left, taking with them whatever they could lay their hands on. The sole furniture in the lobby was a set of overstuffed file cabinets. The stairs were no longer jammed with pillaging troops and the sound of boots marching up them no longer echoed through the room. On the second floor Clinton led his guests to the same room they had been in two years ago.

Some of its furniture still remained, the large table especially, though its matching set of chairs were all gone. Covering the table were large-scale maps of Europe and the world. Pinned to each map were small forests of colored flags. Hovering around it all was a familiar figure, moving the flags as if he were planning the strategy for a war.

"Michael, I'm so happy to see you, and Douglas," said Van Hoff, stepping around the table and greeting his friends. "I thought you wouldn't be here until much later but I see that the roads and the border guards weren't as bad as I feared."

"We made good time once we were in your country," Woods replied. "So, is this what you've been doing since you left the Royal Air Force? It looks like you're doing research on the war. If you're going to write the history of World War Two, I'm afraid General Eisenhower and Winston Churchill have stolen a march on you."

"No, I am waging what is now a more important battle. Come here, I'll show you . . ."

Van Hoff took his friends to his strategy maps and began to explain their meaning and what he was doing.

". . . The last time we were in my home, in this room, I made a promise to find those who imprisoned and killed my family. For the last eighteen months, I have been doing precisely that. I am hunting down those Nazis who have eluded capture by the Allies."

"But aren't the Nuremberg Trials taking care of them, Claus?" Ward asked. "I mean they've been going on for almost two years, mate. And take a look at all the bigwigs they've caught and sentenced."

"Yes, most of the major figures have been caught and put on trial," Van Hoff admitted. "But for every one of those, two more have escaped. Including some of your 'bigwigs' . . ."

Also on the table was a large stack of folders. Van Hoff reached for them and skimmed off the top few. He opened the cover of the first one and started to read from it. As he finished each, he slapped it back on the stack.

". . . Martin Bormann, deputy Fuhrer under Hitler from 1941. One of the most powerful men in Germany during the war years. He is believed to have escaped from Berlin as it fell to the Soviets and has not been seen since. Adolf Eichmann, from 1939 the commander of the Jewish Section of the SS. Not seen since 1945 and believed to be in either Spain or South America. Doctor Josef Mengelé, member of the SS medical department, called the Angel of Auschwitz and responsible for all 'experiments' carried out in that camp. He too, disappeared in '45 and is believed living in Egypt. These men alone are responsible for crimes without number, for crimes that are almost beyond human comprehension. They, and all the others that are identified here, came from some of the most civilized countries on Earth and are responsible for atrocities against humanity and civilization. What they did to my family is but one crime they committed. I have since realized that these animals must be called to judgment for all their crimes, not merely one."

"And you're going to do it all by yourself?" Ward asked, a little incredulously.

"No, there are others. There are of course the governments you made mention of. The victorious Allies and the new governments of Austria, Italy, Czechoslovakia and nearly a dozen others. There are the Jewish groups, including one based locally. It's called the Jewish Documentation Center and it's run by a Pole named Simon Wiesenthal. I've exchanged information with him, his center is in

Vienna. And finally there are the individuals like Captain Clinton here and myself. Each trying to settle his or her own personal injustice. Most have given up, or have settled for the Nuremberg Trials. It's not that they didn't have the same determination I have, they simply don't have my resources."

"What resources?" Now it was Woods's turn to be incredulous. "We've just come through a big, drafty house that's practically empty. I wonder if you even have a bed to sleep on and you're looking a little thin, Claus. You don't look much different than the day you left the RAF, a titled nobleman with little more than his title."

"And I always thought I couldn't slip much by you," said Van Hoff, smiling slyly. "Though perhaps I should say it was my father who slipped it by you, and not me. In the weeks before the German invasion of my country, my father transferred a large portion of his wealth to special accounts in Liechtenstein. Everyone thinks a Swiss bank account is secret, those in Liechtenstein are even more so and much of the wealth my father transferred was in gold. When I left he gave me the account numbers and beyond him, I was the only one who knew.

"That fortune has funded my operations in many ways. The price of gold on the black market is many times its legal value and I've found people are more willing to talk for a few ounces of the precious metal than for any amount of paper money. So far, Captain Clinton and I have been doing rather well, but we could do better if we had more manpower."

Van Hoff was smiling slyly again; it took a few

moments for his friends to catch on to what he was suggesting.

"I don't know, Claus," said Woods, still giving the idea consideration. "I promised my wife I would be home soon and both of us have far to go."

"Speak for yourself, mate," said Ward. "I'd like to help for a little while but, Claus, are you sure you can use us? I mean all we are is a couple of ex-fighter pilots."

"That's all I am. I had to learn how to become my own intelligence officer. It is easy, I will teach you how. Even if you don't feel you can do it, I need you because of your contacts inside Allied military forces."

"Contacts? What contacts?" Woods asked. "All we know best are other pilots. What can they tell you?"

"A great deal, especially if they're assigned to the various Allied occupation headquarters in Berlin. Or are part of units stationed there. For instance you, Douglas are the friend of Squadron Leader Desmond Kain, of the Royal Australian Air force. Friends since childhood as I recall. Squadron Leader Kain is currently an exchange officer with the Royal Air Force and is assigned to British Occupation Headquarters in West Berlin. You, Michael are acquainted with Colonel Reynolds of the American Army Air Force. His fighter group is stationed at the Berlin-Tempelhof airfield. What he doesn't know, his friends in the American Army will. So you see, you two can be very useful to me for the next several days."

"It won't be for long, Michael," said Ward. "And

you did say you wanted to make a couple of side trips."

"Yes, but this isn't one of them," Woods protested. "I'd like to look for photo-reconnaissance aeroplanes."

"If it's focus birds you want, perhaps I can help," Clinton offered. "There's a lot of surplus airplanes in storage in Italy and North Africa. American, British, even German and Italian, and you can get them for scrap metal prices."

"I know, there's dozens of those centers scattered over Germany. Filled of course with Luftwaffe aircraft. All right, Claus, I'll see what I can do for you, for a short time. But why can't Mister Clinton help you in Berlin? After all, he was once part of the Army Air Force."

"He has to stay and work," said Van Hoff. "Someone has to update the files and be here to receive new information, should any come in. Besides, he served in the Mediterranean Front with the Fifteenth Air Force. His circle of friends does not extend to Germany. That is why I need you."

"I see your point," Woods admitted, finally. "If Mister Clinton will find me the planes I want, I'll help you attain the information you need. It's too late to start back into Germany today. We can leave tomorrow morning, I think my car has enough petrol to make it back."

"There's no need to use your car, my friend. The very least I can do is provide transport. You shall stay tonight in my guest rooms and in the morning, I will drive you to Vienna, and from there we'll head for Berlin."

Early the next day Van Hoff woke up his guests and gave them a large breakfast, warning them that it would probably be their best meal of the day. Leaving Jesse Clinton to watch over things, they left in one of the estate's cars.

Though Vienna was only a few miles away, it took almost an hour to reach the city because of the checkpoints they had to stop at. Inside the city they crossed rapidly from one zone of occupation to another and every time, they had to stop for inspection. Beyond the checkpoints however, Van Hoff drove straight through Vienna. Bypassing its railway stations, crossing the Donau River and eventually ending up at a small airfield on its eastern outskirts.

"When you said transport, I thought you meant an auto or a train," said Woods. "Never for a moment did I think of an aeroplane. You must have the only one in all Austria."

"No, there are a few others on the Austrian civil register," Van Hoff corrected. "But mine was the first. Here, help me open the doors."

They walked to one of the airfield's few hangars and rolled open its main doors. Inside were more than just airplanes; cars, a tractor and other farm equipment. There were in fact just two airplanes. A dismantled biplane that looked like a DeHavilland Gypsy Moth and a powder blue Me-108.

Externally very similar to the '109 fighter that came after it, the dainty Messerschmitt was easily pushed out of the hangar by the three men.

Roughly the same size as the fighter, it weighed less than half that of the '109 and had cabin seating for four, instead of a single-seat cockpit. Three pilots made the pre-flight check of the aircraft a very quick procedure, then Van Hoff climbed onto one of its wings and opened up its canopy.

"This aircraft was captured from the Luftwaffe at the end of the war," he said, as he folded the first, then the second clamshell door forward so his friends could enter the plane. "It was held in storage briefly before it was 'requisitioned' by a Royal Air Force unit stationed near Vienna. They used it as a squadron hack for nearly a year before they received some official equipment and I bought it from them. The instant the Austrian civil aviation authorities allowed the registration of private airplanes, I had the *Taifun*'s papers all drawn up."

"*Taifun*, that means typhoon in German doesn't it?" Woods asked. "I certainly hope she doesn't fly like one of our Typhoons. Took one up once, damned crate almost ran off the runway even after I kicked in full right rudder."

"No, she's a pleasant flying kite, almost impossible to stall. She doesn't have the performance of a fighter but I think she will surprise you. Michael, you can have the other front seat and, Douglas, the back is all yours."

While Woods took the co-pilot's position, Ward climbed into the Messerschmitt's spacious rear bench seat. Van Hoff came in last and closed the canopy around them. The leather upholstery and uncluttered interior were a radical change from the fighters Woods and Ward had so recently flown. Van

Hoff had to gently remind them to strap in for take off.

"Your seat belts, gentlemen, your seat belts," he said. "And when you're finished, Michael, could you hand me the flight chart for Berlin? You'll find it in the map case in front of you."

"Of course, have you already filed a flight plan for Berlin?"

"No, but I'll file it with Vienna Control as soon as we're airborne. In case you didn't notice, there is no tower or any other facilities at this field. All we have is an airstrip, some hangars and a pile of wrecked aircraft."

"Yes, I took a glance at'em when we first arrived," said Ward. "They're Focke-Wulf One-nineties, mostly. Plus a few Eighty-eights and an M.E. or two. I'll bet you'll find them a good source of spare parts."

"I can obtain a few items from them but mostly I rely on the Nord aircraft factory in France, where they still build the Me-one-oh-eight as the Nord One thousand. Watch your knees, Michael, I may have to use the fuel reserve switch and don't put your feet on the rudder pedals. Standby to start engine."

Van Hoff cracked open the throttle and punched the starter button. The Messerschmitt's Argus engine coughed and its propeller spun hesitantly. As jets of blue smoke came out its exhaust ports the propeller became a soft blur. Once the warm-up checks had been made, Van Hoff released the brakes and steered the Me-108 to the field's one runway where he did the magneto tests and other pre-flight procedures. Then he pushed the throttle to the gate stop and let the Messerschmitt sail down the strip, picking up speed until it lifted off the ground on its own accord.

"Thank you, Vienna-Schwechat, this is Oscar-Delta-Lima, out," Van Hoff replied, hanging his microphone back on its hook. "We're cleared to Berlin. We'll take a direct route across Czechoslovakia, three hundred and fifty miles. I don't know if we will always be able to do that, its government may fall to the communists."

"And you'd better watch it when we reach the East German-Czechoslovakian border," said Woods. "Make sure you stay well inside one of those air corridors the Russians have marked. About a week ago an RAF Lincoln wandered over the border and the bloody Ivans shot it down. They might've had me and my entire flight if it weren't for the timely intervention of another Lincoln. He had the nav systems to lead us back home. I don't think your aircraft is so equipped."

At cruise altitude, Van Hoff levelled his *Taifun* out and set course west by northwest. At cruise speed, it took a little over two hours for them to fly from one divided city to another. On reaching Berlin, they had three airports to choose from but only one would put them down in the middle of the city—Tempelhof, in the American zone.

For its size, the Messerschmitt was a rather conspicuous sight, flying the pattern with civilian airliners, military transports and sharing the flight with such giants. Once on the ground, Van Hoff taxied over to a group of U.S. Air Force Mustangs and parked as close as he could to them. The arrival of the sleek, little *Taifun* drew the attention of some air force personnel and that made it easy for Woods to get word to Reynolds.

"God, this is a surprise, I thought I'd never see you two again," said Reynolds, greeting Woods and Ward out on the airport apron. "Not unless I went to Sydney or Cape Town for a vacation. What brings you to Berlin?"

"He does, I'm sure you recognize him," Woods replied, pointing to Van Hoff, who was busy postflighting his plane. "He has some questions he'd like to put to you."

"You're the Count we went hopping all over Austria for during the last days of the war. Van Hoff isn't it? Mike talked about visiting you at his discharge party. How've you been and what are you up to?"

After exchanging some pleasantries with Colonel Reynolds, Van Hoff started on an explanation of his activities over the last two years. Then he made his requests, for information on the war criminals still at large and in particular those who worked in Austria during its annexation.

". . . Many of those survived the war and have escaped capture," added Van Hoff. "I have traced some of them through Italy, others through Spain. I suspect they've gone to South America but I'd like to be positive. Can you help?"

"I'd sure as hell like to, I just don't know if I can," said Reynolds, thinking for a few moments about his answer. "U.S. intelligence is all screwed up. You see, not only are we forming a new military force, we are also creating a new intelligence service. The old OSS is long gone. In its place they're building something called the Central Intelligence Agency. It's a civilian outfit and they're having jurisdictional disputes with Army and Navy intelligence, even the FBI. They used to run spy operations in South America and now the FBI has to turn them over to the new guys. There's friction in Army intelligence itself over who will stay and who'll go into the new air force."

"So, you're telling me that you can't be of much help?"

"Yes, but I'd like to help anyway. Let's go to my office, I'll write you a letter and give you some names you can try at occupation zone headquarters. And if you'll push your plane a little closer to my flight line, I'll have her gassed up and ready to go when you return. I hope when you go to headquarters, that you'll have something to bargain with. Otherwise, they might give you a sympathetic ear, file your request and forget you."

"I believe I have some information that might interest them." Van Hoff held up his briefcase and shook it, rattling the contents inside. "About a Condor named Hessen."

In Reynolds's office they also ordered a civilian taxi, which was waiting for them at the airport entrance. From Tempelhof it was a short drive to the headquarters for the American zone in Berlin. Van Hoff told his friends to wait with the cab while he went inside. It was their only means of travel around the city and at any rate, if the Americans had what Van Hoff wanted, he would not be long.

Forty minutes later, they were still waiting for him to appear.

"Claus, what on earth went on in there? Our driver's becoming impatient," said Woods, the moment Van Hoff came storming out of the entrance.

"Why should he be impatient? He's being paid well for this, I'm not. Come, we shall try the British next."

Van Hoff brusquely led Woods back to the cab and, with Ward, piled into its rear seat. He was equally curt with its driver, barking orders at him to head for the British section of Berlin.

"I'm sorry my contact wasn't of much help to you," said Woods. "I'm sorry you came all this way for nothing."

"Don't apologize, it's not your fault," Van Hoff replied. "And we have come away with something. I now know how difficult it will be to work with the Americans. This new service of theirs, the CIA, has yet to properly set up its offices in Berlin and it is, shall we say, at crossed swords with U.S. military intelligence. I think if Russian tanks were to start rolling past the Brandenburg Gate, they would still be arguing. They treated me as if I were a Soviet agent and refused to share any information with me. At least we know how disorganized and paranoid they are and we do have a full tank of free petrol. Only an American could've given us that, everyone else still rations it."

"I hope Donny Kain can be of more help," said Ward.

"I hope so as well. In due time we shall find out, the British checkpoint is just ahead of us."

From the checkpoint it was not far to the headquarters for British occupation forces. This time, Van Hoff took his friends with him into the building where Ward asked to see the Australian exchange officer, Squadron Leader Desmond Kain.

They found him in a tiny office among a rabbit-warren of rooms. His desk was piled high with paperwork and he was staring absently out the window at the aircraft heading in for Tempelhof Airport. When Ward announced himself, Kain bolted out of his chair and embraced his friend.

". . . And I see you've brought along some of your squadron mates," Kain noted, looking over Ward's shoulder. "I've seen you before, you're Mike Woods. You're Doug's CO. You I haven't seen but I think I recognize you. You're that mad Count who flew with these two during the war, aren't you?"

"Yes, I am Claus Van Hoff. Though I won't admit to being mad, at least not for now. Douglas, would you care to explain to your friend why we're here, or shall I?"

"Look, Donny, Mike and I have come here to help Claus with an investigation of his," said Ward, his warm smile getting replaced by a more somber, serious expression. "Remember that story I told you about the last days of the war?"

"You mean the one where you had to chase the mad Count all over Austria? You bet I do."

"Well the reason he was hopping around Austria was to find his family. He found they had been killed at the Dachau death camp and for the last two years he's been tracking those responsible. He'd like to know, I'd like to know, if you can help us."

"Believe me, mate, I'd love to, but how?" Kain asked. "I'm stuck here in a desk job, out of my element. What I know best is flying fighters. If you know where these bastards are, I'd be happy to lead an air strike against them."

"You don't have to do anything quite so extreme," said Van Hoff. "Merely give us a name or two from your intelligence staff. Particularly those working on this problem."

"I don't even know if I can do that. I spend the day here pushing paper from one cubbyhole to another. I never thought I'd envy transport pilots but I do, at least they're flying. Come along, mates, let's see if we can't pin down someone from MI-Six. I'm sure they'll help."

They didn't. The MI-6 officers that Kain and the others were able to talk to had little information to offer Van Hoff in exchange for his and didn't really seem interested. In essence their reaction was similar to the Americans and Van Hoff's disgust was the same. After an hour of evasive answers and dated information, he stormed out with the others in tow.

"I'm sorry I couldn't help your friend, Doug," said Kain. "But I simply don't have much authority with military intelligence or the Foreign Office. As I told you before, aircraft I know, spying I don't."

"There's no reason for you to apologize," said Van Hoff. "I shouldn't have expected anything more from you. I think aviation is all we really know."

"Look, I can give you one lead, Mister Van Hoff. A few weeks ago, I met this chap from the French occupation headquarters at a party. Like me, he's an air force officer grounded to a desk. Unlike me, he wanted the assignment so he could hunt Nazis. His name is Captain Clostermann, André Clostermann and he wants the men who killed his fiancée. She was a resistance fighter in their home town. I think he'd be the best man in Berlin for you to talk to."

"Very well, Michael, tell the driver that our next stop will be French headquarters."

"The Frogs? I suppose I'll have to have me passport ready for inspection again," sighed Ward. "It's been fingered so many times it's beginning to fall apart."

To reach the French zone of occupation they had to drive back across the British and American zones; which meant being stopped once more at the various checkpoints. French headquarters was almost exactly like the others, save for the flags hanging from its facade.

This time Van Hoff went in alone. He found Clostermann cloistered in a tiny office like Kaine, half-heartedly pushing papers for some useless duty. All Van Hoff had to do was mention the Australian's name and what his mission in Berlin was for the Frenchman to abandon his work.

"In a way, I already know of your work, Mister Van Hoff," Clostermann admitted. "We share a mutual friend. Major Daniel Green of the U.S. Army Air Force in Italy. We correspond, write letters to each other on occasion. He's told me what you have done, I am glad to have met you."

"Thank you, Captain, it's nice to know I'm gaining a reputation. Then you should know why I'm here. I've gone beyond hunting down the butchers who exterminated my family. I want the rest, as many as possible if I can have them. I've come to Berlin to gather information on which of the escape routes the uncaptured Nazis are most using and which country is providing them with the best sanctuary."

"I'm afraid you're asking for something that's beyond my knowledge and, unfortunately, beyond the care of French intelligence. Unlike the Americans and the British, Berlin is not quite as important to my government. Indochina and Algeria are. My government does not choose to hunt Nazis, it recruits them for service in the Foreign Legion. As a French officer, it is something I'm not proud of. For all I know, those who killed the woman I loved are in the Legion."

"Squadron Leader Kain told me about that. Tell me, was she in the resistance?"

"She was a courier for the local cells. Our home town is near Lyon and when she was caught, they took her to prison there and later executed her."

"I have information as to the location of Klaus Barbie," said Van Hoff, dropping a name that made Clostermann miss his step. "The Butcher of Lyon, though I need not tell you that. I had thought the Americans were using him but I now know he's in Italy, probably in Genoa, probably trying to leave Europe. I want to know if that's the major escape route, or is it Spain or is it Sweden?"

"I couldn't tell you that," Clostermann replied. "At least not officially. My job here is not an intelligence. But based on what I have heard, I can tell you to stay with Italy. A great many Nazis seem to be using it, more so than Spain or Sweden or any other European country. As to where they're finding the best sanctuary, I would say South America. In any event, please tell me should you find anything. I want very much to help but, remember, all I am is a fighter pilot chained to a desk."

Chapter Three:
ITALY.
UNCOVERING THE PIPELINE.

"Tempelhof Control to Messerschmitt Oscar-Delta-Lima, we are handing you over to Prague Control. Maintain current speed and heading and you should cross the Czechoslovakian border in the next eight minutes. Tempelhof Control, out."

"Thank you, Tempelhof," said Van Hoff. "I'll be calling Prague on their frequency. This is Oscar-Delta-Lima, out."

"Claus, did you ever share that information you brought with you?" asked Woods. "About a Condor as I recall. I take it you mean a Focke-Wulf Two Hundred?"

"Yes, it is about a Focke-Wulf and no, I didn't share it with anyone in Berlin. The British and Americans who I talked to weren't interested in what I had and Captain Clostermann said I didn't have to pay him for what he gave me."

"What exactly do you have on this plane? Would you mind showing it to me?"

"No, I wouldn't mind. Here, take the controls while I retrieve my case." Van Hoff reached behind his seat

64

and brought forward his briefcase. Balancing it on his knees, he opened it; making sure its lid didn't bang against the control yoke. He pulled out of the case one of several folders, slapped the lid back down and spread the folder's contents on top of it. "The Focke-Wulf Condor in question was one of the very early models. Built before the Germans converted the type from an airliner to a maritime patrol bomber. It was given a civil registration, Alpha-Sierra-Hotel-Hotel and was turned over to Lufthansa who called it 'Hessen'. On April twenty-first, 1945, it took off from Berlin on Lufthansa's last scheduled flight. Its destination was Barcelona, Spain via Munich. It reached Munich safely, departed on time and was never seen again.

"Alpha-Sierra-Hotel-Hotel never arrived in Spain. It was not shot down by Allied fighters. It did not detour to Sweden or Switzerland. It crashed in bad weather, near a small village in Bavaria. Piesenkofen Kreis Muhlberg. My groundsman has relatives who live in the area. They told me of the crash though they didn't know what type of plane went down. I investigated the wreck two months ago and uncovered its secrets.

"The Condor's passengers were members of the Berlin Headquarters Staff of the SS. None of the passengers or crew survived the crash and everything was badly burned. Some of the passengers' baggage was intact though, and I uncovered partial plans for what appeared to be a Nazi takeover of another country. From the ashes of the Third Reich, the Fourth Reich will arise."

"Claus, are you sure about that?" Woods asked, not

quite believing his friend. "It sounds so incredible. What country are they planning to take over? How are they going to do it?"

"Those are things I do not know. As I said before, the plans I uncovered were only partial. They came from an SS long-range planning group. I don't have the name of the target country, if indeed they had decided on one back in '45. I don't have any lists of people who would be involved in the takeover and I don't have the actual, tactical plans for the operation. Much of what I have is fragmentary but it all points to a project to establish another Nazi state. I have deduced that the country which is providing the best sanctuary would be the most likely candidate."

"Or the best springboard for such an operation. You shouldn't overlook the fact that they may want to exploit some local situation. I can't believe the Allied governments wouldn't be interested in such information. Even if it's only fragmentary and, shall we say, somewhat speculative."

"Well, they weren't. And in a way, I can't blame them," said Van Hoff, opening his briefcase and sliding the folder back inside it; he then returned the case to its original position behind his seat. "Here, I'll take the controls. Careful removing your feet from the rubber pedals, she tends to be a little sensitive. I can understand why the Allies, indeed why everyone, doesn't have the same desire I have for vengeance. There are so many problems they face, pursuing war criminals is not a national goal. The British and the French are trying to hold on to what's left of their colonial empires. Russia is busy building an empire of its own and the United States has to take on the responsibilities of a world power. The smaller European countries are struggling to merely survive against the devastation of war or, in the case of Czechoslovakia and Greece, communism. Private groups are mostly mismanaged, in financial trouble and the Jewish groups appear to be preoccupied with forming a Jewish state in Palestine."

"You might want to add to your list the size of peacetime armed forces," said Woods. "Perhaps during the war we had enough solicitors and legal personnel to try all these cases. But now, everyone's military is being heavily demobilized, save for the Bolsheviks. All things considered, it's a wonder that any trials are taking place."

"True, which makes our operation even more important. Would you and Ward be willing to help me again?"

"I think so, looks like Doug's fallen asleep back there but I'll volunteer him. Why not, I've done it in the past. Since you've exhausted our Berlin contacts, what do you propose doing with us?"

"You'll go to Italy. Captain Clostermann told me to concentrate on that country, instead of Spain or Switzerland or Sweden. You'll go with Captain Clinton, perhaps he can help you locate those planes you want."

Van Hoff had to land at Vienna-Schwechat airport and go through a customs check; it was not until nightfall that he and his friends got back to the estate. The next day, they planned for the trip south with Jesse Clinton. A few phone calls were made, passports revalidated at the Vienna consulates, the Messerschmitt was checked and baggage was packed. The following morning they all turned up at the airport, where Van Hoff gave his friends some last minute instructions.

"Now your destination is the Foggia Air Base in southern Italy. You will refuel in Trieste and avoid Yugoslavian airspace if you can. The Italians have been having some trouble with them. Major Green will meet you at the field. Jesse, you know what information to trade with him should he have anything useful. Michael, if you need any further funds, cable me directly. Douglas, try to stay out of trouble. I don't have much influence with the Italian authorities. Good luck, gentlemen, contact me immediately when you discover something."

With their baggage loaded and the *Taifun* preflighted, the pilot and passengers climbed inside, though not before there was a disagreement over who would be pilot.

"I think to be safe, we should have someone more experienced at the controls," said Ward. "I mean, we are heavily loaded."

"Oh really, Mister Ward, and how many hours have you had on Me-108s?" Clinton asked. "I've had nearly one hundred hours on this plane. You wouldn't even know how to turn the engine over."

"Don't start trouble now, Doug," said Woods. "You're not even in Italy yet."

"I'm not trying to start something. Why I haven't caused any trouble for the last two days."

"That's only because we've been too busy for you to become involved. You may have the rear seat again. If we crash, you'll stand a better chance of surviving."

"You know something, considering that you're South African, I would've thought you'd be the bigot," Clinton admitted, as they watched Ward clamber up the Messerschmitt's wing.

"Just goes to show you can't trust stereotypes," said Woods. "Not every South African is a pro-fascist Afrikaaner."

Ward didn't say too much after Clinton had safely and successfully flown the Me-108 off Vienna-Schwechat's main runway. In fact about the only thing he did say was that he needed a short nap as he was still tired. Clear of Vienna air traffic control, Clinton steered a course over the Austrian Alps, staying well away from the border with Yugoslavia.

"Sleep, that's all Douglas did on the flight back from Berlin," said Woods. "He didn't really mean what he's been saying to you. He just finds it very odd for a Negro-American army officer to be working with an Austrian count. I must admit I found it odd as well. It's a rather unusual combination. Why are you with Claus?"

"The son of a colored school teacher and a member of European nobility? Yeah, I guess it is strange," said Clinton. "And Van Hoff told you partially why I'm working for him. I'm out to settle an old score with some Nazis. One older than World War Two itself.

"I had an older brother, Raymond Clinton. Back in '37 he tried to join the Air Corps but they were even more racist then than they are today. So he went to Spain and fought on the Republican side during the civil war. He became an ace flying Russian fighters.

In 1939, he was ferrying DC-3s converted into bombers to the Republicans when the Nazis captured him. They tortured him, killed him and when they sent his body back to his friends, they had hacked it to pieces.

"All throughout the war, I carried my own personal grudge. When it ended, I still hadn't found all of those who were responsible. I got out of the Army, came back to Europe and started running down leads. One of them took me to Austria. I met Van Hoff and that was eight months ago. The rest you know, I've been helping him ever since."

"I'm sorry about your brother, Jesse," said Woods. "I never lost a family member to the war. They were all safe in either Port Elizabeth or East London in South Africa. That's where my wife is now. In East London at my mother's home, expecting our first child."

"Then you have a lot waiting for you when you get home. Starting a family as well as a business. I think we'll be able to help you along with your business while you're in Italy. I put together a list of aircraft storage sites we can check out. It's in my bag, why don't you take a look?"

For the duration of the flight into Italy, Woods, and later Ward, were preoccupied with the list. Daydreaming mostly, about which aircraft they'd like to buy, though they did ask Clinton what storage centers were closest to Foggia. By the time they reached the air base, Woods had devised his own list of locations he'd like to visit.

Following its brief stop at Trieste, the pale blue Messerschmitt flew down the Adriatic Sea and cut over the southeastern Italian shore line. Foggia was mostly an Italian Air Force base; very few U.S. Army Air Force machines could be seen on the field as the Me-108 puttered over it, waiting for a slot in the landing pattern to appear.

As in Berlin, the plane was a conspicuous sight. Touching down on a base filled almost entirely with military aircraft; taxiing past rows of silver T-6s and olive drab P39s used for advanced training. Clinton turned the Messerschmitt in at the end of one row of Texans and parked it. A jeep with an American officer sat waiting for its arrival; he was walking to the plane even before its engine had been switched off.

"Jesse, it's great to see you again," said the officer, shaking Clinton's hand as he climbed off the Messerschmitt. "I see you brought along Van Hoff's friends."

"Yes, this is Michael Woods and Douglas Ward. Until a few days ago, they were in the Royal Air Force but they've since been promoted to civilians. They helped us in Berlin and now they've come to help us in Italy. And by the way, we're to help them. Mister Woods is in the market for some focus birds, he'd like to see what's in storage around here."

"We can do that later," said Woods. "You must be Major Green. I do hope we're not interfering with your duties."

"Hell no, this is the Italians' advanced training base. I'm part of an army advisor group assigned to help them. I'm not part of any operational unit."

"Oh, then you're not an intelligence officer? It seems like all Doug and I have been used for is to gain an audience with someone in the intelligence community."

"No, I'm just a fighter pilot like you," Green replied.

"Then what's your stake in all this Nazi hunting Van Hoff is doing?" Ward asked, as he finished pulling everyone's luggage out of the Messerschmitt's baggage compartment.

"That's easy to answer, Mister Ward, I'm a Jew. I'm doing it for my people and my homeland."

"Oh, you mean Palestine?"

"Israel, Mister Ward, Israel. After almost two thousands years, there will be a Jewish homeland once more. In spite of what the Nazis did and what the Arabs are trying to do. I'll be leaving the Army Air Force soon and when I do I'll be going to Israel. But for now, let's get out of here. I'll take you to my quarters, they're off base."

Green had an apartment in the town of Foggia, as did most other American officers assigned to the base. What they were given in their monthly rent allowances allowed them to live like princes and Green was no exception. His apartment was on the top floor of the building he lived in and was quite spacious. He could easily accommodate his guests.

"My favorite restaurant will be opening soon," said Green. "Dinner will be on me tonight. Well, what have you come down for this time, Jesse? Are you tracking someone specifically or is this a general investigation?"

"You should know why I'm here, Daniel. Van Hoff told me that the French officer he talked to was a friend of yours. You could say this is a general investigation."

"All right, Clostermann did give me a call yesterday. He said you're looking into the escape routes the Nazis are using to flee Europe. He also said Van Hoff had some very startling information on a missing German plane."

"Indeed he does and he'll be glad to let you see it, if what you have is useful to us."

"God, you people must really think you have something hot," Green noted, surprised at the rules Clinton laid down. "I see negotiating is going to be difficult. What if I don't want to exchange any information until I see yours?"

"You'll just have to trust us this time. Our info has always proven to be accurate in the past."

"Up-to-date too. Okay, just this once. What I have to tell you is pretty much an open secret anyway. We'll discuss it over dinner, along with your travel plans. If you want to follow my leads, you'll have to go to Rome and other cities. Just drop your bags anywhere, you guys, we'll worry about who sleeps where later."

For the first time since their discharge, Woods and Ward got to sleep in late. Green left early for the air base and Clinton made breakfast for his friends. It was still mid-morning when they left for the air base as well, where they filed a flight plan for Rome and departed, following the mass departure of Italian T-6s.

"Look, there they are," said Woods, pointing at a cloud of silver specks. "Forming up over the Gulf of Manfredonia. I estimate thirty-plus, what do you say?"

"Let's not get anywhere near them," Clinton responded. "I've had more close calls with formations of students than squadrons of Germans. Besides, we're heading for Rome and not the Adriatic."

"What will we do when we arrive there, mate?" Ward asked. "In Rome I mean."

"We'd cover more territory if we were to split up. Mister Ward, you and I will go to the offices of the International Red Cross and the Displaced Persons Board. Michael, you're to go to the Italian War Assets Commissions for Aircraft. Claus promised we'd help you get your planes and this is your chance. Find out which center or depot has what you're looking for and when we're through, we'll go there."

They landed at a small, civilian airfield just outside of Rome. It was easy for them to order a taxi and drive into the city where Clinton and Ward, then Woods were dropped off at various government ministries. By noon they were all working at their assignments when, suddenly they found themselves alone. It was lunch time and virtually every worker was streaming out of his or her office; not to return for several hours. For Woods at least it meant unrestricted access to information.

"What on earth are you two doing here?" he asked, when Clinton and Ward appeared at the offices of the War Assets Commission. "I thought you were buttonholing officials over at the International Red Cross?"

"The truth is we were the ones that got buttonholed," Clinton admitted. "We didn't get anywhere with those people. Or the Displaced Persons Board. Daniel Green was right, they never did clean all the fascists out of the Italian government. There's lots of people still sympathetic to Nazis in this country. We couldn't get a word out of anybody when they found out we'd come looking for war criminals."

"I can now see why the ruddy bastards use Italy instead of Spain," said Ward, sitting down at an empty desk. "Spain may still be a fascist state but it's the outcast of Europe. You can enter and leave Italy easier than you can Spain and Spain never suffered much during the war. It doesn't have a Displaced Persons Board or an army of Red Cross workers for a Nazi to hide in and get documents from."

"It also doesn't have a War Assets Commission for Aeroplanes," added Woods. "Jesse, come here and have a look at this."

Clinton moved over to the file cabinet Woods was rifling and began to examine the folders he had removed.

"These are files on Luftwaffe aircraft," said Clinton, "What the hell are you looking at them for? I thought you were interested in buying photo-recon planes?"

"Out of curiosity mostly. I thought it might be interesting if I could buy an Me-410 or some other German reconnaissance machine. Then I saw something that just became curiouser and curiouser. Look at the sales."

"So what, lots of Luftwaffe planes are being sold off. They're cheap and it's keeping a lot of scrap dealers in business. What's so special about that?"

"You're looking but you're not seeing. Take note of the number of sales and subsequent shipment overseas of the remains. Now, compare that to this file on Allied aircraft. Notice the much smaller ratio of overseas shipments to sales. I find it very strange. What's more I'd like to know what countries these machines are being shipped to."

"I understand, it is strange," said Clinton. "We should copy down the names of these scrap dealers. Then go to shipping offices or the Ministry of Trade and find out what freighters are being used and what their destinations are. Here, Mister Ward, you seem all set up and ready. You copy these names, especially those in the area of Rome, Naples and Foggia. And hurry, I think the workers will start drifting back in here at two o'clock."

"I should've known someone would find me work the minute I got comfortable," Ward groused, hunching over the folders Clinton handed him. "Maybe one of us should stand by the window and watch for the people returning? I feel like a ruddy spy."

"Now you know how I've felt from time to time, since I started working for your friend. I feel so out of place, I wish I could get my hands on a fighter. Speaking of fighters, did you locate any that would suit you?"

"A lot of photo-recon P-38s," said Woods. "I wish I knew how to fly one. However, there are some reconnaissance Spits at a center near Foggia. Should we investigate one of these storage areas, may I suggest we go there?"

"Sure we can, if we get out of here in time," said Clinton. "C'mon, let's hurry up and finish it."

"As Michael would say, just a sec," Ward countered. "I'm even less good at being a secretary than a spy. If you've had so much experience at being a spy, why don't you have one of them little cameras to snap some pictures?"

"Because it would take too long to develop pictures." Clinton pulled from his pants' pocket a small

Leica camera, which neatly fit in the palm of his hand. "We need what you're copying now, if we're to get to the bottom of things today. Mike, do you have the information you need?"

"Oh yes, I copied it all quite some time ago," Woods advised, returning some folders to their proper cabinets.

"Here, I'm done," said Ward, closing the last folder and pushing it away. "Let's grab our notes and leave."

The Ministry of Trade was just a few blocks from the offices of the War Assets Commissions. By the time Woods and the others arrived at the ministry, there were enough workers returning from their long lunches to help them. However, like any bureaucracy, it took time to track down expert permits, copies of shipping orders, what ports the shipments left from, what vessels they left on and what their destinations were. It was late in the afternoon, almost closing time, when at last all the information they had requested was found. While it was still light out, they returned to the airport where they climbed back in the Me-108 for the trip back to Foggia.

"What are we going to tell Major Green when we turn up at his apartment?" Woods asked, after contact was established with the Foggia control tower. "I mean, we did promise him we'd share our information."

"Only if what he gave us was useful," said Clinton. "And what we found wasn't the result of his info but your digging through dusty files. And we still don't really know what we have. Just an unusually high number of scrapped German planes being sent to South America. We don't know what condition they're in or who gets them at the other end. For all we know they're being turned into aluminum ingots and sent to a spoon factory. Let's just keep what we have under our hats for now. Tomorrow we'll go to this depot of yours and then to one of these scrap dealers who does business with it."

It was difficult to keep Daniel Green in the dark but they succeeded. In spite of another free meal, he went to sleep without learning what they had uncovered and the next morning he was gone before any of them were awake.

This time what they needed was a car and not a plane. From a rental agency they got a dilapidated, pre-war Fiat; it didn't look good but at least it ran. They drove out of Foggia and headed south, following both the directions Woods had written down and those from the locals.

The storage center in question was a one-time airfield located near the Gulf of Manfredonia. It was filled with both Allied and Axis aircraft. Most were little more than hulks, often without propellers or tail surfaces; lying on their bellies with their wings stacked beside them. Some looked factory new though even they had all their guns removed and their plexiglas was long since frosted over by the Italian sun. There were acres of them, American and German mostly, with a smattering of British and Italian types. They stood, silent except for the sounds of scrapping crews carting off the aircraft they had bought.

"This is a depressing place," said Woods, as he and Ward moved down a line of B-25 Mitchells in U.S.

Army Air Force colors. "Most of these planes will be cut apart and smelted down. Turned into pots, or spoons, or perhaps into next year's line of passenger cars. They deserve better, I wish I could buy the whole lot. If I had Claus's money I would. In our hands, these planes defeated the greatest threat ever faced by our countries, our civilization. How soon they are forgotten, in a few years I fear they will all be gone."

"I'd like to just have 'em around because it's so wonderful to fly them," Ward added. "Even these bombers would be fun. Are you sure the Spits are located in this row?"

"That's what they claimed at the office. They told me the Spitfires would be here with the Mitchells and they would be in RAF markings. Will you take a look at the colors these bombers are painted in? Why they must be from every unit the Yanks had flying in Italy."

"And where's that overgrown aborigine of ours? He disappeared the moment we left the office and I haven't seen him since. If he's lost I say we leave him here."

"You better ease off those remarks or he'll start calling you a kangaroo puncher and that's just to start with."

"That's not a bad crack, maybe I'll use it some time," said Clinton, walking out from under one of the B-25s. "Have you found your focus birds yet?"

"Michael, look, there they are," said Ward, pointing at the end of the flanking columns of medium bombers. Almost hidden behind their bulky fuselages was a collection of slim-bodied fighters standing on narrow track landing gear. Lying against them were sets of broad, elliptical wings; the unmistakable mark of the Spitfire. "I'd say there's about a dozen. C'mon, mate, they're what you're looking for."

"What do you want, Jesse?" Woods asked, torn between following Ward's summoning and finding out what Clinton needed.

"I think the both of you had better come with me and take a look at this. You'll find it interesting."

"Can't it wait, mate? This is what Michael came to Italy for in the first place."

"Those planes aren't going anywhere. But what I've found is going and we'd better hurry before they leave."

Woods gave the Spitfires a long, desiring glance before he followed Clinton under the fuselage of a Mitchell and on to another section of the depot.

They passed through more rows of B-25s, then P-38s until Clinton signalled for Woods and Ward to stop and crouch behind the tires of the nearest available Lightning. The next row of aircraft beyond them were all German. Focke-Wulf 190s mostly, with a scattering of Me-109s thrown in. Like the Allied aircraft around them, some were little more than hulks while others looked almost untouched. The scrapping crews were working busily on them, the only activity at the otherwise quiet center.

"Those guys have been here since seven o'clock this morning," Clinton noted, as they watched the noisy operation from underneath the Lightning. "Soon they'll have their quota of planes for the day and they'll be leaving. Mister Ward, go bring the car to the back of this lot. Near where that truck is leaving,

80

we're going to follow one of them."

Clinton tossed the car keys to Ward who backed out from under the P-38 and scuttled away as quietly as he could.

"We'll have a few minutes before he brings the car into position," said Woods. "Shouldn't we be sneaking down to the back gate and finding a way out?"

"I've already found us a way out. The fence goes over a drainage ditch, that's how we'll leave. Have you noticed how those crews are removing the planes? Or that the crew leaders aren't Italians?"

"You're right, they are rather Aryan-looking aren't they? As for handling the aircraft, I don't quite see what you mean. Are you referring to the fact they're only moving fighters?"

"No, it's not that. I guess you'd have to sit here a while before you'd see what I'm talking about. Notice how they're handling those long-nose Focke-Wulfs and the Messerschmitts with the tall tails."

"Now I see what you mean," Woods admitted. "The late-model planes are being handled far more carefully than the earlier ones. In spite of their condition. How odd, I wonder if this could have something to do with those plans Claus discovered in the Condor?"

"That's a mighty long link you're trying for but, who knows where this may lead? C'mon, it's time for us to go and look, I'm sorry for dragging you away from those planes."

"No problem, I feel they will still be here in a few days, when everything is done. All right, let's go."

The Fiat stood waiting for them on the road beyond the fence. As soon as they reached it, Clinton told

Ward to follow the next truck to leave the depot. Barely a minute later one pulled out from the back gate carrying a trailer load of Focke-Wulfs and Focke-Wulf pieces.

The truck bounced its way down a series of dusty, unpaved roads until it had almost reached the foothills of the Apennines. In one of the many small villages which dotted the landscape, it turned into a scrap yard filled with the wreckage of war; most of it airplane parts. Ward drove past the yard and finally parked the car where they could overlook it. From his briefcase Clinton produced a pair of army-surplus field glasses which he used to scan the busy operation.

"Well, mate, what're they doing?" Ward asked.

"They're using hydraulic choppers on the planes," said Clinton. "But again it's only on the old ones. Here, take a look for yourself."

He handed the binoculars forward for the others to use; then he started rooting through his briefcase again.

"What the hell do you mean old?" said Ward, it was now his turn to use the glasses. "That plane they're hacking apart is almost new."

"It's a Gustav-model, Doug," Woods pointed out. "It was obsolescent back in 1943. Why a Spit Nine can outclass that. Take a look at how they're working on those Focke-Wulf Doras. Even today they're still one of the best piston-engined fighters in the world."

"Oh, you mean the long-nose 190s?" Yeah, I see'em. They're taking those apart too."

"They're dismantling them. And taking the parts inside the main building. Now, have a look at the building's other end."

Ward shifted the binoculars a few inches, from the front of the yard's largest building to its rear. What emerged were sections of aircraft, trussed up in wooden frames and being loaded into crates. The crates were also being filled with the remains of the aircraft which had been sent through the choppers. The scrap was scarcely recognizable as ever having been flying machines.

"God damn it, they're smuggling those planes out of the country," Ward finally realized. "This is incredible. How on earth can they do it in broad daylight?"

"When you become a spy, you learn all kinds of things take place in the open," said Clinton. "You'd be surprised at what you can get away with, especially here. In Italy they smuggle cigarettes openly, all kinds of drugs, even gold. If the black market were to ever dry up, I think the country would come crashing down. So the fact that these guys can get away with smuggling aircraft is hardly surprising. I wonder if they're doing as good a business in infantry weapons and tanks. There's mountains of that stuff lying around Europe as well."

"They no doubt are," Woods added. "And you have to remember, Doug, we're sitting on top of the town looking into it. That scrap yard has a high brick wall around it. From street level you'd never see what was going on inside. And even if the people in the town knew, they're probably grateful for the jobs the work's providing."

"Okay, I think we've seen enough. Get us out of here before we get noticed, Mister Ward. Once we're back at the apartment, I'm calling Claus. We're on to something and I think it's time to bring him in."

The silver Ju-52 taxied out of the darkness and into the bright lights at the arrival gate. A handful of passengers disembarked from the converted, ex-Luftwaffe transport; among them was a blond-haired businessman. At least he appeared to be a businessman, wearing a perfectly fitted, three-piece suit and dragging with him a large briefcase. On the other side of the fence he met with four men who bundled him into the airport lobby.

"Welcome to Naples, Claus," greeted Woods. "Do you need to go through customs?"

"No, I went through it at Milan where we made a refueling stop," said Van Hoff. "The Junkers is a fine aircraft though it doesn't have the range to make it from Vienna to Naples in one jump. I swear, that aircraft is so stock it still has the machine gun mount at the rear of the flight deck. Where are we going once we leave here and why did you have me come to Naples and not Foggia?"

"Because this is where the evidence is," said Clinton. "Not Foggia. We've come across something more important than a Nazi escape route. We've found a weapons pipeline. I think there's something to that take-over plot you found."

"What take-over plot?" Green asked. "Is this the information you guys have been promising me? I chased a truck over the Apennines, wasted valuable leave time, to hear about some harebrained plot?"

"I can assure you, it is not a joke," Van Hoff promised. "Once we leave here, I'll show you the evidence I brought with me. Do you have a car, or a taxi cab?"

"In fact, we have two cars," said Woods. "The one we rented and Major Green's. I suggest you and Jesse take his car and Doug and I will follow in the other. We're heading for the Naples dockyard. That is where our evidence is located."

Fortunately, Van Hoff didn't bring much luggage with him and the tiny, two-car convoy was able to leave the airport soon after his arrival. They wound through the narrow, often clogged streets of Naples to its port area. Even at night its facilities were busy; either offloading newly arrived ships or preparing others to sail with the morning tide. And there was the ever-present roar of outboard motor boats buzzing around the harbor. Not long after they entered the port area, the cars parked at the base of one of its smaller piers and their passengers met by Green's sedan.

"Well, Major, what do you think of the plans Claus discovered?" Woods asked.

"They're dynamite," Green responded. "I'm surprised none of those G-Two boys showed any interest in them. They're not complete but they're convincing as all hell. I believe 'em, now I understand why I chased that truck here. I'm glad you let me see what you had, I know of some people who'll be very interested in it."

"For the time being, I'd prefer you not talk to any officials about what you saw," Van Hoff asked. "We still have to find out if this is part of that plan. Where's the truck you followed and the ship it's destined for?"

"Right this way, it's called the *Princesa*. It has Liberian registry and it's owned by a Spanish outfit."

Green described the ship as he led the way to it. The S.S. *Princesa* was anything but a regal ship. A small, unkempt-looking freighter, it was the second ship tied to the pier and had the most activity around it. Lights burned all over the ship, there was a line of trucks dockside and its cargo hoists were busy lifting crates into the holds. The group slowed its pace as it approached the freighter, even tried hiding among crates destined for another ship.

"We don't have to be quite so secretive, Doug," said Woods, when he noticed Ward moving between the crates and the edge of the pier. "I doubt they have many lookouts."

"I'm not trying to hide, mate. I want to get me a look at these speed boats." Ward motioned to the tiny craft darting about the harbor. "Bloody damn noise makers. Is that all the ruddy I-ties have time for? Running off and having fun?"

"They're not playing," Clinton advised. "Those guys are working. They're heading out to a ship anchored at sea where their boats will be loaded with cigarettes. If the Italian customs and the Finance Police can overlook these seagoing hot rods they can damn well overlook what's going on here. C'mon, move in a little closer, you're missing it."

Clinton led them back to where they could see the freighter and the continuing operation of filling its holds. They found Green already explaining to Van Hoff what they had been doing for the last several days and what he was watching.

"About a third of this ship's cargo is from the Sparviero Scrap Works," said Green. "The rest is machine products and shoes. The truck I followed from Sparviero is the red one with the flat bed trailer. As you can see, the check done by the inspectors is perfunctory.

They just open the top of a crate or two and look inside. Naturally, all they see is a box filled with chopped airplane parts."

"And secreted in that scrap are complete aircraft?" Van Hoff inquired, as the crate from the truck Green had followed was hoisted aboard the ship. "I would think weighing the crates would prove they aren't filled with solid metal."

"Well do you see them doing that? And who has a scale to weigh a crate that's forty feet long?"

"We watched the scrap yard workers load two long-nose, Focke-Wulf 190 Ds into a crate like that," said Woods. "They were complete, down to propellers, canopies and undercarriage. I don't think the weight discrepancy would be that much."

"I see, and what were you doing, Michael, while the major here was chasing a truck all over Italy?"

"We were in the shipping office, asking a great many questions. Doug and I found out the number of shipments Sparviero made from Naples. The number of other scrap dealers and the shipments they made. Since the middle of last year, some fifty shipments of scrapped aircraft have left Naples and that's just Naples. We don't know about other ports in Italy, or France or any other country. Who knows how many aircraft have been smuggled out of Europe? I don't but I do know the destination of the planes that left Naples. All those shipments went to South America. To the port of Montevideo, Uruguay."

Chapter Four:
MEETING IN AUSTRIA.
SOUTH AMERICA.

They watched the *Princesa* for another half-hour and then left. Van Hoff had seen enough and in spite of their attempts to conceal themselves, they were beginning to be noticed.

Rather than spend the rest of the night in Naples, the group drove back over the Apennines to Foggia. They got some rest at Green's apartment before driving to the air base where Woods, Van Hoff, Clinton and Ward all piled into the Messerschmitt. With their luggage, the Me-108 was fully loaded and required two refueling stops to make it all the way back to Vienna.

"I would've thought you'd prefer we stay in Italy and continue our work," said Woods, after they had cleared customs. "I don't see why we had to come back to Austria simply to hold a meeting."

"You'll understand once you discover who we're going to meet," said Van Hoff. "Come, I left my car in long-term storage. You're about to discover that I've been busy as well."

The moment they returned to Falkestaaten, Van

Hoff sent Clinton back to Vienna-Schwechat with orders to pick up several passengers from an afternoon flight. While he was gone, Woods and Ward unpacked the information they had gathered in Italy and laid it out on Van Hoff's 'campaign' table. Along with other files Van Hoff took from his cabinets, they had it all ready by the time they heard Clinton return.

"Just who are we making this presentation to, mate?" Ward asked, surveying what was on the table. "Are we doing this for that chap you mentioned from the Jewish Center?"

"You mean Simon Wiesenthal?" Van Hoff inquired. "No, it's not him. Someone familiar to you though you'd least suspect."

"They're on the stairs," said Woods. "Whoever they are, they'll be here in just a sec or two."

When the office doors opened, Clinton was the first to appear. Followed by two men who were both familiar and found the room to be equally so.

"Well, the last time I saw this place it was filled with Nazis and Ivans," Brandon recalled. "It's been years, Claus and you haven't changed."

"Dennis! My God, I thought it'd be years before I saw you again." Woods charged to the doors and embraced Brandon, slapping him on the back repeatedly. "And Eric, what on earth are you doing here?"

"The same reason he is," replied Kingston. "I hope I rate the same welcome as he did."

"Of course you do, this is quite a gathering."

And they both received the same greeting when Ward came to the door; though Van Hoff's welcome was a bit more formal.

"Shall we start our work, friends?" he suggested.

"I'm afraid you and Eric must leave soon if you're to make it back to Germany by nightfall."

"I should've guessed it would be you two," Woods admitted. "Especially when Claus said Mister Clinton would be meeting a flight from British European Airways. But why do you two have to leave so quickly? I take it you both are on leave."

"They must meet with more friends of ours. Those we saw recently in West Berlin. And they only have two days to accomplish it all and return to their base. I've been communicating with them since the day all of you left and, fortunately, this is the first time they could break away from their duties."

Van Hoff went on to explain his operations to Brandon and Kingston, before they had even walked over to the room's large table. Once there, he showed them the information that had been recently gained and what it might indicate. Van Hoff at several points allowed Woods and Ward to help explain what they had found. It didn't take long for them to make their presentation and when it was over, Brandon and Kingston got a chance to give their views and ask a few questions.

"In my opinion, I think someone here should go to South America," Brandon noted. "It's the obvious thing but tell me, why have you switched from tracking war criminals in this case to aircraft?"

"I should think that's obvious as well," Van Hoff replied. "Where the planes go we will find the Nazis. Not unless you actually believe they're being sent to some smelter, or being purchased clandestinely by some air force. I doubt they'd do that, when the Americans and you British are virtually giving away thousands of aeroplanes. No, what Michael's uncovered follows what is in these plans. Not everyone who worked on then died in the crash. Of that I am certain, however, I would like to be positive. You're quite right, someone has to go to South America. The question is who?"

"Well, we certainly can't," said Kingston. "Dennis and I are still in the RAF. Why not you or your friend here? He's American, he should be able to get along with the locals."

"I'm not afraid not, neither of us can go. We must stay and track down the leads we have. I'll work with my European contacts, Jesse will work with his American ones. Which means there are only two others who can do it."

"Somehow, I expected it would come down to us," said Woods. "Another little trip for an old friend? This is really beginning to grow out of hand."

"I know, but you must see how important it is?" Van Hoff pleaded. "It would mean so much. You and Doug have done more than you needed to, but you're the only ones available. Of course, I will pay for all your expenses and perhaps I'll put in a bid on some of those reconnaissance Spitfires you're so interested in."

"You do know a man's weak spots, don't you, Claus? All right, if you'll purchase for each of us a recon Spit, we'll go to South America and track those planes. One thing is for certain, this is the damndest, most roundabout way I've ever traveled to South Africa."

"Before I agree, I have a question for you, mate," Ward injected. "It's not about the assignment. It's about Dennis and Eric. There must be another reason why you brought them here. More than just running the latest bits of gossip to our friends in Berlin. Why?"

"Very well, the truth is they contacted me the day you left for Italy," said Van Hoff. "Colonel Reynolds told them of our visit and they didn't want to be left out of anything. Even if they were merely fighter pilots, they wanted to help. That's been a recurring phrase this past week and I'm beginning to believe that as fighter pilots we can do more than as spies or diplomats. I'm not certain of what we can do as fighter pilots and I would still like to give the law of nations a chance. You can call Dennis, Eric, Colonel Reynolds and the rest my contingency plan. I hope I don't have to use you as fighter pilots, let's continue for now as spies."

Brandon and Kingston made it to Vienna-Schwechat in time; they left on the last flight of the day for Berlin. It took two days for Van Hoff to make the travel arrangements for Woods and Ward. Few flights to South America left from Vienna and the Uruguayan embassy proved hard to get hold of. Unlike Brandon and Kingston, Woods and Ward left on the first flight of the day. For Paris.

At Le Bourget field they switched from an Air France DC-3 to one of Pan Am's new Lockheed Constellations. The four-engined, triple-finned giant didn't rattle like the war veteran Dakota. It reared off the ground smoothly and cruised at an airspeed which, just a few years ago, only fighters could reach. The Lockheed gave a level ride, as fine as a luxury train and with scarcely any greater noise. It was a pleasant change for those accustomed to the ride of fighters.

After several hours, the airliner landed briefly at Lisbon, Portugal to take on more passengers and the fuel necessary to reach its final destination, Rio de Janeiro. Then, it was across the Atlantic on a ten-hour flight that took Woods and Ward south of the equator and to a new continent; one untouched by war.

The Pan Am Constellation landed at Rio de Janeiro's Santos Dumont airport at a little before eight o'clock in the evening. The first flight for Montevideo didn't leave until the next morning, something which Van Hoff did take into account, and he arranged a layover for Woods and Ward at a hotel near the airport. Something neither of them really needed as they had both managed to catch some sleep on the airliner.

Beyond the hotel, all they saw of Brazil's capital city was the airport lobby. At least in the morning Woods and Ward got to see Rio's skyline and Sugar Loaf Mountain when they took off in an ancient Ford Trimotor.

It followed the Brazilian coastline south, stopping at Sao Paulo, Pôrto Alegre and other cities along the way. This plus the Trimotor's slow cruising speed made the trip to Montevideo a long, uncomfortable one. Finally, near midday, the airliner entered Uruguayan airspace and was soon circling over the River Plate estuary.

"So that's what a city that hasn't been bombed looks like," said Ward, leaning over the aisle so he could see through Woods's window. "I've almost forgotten such places existed. I'd bet most any country in

Europe would be willing to trade one of their gutted cities for this."

"It reminds me of Cape Town," said Woods. "Except of course it doesn't have Table Mountain behind it or the Twelve Apostles Peaks to the south."

"You made the same remark when we left Rio de Janeiro. Are you becoming homesick, mate?"

"I suppose I am. Until this flight I've been too busy to miss my home and wife but now I do. I wish I could be with Margaret. She's having a baby, our first, and damn it she needs me. What am I doing chasing planes and war criminals my government's forgotten about?"

"You're doing it for a friend and you, at least, have a high sense of justice, mate. I'm here for the hell of it. There's nothing in Australia for me to return to. Not unless Claus does buy me a recon Spit. Maybe I'll start a photo business like you."

"Good but remember, starting a business is something you don't do on a whim. It takes a great deal of thought and planning," Woods advised.

"I know, I'll do me worrying about it later. You know something, mate, it angers me to see a city like this. We just fought the most devastating war in history, to defeat the bloodiest race of madmen the world has ever known and these wogs sat it out on the sidelines. Watching the rest of us put on a great show. Why England's little colony in the Falkland Islands suffered more during the war than the entire South American continent."

"I wouldn't say that about all of South America. Brazil fought on our side, Jesse Clinton told me they had a group of Thunderbolts in Italy during the war.

And even Montevideo saw its share of the war, long before any city in England was bombed. Take a look below as we come around, that's the wreck of the *Graf Spee*."

Some six miles outside Montevideo harbor lay the shattered, rusting hulk of the pocket battleship *Graf Spee*. She rested in comparatively shallow waters, her entire superstructure could be seen though most of her upper decks were awash. Only her bridge and control tower stood above the surface; blackened and buckled by the fires which had consumed the Nazi warship eight years earlier.

The Trimotor circled the *Graf Spee* several times; coming so low it scared off the sea gulls perched on its upper works. When given clearance to land, the Ford swung around slowly and proceeded into Carrasco Airport, Montevideo's main airfield. On landing it taxied to the international arrivals terminal where Woods and Ward got their passports ready for customs inspection.

". . . And what is the purpose for visiting our country, Mister Woods?" the official behind the table queried, while still looking at the passport he held in his hands.

"Well, it's like what my visa says," Woods replied. "I'm here as a tourist. There are many countries I've always wanted to visit and since my discharge from the Royal Air Force, I've been doing precisely that."

"Yes, I can see. Austria, Italy, Austria again and Brazil. You did not stay long in Rio de Janeiro, a stopover only. Do you have a specific reason for coming to Uruguay?"

"As a matter of fact, I have." Woods's voice started

to tremble, now he had to come up with one. "I have a brother in the Royal Navy. He served on board the cruiser *Achilles*, one of the ships which trapped the *Graf Spee* here in Montevideo. I promised him I'd come here one day, to see first hand the victory he'd played a part in."

"I understand. And you, Mister Ward, what is your reason for coming to Uruguay?"

"Oh I'm a bird watcher, mate. The New South Wales Bird Watching Society would like to know how many Urus you have here."

"Douglas, shut up," Woods barked, then, turning to the customs official. "I'm sorry, you'll have to forgive my friend. You see, he's Australian."

"I can see that, I also note he has been in all the same countries you have. Why?"

"I'm his friend," said Ward. "Can't I just be someone's friend, mate?"

"Of course you can. Where do you plan to go after my country, Mister Woods?"

"If we have enough money left, we'd like to visit Argentina. Then I'll take my friend to South Africa and show him the country I've been talking about all these years."

"Thank you, Mister Woods and may I suggest you leave yourselves enough money to travel to Argentina? Only Buenos Aires has flights to South Africa. May I ask where you'll be staying while in Montevideo?"

"I haven't decided on that yet," said Woods. "And I hope this airport has a car rental agency."

"You will find the rental desk in the lobby and if I may make a tip as to where you might stay? My uncle owns the Hotel Avenida. It has a hundred rooms, with new beds and running water. It is not far and in the perfect location."

"Does it have a view of the harbor?"

"Of course, especially from the higher floors. Here, let me give you its address." The official reached into one of the table's many drawers and came up with a business card which he handed over to Woods. "Those rooms you want will cost slightly more. Enjoy your stay in my country, gentlemen."

After picking up their luggage from the claim area, Woods and Ward entered the busy, spartan lobby and went to the rental desk to see what kind of car they could get.

"That was an extremely stupid remark to have made," said Woods, once they were in the terminal and beyond the earshot of customs officials. "New South Wales Bird Watching Society, I'm here to count your Urus. Don't you know we're not supposed to attract attention to ourselves?"

"I don't think what I said was so bad, mate. Not much worse than you claiming you had a brother on the old *Achilles*. You better hope your friend isn't a navy buff. Even I know the *Achilles* was part of the Royal New Zealand Navy and manned entirely by New Zealanders."

"And you'd better hope that he wasn't part of some intelligence unit. The last problem we need is for us to be watched while we're watching the harbor."

"Don't worry about it, Michael," said Ward. "I think he's more interested in getting business for his family than spying on us. I only hope this hotel is as good as he claims it is. I have the feeling that in this country, 'running water' means there's your water, now run it up to your room."

The car they ended up with was a Ford sedan from the early 'thirties; one of the newer cars they saw on the streets of Montevideo. The hotel had a view of the harbor, though only from the upper floors as warned, and its running water was little better than what Ward had expected. With a room rented, they set out in search of the harbor shipping office and a restaurant. They had not had anything substantial to eat since breakfast in Rio de Janeiro.

"Remember, we drink only coffee, or tea or alcohol," Woods instructed, as their meals arrived. "And then only wine or hard drinks, no beer. Neither of us had better end up with dysentery and a spell in the hospital. Claus'll kick our backsides off, provided we haven't shit them off."

"Understand, mate. Are you sure this is a steak?" Ward dug his fork into the blackened slab of meat on his plate and lifted it up for Woods to see.

"Of course it is, that's good Argentine beef. It helped us win the war. Perhaps they didn't give you the best cut. Enjoy it anyway or would you rather have Spam?"

"No. No thank you. I'd even take K-rations over Spam. I'll wager when we leave here we'll be looking for the shipping office. What ships will we ask for?"

"Well one thing is for certain, we won't be looking for the S.S. *Princesa*. That tub is most likely still in the Mediterranean. We have our list of suspect ships which left Naples in the last three months, bound for Montevideo. We'll find out if any have arrived, or when they will arrive. What docks they have used or will use. Who picks up the cargo and where it ultimately goes. We have a lot of work in front of us, more so than when we were in Italy. There we had other people helping us, experts like Green and Jesse. Here, we're on our own and I'll admit, I haven't been this nervous since June of 1940. When I flew my first mission."

After their lunch, Woods and Ward drove down to the dock area and began a frustratingly long search for the shipping office. Few people on the Montevideo wharves could speak English. In fact it was an American who gave them accurate enough directions to locate it. Fortunately, there were people in the shipping office who did speak English; though they were curious as to why a South African and an Australian would be so interested in the movement of ships from Italy.

"Me brother's a first mate on one of the ships," Ward answered, scanning the list Woods handed him to decide which ship his brother was first mate on. "I haven't seen him for years, what with the war and all. And I was too late to catch him in Italy. So I decided to meet him here. He has some friends on the other ships and I'd like to talk to them to find out how he's been. Me brother's on the *Giuseppe Colombri*, when's she due in?"

"You're in luck, Mister Ward. The *Colombri* will arrive in two days' time," said one of the office clerks, scanning a list of his own. "She will dock at pier thirty-six, slip B. Call us back on the day of arrival and we'll tell you her exact docking time. She's just in radio range, if you'd like us to, we'd be happy to send your brother a message telling him you're here."

"No thank you, I'd like this to be a surprise. Could

you tell me if any of the other ships are in?"

"Yes, the S.S. *Tyrrhenian Sea* is at pier thirty, slip A. In Italian, the name would be *Mare Tirreno*. And the S.S. *Cosenza* entered the harbor today. She's just taking on her tugs, she should dock by six this evening, alongside the *Mare Tirreno*. Again, we could use our radio to contact your brother's friend on board her."

"No, I'd like to surprise him too. Thanks, mate, you've been a help. C'mon, Michael, it's time to leave."

"So, your brother's a first mate on an Italian ship," said Woods, once they were out of the shipping office and walking to their car. "Don't you think they'd find it a little strange that an Australian would be on board?"

"No more so than your brother being on a New Zealand cruiser," Ward pointed out. "Between your brother and my brother, we're starting to run out of brothers. Next time we have to use our relatives, let's try someone else. Like uncles or cousins, I have plenty of those."

"It would be more realistic anyway. I'm the only son my parents have and I know your brother's only sixteen."

"There, you see, a real sea dog. It's what you should expect for a family that can trace its lineage all the way back to Nelson and Francis Drake."

"What, Sir Francis Drake?" Woods responded, incredulously. "You're about as related to Drake as a sea gull is to a Supermarine Spitfire."

"Now that hurt, mate. That hurt almost as much as the time you confiscated my liquor supplies."

They scarcely needed to use the car to reach the *Mare Tirreno*; they could see it from the shipping office's parking lot. There was activity around the freighter, cargo was being off-loaded, though curiously; no bulky crates with the name Sparviero stamped on them were being removed. Woods went so far as to use what little Spanish he knew on dock workers to find out if any had been.

It proved to be a frustrating exercise, with most workers shaking their heads in bewilderment at the 'anglo' who asked strange questions in butchered Spanish. Woods and Ward left without gaining any additional information. They decided it would be easier to watch for any suspicious activity from the balcony of their hotel room.

"Perhaps as in Naples, they won't be moving anything large until the evening," said Woods. "If we're to see anything of it from our room, we should unpack those Army field glasses of yours. All right, Doug? Doug? Douglas, what on earth are you looking at?"

"That green sedan two cars behind us. I've seen it before."

"Indeed, such as where?"

"Such as in front of our hotel and in the parking lot at the shipping office. I have that feeling, mate. The hairs on the back of me neck are standing up. Just like whenever I'd get some Jerries sitting on my tail."

"In other words, you think we're being followed."

"Think? I know we're being followed. Here, make a right turn at the next block and I'll prove it."

The Ford's tires squealed loudly as Woods cut a sharp right. He had to swerve to avoid cars parked on the street and floored the gas pedal. The Ford responded sluggishly, though it did widen the gap with the green sedan, which came roaring after it a few seconds later. Ward's feelings had been confirmed.

"I told you we were being followed," he said, glancing through the rear window. "I wonder who they are?"

"We may find out soon," Woods warned. "This car isn't like my Mercedes. The tires are almost bald and I've seen trucks accelerate faster than this. Which way shall we go next?"

"How the hell should I know, mate? I don't know this city. I haven't been here any longer than you have. I wish I had me service revolver, why did I ever sell it?"

"Because you received fifty pounds for it like I did. Hold on, let's see where this road leads."

The sedan was rapidly overtaking them when Woods swung left. He did it against the traffic light, causing a number of vehicles to careen out of the Ford's way. The new street seemed to lead away from the city; to a section of slums and shacks made out of corrugated sheet metal. Soon the Ford and the sedan pursuing it were the only vehicles on the road.

"You're getting us into a fine mess, mate," said Ward. "Whoever's in that car could kill us here and the police will never find our bodies. I bet those are Nazis following us."

"It may also be the police," said Woods. "Your smart remarks at customs may have made local intelligence suspicious of us. We may end up in jail. My wife and child can fly over and visit me once a month."

"I say we head back for the airport. You saw that line of Harvard trainers when we flew in didn't you?

Let's pinch one of those and nip off to Brazil or Argentina or wherever you'd like to go."

"That's crazy but I'll head there anyway. It may scare off the car behind us. Let's see where this road leads."

Woods made another left turn and, much to his horror, found the road he had chosen led to a dead end. It was too late to turn around, the pursuing sedan was at the intersection; making the same maneuver. Instead Woods gunned the Ford, speeding down to the road's end where he spun the car sideways and killed the engine.

"Quick, bail out!" he urged as he opened his door. "And get behind her. Pretend we're armed, let's see if we can bluff our way out of this mess."

Ward had only to open his own door and roll out. Woods needed to scurry around the car's tail before he could find some protection. The green sedan screeched to a stop a few moments later. It was barely a dozen feet in front of the Ford and at last Woods and Ward had a good look at the people chasing them.

"They're definitely not Latin-types," said Woods. "They don't even look Italian. Oh my God, maybe they are German."

The sedan's engine sputtered and died. Its driver and passengers, all four of them, eased out of the car and started to walk toward the men they had trapped.

"Hold it right there, mates!" Ward shouted. "Both of us are armed. We'll kill the lot of you before you can get your guns out."

"Mister Woods, Mister Ward, we have no weapons," said the man who raised his hands. "And we know that neither of you have any weapons either. Major

Green told us you wouldn't be armed, that Count Van Hoff supplied you with information but no guns. We've all had enough excitement for one day, my friends, let's not continue this any longer."

"Who on earth are you people?" Woods asked, raising his head cautiously above the car's trunk.

"It should be obvious we aren't with the Uruguayan government. We aren't with any government, not yet anyway. We're Jews, from America, from Europe and like you, we came here to hunt Nazis. Daniel Green is a very good friend of ours. He told us everything about you and when to expect you . . ."

Woods and Ward slowly emerged from behind their car. The man speaking to them dropped his hands and came forward; extending one to Woods in friendship.

". . . My name is Samuel Ephron. You might say I'm the leader of my group. Which one of you is Michael Woods?"

"You might say I am, mate," Ward responded, cutting in before Woods could open his mouth.

"No, I'm afraid you aren't. I was told Michael Woods is South African. You're Australian, I'd know an Australian accent anywhere. I served in the Pacific during the war. I think your friend here is Mister Woods and that you're Douglas Ward."

"You're right, I am Mike Woods. Sorry for leading you on a merry chase and all but we're new to this world of spying. You could say we were on edge."

"It's understandable. I served in Navy intelligence but my friends here didn't and they acted much like you two before I arrived. We're lucky the local police didn't see us or we'd be in jail by now. Let's get the hell out of here and go to our headquarters where we can discuss our common problem. This is Lee Mendelsohn, he'll give you directions to the house we're using and will make sure you get in. Our security is rather heavy."

The man Samuel Ephron indicated, a short, stocky type with wiry black hair, climbed into the Ford's front seat along with Woods, much to the consternation of Ward.

"Christ, I'm always getting kicked to the back seat," he grumbled, before Woods started the engine and latched onto the green sedan's tail.

The headquarters Ephron referred to was on the outskirts of Montevideo and proved to be not much smaller than Van Hoff's Falkestaaten, though its location was entirely different. It didn't sit atop a hill in the Vienna Woods but on the Uruguayan shore of the Plate River Estuary. Its architecture was lighter, more open; though in spite of this and the oppressive, late-afternoon heat of South America, the estate did remind Woods of his friend's home in Austria. More by its remoteness than anything else.

At its main gate, there were armed guards who searched each car as it passed through. There were more guards on the estate grounds and even inside the house itself. It did give the place the atmosphere of being a headquarters. On an airy veranda overlooking the South Atlantic, Woods and Ward met with Ephron again.

"I'm glad your Mister Mendelsohn isn't sitting down with us," Woods admitted, as the parties gathered around a large, circular table. "I have scarcely met a more abrasive individual. Doug and I may have been in the Royal Air Force, but we are not responsible for British foreign policy. Most especially with regards to Palestine. I wasn't even born and my parents weren't even married when the Balfour Declaration was signed!"

Woods banged the table at the end of his last point. Ephron leaned forward and put a hand on his fist. Coming from someone else, Woods would've considered the gesture both effeminate and patronizing but it wasn't. Instead it was calming and said much quicker than words that he understood why Woods was so angry.

"Lee is not the most diplomatic of men, Ephron said, with an acknowledging smile. "Which is one of the reasons why his father sent him here and not to the Middle East. Lee has friends in the Irgun, he would probably be killing British soldiers with the other fools if he were there. We're not happy with him either but he's useful. We'll try to keep him away from you and your friend. Now if we could begin?

"Major Green said you would have information that we'd find extremely interesting. And what you would find interesting is our operation here. Our intelligence network is excellent, better than the Uruguayans or what the Nazis hiding in this country have. I think we have the basis for a trade. You give us the information, we give you the manpower."

"Another trade?" Woods sighed. "Is this all there is to spying? Bartering?"

"No, there's also sneaking around, collecting what you want to barter, buying it, even blackmailing for it, though that's rare. None of this should really surprise either of you. From Major Green's report, you've both become rather proficient at gathering information.

That should make you appreciate my offer of manpower. You're in a country of which you know little and you have no friends or contacts to turn to. There's just us and we can do in a few days or a few hours what might take you weeks to accomplish. You have everything to gain by cooperating with us, and a lot of time to lose."

"All right, now I know how Daniel Green felt when he was given a take it or leave it proposition." Woods handed the manila envelope he'd been holding over to Ephron.

His long, elegant fingers pried open its clasp and he pulled out the few sheets of paper he had bargained so much for. At first he examined them silently, then he spoke as he continued to read through the information.

"This is what Major Green told us to expect. The names of ships on which you and Count Van Hoff believe German fighters are hidden, in crates of scrap metal. And these names of Uruguayan companies? I take it those are the destinations of the aircraft?"

"Of the scrapped aeroplanes, yes. The intact ones we don't know. That's what we're here for. At one point we thought the Uruguayan Air Force might be the purchaser but when we landed earlier today, we saw it has nothing more than transports and Harvard trainers. Those intact aircraft must be going to a third party, probably outside of Uruguay."

"I would tend to agree," said Ephron. "This country isn't a haven for Nazis. Like Spain or Italy or Egypt, it's part of an 'underground railroad' for them. It's a transit point, not a destination. This country is too open and it's a democracy, something rare in

South America. The Nazis like countries that are more remote or have oppressive regimes. Paraguay, Bolivia, Argentina are more likely candidates. I'll have my men look into these companies and watch the harbor. We'll have some answers soon. Until then, let me treat you and Mister Ward to dinner. I guarantee it'll be better than the lunch you had."

Ephron also offered Woods and Ward rooms at the estate and had their belongings brought in from the hotel in Montevideo. They had their first good meal, and later, their first real sleep in days. They were allowed to sleep in the next morning, while Ephron's men worked on the leads they had provided.

"What you've given us is beginning to pay off," he announced, walking in on his new friends after their mid-morning breakfast. "I've rarely had an operation move this quickly."

"Why do you think that is, mate?" Ward asked, mopping up the rest of his fried eggs with his toast.

"Because we've been watching for people, not machines. I think you and your Austrian friend have hit upon something new. We've been watching houses and apartments when we should've been sitting on harbors and industries. This has probably been going on right under our noses for a long time. It would've continued if your friend hadn't come across that wrecked airliner. Who would've guessed the Nazis would be embarking on a rearmament program and not trying to hide in some deep, dark corner of the Earth."

"Chances are no one would have," said Woods. "Not until there was a two-minute radio report or a small headline in the papers, of some Godforsaken country nobody gives a damn about falling to a fascist coup. It would take a long time before anyone noticed that a Nazi state had been created."

"And I fear no one would do anything about it. By becoming an official, national government, these criminals would gain a certain legitimacy. That may sound outlandish but we have to remember that Hitler was a former convict when he rose to power and Goering was a wanted felon back in 1923. The world will have other problems to worry about by then, it has so many now it's a wonder our governments are doing anything about these criminals."

"Are you getting any help from our governments?" Ward asked. "And why's your operation here so big? Yesterday you said this country was just a transit point."

"No, we're not receiving any help officially and the reason why we are in Uruguay is: it's friendly. We'd have a great deal of trouble working in Argentina or Paraguay. Apart from Spain's Francisco Franco, Juan Perón was Adolf Hitler's most ardent admirer. Perhaps if the regime changes things will be different but until then, we'll have to stay in Montevideo. We're busy enough here anyway. The freighter *Mare Tirreno* has finished unloading though the *Cosenza* has just started. Most of its cargo is destined for one smelting company. We're watching it and when something happens, we'll be there to see it."

"C'mon, you schmucks, this way," urged Mendelsohn, leading Woods and Ward down a narrow path. "You'll be able to see the whole plant from the post we set up. C'mon, Sam's there already, damn it."

It was nightfall; some time after sunset though not quite midnight. A time when most people were either enjoying the night life in Montevideo or going to sleep. But not in the industrial plant below the observation post Ephron's men had set up. Once they reached it, Woods and Ward were given binoculars so they could have a better view of what was going on.

"Apparently this type of activity is not at all unusual," said Ephron. "It's easier to keep the smelters going around the clock than to restart them in the morning. The level of activity is odd however. It's up over the last few days as a result of those shipments from Italy. Can you see the crates by the fence? Those are from the *Cosenza* and you can see one of them being unloaded now."

Woods and Ward trained their field glasses on the facility below, at one of its warehouses where, through a large set of open doors, a crate could be seen being dismantled and its contents separated. The scrap metal was dumped into huge bins mounted on trolley wheels while the intact aircraft were lifted, section by section, onto a flat bed trailer. As each bin was filled, it was dragged off to the smelters; as each complete aircraft was extracted from its crate, it was towed through the warehouse. Its eventual destination was a rail head on the plant grounds.

It was almost the same operation Woods and Ward had seen earlier at the scrap yard they had watched in Italy, only in reverse. At the rail head the complete aircraft, Me-109s mostly, were transferred from the flat bed trailers to flat bed railroad cars. Once on the cars, the German fighters were tied down and wrapped in tarpaulins. In the whole train there were a half-dozen or so flat bed cars; along with boxcars and tank cars. Some twenty aircraft had been loaded on the train so far, and from appearances there were more to come.

"Those planes are being shipped as 'mechanized farm machinery'," said Ephron, pointing a flashlight at a sheet of paper he held. "At Salto, the train will enter Argentina and cross its northern provinces to Pocitos, where it will enter Bolivia. The final destination of the farm machinery is San José in Santa Cruz province in Bolivia. We've tracked a number of war criminals to that area before losing them; I doubt those planes of yours will be going anywhere else. I can't believe all this was going on under our noses but, as I told you earlier today, we never watched for the movement of arms. Just fugitives running from the justice of civilization."

"I think we've seen enough," Woods remarked, lowering his binoculars. "Our report, plus those shipping orders you managed to steal, will be enough to convince Claus that we've discovered where the planes are going. What's the political situation in Bolivia like?"

"A true mess. There was a bloody revolt in the country last year. The left is trying to form a coalition government but it isn't working. The situation is unstable and ripe for another overthrow."

"Then it fits perfectly the situation called for in the papers Van Hoff has," said Woods. "It's an opportunity the Nazis wouldn't pass up. If it can be done, I think we should put a call through to Claus. I know it's expensive so we'll pick up the cost. Doug, it's time for us to go."

"Okay, mate," said Ward. 'I wish we could find

ourselves a squadron of Mosquitoes. They'd take care of this in fifteen minutes. I'm bleeding tired of being a spy."

The plant was north of Montevideo, closer to the city of Canelones than Uruguay's capital, and it took more than an hour to reach the estate Ephron's group used as a base of operations. It was after midnight when they arrived, which meant it would be five o'clock in the morning on the European continent.

To make the call, first Ephron had to get on the phone and use his limited Spanish to have the local operator switch them to the international operator. Woods took over and gave the operator Van Hoff's number. After being routed through a Vienna operator, a phone at the other end finally started to ring. When it was answered, the voice from Austria sounded weak though recognizable. It was Jesse Clinton, who in turn got Van Hoff on the line. Of course he was groggy with sleep and Woods had to repeat what he shouted into the receiver.

". . . Major Green contacted some of his friends down here," he continued. "They were of great help to us. They tracked the aircraft and discovered their destination is Bolivia. Yes I can confirm that. They have copies of the shipping orders for the planes. They're going into Bolivia as mechanized farm machinery. Major Green's friends say that a number of war criminals have also fled to Bolivia. What shall we do next, Claus? Would you like us to go to Bolivia?"

"No, that won't be necessary," Van Hoff answered. "You have gathered enough information. I believe completely in what you're telling me. It's time for us to do something and I've decided to change our plans. If you and Douglas are still willing to help me, I'd like you to leave Montevideo on the first available flight."

"Certainly we do, would you like us to fly back to Europe?"

"No, don't come back here. I want you to go to the United States. To Miami, Florida. We'll meet you there in a few days' time. I'll send you our flight number when I can. I've decided we can't do anything more as spies. We can't rely on governments to do what has to be done. We must deal with this problem in the ways we know best, as Eagles and we have one last mission to fly. Good-bye, Michael, we'll see you soon."

Woods signed off a moment later and carefully laid the telephone's handset back on its cradle.

"Well, mate, where do we go now?" Ward asked, he'd been hovering around Woods since the conversation began. "Bolivia? Europe? And what are we supposed to do when we get there?"

"It's neither. We're flying to America and while I don't know what we'll be doing, my guess is our cloak and dagger days are over."

Chapter Five:
RENDEZVOUS.
A GATHERING OF FORCES.

The first available flight from Montevideo to American territory wouldn't leave until the morning; Carrasco airport lacked even the most rudimentary night landing aids. At least it allowed Woods and Ward a chance at some sleep while Ephron's group got them reservations and lined up early meetings at the South African, Australian and American embassies.

Unlike the previous day, Woods and Ward were up at first light, packing, having a last meal and meeting with Ephron before being driven to the city. At the embassies they had their visas and passports stamped for U.S. entry. The procedures took longer than expected, causing them to arrive at the airport only minutes before their flight was due to depart.

A Trans World Airlines DC-4, the most modern aircraft on the field, lifted away with Woods and Ward on it. After reaching cruise altitude, the red and silver airliner set course due north; across Brazil to Caracas, Venezuela where it picked up more passengers and fuel before setting out over the Caribbean for the United States.

Woods and Ward spent a full day in transit and most of it in the air. They were weary though hardly saddle sore; twenty-one hours in an airliner was much less excruciating than the cramped cockpit of a fighter. The DC-4 circled over the hotels of Miami Beach and the waters of Biscayne Bay before heading into Miami International.

At last, a busy airport filled with modern aircraft. There were even jets, U.S. Air Force F-80s at the military side of the field. Woods gave them a long, admiring look while he and Ward made their way through customs. They went to a hotel near the airport where they took out a room for themselves and asked if they could make a long-distance phone call to Europe.

"That's excellent, Michael," said Van Hoff, this time the connection was much better, much clearer. "We should arrive on Thursday, two days from now, on Pan American flight Two-thirty-three. If you can, rent out an entire floor of the hotel for us. If you don't have enough money to do so, phone me again and I'll wire you the money. See you soon, Michael."

"Well that was certainly odd," said Woods, hanging up the phone and turning to Ward. "Claus wants us to rent an entire floor of rooms for him. I wonder what's going on? I thought just he and Jesse Clinton were coming?"

"Maybe our friend's becoming a real count?" Ward offered. "I heard them royal types do things like that. They always take the best rooms, go first-class. Not that I mind it, mate. If he goes first-class, then we'll go first-class."

They had enough money left from their travels to do as Van Hoff requested, provided they didn't eat too lavishly or act like tourists while in Miami. They spent their days quietly, watching a new device recently installed in the hotel's bar, television. Then, just after lunch on Thursday, they went back to Miami International where they waited at the customs gate for the arrival of their friends. On time, a Pan Am Constellation droned into sight and spiralled down for a landing. The customs area had no viewing windows and as a result, Woods and Ward couldn't see who Van Hoff had brought with him until they came through the doors.

"Jesse, well I knew Claus would bring you along," said Woods, when Clinton appeared. "Do you know why he asked me to reserve an entire floor? What's he doing, bringing a whole squadron with him?"

"He is, in a way. Just wait and see."

One by one, they filed through the customs gate. Jack Reynolds, Daniel Green, André Clostermann, Desmond Kain, Eric Kingston, Dennis Brandon and finally Van Hoff himself. There were so many, they crowded the hallway outside.

"Claus, what the hell is going on?" Woods demanded, flabbergasted at the collection of friends and fellow pilots. "Why are they all with you? What is this, reunion time?"

"It's a change of plans," said Van Hoff, calmly. "I don't think this is the place to explain to you at length what's happened or what we'll be doing. But suffice it to say, we will all be flying one more mission."

It took four taxicabs to transport the men and their luggage to the hotel. They stormed its small lobby like an invading army; it was a half-hour before the turmoil died down and they were assigned to their rooms. Not that they remained in them for very long, as soon as they threw their suitcases and bags on their beds, they made for the room assigned to Van Hoff. In minutes it became so crowded there was scarcely room to move or breathe.

"Okay, mate, now will you tell us what's going on?" Ward asked. "It looks to me like you're creating your own private air force."

"No, my friend, just a squadron," Van Hoff replied. "We will stop what you've uncovered not as spies or bureaucrats but as fighter pilots. In a very real sense, World War Two is not yet over, we have one more mission to fly."

"Wait, wait. Are you seriously suggesting that we take the law into our own hands?" Woods asked.

"What we've uncovered no tribunal can handle and no government will believe. They have more pressing problems to deal with, stopping the Russians or merely trying to survive. We can take care of this ourselves because we have the skills, the resources and because the plot hasn't grown too big yet. Once we locate the target or targets, a single air strike will destroy everything. In a way this really isn't my idea, it's yours, all of you. To a man, each of you told me you were only a fighter pilot, so how could you help me? Well, here's a way you can help me, as fighter pilots . . ."

"Yes, I do remember saying that to you," Woods admitted.

". . . This situation is perfect for our kind. It can't be resolved legally, it's gone beyond that. It has to be stopped tactically and we are the best people to do so. We're the experts and we have the resources."

"What resources? You don't have an air force here, just a collection of friends," said Woods.

"It's a beginning and we have the information you and Ward gathered. In due time we will acquire everything else we'll need. For now I, and all of us, would like to hear what you've found. I've shown everyone the plans I discovered so you don't have to worry about whether or not they'll understand. They will and afterwards, I'll explain why the Nazis seem to have chosen Bolivia."

As Woods explained how they got to Montevideo, Ward opened his suitcase and started to display what they had found during their short stay in the city. He even produced photographs, of the ships in Montevideo harbor, of the smelting plant where the intact aircraft were extracted from the crates of scrap metal and of the trainload of thinly disguised fighters. They had all been taken by people in Ephron's group, who, Woods went to great length to explain, had been so helpful.

"If it weren't for him and the services of his organization, Doug and I would still be in Uruguay," he maintained. "Chasing our own shadows probably. They did all this, really, in exchange for the lists we let them see."

"It's incredible," said Reynolds, looking at one of

the photographs. "A pity you can't put these in *Life* magazine. But that wouldn't achieve what we want. It would only create a furor and drive the bastards deep underground where they'd be almost impossible to find and stop. Do you know why they chose Bolivia and not some other South American country?"

"I don't actually know, the Nazis didn't tell me," said Van Hoff. "Though based on those plans I showed you, I can well understand why Bolivia was chosen. It's the perfect country for them in every respect. It's small, it's remote, even by South American standards. Bolivia is landlocked, so they won't need a navy, just an army and an air force. And it's unstable, has been for years.

"In 1932, a war started between Bolivia and Paraguay over a long-standing border dispute. It was provoked by then Bolivian president Daniel Salamanca, in order to stop political opposition to his regime. Bolivia went into the war better armed and trained than Paraguay; however, because of poor tactics and leadership, it lost the war after three years and one hundred thousand casualties. The returning Bolivian veterans were called the Chaco generation, it was they who overthrew the civilian government in 1936 and started a dictatorship.

"By 1940 civilian dissidents had organized into two opposition parties. One, the Nationalist Revolutionary Movement was fascist and the other, the Party of the Leftist Revolution, was of course communist. In 1943, a secret military group allied with the fascists overthrew General Peñaranda and set up a Colonel Villaroel as president.

"Both Villaroel and the NRM were controlled by the Nazis. When they lost the war, Villaroel lost control of his country and last year there was a bloody revolt. Villaroel was hanged in front of the presidential palace at La Paz and the communists gained power. Since then they've tried to rule in coalition with other parties but nothing has worked. The country is in turmoil, the government is ineffective, it's exactly like the last days of the Weimar Republic. A small, well-armed group could easily take absolute control. For the Nazis, it would be like reliving their days of glory."

"All right, I buy the idea," Reynolds conceded. "But why are they using German aircraft? There's whole fields of U.S. planes they could buy for a song."

"There are too many restrictions on their sale," said Green. "Especially if those planes are going out of the country. The German aircraft, on the other hand, were sold as scrap metal, supposedly chopped into scrap and who gives a damn about where they go? I know a little bit about these things, I have a few friends who are trying to buy aircraft for the future Israeli Air Force."

"And where else can they obtain high-performance aircraft?" Van Hoff added. "Tempests, late-model Mustangs and Spitfires are simply not being sold. What the Nazis are buying, at a fraction of the cost, is the cream of their war machine. Focke-Wulfs and 109s that could equal our best fighters. We won't have as good a choice."

"Yes, that's another problem," said Woods. "What type of aeroplane will we use? Most of us can fly Spitfires but there are damn few Spits in the United States. And there's a hundred more problems we have to solve. What about logistics? Where will we find weapons and munitions? What about petrol? Spare parts? We are merely pilots, we never had to worry much about those problems."

"I know, I understand. We have a hundred questions which need to be answered. Don't worry, in due time they will be solved. Mister Reynolds told me of an American way to solve problems. Throw money at them. Now that is something I have the resources to do."

"Why are you so against this idea, mate?" asked Ward. "Simply because it's illegal never stopped you in the past."

"I know," said Woods. "It's just that we'll encounter so many problems and setbacks we may become discouraged. How much time will we take? Claus, many of the men you have here are still in the military. How much leave do they have? What will happen when it starts to run out and they have to go back or face a court-martial? Have you thought of that? Or are we doing this the same way you pulled off your little flight to Austria at the end of the war?"

"Michael, you're not being fair," said Brandon, interceding on Van Hoff's behalf. "We all put our heads together on this. We each took the maximum amount of leave time and called in a few favors. Some of us even took an early discharge. Such as Colonel Reynolds, he's out months ahead of time. I think I know the real reason why you're against our plan. You miss Margaret, don't you? I miss my own Margaret as well, and my daughter. It's difficult, I know, but we made these sacrifices in the past and we won't be away for too long. Besides, you married an Englishwoman, not some little Afrikaaner. I'm sure she'll understand."

"I hope you're right," Woods replied. "I'll be in for it if you're not. Since we have a hundred problems facing us, which one shall we solve first?"

"The most obvious one," said Van Hoff, "decide which fighter we're to use. All of us have flown a variety of types. Reynolds and Jesse last flew Mustangs, Green and Clostermann, P-47s and the rest of us flew either Spitfires of Tempests. At one point we all must've flown the same aircraft. Everyone make a list and we'll find out which one. Jack, you do the list for Mister Acerrio and Dennis, you do it for McCloud."

"Acerrio? Jeffrey McCloud? Why are we including them?" Woods asked.

"Simple. Every squadron I've been in needs at least twelve pilots and there are only ten of us here."

There was a search for paper before anyone could start a list. Van Hoff eventually found a note pad among his luggage and distributed sheets of paper among the others; then they had to share the small supply of pens among them. As each finished his list, they were handed over to Van Hoff and Reynolds.

"We can ignore all the British aircraft they've written down," said Reynolds, looking over the first lists to be turned in. "Apart from some Hurricanes and Mosquitoes built in Canada, none of these aircraft exist on this side of the world. We'll have to concentrate on the American types."

"Nothing so far is adding up," said Van Hoff. "There is no common aircraft among the ones we've flown."

"Yes there is, you're just not seeing it because of the different names we're using. Look, what you, Woods and Kingston call the Kittyhawk, I call the Tomahawk and Danny calls the Warhawk. It all adds up to the same airplane, the Curtiss P-40. That's the one for us."

"What? The Kittyhawk?" cried Ward, incredulously. "That crate was obsolete in 1942, when we first received it. How are we supposed to fly against late-model 190s and win?"

"I would prefer a more advanced aeroplane," said Van Hoff. "But the choice is being forced on us."

"You can 'speak for yourself, mate' about taking on Focke-Wulfs," said Kingston. "I can go up against an Me-262 in a bloody Tiger Moth and win. You're forgetting all of us now have four or five years of combat flying under our belts. That kind of experience will cancel out any advantage in performance the enemy will have."

"And what if their pilots are just as good as we are?" Woods asked. "What then?"

"We shall always have the advantage of surprise," said Van Hoff. "In any case, we can find out if ex-Luftwaffe pilots are being imported. Daniel, do you think your friends in Montevideo could help us there?"

"They're on the watch for war criminals," Green replied. "Not pilots, but I'm sure they can do it."

"Good, that at least is settled. I'm afraid it's

unanimous, Douglas. The only aircraft all of us have in common is the Curtiss Kittyhawk, or as Jack calls it, the P-40. Jack, are you sure what you wrote for Mister Acerrio is correct?"

"I'm sure it is," said Reynolds. "Tony's first assignment was to the Forty-fourth Pursuit Squadron, Wheeler Field, Hawaii. He shot down his first enemy plane on December seventh, 1941. Ten days before I bagged my first."

"And all of us who served with Jeffrey know he flew Kittyhawks in Alaska," Brandon added. "In fact I believe he shot down the only Japanese plane to fall to a Canadian fighter during the Aleutian campaign."

"Well, finding enough of those aircraft to suit our needs should be easy," said Green. "There's whole fields of P-40s out west. Again, that's a little tidbit of info from my friends in the future Israeli Air Force."

"And once we buy the planes we want, my brother's company can take care of them," said Reynolds. "That's how we'll take care of part of our logistics problem, Mike. And don't worry about weapons, either. I have a source for those as well."

"You see, we'll solve many of our problems in the next few days," said Van Hoff. "For the time being we need a meal and some rest. Fourteen hours even in a luxury airliner can be tiring. Michael, you and Doug are going to have to do a little work for us. We'll be needing airline tickets for tomorrow and we have to send out telegrams, also wire some money. Jack, how much money do you think Mister Acerrio needs?"

"I'd say about eight hundred dollars, to cover both the cost of tickets and to pay off some of his debts."

"All right, I'll draw the money from my new American account after we've finished our lunch. Michael, can you recommend a good restaurant in this area?"

It was Daniel Green who ended up picking them a restaurant, one his family went to every time they vacationed in Miami. Following lunch, Van Hoff and most of the group retired to the hotel while Woods went to the airline ticket agencies and Ward to the nearest Western Union office. When they got back to their rooms, they found all their friends asleep; though Van Hoff had left them some additional instructions as to when they should wake up the rest of the group.

"It seems like we'll be having an early day tomorrow," Woods remarked, looking over the sheet of orders. "Dennis and I will be the first to leave. We'll fly to Toronto to collect Jeffrey McCloud. The rest of you will head out to a Des Moines in a state called Iowa. Apparently Iowa is where Jack Reynolds's brother has his air service. Claus wants us all to be up several hours ahead of time."

"Makes sense," said Ward. "This is starting to sound like the old days. Soon we'll be having predawn briefings. I only wish we could've had quarters like these during the war."

"Yes, how much easier the war would've been to fight if we could've waged it from such luxury. Only this doesn't do much for the loneliness I still feel."

"Well, mate, there is a way to handle it." Ward

sat down on the bed and reached for the telephone on the night table. "The telephone network in the U.S. is much better than down in South America or over in Europe. Why don't you call Margaret? I'm sure it's not too late in South Africa."

"No, it would only be nine-thirty at night in East London. I don't think I should try. It would only make the whole situation worse. I think I'll just go to the bar, look at my wife's picture and drink until I pass out. Care to join me?"

"Pardon me, madame, my friend and I are looking for Squadron Leader Jeffrey McCloud," Brandon announced, stepping back from the door as an elderly woman pushed it open. "We were told he's living here, would he happen to be in?"

"He is," she answered, eyeing Brandon and Woods suspiciously. "But first things first, are you his wife's lawyers?"

"Indeed no, we're his friends, we served in the same wing during the war. This is his commanding officer."

"Oh, you'd be that Michael Woods he's talked about. He's here all right, you'll find him out in back. Just go around the side there and lift the gate. He'll be building model airplanes, it's the only thing he does these days."

After thanking the woman, Brandon and Woods circled around the house as she told them and found their friend sitting at a table; doing what she claimed he would be, constructing balsa wood model aircraft.

"Jeffrey, old boy," said Brandon. "I see you're back at your favourite hobby."

"My God, where did you two come from!" McCloud shouted, jumping up and spinning around.

"Miami, about six hours ago," said Woods. "Before then Dennis came from Europe and I came from South America."

"I thought Claus would come for me. Please, sit down."

"No, we were sent to collect you," said Brandon, taking McCloud's offer. "Van Hoff and the others are flying on to a place called Des Moines, Iowa. We've decided to mount a combat operation. We've even decided which aircraft to use."

"I thought you would, I didn't think you'd come here to see if I could influence the Canadian government for you."

"The woman we met at the front door asked us if we were your wife's solicitors," Woods informed. "I take it that means you've separated from Lynn?"

"Yes, the ten-month seige is over. Now I know how those poor bastards at Dunkirk, Anzio and Arnhem must've felt. It's all finished except for deciding who gets what."

"We're very sorry to hear that, Jeffrey," said Brandon. "What happened to the crystal Margaret and I gave you as a wedding present?"

"Dennis, that's mercenary," Woods admonished.

"No, it's okay. I think we smashed most of it in one of our last fights. A smashed marriage, a smashed job, I guess you could say I really pranged up my life. It seems as though the only thing I can do right is this." McCloud held up the fuselage of a

Spitfire he was in the middle of making. "I make 'em for the neighborhood kids but I don't think I can earn a living off them."

"Why aren't you in the Royal Canadian Air Force?" asked Brandon. "A veteran with your record. An ace. Why they'd snap you up in a second."

"They probably would but I don't want to be part of an air force that has three thousand trainers and only thirty fighters. They'd stick me behind a desk or make me an instructor and that I couldn't stand."

"I know, you want to fly fighters again. Well, we've come here to give you back that job. We can't promise you much money or the latest in equipment. What we're doing is illegal and possibly dangerous but it is a chance for you to fly once more."

"Claus told me something of this mission when he phoned me," said McCloud. "That it would take place in South America and would have something to do with aborting a Nazi take-over. Right now I wouldn't care if it entailed flying ruddy Piper Cubs against German jets, I'd take it anyway. You're right, it's a chance for me to get back in the air and to escape this damnable mess I've found myself in. By the way, what type of aircraft will we be using? I trust it'll be fighters."

"Of course we'll be using fighters," Brandon answered, a little indignantly. "Most of us aren't qualified to fly any other type. We have to use an aircraft all of us have flown at one time. Unfortunately, with the Americans, the Australians and even a Frenchman among us, our backgrounds are so varied only one fighter qualifies. The Curtiss P-40

Kittyhawk."

"Well, at least she's better than a Piper Cub. You have any idea what we'll be flying against?"

"I do," said Woods. "Doug Ward and I saw them being transported. Late-model Focke-Wulfs and Messerschmitts. The long-nosed Doras and maybe some of those fighter-bomber 190s. The 109s we saw were all R-models, with those tall tails and frameless hoods. From what we can guess, there might be as many as fifty all told."

"And how many of us will there be?" McCloud inquired.

"Twelve so far, I don't think Claus will try for more."

"My God, that's four-to-one odds. I certainly hope you plan to catch 'em on the ground and not engage them in the air. I don't care how good we are, those kind of odds could get us all killed."

"I'm certain that's what we'll do once we reach South America. But first we have to find some Kittyhawks and fly them to Bolivia before we decide how to attack."

"I know where you can locate a few P-40s," said McCloud, collecting his unfinished model and the tools he'd been using to build it. "There was a fighter OTU based at Portage La Prairie during the war. They used a few Hurricanes and a lot of Kittyhawks. I have a friend who works at the base and a few months ago he said they were going to sell off the planes stored there. If you're willing to pay the charges, I'll call him and find out how many are left. Then we can meet Claus and the others in Manitoba."

"I take it that means you're joining us?" Brandon asked.

"As I said before, I don't care if it means flying Piper Cubs against jets, I'll do it. Your offer puts me back in a fighter, it gets me out of this mess with my wife and I'll be back with friends again. Right now, I wouldn't dare ask for anything more. C'mon, let's go to my room and make some calls. As soon as they're done, I can start packing."

From Miami, Reynolds took the rest of the group to Love Field at St. Louis where they changed airplanes and air lines to complete the trip to Des Moines. They practically filled the war-surplus Lodestar Ozark used for the run to Iowa. As it lined up on final for Des Moines Municipal Airport, they could see a hangar with Reynolds Air Services painted on it. At the terminal, the group was met by Jack Reynolds's younger brother.

Robert Reynolds was some six years younger than Jack, had darker hair, even different colored eyes but he still looked like his brother. They shook hands and embraced like brothers, then Jack introduced Robert to the rest of the group.

"A great bunch of guys," said Bob as he led Jack away from the baggage claim office. "Except for their accents, they remind me of the men I flew with. Whatever mission you guys are on, it has to be big. You don't line up talent like that to strafe some gun position or truck convoy."

"It is big, I'll fill you in later. Bob, why are you taking me over here?"

"Because I have an introduction of my own to make."

"Oh, who is it? Your top pilot or mechanic?"

"No, it's someone you know. Someone I don't think you ever thought you'd see again."

Bob took his brother out of the terminal and over to a small line of cars. The driver's door opened on one of them and out stepped a young, dark-haired woman. She had clean features, short cut hair and looked to be less than half the age of the older Reynolds. She also looked nervous, apprehensive; and she had his eyes.

"She came to us about two months ago," Bob Reynolds explained. "When she heard you were retiring. She's eighteen now, by California law she can decide where to live and it's not with her mother any more. She wants to be with you."

"Marilyn?" Reynolds uttered, halting his stride for a moment, then holding out his hands to her.

"Daddy!" Marilyn shouted, bolting away from the car and running into his arms. She embraced him tightly, buried her head in his rumpled flight jacket and began to cry. "Daddy, please don't be angry with me but I had to see you. Mother wouldn't bring me out to see you so I came alone. Please don't send me back, I don't want to go back. I want to be with you. It's been years since I saw you."

"I know, it's been almost seven years," said Reynolds, holding onto his daughter. "Ever since your mother divorced me for not leaving the Air Corps and joining some air line like she wanted. You took me by surprise, Angel."

"I'm sorry but I didn't know how to tell you I was here. I didn't know if you wanted me."

"I didn't mean you surprised me that way. I expected to see a little girl in pigtails. I forgot that in seven years you'd have grown into a woman. And of course I want you, I wanted you from the day your mother took you."

"We're not ten minutes on the ground and already he's found himself a local girl," said Ward, as the rest of the group emerged from the terminal. "Don't you think she's a bit young for you, mate?"

"That's not a girl friend, you twit," Kingston pointed out. "That's his daughter, didn't you hear him say so? Stop coming to such unsavory conclusions."

"Jack, this is a side none of us knew you had," said Van Hoff, stepping up next to Reynolds. "We knew you had been married but you never mentioned a daughter."

"I had little reason to, Claus. My divorce wasn't one of my life's better experiences. In fact it was the reason why I jumped at Claire Chennault's offer to fly fighters in China a few months later. I didn't think I'd ever see Marilyn again but it looks like I was wrong. Oh, Marilyn, I'd like you to meet my friends. This one is Count Claus Van Hoff, he flew with the Royal Air Force."

"Charmed to meet you, Miss Reynolds." Van Hoff took Marilyn's hand in his and kissed it. "You look so much like your father, you have his eyes. Jack, I hate to ruin this reunion, but how will you take care of your daughter and where will she stay?"

"She'll stay with us, Mister Van Hoff," said Bob Reynolds, "with my wife and I. She's really been helpful to us, Jack. She's one of our secretaries at the air service, she helps clean our planes and is even learning to fly. Everybody into the cars, I'll take you to see our operations."

Reynolds had to cut short showing off his daughter to his friends. Instead, they piled their luggage in the waiting cars then sped off, driving around the airfield perimeter until they reached the general aviation side. The cars were parked behind the hangar owned by Reynolds Air Services and Bob led the group in through a side door.

"Like we agreed, Jack, we offer air freighting, crop dusting and photo surveying," Bob explained. "These are the planes we use for crop dusting. We have eight altogether."

"But these are Wildcats," his brother replied. "They're Navy fighters. I thought you were getting Stearman biplanes?"

"Hell every spray outfit uses Stearmans. We had to come up with something better. These FM-2s have a much better performance, they can carry bigger loads and, by virtue of their folding wings, can be stored in less than half the space of a PT-17. In the Pacific, I saw how useful that can be. And these Wildcats didn't cost too much more than Stearmans would have."

"Okay, I guess we're stuck with them. What type of transports did you buy?"

"C-46 Commandos," said Bob. "They can carry almost twice the payload of a Gooney Bird and can stow far bulkier items. We have four of them, one of which is out on assignment. I also bought us a B-23 Dragon, to fly around executives and that too is on assignment. It's a sideline to our freight hauling, I think it'll be very profitable. Our last two airplanes are an F-5-G for photo survey and an AT-6 for conversion training."

"F-5? Are you referring to a reconnaissance Lightning?" asked Clostermann.

"Yes, it's based on the last model of the P-38 to be built. It carries three, six-inch chart cameras, one twelve-inch and two twenty-four inch recon cameras. She's a thirsty bird but we've had a lot of success with her. Is there any other plane you guys would like to know about?"

"There is. P-40s, we'd like to buy some," said Reynolds. "A dozen in all. You know where there are any?"

"Sure I do, but why do you want so many? You guys setting yourselves up as a private air force?"

"You could say so, we need them for the special operation I told you about when I called you. Well, Claus, what do you think of Reynolds Air Services?"

"It will suit our needs," said Van Hoff. "Especially the air freight and photo survey branches. As we should all remember from the war, without reconnaissance, we're blind. I would like to discuss this further, in your brother's office perhaps? And just the three of us."

"Okay, my office isn't too big anyway."

"Daddy, Uncle Bob, why are you talking about war and special operations?" Marilyn asked, Reynolds had almost forgotten about her. "I thought you came here to run a business?"

"I did but there's something else we have to take care of first," he explained, trying to be vague. "Angel, could you show my other friends the rest of our air fleet? She'll answer any questions you have, except if she's free on Saturday night. You're my friends and I'd trust any of you with my life but not with my daughter."

While Marilyn took the balance of the group over to the white and red trimmed Lightning; Bob Reynolds showed his older brother and Van Hoff to his office.

"Your daughter could be a problem for us," said Van Hoff, looking at her from the office window.

"Well if any of you young bucks start fighting over her, I'll kick your heads in," said Reynolds.

"No, I don't mean that way, though she is a beautiful young woman. She might not understand why we're on this mission, this crusade. Try to keep her in the dark as much as possible, Jack. Develop some other story as to why we're buying so many fighters. Mister Reynolds, have you found a place where we might buy Kittyhawks?"

"Bob, please. If you're gonna call Jack, Jack, you should call me Bob." The younger Reynolds thumbed his way through a tiny box of file cards; suddenly he stopped and pulled out one of the cards. "Walnut Ridge Army Air Base, Arkansas. It had a large number of P-40s on surplus last year. Let's see if there are any still available."

Bob Reynolds picked up the phone and asked for the long-distance operator. After several minutes he had the answer, there were none left. All had been sold to scrap dealers months before. He returned to the file box and produced a few more names of bases and storage depots that might have P-40s. During the third call there was a knock at the door which Jack Reynolds went to answer.

"Daddy, there's a man here to see you," said Marilyn. "He walked over from the airport terminal and it looks like some of your friends know him."

Reynolds could almost guess who it was. He had only to catch sight of the short, slight frame and the wiry black hair of the recent arrival to know it was Acerrio. The group had by then clustered around the company's one T-6 Texans; apart from the Curtiss P-40, it was probably the only other plane the pilots were all familiar with.

"Hey, Colonel!" Acerrio shouted, he turned around and ran for the hangar the moment he caught sight of his old commanding officer. "I just got in from Chicago. Jeez, what's going on around here? Are you and your brother holding some kind of fighter pilot's convention? Or are those guys applying for the same flying job you offered me?"

"You could say it's a convention of sorts," said Reynolds. "But one with a purpose. You can't say what I'm offering you is really a job, though it is a chance to fly. Our friends are here for the same reason you are. We have an extra special mission to fly and a dozen positions to fill. How'd you like to fly a P-40 again?"

"I'd prefer one of those Mustangs the Air National Guard's got over there but I'll sure take it. Will I get paid anything and where will we be flying?"

136

"Like I told you, I don't know what we'll be paid. That's all up to Claus Van Hoff, he's financing the operation. We'll be flying to South America, a country called Bolivia, which is old territory for me. We didn't catch and kill all the Nazis after the war. A lot of them fled to Bolivia and we think they're going to take it over. Michael Woods and one of the Australians over there have traced shipments of German fighters to Bolivia. You remember Woods, don't you?"

"Hey, yeah, he was one of those guys we flew to Austria with back in '45," Acerrio replied, after he took a moment to recall the name. "And wasn't this Van Hoff the guy we flew in to get? Did he ever find out who killed his family?"

"Yes, in a way. Part of the Nazi hierarchy still exists. And we think they're the ones in Bolivia."

"Well no wonder he's paying for the show. When do we start, Colonel?"

"As soon as we find some P-40s," said Reynolds, before his brother appeared at the office door and called for him. Reynolds quickly excused himself and ran to find out what he wanted, asking his brother about the obvious. "Bob, did you find a base where they have P-40s?"

"There's one all right," said Bob. "Only I didn't find it. One of your friends, Mike Woods, just called and claims that Canadian ace you're recruiting knows of a field in Canada where we'll find P-40s. Mister Van Hoff is taking down the information. Once he gets it all, I'll see about filing a flight plan for us. Looks like we'll be traveling tomorrow."

Chapter Six:
THE PURCHASE.
RETURN FLIGHT.

"Tower to Reynolds-Four-Five-Victor, you are cleared to land. Use exit ramp A-four and proceed to the western side of the field where the storage depot is located. Tower to Reynolds-Seven-Three-Three-Charlie, you may land once Four-Five-Victor is off the runway."

First the C-46 Commando swung onto the final approach, then the T-6 which had escorted it all the way from Des Moines. They each wore much the same markings; red and white trim lines with the name Reynolds Air Services somewhere on the fuselage sides. Overall the planes were bare metal with an occasional hint of faded Army Air Force insignia.

The directions the transport had been given were easy to follow. Once off the runway it taxied over to the densely packed rows of fighters, bombers and trainers on the field's one side. The Commando was met by a small entourage of R.C.A.F. officers and a trio of civilians.

"Welcome to Portage La Prairie, Mister Van Hoff," said the highest ranking officer in the group, as the passengers stepped out of the transport. "My friend, Jeffrey McCloud, claims you're interested in purchasing some of our excess Kittyhawks. I'd be delighted to help you but as a foreign national, you must be aware that you'll have to pass a security check before you're allowed to buy any war materials. I'm afraid the check will take some time."

"I already know of such procedures, Wing Commander," said Van Hoff. "Which is why Jack Reynolds and his brother will actually buy the aeroplanes. They are the co-owners of Reynolds Air Services and they have the authorization to purchase government surplus equipment in both Canada and America. This is Bob Reynolds and Jack is just arriving."

The T-6 rolled in beside the Commando and shut down. It had only Reynolds on board; as he climbed out the civilians who'd been waiting with the officers came over to greet him. The first to shake his hand was Michael Woods.

"I take it this is part of your air fleet," he said. "The rest of what you have must be impressive. Tell me, why did you decide to bring along the Harvard?"

"Actually, this is a T-six and the reason why I flew it in is to give you guys proficiency flights before turning you loose on P-40s. Not all of us have had time recently on high performance, single-engine aircraft."

"And considering what civilians think is high-performance, I suppose this aircraft qualifies," said McCloud, running his hand across the leading edge of the T-6's wing. "There was a day when I turned down the offer to fly a Harvard. These last few months, I would've given my eye teeth for just a ten-minute hop in one. When can we start?"

"As soon as we buy our P-40s," Reynolds replied. "I see my brother has already started talking with the base officers. Have you looked over the planes here?"

"Yes, there's forty-two Kittyhawks in all," said Woods, pulling a slip of paper from his pocket. "Eleven are little more than hulks, they were pranged up in training accidents and not repaired. It would take some doing to put them back in the air. The remaining thirty-one are behind us. Most of those are Mark Four Kittyhawks, P-40-Ns to you Yanks. They're in much more reasonable shape, I don't think it would take long to make them flyable."

"If I may suggest, you should purchase as many early-model Kittyhawks as you can," said Brandon. "Few of us have flown the later Mark Fours."

"I'll try but what we should take are those planes that have the lowest number of flying hours and the most recent engine overhauls. Let's see what Bob's up to."

Reynolds joined his brother, who was busy showing the base officers the papers which allowed him to buy surplus war material from the Canadian government. Once they were sure of their authenticity, they took the two brothers on what amounted to a guided tour of the stored fighters. They brought along the service records of each P-40, handing over to the brothers the file of whatever plane they stopped at. They took their time walking through the rows of Kittyhawks. After all, they were deciding the fate of all the aircraft; for those they did not choose would probably end up in the hands of scrap dealers.

The rest of the pilots busied themselves with inspecting the other aircraft in the storage area. Especially with the Hawker Hurricanes parked next to the Kittyhawks. It was among them that Jack and his brother found the other pilots when they finished their inspection.

"Well, I think we've found twelve planes that will suit us," Reynolds announced, waving a handful of folders at Van Hoff and the rest. "Bob, go get your mechanics and start pulling the airplanes we want out of the rows. Claus, if you're willing to accept our choices, it's time for us to go buy ourselves a squadron."

Reynolds had chosen an equal number of P-40Es and later-model P-40Ns; a half-dozen of each. While he, Van Hoff and McCloud drove away with the Canadian officers; the rest of the group spread out among the fighters to find which ones they would hopefully soon be flying.

"This Kittyhawk's a Mark Four," said Ward. "And so's that one. I've never flown a Mark Four, just Ones and Threes. I'd rather fly one of the earlier Marks."

"They're not too different," said Clinton. "I've flown every model of the P-40 from Tomahawks at Luke Field to the Warhawk Ns. There isn't a lot of difference, just don't look for a wheel and flaps indicator in the cockpit of a Warhawk."

"I'll have to relearn how to fly aeroplanes that have one-half the horsepower of a Tempest," Brandon noted, cracking open the canopy of a P-40E and looking inside the musty cockpit. "God, this takes me back. To North Africa in 'forty-two when I first flew the Hawk."

"I wonder how much it will cost the Count to purchase these fighters?" asked Kain. "I remember my first C.O. in New Guinea, telling me it cost the Yanks forty-five thousand dollars to build a Kittyhawk so I'd better not wreck one or he'd make me pay for it."

"In the States, you can buy a B-17 for around fourteen thousand dollars," said Green. "About one-twentieth what it originally cost to build. I think the Royal Canadian Air Force or the War Assets Corporation, or whoever owns these planes, will probably let them go for two or three thousand apiece. That'll include full tanks of gas and oil but no machine guns or gun sight or bombing equipment. Those things we'll have to get some other way."

"Hey, look, there's the jeep," said Acerrio. He was standing on the wing of one of the P-40s and from his vantage point he could see almost the entire base. "It's got the Colonel and McCloud and the Count in it."

That was all the group needed to hear, they scrambled around the P-40s; reaching the front row as the jeep pulled to a stop. Neither Reynolds, or Van Hoff or McCloud had to say a word; from the smiles they were wearing, everyone knew a sale had been made. For the grand total of thirty thousand dollars Canadian, Reynolds Air Services had just purchased a dozen Kittyhawk fighters.

". . . And we've also bought ten thousand dollars worth of spare parts," Reynolds added, showing everyone the bills of sale. "Everything from Allison engines to formation lights. Enough to run a squadron for a few weeks at least. It all has to be packed into the Commando or used to get the P-40s flying. That will take time, and the base commander will let us use his maintenance facilities and has opened up his spare officers quarters so we don't have to rent rooms at some hotel. There'll be a couple of mules here soon. They'll take our planes over to hangar Two-A, where all those T-6s are located. Excuse me, since we're in Canada, they're Harvards. We'll work on 'em in there. Now I know some of you are going to say, 'I only know how to drive them'. Well, today you're going to learn how to fix them."

The mules—handling vehicles—arrived dragging tow bars, which were attached to the main landing gear struts of the first two Kittyhawks to be hauled away to the hangar. The mules didn't stay to help extract the other ten from the rows of stored aircraft. With nearly two dozen men to call on, Reynolds found it easy to push the unwanted planes out of the way to retrieve those he had bought. And when the last was being pulled down the flight line of bright yellow trainers, he ordered the remaining fighters to be put back in some kind of order. At least the storage area would look neat.

Those who were left at the site had to hike it to the hangar. They arrived to find the process of restoring the P-40s already well under way. The mechanics Reynolds had brought along were pulling off the cowling panels to inspect the engines. While there weren't enough to work on all the planes at once, some off-duty R.C.A.F. ground crews helped increase their ranks and Reynolds assigned the pilots to work with them. Even himself.

"The plane you work on will be the one you'll fly," he told the other pilots. "Now if it happens to be a version you've never flown before, just pick up a flight handbook when we leave today. Consider it something to do before turning in tonight, instead of reading cheap novels or listening to the radio."

There was some grumbling as the aircraft assignments were handed out though no one openly objected. For most of the pilots, a P-40 was a P-40 no matter what its model or mark number. The hangar was alive with activity until early evening, when the rest of the air base closed for the day.

The officers quarters were damp and cold from months of not being used. It took hours for their primitive heating systems to warm them up and then the amount of coal issued to the building wasn't enough to keep it warm all night long. By early morning everyone was shivering.

The day was spent getting the first P-40s ready to fly. Bob Reynolds contacted the Civil Aeronautics Administration to obtain both permission to fly the fighters into the U.S. and temporary registration certificates for the ferry flight. His brother flew check rides in their company's T-6 for those pilots who had no recent time in military aircraft. By early-afternoon the first trio of P-40s had had all their systems checked and the bird nests, wasp nests and cobwebs cleaned out of them. They were towed onto the flight line and, one by one, their engines were started.

The smooth, muted thunder of the Allison engines was a marked contrast to the deafening howls of Pratt and Whitney radials. It was even different from the sound of Rolls-Royce Merlins and it made all those within earshot stop for a moment and listen. By the end of the day, another trio of P-40s had been brought out and their engines turned over.

On the second day flight testing of the fighters began. They took off singly and made a circuit or two of the airfield; with the Reynolds T-6 following as a chase plane. Reynolds himself made the first flights, later he was joined by Woods, Brandon and Van Hoff and by the end of the third day, every pilot had made a test of some sort.

"You see, I told you guys it'd be easy," said Reynolds, as he stood before the rest of the group in one of the base's briefing rooms. "Now the hard stuff begins. We have to ferry the planes into the U.S. It has to be done in two stages. First, we leave from Portage La Prairie and fly to Grand Forks, North Dakota. That will be our point of entry into the states and we'll be inspected by the customs authorities. They'll inspect the fighters, the spare parts on the Commando and ourselves. Now for you foreigners, make sure you have your passports ready. Jeffrey, I don't know if that includes you too but have your passport ready and make sure it's stamped multiple entry.

"The second stage of our flight will be from Grand Forks to Des Moines. We'll base the fighters at the Air Services hangar for the next week or so, while they get a more complete going over and their permanent registration numbers. Then, we leave for South America, by a route we have yet to determine. If there are no questions about all this, I'll show you our flight plan . . ."

A truck stood outside the briefing room entrance, the R.C.A.F. would provide the pilots with transportation to the flight line. They also provided the P-40s with full tanks of gasoline and oil, as had been promised. The C-46 and the Texan were already leaving when the pilots were driven to the field. In spite of their later departure, the fighters would arrive at Grand Forks at around the same time due to their higher speed.

The P-40s had been arranged in a single line in front of the base's rows of Harvards; their bare metal surfaces and faded markings were quite different from the bright yellow, smartly kept Canadian trainers. With the mechanics from Reynolds Air Services long gone, R.C.A.F. ground crews helped the pilots with their pre-flight procedures.

"Your radiator shutters are working fine, Mister Reynolds," said the flight sergeant, climbing back on the P-40's wing. "You're ready to crank her up."

"All right, Sergeant. Have the ground crews stand clear of the planes and thanks for your help."

"No, thank you, sir. Working on your planes these last few days made me recall the time this was a real training base. It really hummed with activity back during the war. Today, we don't train enough pilots to replace what we lose every year, what with demobilization still going on and all. So it's we who should be thanking you, Mister Reynolds, you brought back the good days."

As the propeller on Reynolds's P-40 started to tick over, so did the others. In less than a minute all twelve Allison engines had fired up and were running smoothly. Their combined thunder rolled across the base, filling it. The sound made everyone pause and turn toward the flight line with a touch of envy. Someone would be flying fighters soon and what really made them envious, they were privately owned.

Reynolds was the first to move out of the line and start down toward the runway. He was followed by Van Hoff, Woods, the other Americans and the rest of the group. He swung onto the runway's far end and halted his aircraft. The rest of the snaking procession had to stop while he did his last set of checks. Then he cranked his canopy shut, released the brake pedals and pushed the throttle forward.

The Curtiss picked up speed rapidly, by the runway's midpoint its tail was rising into the air. A hundred yards later its main gear was skipping across the concrete and by the time the fighter had reached the runway's opposite end, those wheels were rotating ninety degrees to lie flush in their wells. And already, Van Hoff had aligned his fighter on the runway.

Reynolds let his aircraft climb gently as he finished cleaning it up; reducing drag until it was a clean, efficient flying machine. He swung it back over Portage La Prairie, where he was joined by Van Hoff, then Woods. Each ascending Kittyhawk joined the formation on the preceding ship's right wing. Eventually they formed a slanting line of silver aircraft, droning across the sky in a loose, stepped rank. They roared over the air base that had been their home for so many years for one last time; afterward, Reynolds set the formation's course due south. To a new home and a new career.

Their arrivals at both Grand Forks, North Dakota and Des Moines, Iowa were preceded a few minutes by the touchdown of the Commando and the Texan. This despite the fact that they departed up to an hour ahead of the P-40s. Apart from some radio problems, the ferry flight went off without incident. The fighters taxied up to the apron in front of the Reynolds Air Services hangar where they shut down. Now the more important work would begin. The aircraft had to be certified, prepared for the flight to South America and the pilots had to become familiar with their old mounts once again.

"You and your Austrian friend picked the perfect time for this," said Bob Reynolds, as he and his brother walked across the fighter-filled apron. "The crop dusting season is all but over and I would've had to start laying off pilots and mechanics. I can keep most of them on, for a few weeks anyway."

"How long will it take to register these?" asked Reynolds.

"Not long, maybe two weeks or so. I have friends in the CAA regional office, they'll make sure our paper work moves fast. It normally takes up to ten weeks to get an aircraft its permanent registration. I also happen to have friends in the Air National Guard squadron over there. They know something about your mission, that you've recruited your own squadron of hot shots for some purpose. Marilyn's told them it's to make a movie about the Flying Tigers. The Guard hot shots would like to know if your hot shots would care to meet them sometime for a friendly dogfight or two? They've become bored with peace time flying, they long for a little excitement."

"I can understand that. I think my friends'll be happy to comply. In a sense it's perfect. Since what we'll be going up against are high-performance aircraft, we should train with something that's superior to our planes. I'll talk it over with the others. By the way, where did they go?"

"Marilyn's driving them to a boarding house where they'll live during their stay in Des Moines. It's right by our house, where we've got a room all set for you. It's your old bedroom, back when our parents had the place."

"I've really come along in this world, haven't I? At age forty I'm back in the same room I had when I was twelve years old. Why's Marilyn driving those guys around? Shouldn't she be in school?"

"No, she graduated last May from her high school back in California. She should go to college, she got out a year ahead of schedule. I think the reason Marilyn's helping us is she's developing a crush on one of your friends."

"Oh God, I should've guessed something like that would happen," Reynolds sighed. "Get an impressionable girl mixed up with so many handsome young men. Do you know which one it is? I hope it isn't one of the married men?"

"I don't think so, she's taken a liking to your Austrian friend, Count Van Hoff. I suppose it's because she never met any nobility before."

"It may also be his life. These last few years it's been rather sad. I first met him when he flew into Austria at the end of the war. He was looking for his family and discovered they had all died in a Nazi death camp. More than helping humanity, I still think that's the real reason why he's on this crusade and probably why we're on it as well. Claus is a difficult man to understand and I hope she knows that."

"This is Racoon Lead to Racoon Flight, climb to level six and maintain current heading until we hit the Loran station. Then it's back to base."

The four Iowa Air National Guard Mustangs raised their noses gently and climbed the extra thousand feet their leader had ordered. They were on a navigation flight, a boring exercise which pilots had to perform if they wanted to get flight time. They were on their final leg, another few minutes and they would be turning back for home. The pilots were growing tired, eager to end the mission and the perfect targets for an attack.

"Bandits eleven o'clock low, tally-ho, lads."

Above and behind the P-51s were a trio of P-40s. They had changed slightly after their flight from Canada; now they only wore anti-glare panels and their permanent registration numbers. One by one they rolled to the left and dove; coming in directly behind the Mustangs. As they did so, their pilots switched over to Air National Guard frequencies. A barrage of simulated machine gun noises startled the Guard pilots out of their tedium and forced them to break formation.

"Splendid, lads, splendid," Woods commented. "Now keep them from regrouping and don't let them on your tails."

Most of the P-51s dove to escape the attack. They thought it would allow them to build up speed but diving was something the P-40 could do almost as well. Only the leader chose to climb, with Woods stuck to his tail. He would've shot him down again if it weren't for the intervention of the leader's wing man.

Suddenly it was Woods who had to break and dive.

He opened his lead over the wing man, his airspeed jumped past four hundred miles an hour and just as quickly as he had thrown the control stick forward, he hauled it back. The speed he had built up allowed him to climb to ten thousand feet before his inertia started to run out. Then he kicked his P-40 through a hammerhead turn and came around to face the Mustang.

"Will somebody come over here and pry this chap off me?" Kingston requested, growing irritated.

"Pry him off your own tail," said Green. "Can't you shoot him down on your own?"

"I have shot him down, twice already. But he's such a damned eager chap."

The other two P-40s were by now down to skimming across the Iowa corn fields. Fortunately the crop dusting season had ended, so none of the combatants had to worry about colliding with some frail biplane. They tried to evade each other by dodging around the few stands of trees, telephone lines, even grain silos and barns.

At low altitude, the superiority of the Mustang over the P-40 was marginal. But it still enjoyed a speed advantage and could outclimb the older fighter, which they used whenever they found themselves in trouble. At higher altitudes Woods found himself being completely outclassed and he had to deal with two P-51s boxing him in. After less than ten minutes of combat, and with the Mustangs consistently winning, Woods contacted the Air National Guard flight commander to surrender his aircraft.

All seven fighters returned to Des Moines in one mass formation. It wasn't until they were all down that they separated; with the P-51Ds taxiing over to the Guard hangars at one side of the field and the P-40s to the Reynolds Air Services hangar at the other end.

"These simulated dogfights are proving quite useful," said Woods, as he met with Reynolds and Van Hoff. "I'm finding that, if your enemy is flying a superior aircraft, you had better shoot him down quickly if you want to win. Even inexperienced pilots soon learn to use the better qualities of their aeroplanes. And, as most of those Air National Guard pilots are war veterans, I'm finding it difficult to shoot them down more than twice. I hope these Nazis aren't importing any ex-Luftwaffe pilots into Bolivia!"

"Daniel Green's friends say they are," Van Hoff reported. "Though their numbers are small. Probably no more than enough to equip a training cadre. Most of the pilots we might encounter will be Bolivians sympathetic to the fascist party. How would you say the integration of the group as a whole is coming along? Since we were all commanders of squadrons or wings or groups, some of us might not like being wing men again and being given orders."

"Well, there's some grumbling but it's nothing serious. Doug Ward and Tony Acerrio claim the choice of flight leaders should be made on the basis of the number of hours flown and planes shot down. While we may have a personality clash or two, we're professionals first and we're the best. We'll become a squadron soon enough. What we need above all else are fighters. How's the certification of the rest of the Kittyhawks proceeding?"

"The rest will get their papers by the end of the week," said Reynolds. "Bob and I flew two more P-

40s today for the CAA. Since our company bought the planes, we own them and we have to fly them for certification and airworthiness. The rest of you guys don't even have to worry about needing pilot's licenses. Since we're renting the aircraft to you, it's we who have to worry about whether or not you're qualified to fly them."

"Excellent, once we have all the fighters done, we can stage large-scale exercises," said Woods. "And we can leave for South America. Have you two been deciding when we'll go and how we're going to fly there?"

"Yes, and I'm beginning to realize how difficult it was to fight the war," Van Hoff admitted. "You were right about it, Michael. All we had to do as fighter pilots was fly the planes and fire the weapons. We never had to worry about maintenance, or logistics or even where to obtain reconnaissance pictures. Now we have to do it all ourselves. Do you realize what the logistics are for just twelve P-40s? Why just to ferry them to our forward base in South America will require almost nine thousand gallons of gasoline. That doesn't include the fuel the cargo planes or the P-38 will need. And what about oil, hydraulic fluid and coolant? What kind of spare parts stores should we take with us, and how many mechanics will we need?

"These are all questions we have to solve before we leave. Fortunately, we're already on that road. Jack and I are finalizing our flight plan to Bolivia, his brother is deciding which of the mechanics will go with us and we've picked the cover story we'll use to hide our true mission. We're flying south to do location filming for a movie about the Flying Tigers. It was an idea Jack's daughter first proposed. She's a very smart young woman, you should be proud of her."

"I'm also protective of her," said Reynolds. "I know you're going to be taking Marilyn out to a movie tonight, Claus. You're even borrowing my brother's car to do so. Make sure you have my daughter back by ten o'clock or I'll start sending out search planes."

"I don't think I can promise that," said Van Hoff. "The movie your daughter wants me to see is a long one, more than three hours. Something called "Gone With the Wind." Next I predict you will tell me to take care of the car as well."

"No, I'll let my brother do that."

It was Marilyn who came around to the boarding house to collect Van Hoff. While the other pilots stayed to watch whatever the television had to offer, they went into town, not to return until nearly midnight.

"That was a fine movie, it told me much about your country's history," Van Hoff commented, as he walked with Marilyn back to the house. "Though I find it odd that three of the four actors who played the lead roles were British. Only this Clark Gable was American. Tell me something, why did you take me to see this particular film?"

"Because in a way, you remind me of its main character," said Marilyn. "She lost her family, everything during the war and yet she didn't go out for revenge."

"Well she didn't have anything to truly take revenge against. Her mother died from an illness and her father died in an accident of his own making. And she still had her sisters at the end of your civil war. I have no one, only my friends and my enemies. And I've come upon a situation in which one can help me destroy the other. Do you always try to relate life to what you see in films?"

"Why not? It's what we all did in California. I remember when I was thirteen and a movie called 'The Flying Tigers' came out. I must've seen it a hundred times. I kept wondering if my father would be like John Carroll and kill himself on some mission or John Wayne, and fall in love with a nurse while in China."

"Well he did neither," Van Hoff pointed out. "He went on to command a fighter group in Europe and retired an air ace. So you can't really draw conclusions on what life will be like from what you've seen in motion pictures."

"I know. But it's just that I don't want to see you consumed by this," said Marilyn, easing her arms around Van Hoff's neck. "You're becoming very special to me."

His arms encircled her waist and they pulled each other closer until they kissed. They would not have parted for many minutes had it not been for the smattering of applause and unrequested advice that rained down from the upper floor of the boarding house.

"Better let her go, Count," Acerrio warned. "She'd better be home in five minutes or the Colonel will send out search planes."

"I think you should put that one back in the perambulator, Claus," said Brandon. "There may be laws in this country against stealing children."

"All right, the lot of you," Van Hoff answered. "We both know it's long past time for her to leave. You see, Marilyn? You must go. I don't think you should say anything more in front of this audience. Go now, before your father does come looking for you in a Kittyhawk."

"Well, there they are," said Bob Reynolds, laying a sheaf of papers before his brother, Woods and Van Hoff. "The permanent registration certificates for all twelve P-40s. Without them, the CAA wouldn't have let us fly them out of the U.S. The temporary certificates weren't valid for that purpose. The P-40s have been registered in the Limited category, which is the best we could've hoped for. No ex-military fighter or bomber has ever been registered in the standard category. The mechanics have checked over every fighter and they've replaced anything which might have given you trouble. That includes one engine, three complete sets of coolant radiators, four oil coolers, seventeen hydraulic cylinders, six fuel pumps, four full sets of radio gear and probably half a mile of new feed lines and vent lines.

"They have also installed underbelly racks on all 'E' model P-40s and underwing and underbelly racks on the 'N' models. We've managed to locate twelve complete sets of gun charging cylinders. In short, with the exception of machine guns and gunsights, Count, your squadron is combat-ready. Have you and Jack mapped out a flight plan?"

"We have," Reynolds answered, unfolding a set of charts. "It's five thousand miles long, stretches across six countries and one territory. It starts here in Des Moines and has refueling stops at Huntsville, Alabama. Fort Myers, Florida. Havana, Cuba. Holguin,

Cuba. Santo Domingo in the Dominican Republic. Oranjestad, on the island of Aruba, the Dutch Antilles. Puerto La Cruz in Venezuela. Boa Vista in Brazil. Manicore, Brazil. And finally, San Joaquin in Bolivia before we go on to our forward base. Which will be a ranch, or hacienda if you will, on the border between Santa Cruz and Beni provinces.

"Back in the late 'thirties my father, our father, flew for the airlines in South America. He met and made quite a few friends, one of them owns a ranch on the San Miguel River. It has an air strip long enough to handle both our fighters and our Commandoes. It's rather primitive, though it does serve as a headquarters for a local flying club and our father's friend has welcomed all of us . . ."

To prove his point, Reynolds produced a telegram which had been sent from the Western Union office in La Paz, Bolivia's capital. As Woods and Van Hoff read its short, staccato message, Reynolds went on to explain why he had chosen that particular location.

". . . The ranch is close enough to the border to allow us coverage of most of Santa Cruz province within the P-40's standard tactical radius. My father did have another friend who lives in Santa Cruz itself, and the airfield near his house would give us a better base. However, we don't know how extensive Nazi infiltration of the province is and I don't think we should tempt fate by setting up operations right in their midst. For you and the Lightning, Bob, we've drawn up a separate flight plan.

"You'll also take off from Des Moines but you'll head directly south. First to Houston, then Mexico City. Guatemala City, Guatemala. Fort Kobbs Air

Base in the Canal Zone. Quito, Ecuador. Lima, Peru and La Paz, Bolivia, your destination. If anyone asks why you're there, tell them you're doing an aerial survey for an oil company. We don't think you'll run into any trouble but if you do, we'll be close enough to come to your aid."

"What do you mean by that?" Woods asked. "You want us to strafe a country's capital city? Are you crazy? That could start a real war."

"I don't give a damn," Reynolds snapped. "It's my brother we're talking about and a hole in the wall country even our twelve planes can knock off. If we can't protect ourselves, or our brothers, then maybe we shouldn't go in the first place."

"Wait, you two," said Van Hoff. "You are dealing with hypothetical situations. There are a great many of those, let's not worry about them until one happens. Bob, have you decided how many mechanics we'll use?"

"Well according to Army Air Force regulations, we would need over a hundred and twenty men to care for your planes," said the younger Reynolds. "But we don't have to follow Air Force regs. I think we can get by with sixteen mechanics. Twelve for the fighters and four to keep the transports flying. I'd say you'll need at least three of our Commandoes. Each with its own two-man crew and carrying eleven thousand pounds of equipment and spares. With you guys helping out in the maintenance, that should keep the P-40s operational for at least two weeks. I've made the choices of both the mechanics and the flight crews, give us a few days to get the C-46s ready and you can leave. Would you care to discuss the cost of any of this, Claus?"

"No, I won't haggle over expenses like a merchant. Draw up a bill of sale and I'll see to its payment. I've only spent a small part of my family's fortune so far."

"Wait until we reach the Dominican Republic," said Reynolds. "That's where we'll buy our gunsights, machine guns and munitions. We'll have to pay black market prices for them. It's bound to be steep."

"Is there anything else we have to talk about?" Woods inquired, impatiently. "I would like to do some flying before this day is over."

"Not really, though I would like to see us fly a mass exercise prior to our departure," said Van Hoff. "Do you think your friends in the Air National Guard can help?"

"I'm sure they can," said Bob Reynolds. "There's a unit or two that'll be on active duty during the weekend. Let's see what we can arrange."

The neat rows of P-51s and T-6s gleamed in the mid-morning sun. Beyond some activity around them, the rest of the airport was quiet. The civilian side had been closed down. And since the field was a small one, smaller than Des Moines, there would be no interruption of regular airline service. There in fact could be no civilian traffic while the maneuvers were under way.

Stationed along the tarmac perimeter were quad-fifty anti-aircrafts guns and at one end of the field was a mobile radar set. For peacetime, the conditions were as war-like as was possible. In a half-hour they would launch their first sortie of the day, against an 'enemy' airfield; provided they were not put out of action first.

"Hawk Lead to all flights, target ahead. Eagle Flight, follow us in. Falcon Lead, take your guys around to the west and make sure you get that radar station."

They came skimming across the barren farm fields and the autumn-colored trees. The four-ship flights of silver P-40s had arranged themselves in a vee formation, with Reynolds and his Hawk flight in the lead. While they and Woods's Eagles continued to bear down on the airport, Van Hoff turned his flight away, as he had been ordered.

They came in so low, it was not until the P-40s had cleared the last stand of trees on the airport boundary that they could be clearly seen. Reynolds dropped his aircraft closer to the ground, as did the other ships in his flight. Their prop wash kicked up tracks of dust as they closed on the flight line.

The anti-aircraft guns stood unmanned, most of their crews were just coming out of breakfast. The lead group of P-40s hopped over the guns and continued on to the lines of Mustangs and T-6s. Moments later smoke charges were going off around the quad-fifties; signifying that they had been destroyed. There were additional charges among the P-51s and some of them were ignited as the Kittyhawks roared overhead. The air raid sirens had barely started to wail when Woods and his Eagles came screaming in.

"Hawk Lead to all flights, we've caught 'em with their pants down," said Reynolds. "Continue and we'll have this base neutralized in no time. Hawk Three, Hawk Four, break off and form a fighter cap. They may have some planes up."

"Hey, Colonel, what the hell are they doing on the

ground?" asked Acerrio. "Trying to make smoke screens?"

"No, they're trying to simulate an air attack. There's an army demolition team setting off small charges. If it were any more realistic we'd be firing machine guns."

As the first group of P-40s pulled away from the airfield, it split into its separate elements. One pair of fighters, Reynolds and Acerrio, turned back to continue the attack; while the other two, Green and Clinton, climbed to form a combat air patrol.

Woods's flight arrived over the flight line seconds after the lead one had departed. They swept through the growing columns of smoke, causing more to be exploded by the demolition team. Their thunder had barely started to ebb away when the scream of more fighters became audible.

Van Hoff and his flight pounced on the radar site, attacking it in train. One fighter after another swooped down on it then pulled away; reforming into pairs to continue strafing the Air National Guard planes on the airport's far side. They had yet to complete their run when Reynolds and Acerrio returned; slicing across their line of attack.

They 'strafed' most of the remaining anti-aircraft guns; putting them out of action the moment they were being manned. On their return runs, Woods and Van Hoff's flights concentrated on the aircraft. Soon there were so many smoke charges going off, that the Air National Guard hangars, and the planes on the apron in front of them, were becoming obscured.

No ANG fighters attempted to stop the attack, not a single Mustang tried to taxi from the hangar apron.

In fact the P-40s scored a 'kill' when they shot down a C-47 attempting to land while they were still over the field. After fifteen minutes of mock strafing runs, the Kittyhawks regrouped and departed. Their pilots had proven they could fly as a squadron and not as a pack of lone wolves. Now all they had to do was get to South America.

Chapter Seven:
DEPARTURE.
THE EAGLES GET THEIR CLAWS.

For several days after the weekend operation, none of the P-40s were flown. Instead they all received one final, thorough exam in preparation to their ferry flight to South America. The C-46 Commandoes were also examined and loaded with the thousands of pounds of spare parts and equipment the Curtiss fighters would need.

Far more than what had been brought from Canada, the transports were filled with almost every conceivable Kittyhawk part. From Allison engines and Curtiss Electric propellers to canopy plexiglass, outer wing panels and landing gear struts. All were tagged, catalogued and placed on board one of three Commandoes being prepared for the operation. Even spares for the transports themselves were taken along.

All the pilots and mechanics were given physical exams as well and received full batteries of inoculations to prevent illness; in spite of protests.

"The last thing we need is to lose an operational fighter because its pilot has come down with malaria or some intestinal malady," said Van Hoff, turning to the others in the doctor's waiting room. "I don't care what you've been through in North Africa or the Pacific. I've been through the same and I say we don't take chances. I remember when dysentery kept four out of ten pilots from flying, and the rest weren't in top physical condition either. So roll up your sleeves or, if you can't stand to see the needle go in, let down your pants."

When all was done, those who were part of the mission returned home and went to sleep early. They were ordered to and next morning they were up before sunrise. Packing away what belongings they needed and rendezvousing at the Reynolds Air Services hangar.

". . . There, that's the whole route we'll be taking," said Reynolds, putting down the maps he'd been using. "And the one my brother will use. We'll be flying independent routes because we can't have Bob being identified with us. He's on a survey job for an oil company and that's what we want everyone to believe. Because of the P-38's longer range, it'll need fewer refueling stops. And because its route is five hundred miles shorter, Bob will arrive some time ahead of us. Hopefully, he'll have completely photo-mapped Santa Cruz province when we reach our destination. Now I know there are lots of questions, so let's hear them all before we get started."

The last things to be loaded into the P-40s, apart from the pilots, were their belongings; packed tightly into Army-surplus duffle bags instead of the suitcases they had been using. The Lightning took off while the Kittyhawks and the transports were still being readied for flight. Its twin Allison engines gave a smooth, powerful thunder as Bob Reynolds swung his fighter back over Des Moines International. He waggled his wings then set out on the first of his eight hundred mile hops to Bolivia.

Because of their much longer range, C-46s were allowed to depart first. Even though most of the P-40s were ready ahead of them and it forced Reynolds and the other fighters to wait impatiently while the rotund Commandoes waddled out to the runway. Their brutish, Double Wasp radials filled the airport with ear numbing howls as they lifted off. Before the last of the transports had started down the runway, Reynolds signaled the fighters to start engines.

"Tower to Curtiss-One-One-Seven-Nine, you are cleared to taxi to the runway. As we have no other outbound traffic, the rest of your group are cleared to taxi as well. Please notify us when you're ready to leave."

Reynolds, followed by a long, snaking line of silver aircraft, moved to the end of Des Moines's longest runway. All twelve P-40s lifted away without incident and joined formation above the vee of transports. Like the P-38 before them, they swung past Des Moines International before setting off to the southeast. The odyssey was under way.

For about an hour the fighters and the transports maintained their formations. Then slowly, their ranks became more casual until the formations dissolved and everyone decided what altitude and with whom they wanted to fly. A cruising speed of two hundred and twenty miles an hour was compatible with both the P-40s and C-46s; which meant the fighters wouldn't have to weave back and forth to maintain pace with the Commandoes.

After three hours and overflying parts of four states, the gaggle arrived at their first refueling stop; Huntsville, Alabama. Because they were near the end of their ferry range, the P-40s went in first while the transports circled the sleepy-looking field. It was almost noon and in addition to their planes needing fuel, the pilots were starting to get hungry.

"I don't think this place has the facilities to refuel fifteen planes simultaneously," said Reynolds, as the others gathered around him. "We're going to be here for a little while and I don't know about the rest of you but I'd like to have some lunch."

"And where will we do that?" asked McCloud. "I've traveled in this part of your country before. Often the only restaurant in town is a homey little place called 'Eats'."

"There's a bar and grille here at the airport. One of my Commando pilots has been to it before and says it's okay, especially the southern fried chicken. C'mon, I'll pay."

"I'll just wait out here by the planes," said Clinton. "Bring me some chicken, fries and a coffee to go."

"Why that's nonsense," said Van Hoff, grabbing the reluctant Clinton by the arm. "Come, I am sure there's plenty of room for all of us. Why it looks almost deserted."

In spite of his protests, the entire group dragged Clinton to the airport's small restaurant; which was located almost underneath the control tower. Van Hoff was indeed right, save for a few people in the booths, it was empty.

"I hope you guys can handle volume business in a

hurry," said Reynolds, as he led his contingent up to the lunch counter. "We're all hungry and we'd like to see some menus please."

"What you see up there is what we serve, mister," replied the scowling, reed-thin man behind the counter. He was pointing at the blackboard above the grille. "But I can tell you one thing, we don't serve watermelon."

"What does that mean?" Van Hoff asked, naïvely.

"It means he won't serve me," said Clinton.

"You're damn right, boy," the reed answered. "Why it's only been in the last few years that we allowed his kind to eat in here."

He pointed at Green who, along with the others, stepped forward and spread out along the counter.

"Well you're going to desegregate your establishment real quick," said Reynolds, leaning over the counter. "That man over there shot down eleven enemy planes during the war. Including an Me-262 jet."

"I don't care if he shot down fucking Hermann Goering, we don't serve niggers. You can wait outside for the honey wagon, boy. It'll be by soon."

"How strange this country is. It will not allow a colored man to eat with whites but yet will supply him with honey," said Van Hoff; again, naïvely.

"God, are you stupid," laughed the reed. "Where the hell are you from? You certainly ain't no American. You don't even sound like a damn Yankee."

"Of course I'm not. I am Austrian."

"Jesus Christ, a Nazi."

"He is not a Nazi!" Brandon shouted, indignantly. "He served with most of us in the Royal Air Force. Throughout the entire war. Why he lost his whole

167

family in a German concentration camp."

"Then he and the Jew boy should like the house special. Dachau burgers."

"Hold it, Claus," said Reynolds, grabbing Van Hoff by the shoulder. "We don't want any trouble here. Not yet anyway, let's see if we can try reasoning a little longer."

"Watch it you guys!" Ward shouted. "Heads up!"

In spite of their small numbers, the restaurant's patrons tried to jump the group at the counter. Ward and Kain were the first to intercept them; followed by Green, Kingston and Clinton. In seconds they were involved in a fight which they were easily dominating. It raged on like a tornado, fury around the edges, calm at the center.

"Don't break the furniture," said Reynolds. "I don't want to pay a damn repair bill."

"All right, boys, let's say you all leave now, before I call the sheriff," the reed ordered, in the diversion the fight had momentarily caused, he had grabbed a large butcher knife off the wall rack.

"Tony, you're good with knives. Disarm him."

Reynolds barely finished giving his order when Acerrio responded. He picked up a sugar dispenser, pried off the cap and hurled its contents into the reed's face; who screamed and tried to wipe the granules out of his eyes but refused to drop the knife. To accomplish that, Acerrio had to break a ketchup bottle over his head.

"There, that's the last of 'em," said Ward, watching the fourth southerner collapse unconscious to the floor. "I haven't had this much fun since the squadron and I took on those Frogs at a German bar."

"My, but aren't we modest," said Kingston. "Your friend has much more to boast about. I believe he finished off two of those blighters by himself."

"Well, now you know why Desmond Kain is called 'Donny' Donnybrook Kain. He's one of the best scrappers to ever come out of Sydney."

"Jeff, check the windows," Reynolds ordered, as he helped Acerrio to climb over the counter. "See if anybody's coming."

"No one's coming," McCloud answered, "the field's just as sleepy as ever. The only activity is around our planes."

"Hey, I really put this guy's lights out," said Acerrio, admiring his work. "He won't wake up for hours."

"What a God awful mess we're in," said Woods. "Let's fly out of here now. Before we land in real trouble."

"Not yet, I'm still hungry," said Reynolds. "We have time for something quick. Tony, what's behind there?"

"Hey, he's got a lot of hot dogs in a steamer, Colonel. And some stuff in a pot that looks like cream of wheat."

"Skip that, it's hominy grits. Find some buns and let's have thirty hot dogs to go. Open some bags of potato chips if there are any and let's see what's in the soda machine. Think you can handle it, Tony?"

"Sure thing, I used to sling hamburgers back at a diner on my block." Acerrio was already hard at work, splitting open hot dog buns with a knife. "This'll be easy. I have more dogs on the boil. What would you like on yours?"

In a few minutes Acerrio was handing out frankfurters to the pilots and mechanics. There were more bottles of ketchup, and jars of mustard and other condiments along the counter top; enough for the men to prepare their hot dogs in their own way. They ate as quickly as they could, with some watching for the approach of any restaurant patrons and others guarding those who were already there.

"These are very much like sausages," Van Hoff noted, finishing his off. "Only not as highly seasoned. I can see why you need all these sauces and vegetables to put on them."

"All right, the Commandoes have all been refueled," said Reynolds, looking out one of the windows. "Greg, you and the others get out to your planes. I want you to leave first. I want you mechanics to go as well. Pre-flight the fighters, we may have to scramble to get out of here. The rest of us will follow in a minute or so."

The men Reynolds gave orders to sauntered casually out toward the planes. They climbed aboard the transports and checked out each of the P-40s. When the propellers on the C-46s started to tick over, Reynolds told the rest it was time to depart.

"Hey, mate, this one's coming to," Ward advised, standing guard over the southerners they had beaten.

"Good, I did want to leave a message," said Reynolds. "Looks like I won't have to write it down."

Ward and Kain dragged the slowly awakening man up to one of the booths and sat on either side of him while Reynolds sat in front of him.

"Wake up, asshole," he demanded, slapping the man's face. He continued until he got a mumbled oath from the rebel. "There's fifteen dollars and a bill for what we ate sitting on the cash register. We've rung it through the machine so don't try to steal it. And don't try to make trouble for us, boy. Never fuck around with people who own their own fighters. You can tell that to your friend behind the counter as well. You understand me, boy?"

"You're a dead man," said the rebel, slurring his words. "When we catch you we'll hang your Yankee ass from a tree!"

Reynolds reached across the table and grabbed the man by the hair. He dragged him onto it and pointed him at the window; so he could see the line of fighters outside.

"Make trouble for us, you shit head, and we'll be back with those planes," Reynolds warned. "And they'll be armed with machine guns. Tell that to your friends . . ."

Then he lifted the rebel's head a little higher off the table and landed a haymaker on his jaw; sending the rebel back into unconsciousness.

". . . Leave him there. Let's get out of here."

"God, mate, and I thought your Italian friend was nasty," said Ward, marveling at Reynolds's performance.

"Of course I'm nasty, how do you think I got to be a Colonel? Now as we go out the door, I want one of you to flip around the sign in the window. This place is closed."

The pilots made for their planes in a haphazard series of groups. They walked across the field as if there had been no trouble, even though most of them wanted to dash to their planes and take off as quickly as possible.

"I suppose what happened back there put you in mind of your homeland," said Clinton, joining Woods.

"It did and again it didn't," he replied. "You would scarcely be allowed onto an airfield in South Africa. And if a fight like we had were to break out, the police would've been on us in a minute. Most of us would receive heavy fines and you'd be locked in prison for years, for inciting a civil disturbance. It's something I'm not proud of and I hope it will change in the future. At least in your country, not all of it is as bad as this place."

When they reached their planes, the pilots helped the mechanics remove wheel chocks and turn the propellers by hand; in order to remove any oil which had accumulated in the engine cylinders. The moment they climbed into the cockpits they switched on their radios so they could communicate with each other and, most especially, Reynolds.

"Stay on the air at all times," he warned them, before turning his attention to the mechanics. "Okay, you guys, get on those transports or you'll be walking to Florida."

The first P-40s were starting up as the third and last C-46 aligned itself on the runway. Half of them still had to get their engines running when Acerrio noticed some activity back at the restaurant.

"There's some pickup trucks parking at that grille, Colonel," he said. "It looks like the clowns in them are heading for the place."

"Thanks, Tony. All right everyone, scramble," Reynolds ordered. "Take off in pairs. Start moving now, I don't care if you've finished engine warm-up or not."

Woods and Ward moved out to the runway, followed

by Van Hoff and Kain. The customers for the restaurant first clustered at its door then spread out along the windows to see if they could glimpse anything inside. Woods and Ward did their fastest engine test and pre-flight check since the war; they had barely turned onto the runway when they opened their throttles and raced down it.

"Hey, Colonel, it looks like they're trying to break in the door," said Acerrio.

"I know, I can see it too. C'mon you guys, speed it up out there. I want us to be specks on the horizon by the time those rebels figure it all out."

When the third pair of P-40s taxied to the runway, the rebels had forced open the restaurant door and piled inside. High above the airfield, the first sets of Kittyhawks had formed into a flight and wheeled around protectively, waiting for their brothers to join.

"Clostermann, Green, move onto the runway now," said Reynolds. "Do it as soon as they've started their take off runs. They're not about to back up on you."

"Colonel, some of those guys have come back out," said Acerrio. "I think they're dragging one of the assholes we beat up. I don't like the looks of this. He could identify us."

As the fourth pair of fighters roared out of the field, they were. The newly arrived rebels jumped back in their pickups and tore off across the taxiways and hangar aprons, narrowly missing the lines of light planes.

"Holy shit, we're in for it now," warned Acerrio. "What are we gonna do? We're a couple of sitting ducks."

"Nothing, we'll let someone else run interference

for us," said Reynolds. "Eagle Flight, get down here and explain things to these bastards."

Woods and Ward peeled away from the growing formation as if they were one aircraft. They screamed down on the airport, sweeping past the fighters waiting for take off and closed on the approaching trucks. Woods edged his P-40 as close to the ground as he could without hitting hangars or parked aircraft. He almost did hit the first of the pickups but then again, that was intentional.

The truck swerved wildly to avoid the oncoming fighter. It veered off the taxiway and plunged into a shallow drainage ditch; tossing out everyone who was riding in the rear. The other two slowed as first Woods, then Ward thundered over them. One stopped to see if anyone in the lead pickup needed help, the third continued on towards the runway.

Brandon and Kingston streaked across the airport next; concentrating on the third pickup. Their effect on it was similar to what Woods and Ward had on its leader. The truck swung out of the path of the strafing fighters; skidded onto a hangar apron, sheared off the left wing of an Aeronca light plane before crashing against the side of a hangar.

Another set of Kittyhawks had leaped away from the ground during the attack. Leaving only Reynolds and Acerrio to align themselves on the runway and do their checks.

"Colonel, let's get the fuck outta here! Those guys in the trucks have guns. They're loading them!"

"Stay calm and do your magneto test," said Reynolds. "And crack open those cowl flaps, Tony. Hawk Lead to Falcon Lead, we need another run. Same targets and be warned, those bastards are armed."

Van Hoff and Kain dipped their wings and broke away from the other half of their flight. The rebels from the first pickup, those who could walk, climbed on top of the second. They carried with them a collection of rifles and shotguns which, as soon as the truck was moving, they started firing at the remaining P-40s.

Van Hoff dove at the truck instead of making a low, strafing pass. It was a dive bombing run, and he pulled out in the last few hundred feet; howling over their heads like an angry bird of prey. By the time the rebels opened fire on him, he was far out of range. Kain repeated the attack a few moments later, distracting the rebels long enough for Acerrio and Reynolds to release their brakes and open their throttles.

Clinton and McCloud came in next, reverting to the more conventional sweep. They paralleled the runway, putting themselves between the last set of P-40s and the rebels. A barrage of ineffective shots failed to hit any of the planes. Reynolds and Acerrio thundered off the ground and stayed low until they were well beyond the airport perimeter.

"I didn't know you could spray crops with a Kittyhawk," said Woods, as the last P-40s to depart Huntsville climbed into formation.

"You could do it with a B-29 if you wanted to," said Reynolds. "Only I wouldn't recommend it. And I don't think the P-40 would make such a good crop duster either. There aren't many places in this ship you can put hopper tanks."

"Do you think what happened back there could cause trouble for us?" asked Van Hoff.

"It will if we land anywhere in Alabama. I doubt it'll cause any trouble for us when we land in Florida. Not even the Alabama State Police has planes that can catch us. The only way we can be stopped is for the governor to call up the Air National Guard and have us intercepted."

Even though such a possibility was extremely remote, everyone breathed a little easier when the formation left the Gulf coastline behind, near the Pensacola Naval Air Station. They flew down the western coast of Florida, rarely venturing more than a few miles into the Gulf of Mexico.

Past Tampa Bay they started hugging the coast a little more and when they reached Sanibel Island, the entire formation turned up the Caloosahatchee River and flew into Fort Myers. Where they all received a much friendlier greeting.

"It was mighty nice of you to park your aircraft right here by the customs office," said the official, looking down the list of planes Reynolds gave him. "We'll have 'em all inspected for you by tomorrow morning."

"Thanks, we'd appreciate that," Reynolds answered.

"Oh, by the way. You wouldn't happen to know anything about some trouble they had at your last refueling stop? Reports we got are a little confused. It seems like something between a red neck brawl and World War Two happened up there in Huntsville. They say some people got punched out and the airport was shot up. They also say that your planes were involved, that you buzzed the airport."

"Well we had to. Some local clowns started breaking

up the airport restaurant as we were leaving. Then they started shooting at us, probably because we were all Yankees and foreigners. I hope it doesn't happen here."

"Now you don't have to worry about that, Mister Reynolds. This here is a more enlightened state than the one you left. Sometimes I think those damn Alabama rebs are still fighting the Civil War. We'll handle things with the Huntsville Police. You know something, they thought the restaurant owner had had his head bashed in but when they got him to the hospital, they found he just had a ketchup bottle broken over it. They say he has a concussion, and he won't be able to talk straight for days."

"Well, Jack, how did it go in there?" Woods asked, when Reynolds emerged from the U.S. Customs office.

"We lucked out. We'll be in South America by the time they figure things out in Huntsville. Still, I would like to leave for Cuba as soon as possible tomorrow. We've avoided one problem, I wouldn't like to run into any more."

"Don't speak so soon, mate," said Ward, looking across the lobby instead of at Reynolds. "I think we've just gone from one to another. Isn't that your daughter over there?"

Even though she was in the middle of a crowd, Reynolds spotted Marilyn immediately. A moment later she identified him and started forcing her way around the people in front of her. With a phalanx of pilots on either side of him, Reynolds found it easier to push through the crowd than his daughter. They met near the middle of the lobby, with Marilyn throwing her arms around her father. It melted most of his anger, but not all of it.

"How did you get here?" Reynolds asked, with a loud, stern voice. "And why on earth are you here?"

"I bought airline tickets and flew here," said Marilyn. "Aunt Eve gave me the money to do so."

"I should've thought so and again, why are you here?" Reynolds repeated, and as he did so, Marilyn caught sight of Van Hoff. She released her father and ran to embrace him.

He looked stunned. Just as stunned as Reynolds had been; it took a few seconds for him to realize that he should put his arms around her.

"Well, I think we now know why she followed us here," said Woods. "It looks as though she's quite taken with him. Doug is right, we do have another problem."

"In the states we call it going from frying pan to fire," said Reynolds. "God damn it, I'm going over there and find out if he had anything to do with this."

"Jack, be easy on Claus. I don't believe he knew."

Reynolds charged off to demand a few answers of Van Hoff and Marilyn, but he wouldn't be quite so angry about it.

"You know something, I wonder if I'll be like him when my daughter grows up and falls in love," Brandon pondered.

"I think you will," said Woods. "And I hope you have the chance to watch your daughter grow up, unlike Jack."

"All right, Marilyn, I want to know why you're here and if Claus had anything to do with it," Reynolds asked.

"No, Daddy, he doesn't," she said. "He didn't have any part of this. But he's the reason I came, and so are you. Don't you understand? I love him and I love you. For the first time in my life I have my father and I've also found someone to love. But now I'm going to lose both of you to this mission. And I don't want to. I want to go with you, I want to be with you."

"No!" Reynolds tried to make his answer sound as absolute as possible. "You're not going any farther than here. What we're doing could be dangerous. We can't afford to have a woman along, not even my daughter. Most especially my daughter. I want you safe."

"I will be safe, I promise I won't get in the way."

"Angel, please. You're only making this more difficult. Claus, explain it to her, will you?"

"I'll try, but I think I should do it in some place other than a busy airport lobby."

The hotel they were booked into wasn't far from the airport; in fact it was just across the street. Inside of a half-hour everyone had been assigned a room and the argument between Van Hoff, Reynolds and his daughter could continue in hoped for privacy.

"How's it going in there, mate?" Ward whispered, since both he and Acerrio were standing next to the door to Reynolds's room.

"For a fight they sure ain't shouting a hell of a lot," said Acerrio. "You'd never mistake these guys for an Italian family. Wait, wait, she's turning on the water works."

"Water works? You mean she's in the bathroom?"

"No, you down under dummy. She's crying. If there's one way a woman can get something, it's by crying. And that's really true when it's a father and a daughter."

"Don't you two think it's slightly unseemly to be seen standing in front of someone else's door?" Woods observed, speaking at a more normal volume.

"Quiet, mate, do you want them to hear us? Of course we don't want to be seen, that's why Kain and McCloud are relieving us in the next five minutes."

"Douglas, you can really be too much sometimes. Of what interest can this be to you?"

"It's of interest to us, mate, because that little lady in there could cause a lot of trouble for us. This operation's dangerous enough without having her around."

"Doug, how's it doing?" Kain asked, coming down the hallway with McCloud in tow.

"She's crying," said Acerrio. "I think it's going to end soon. It always does when the girl starts bawling."

"I should hope so," Ward added. "They've been having at it in there for more than an hour."

Suddenly the voices on the other side of the door grew louder, nearer, and its knob started to move. Those in the hallway jumped from the door and tried to run for the safety of their own rooms. But only McCloud made it; the others were all caught by Reynolds when he stepped out of his room. Including Woods.

"And just what the hell are you guys doing here?" Reynolds asked, with a mixture of surprise and irritation.

"Ah, we're waiting for a streetcar, Colonel," Acerrio hesitantly offered, after an embarrassingly long period of silence.

"What? Inside, and on the fifth floor!"

"Would you believe an elevated streetcar?"

"They were eavesdropping, Jack," said Van Hoff, appearing behind Reynolds. "They wanted to know how we would resolve this, situation. Really, Michael, I'm surprised at you. I'd have expected the Americans and the Australians, even Jeffrey, but you? I thought you were above this."

"But, but, I," Woods mumbled. "I'm not part . . . Oh forget it, I don't think you're in the mood to believe me."

"Well, Colonel, what have you decided?" Acerrio asked.

"After careful deliberation, Marilyn's decided that she will return home. She'll leave tomorrow but for tonight she'll stay with us, with me and we're all going to have dinner now."

By the time they went down to the restaurant, Marilyn had dried her eyes and touched up her streaked make-up. No one could guess she'd been crying.

The entire outfit, pilots, mechanics and transport crews, came for dinner; they needed to use the largest table the restaurant had. Plus an extra chair at one end of the table, where Reynolds sat. Dinner for thirty-one took a while to be served, even longer to eat when everyone was busy talking. The meal lasted until almost closing time for the restaurant. It ended but the conversation that had started continued, though in a rather fragmented form. With discussions going on in various hotel rooms.

"I don't think we have much time, your father will be here soon," said Van Hoff, as he and Marilyn entered her and her father's room. "Jack may be my friend but I don't think he'll like it much if he were to find me with you."

"I understand," she said, embracing him again, kissing him. "I know but it was you who wanted to come here. What did you want to tell me?"

"That I know you. In the brief time we've been together, I've grown to understand you. How you feel and how you think. I don't believe you're returning home like you promised you would. You are a very determined young woman and you won't let what we've demanded stop you. I don't know if you should be stopped. A daughter should be with her father."

"People should be with those they love. I feel so sorry for your friends. They miss their wives, their families. I think Mister Clinton could cry because he can't call his parents. And they're not far away, just Georgia. Claus, I think they should all be with the ones they love. Each of your friends told me about the people they miss. I know it'd be hard to collect them all but I think it can be done."

"Yes. It would, however, be expensive," Van Hoff noted. "But not for me. Such an expense would be insignificant."

"Could you do it, Claus? For them, for me?"

"No, I have so many other duties, among them flying a fighter. This would require someone's full attention. Someone like you. If I were to supply the funds, would you make all the contacts and arrangements?"

"I . . . I don't know," said Marilyn, startled by Van Hoff's request. "If you think I can, then I'll try. I suppose it wouldn't be much different than arranging for a party, only a lot more difficult to bring everyone together."

"I believe you can. You are, as I said before, very determined. This is something that should be done. It's what my friends deserve. After all they have done, and are doing, for me it's the least I can do for my brothers. Tomorrow, before we leave, I will find a way to supply you with money. I hope you have a passport, our destination will be Santo Domingo, in the Dominican Republic, by way of Cuba. Good-night, Marilyn. I'll be thinking of you tomorrow."

"Okay, Mister Reynolds, let's see what you have," said a customs official, looking at the ownership papers, C.A.A. registrations and the flight plan Reynolds had submitted to him. "You are flying three C-46 transports and twelve P-40 fighters to Bolivia via Cuba, the Dominican Republic, Aruba, Venezuela and Brazil. And these planes are owned by your company, Reynolds Air Services of Des Moines, Iowa. You say you're taking these planes to South America to film a movie about the Flying Tigers during World War Two. Everything you have here looks true enough, except for this job of yours. Now why would Hollywood make a movie about China in South America?"

"Well they certainly can't make it in China," Reynolds countered. "There's a civil war raging throughout that country. In spite of what Chiang Kai-Shek's saying, I think he's going to lose it to the commies. And they can't use California, the landscape's becoming too familiar. The Andes look a lot like the mountains of Burma and China. I should know, I was part of the AVG during the war. Panda Bear Squadron."

"Okay, I'll buy that. But where are they going to get Chinese? I don't think there are many Chinese in Bolivia."

"Don't worry, the movie company will import them too. They told me they've rented a steamer and will be sending a few hundred extras south. They're using all the Chinese the Screen Extras Guild has and a whole cast of stars."

"Really? Who are they going to use?" asked the official, perking up and showing some real interest at last.

"Well I . . . I, can't recall." Reynolds had been caught off-guard by the request.

"Clark Gable," said Van Hoff, stepping into the discussion; it was the first actor's name he could think of.

"Hey, that's great. I'm a Gable fan myself. But isn't he a little too old to be playing a fighter pilot?"

"Sure he is, that's why he'll be playing Claire Chennault," said Reynolds. "He was the leader of the Tigers."

"Yeah, I know. I saw that 'God is My Co-pilot' picture two years ago," replied the official. "I think he'll do a better job than what Raymond Massey did. Who else is going to be in this picture?"

"Errol Flynn and Tyrone Power," Ward interjected.

"Hey, wait a minute. Those guys belong to Warner Brothers and Twentieth Century-Fox. How can they be in it when Gable's an MGM man? That don't sound right."

"Well they're not in it," said Reynolds. "You have to forgive Doug. He's an Australian and he doesn't understand our studio system. He just likes pirate movies. MGM wants to use Van Johnson and Robert Mitchum to play two of the pilots. And I know they'd like to get Bette Davis from Warners to play Madame Chiang Kai-Shek. I don't know who's playing Chiang yet. Probably some British actor."

"Sure sounds like it's going to be a good picture," the official said, handing back all the documents to Reynolds. "Do you know when it's coming out?"

"Probably the end of next year. Sooner if we could get out of here today. Know what I mean?"

The suggestion was acknowledged and the remainder of the customs checks were quickly finished; allowing the pilots to head out to their planes. Already the mechanics were hard at work, inspecting the fighters, doing repairs and replacing parts as needed. With the pilots joining in, what was left was soon finished, as well as fueling the planes. By mid-morning the C-46s and the entire squadron of P-40s were taxiing out to the runway for departure.

Because of their success at evacuating Huntsville the day before, Reynolds allowed the fighters to take off two at a time. It cut almost in half the time the formation needed to join up. Once they were all at cruise altitude, the aircraft swung over the Gulf of Mexico and headed south to their next destination. Havana, Cuba.

Across the Straits of Florida and the Florida Keys, the flight was a short hop compared to the earlier ones but it was the first one to jump a body of water and to enter a foreign country. A half-hour after leaving Florida, the fighters and transports were wheeling over Havana; breaking away to enter the landing pattern at Jose Marti Airport, southwest of the city. They scarcely needed to do it for fuel but had to if they wanted to properly and legally enter Cuba. Few other airfields on the island had the necessary customs offices.

"Is this where we start enjoying the benefits of your family's contacts in South America?" Woods asked.

"Not exactly, my father didn't get along with many Cubans," said Reynolds, as the other pilots collected around his P-40. "That won't start until we reach Santo Domingo, where our planes will be rearmed. For now we're just going to have to smile and grease their palms with a few bucks. I hope your billfold is deep, Claus."

While Van Hoff dipped into his wallet for bribes, the Kittyhawks, Commandoes and what the Commandoes were carrying under went a lengthy, unnecessary inspection. It took longer than the hop from Florida did and the bribes ended up costing more than the fuel Van Hoff bought. Finally, they were all allowed to leave and the formation departed Havana as rapidly as they could.

They flew east, following the island's central spine of mountains; a low heavily forested range called Sierra de Trinidad. For the next three hours the formation encountered very little of civilization. Occasionally a village, only rarely a large town or city. They had to dodge around local thunderstorms and, by the time they reached Holguín in Oriente province, the gas tanks in the P-40s were nearly empty.

Now they really were in need of refueling and, fortunately, the Cuban Air Force owned most of the field they landed at. As a professional courtesy, they would sell the group some of their high-octane gasoline and service the planes. They also opened their officers' cafeteria and invited their guests to a late lunch.

"Be careful in here," Reynolds warned. "Don't eat too much, I still think they'll charge us for it. And don't drink anything that isn't bottled or boiled. Learn this thing about South America, 'there are lots of things here that you may drink but stay away from the kitchen sink'."

As it ended up they were charged for their meal, though the bill wasn't as exorbitant as the cost of nearly three thousand gallons of one hundred octane aviation fuel. The Cuban military proved friendly enough, however and on departure, the P-40s dipped their wings in thanks before climbing to join the transports.

The formation turned southeast, skirting the Sierra Maestra Mountains on Cuba's southern end and flying past the huge U.S. naval base at Guantánamo Bay. They hopped across another stretch of water, the Windward Passage between the islands of Cuba and Hispaniola. It was a hundred and thirty miles before they made land again; Gonâve Island and the coastline of Haiti. After getting a navigation fix from the airfield at Port au Prince, to correct their drift caused by the prevailing winds, they continued on toward the Dominican Republic.

They cut across the narrow peninsula of land west of Port au Prince and climbed past its densely forested mountain peaks. On the Caribbean side of Hispaniola, the aircraft followed the coastline to the Dominican Republic. It was a meandering journey, with an occasional shortcut over a bay or cape. As they approached Santo Domingo, a flight of Dominican

Army Air Corps P-51Ds met the formation and escorted them to their air base outside the country's capital.

Compared to the Cuban Air Force base at Holguín, it was alive with activity, and filled with aircraft. In addition to the Mustangs, there were P-47s, T-6 and BT-13 trainers and even a B-17. All of them were painted in green and light tan camouflage paint, making the bare metal P-40s and civilian marked Commandoes really stand out on the flight line. The pilots of the escorting P-51s were waiting for the Kittyhawks when they taxied in and gathered around the lead fighter as it shut its engine down.

"Welcome to Santo Domingo, Jack!" shouted the most senior officer, climbing onto the fighter's wing to greet Reynolds. "It has been many years, hasn't it? But you haven't changed. You look older, you're starting to look like your father but you are still the same."

"You haven't changed much either, Carlos," said Reynolds. "Except I see you're finally wearing those wings you always wanted. I heard you guys got your army air corps started back in—1942, was it?"

"Yes, and at last we have received some real combat planes. Until a few months ago, all we flew were those trainers over there, with machine guns rigged to them. Now we have fighters and bombers, after we signed the Rio Treaty at the start of this year. Next year we will get more and we may become our own separate service."

"That's why we came here. With so much surplus equipment coming in, my friends and I knew you'd have some to spare. For a price."

"Yes, my friend that we do have. And I am happy

you came to us for help. We couldn't help you defeat the Nazis during the war, maybe we can now. Come, show me your friends, I would like them to be my friends."

As they walked down the growing flight line, Reynolds introduced his new friends to an old family friend, Major Rafael Carlos of the Dominican Army Air Corps. He even presented him to the flight crews of the C-46s and the mechanics he brought along. Carlos, in turn, took them all to a base cafeteria where he had a lavish dinner set for them.

It soon became a raucous, festive party instead of just a meal. Stories were told, more food and wine was served until it was late in the evening, by which time everyone was stuffed and drunk. Instead of being taken to their quarters, one of the few unused barracks at the base, Carlos drove them back to the flight line. Even though the airfield had been closed for the night, there was still activity on it.

"In your phone calls, Jack, you were very descriptive of your needs," said Carlos. "An unwise move on your part. It could've been easily overheard but I understand the urgency of your situation. You don't know how far along those Nazi pigs are. Since your stay must be a sadly short one, I will help you along as much as possible. As you can see, we are taking half your aircraft to a hangar. Some of our ground crews are experienced with the P-40, they trained at your Tactical Center in Orlando, Florida. They will do all maintenance and repairs, you will install all your machine guns and gunsights yourself, with the help of our base weapons officer. It's the best way to rearm your planes. No one but Captain Diaz and me will really know what you did."

"How will you handle boresighting the machine guns?" asked Clostermann. "In any aircraft I ever flew, they had to test fire those guns to make sure they were properly aligned."

"Again, that will be done at night. Our weapons test area is in a remote part of the field but I would suggest that we do those tests quickly. A dozen aircraft firing machine guns will, in time, attract interest where we cannot afford more. Your arrival has already raised some eyebrows. Oh, by the way, may I have your passports, all of them? I will have them stamped by the proper authorities and returned to you."

While the Americans and the Australians readily handed over their passports, the Europeans, notably Van Hoff and Clostermann, were reluctant to surrender them.

"Don't worry, you guys," Reynolds assured. "If Rafael says he'll return them, he will. He's always kept a promise."

"It's not that we don't trust your friend, Colonel," said Clostermann. "It's simply that . . . His government is a dictatorship and after you have just defeated one, you're wary of them."

"As the Americans are fond of saying, what's in this for you?" asked Van Hoff, still withholding his passport from Carlos. "Apart from money, of which you're being paid a great deal for your corruption, why are you doing all this for us?"

"Don't pay attention to what he's saying, Rafael," Reynolds quickly advised. "It's the liquor talking."

"Do not worry, my friend," said Carlos. "I understand. To answer your question, Mister Van Hoff, I am doing it for the money, which I have to share with other corrupt men. I am doing it for Jack, his family have been my friends for many years. To me, he is like a brother. And I'm doing it because this is the only way I can help defeat the Germans. You, all of you, fought the greatest war in history. For the greatest cause in history and I could not be part of it. This way, I will. Now all three of those reasons are true but the last two are more true. Have I answered your question, Mister Van Hoff?"

"Yes, you have. And I'm sorry for the way I phrased it," he apologized, handing his passport to Carlos. "Jack, I think we should retire now, before I pass out."

The barracks they were given turned out to be enlisted men's quarters; it was all the base had available. No individual rooms, just rows of double-deck bunk beds. The pilots and mechanics staggered to the beds closest to the door and fell asleep, often without removing their clothes. They were allowed to sleep late, by military standards; nobody woke them up until mid-morning the following day.

"I can see you've already done all the preliminary wiring on the armament systems of your planes," said Captain Diaz, standing on the wing of one of the P-40s. "You even managed to install gun charging cylinders. That is good, it will make installing the machine guns and gunsights much easier, much quicker. If we hurry, we could have it all done today. Come, your weapons are over here."

Diaz jumped off the wing and led the group to one

side of the hangar where several dozen small crates had been stacked. They were rectangular, about a foot wide and more than seven feet long. With a crowbar, Diaz pried the lid off one of them, revealing a Browning, .50-caliber M-2 aircraft machine gun in a protective paper wrapping. Woods reached in and, with one good pull, tore the paper off the gun's long barrel.

"That's beautiful, mate," said Ward admiringly. Then, turning to Van Hoff. "How much did they all cost you?"

"Forty thousand dollars," he replied. "As much as it cost to originally buy the Kittyhawks and all the spare parts."

"Ahh, but for that you're receiving seventy-two machine guns," said Diaz. "Enough to give six to each airplane. And you're receiving our expert aid and use of our test range. Now if you will help, we shall start."

Beyond Diaz, there were just the pilots, mechanics and C-46 flight crews in the hangar. No other Dominican Army Air Corps personnel were allowed inside. Two more crates were opened and the first three machine guns were completely stripped of their protective wrappings and washed of their shipping oil. They were carried over to Reynolds's P-40E, where the access panels to the top and bottom of the gun bay in its left wing had been removed.

Each gun received an arming solenoid before it was slid into the gun bay and anchored in one of three troughs. Then it was hooked up to a hydraulic gun charging cylinder and wired to the arming system. Mostly it was done by the mechanics while the pilots did the rudimentary labor and Diaz supervized it all. They became more proficient as they installed the guns in the right wing. Proficient enough for Diaz to split them up and have them go to work on several fighters.

Next Diaz showed the pilots a dozen small boxes; inside them were K-14 gyro gunsights. In the front instrument panels of the P-40s were notches where the gunsights were meant to go. But these particular sights would cause some problems as they were larger than the older N-3 gunsights originally installed in the Curtiss fighters.

"At least we can use one piece of modern equipment from our Mustangs and Tempests," said Van Hoff, showing one of the K-14s to the other pilots. "The gyro actuated gunsight. I believe you Americans called it the No-Miss-Um."

"Yes, it was a wonderful piece of equipment," Reynolds noted, looking at another one. "Once we got used to working it. This will allow us to make deflection shots without any trouble."

"They were no trouble for me, Colonel," said McCloud. "I always did have a head for numbers. I like the mathematical precision of deflection shots."

"Well you'll get the sight anyway. This is the only type we have and Claus paid six thousand dollars for them. Captain, you think these sights will give us much trouble?"

"Some, Mister Reynolds but nothing great," said Diaz. "We shall have to widen the gap in the control panel and add braces to hold the sights in place. Fortunately, there are not many instruments on the control panel that the sight would hide. Let's go, I will show you."

They returned to Reynolds's P-40, standing alone at

the front of the hangar. With the canopy rolled back, Diaz climbed into the cockpit and showed how the gunsight would be put in place. Then he called for his tool box and took out a hack-saw. He proceeded to carve from each side of the hole a thin, jagged, strip of metal.

It was strenuous work, Diaz was soon sweating, but the notch in the front instrument panel had been enlarged to take the K-14 sight. He asked for an electric drill and punched two holes in the panel, just beneath the notch, for the braces the sight needed for support. The remaining installation procedures were simple; Diaz left them to Reynolds and one of his company's mechanics while he moved on to another P-40 where he would supervise the work rather than do it himself.

By noon four of the six P-40s in the hangar had been rearmed and two had received their gunsights. By mid-afternoon all six fighters had full batteries of machine guns and their gunsights were installed. They were towed out of the hangar and the remaining P-40s, all the N-models, were taken inside. Some work was done on them, mostly in the cockpits for the K-14 sights, before Reynolds called it a day and everyone left.

Though it wasn't for long. At two o'clock in the morning, hours before the base would awaken, the pilots and mechanics returned to the flight line where the newly armed Kittyhawks were towed to the weapons test area. There they had their guns boresighted, two fighters at a time. The P-40s were set up in the revetments, their tails raised, and their guns test fired to see if the streams of shells would converge properly. If all went well, in another twenty-four hours the entire squadron would be combat ready.

"Your flight line looks most impressive, from here," the official observed, glancing out the balcony. "May I see the list of the aircraft you've completed?"

"Of course, Herr Rauchman, we have it ready for you." The man by the table opened a folder and laid it in front of a chair. Rauchman stepped away from the balcony and took the one offered to him. As he flipped noisily through the folder's contents, the sounds echoed faintly around the vast meeting hall. Save for Rauchman and the few men he was meeting with, the hall was empty. "Excuse me but when will our leaders arrive? Everything is ready for them."

"Soon, very soon," said Rauchman. "In the next few days. Currently, they are meeting with Argentinian officials outside of Buenos Aires. Once those talks are done, they will come here. For more meetings, to see the preparations are moving. I see you've done quite well but tell me, what do these asterisks mean beside these serial numbers?"

"Those aircraft were wrecked after being assembled. We've had some flying accidents here during our training program."

"Indeed, were any of them fatal?"

"Almost all, unfortunately. But not to worry, we have cleaned the crash sites and all the debris has been brought here. We use the wrecks for spare parts, along with several of the uncompleted aircraft. I'm sorry but it was necessary, we have no other source for spares."

"I understand and I see where you've marked that in the list," said Rauchman, tapped his pen on one of the report's pages. "I also see where you have managed to assemble six bombers—excellent. You have an entire staffel of Doras and how is work on the Salamanders proceeding?"

"Two are almost ready, we've received four altogether. I'm told we cannot expect more because they are difficult to smuggle out of Europe. I hope these will be enough?"

"Not to worry, they will. When they fly, they shall be the only aircraft of their kind in South America. That will make them enough for us."

Chapter Eight:
A STOWAWAY.
FLIGHT INTO SOUTH AMERICA.

"All right, Dennis, the pit's been cleared," Woods advised. "Everything's ready. You may open fire."

After acknowledging his instructions, Brandon flipped on the machine gun circuit breakers, turned off the safety switch and squeezed the trigger on the control stick grip. The six wing guns on his P-40 chattered noisily, hammering a short burst into the earthen revetment several dozen feet in front of it. The entire fighter shook, and the brace holding up its tail rattled until the test firing ended.

"Gun safety switch, on," said Brandon, hitting a toggle on the front instrument panel. "Gun relay circuit breaker, off. Gun solenoid circuit breaker, off. The armament system is down. Well, how did they work this time, Michael."

"All your guns fired properly," said Woods, taking a set of ear protectors off his head. "That jam from the last time must've been nothing more than a link failure. And the moment we receive a report from the pit, we'll know if your guns are aligned or not."

A few seconds later, the men who had gone into the

revetment came back with their verdict. All the holes the slugs had caused showed that the guns on Brandon's P-40 were properly boresighted. Their fire would converge on a point three hundred yards in front of the fighter, standard combat range.

The brace holding the plane in flying attitude was removed and the tail lowered to the ground. All the access panels to the ammunition and gun bays were put back in place and a tow bar was hooked to the main landing gear legs. While a mule towed the P-40 back to the distant flight line, another was put in its place in front of one of the two gun pits.

The next aircraft in was Doug Ward's P-40N. In fact all the P-40s at the test area that night were N-models; the second half of the squadron. Woods climbed onto its wing and repeated what he had done on Brandon's.

He supervised the removal of all access panels on the wings, the feeding of ammunition belts into the machine guns and the charging of the guns. The tail brace raised the fighter to its flying attitude and blocks were placed around its main wheels. Ward took to the cockpit where he switched on the electrical and armament systems. The pit was cleared and he squeezed off the first of a series of short bursts.

It lasted less than a second but the orange-red flashes at the gun muzzles persisted in people's eyes for some time after and the burst could be heard echoing around the base. Before the dust had settled in the revetment, a detail had scrambled in to measure the holes the shells had dug.

Back at the fighter the measurements were used to make minute adjustments in the alignment of the guns. They were fired again, then a third and fourth time before everyone was satisfied that they had been properly boresighted.

"Well, thank God that's the last of them," said Reynolds, as he watched the two P-40Ns being towed away. "In another half-hour the base will be waking up. It's amazing no one is up, we've been making the devil's own noise with these armament tests."

"If anyone did hear us they were probably ordered not to worry about it or remember it," Woods observed. "I hope someone will order them to keep things quiet while we're asleep. When will we be flying our practice mission?"

"Not until later this afternoon, around three o'clock but we'll be getting up at one for our pre-flight briefing. So let's not waste any more time here and head back to the barracks. We should get as much rest as we can."

Reynolds used a pair of trucks to collect the pilots and his mechanics. One of them stopped by the flight line to pick up those who had towed the fighters back to it. They all retired just before reveille sounded, officially awaking the base to a new day.

For seven hours the group slept, or tried to sleep, while the base went about its normal activities. A little after twelve they began to stir and were ready for Major Carlos when he arrived at one o'clock. He took them to a cafeteria for a late lunch and then on to a briefing room where he explained the mission they would be flying.

"We will proceed along the coastline to the island of Saona, on our southeastern side," said Carlos, using a wall map to outline the route. "This is where our gunnery range is located. You should not worry about being spotted here. The island is sparsely populated and remote even by Dominican standards. Our range is on the island's Caribbean side, down here. There many targets set up along the shore, merely choose which one you want and attack it. Jack, I suggest that you allow no more than one flight to use the range at a time. We had a bad accident with a large operation a few months ago. Two of our planes collided over the range. Do any of you have questions?"

"I have one, why do you keep saying 'we'," Woods asked.

"Because I shall accompany you. I feel you need someone along who knows the route and should anyone see you, they will think you are new aircraft for the Dominican Air Corps."

The tan and green Mustang maneuvered in next to the lead flight of P-40s. It led the entire formation out over the Caribbean, taking them to Saona Island where many of the pilots would fly their first gunnery runs since World War Two. The P-51 seemed to lead them impatiently, as if the Kittyhawks were delaying it, and no wonder; the P-40's maximum speed was some thirty miles an hour slower than the Mustang's standard cruise speed. They had barely left the Dominican Republic behind them when Saona came into view.

It was a low, vibrantly green island with a center rise of small, jagged mountains. There were no towns on it and scarcely even any villages; no roads could be seen, nor were there any airfields. It was the perfect site for a test range.

"Hawk Lead to Squadron, we are two minutes from target area," said Reynolds. "Activate guns and gunsights. Standby, mine will be the first flight to go in. Eagle Flight, Falcon Flight, stay at altitude until we're done."

Over the island's southern coast the lead flight peeled away and split into pairs. They rolled on their backs and dove; levelling off just above the surf. The P-40s roared across the beach; the leaders pulling out in front and the wing men moving in behind them. They closed on a pair of white, corrugated metal shacks spaced a few hundred yards apart. Reynolds and Green opened fire at the same time, raking the shacks with streams of .50-caliber shells. For exactly three seconds they held their triggers down, then released them and swung out of the way to allow their wing men a crack at the targets.

Acerrio and Clinton hit them with the same barrage of fire though not quite as accurately; their bursts quavered slightly and chopped up some of the surrounding foliage. They didn't fire for nearly as long and when they were finished, they streaked over the shacks and pulled into steep climbs. At a thousand feet they rejoined their leaders; who took them back for another run.

"Pull abreast of me, Tony," Reynolds ordered. "We're going to hit those runway marks."

On the beach was an outline, in white, of a runway about half a mile long. It was fairly complete, with center line marks and compass numbers at either end. Reynolds and Acerrio came out of the east and, after several seconds' hesitation, Green and Clinton came diving in from the west.

Wing tip to wing tip now, Reynolds and Acerrio sprayed the fake runway with a dozen streams of shells; neatly covering its entire width. The carpet of miniature explosions walked from one end to the other; where the two P-40s turned away and flew out over the sea. The little fountains of sand barely had time to settle when Green and Clinton made their run, stitching the same stretch of beach in exactly the same manner.

For their third attack the fighters skimmed low across the hills bordering the test range and strafed a set of triangles laid out in some clearings. It proved to the the most difficult of their runs and was repeated on other targets before all four aircraft had exhausted their ammunition. While they regrouped, Reynolds contacted Van Hoff; it was now his turn to use the range.

"All right, Falcon Flight, let's show the Americans what we can do," he said. "Tally-ho, boys."

As Reynolds and his flight climbed back to cruise altitude, Van Hoff's flashed past him to begin their attack. They started out with a similar maneuver. They split into pairs and came thundering in from the sea to hit the two shacks. Only Van Hoff's fire wasn't as accurate as his wing man's, Desmond Kain's. Like Acerrio and Clinton in the lead flight, he was a little rusty in his combat skills after being out of military service for so long. All who had been discharged from whatever air force they had served with found their skills wanting at the start of their practice runs. Though by the time they ran out of ammunition, the rustiness had vanished and their ability to place shells where they wanted them to be had fully returned. The mission was a success.

"So, is that the way you attacked the enemy while in China, Jack?" asked Carlos, as Wood's flight rejoined the formation.

"Yes, and in Europe as well," said Reynolds. "It's the way we all did it. Whether that be in Alaska or New Guinea or North Africa or England. It's how we all more or less fought the war."

"Hey, Major, how do they teach you guys here to shoot-up targets?" said Acerrio. It was all the excuse Carlos needed to hear.

He pulled his Mustang away from the Kittyhawks and rolled it onto its back. For the second he hung there he marked his target and dove toward the beach. He spiralled around his right wing as he descended; finally levelling out a mere dozen feet above the sand. His prop wash kicked up a trail of spray as he aligned himself with the runway markers and opened fire.

The barrage was a little off-center but tracked nicely down the full length of the target. When the P-51 reached the opposite end it turned to the left and all but disappeared amongst the island's rich foliage; its tan and green camouflage was indeed effective. Near the mountains the fighter became visible again, it was swinging around so tightly, it was pulling contrails from its wing tips in the hot, humid air.

Carlos hit one of the shacks next—they had both collapsed under the hard pounding they received from the P-40s. Then it was out over the sea where he turned, paralleled the shore for a few hundred yards, then turned again and thundered across the test range at often less than treetop height. He followed the terrain of the land, hopping over the taller trees and strafing whatever targets appeared in the clearings. When he was done, Carlos climbed smartly back into the formation where he resumed his position next to the lead flight. For a pilot who hadn't flown a single combat mission, it had been an impressive performance.

"That, Mister Acerrio, is how they teach us to fight in my air force," he finally replied. "Now if you'll turn one hundred and twenty degrees to the west, I shall lead you home."

Returning to the air base, the P-40s had barely shut down when the mechanics started to work on them. A combination of little sleep and a strenuous mission left the pilots bone-tired; they scarcely had the strength to crawl out of the cockpits. Like every other flight, they gathered around Reynolds's P-40, where they were met by Carlos.

"Oh Lord, I haven't felt this exhausted since North Africa in 'forty-two," said Brandon. "When we were flying up to four sorties a day. Especially during the El Almein battle."

"I know how you feel, mate," Ward croaked. "We're not even thirty yet and already we're physical wrecks."

"My friends, that was magnificent!" Carlos shouted, jumping out of the jeep before his driver had brought it to a stop. "I wish my pilots had seen your demonstration. They would understand what it means to be professional."

"Don't tell me, he's going to make us do it again," said Green, leaning against the wing of Reynolds's P-40.

"No, my friends. You're going to be the guests of

honor at a grand dinner. Come, I will have you driven to your barracks where you can wash and shave. And then we shall eat and party all night!"

"Bloody hell, he can afford to talk about partying to the wee hours," said Brandon. "He hasn't been working on ruddy aeroplanes for the last two days."

The mixture of exhaustion and freely flowing wine proved too much for the pilots. By nine o'clock many of them were asleep, whether they were back at their barracks or not, and by midnight they were all in their beds, most having been dragged there. At last they were able to sleep soundly for a full night. In the morning they awoke rested and refreshed, and they would need it for what the day had in store.

"In spite of the hospitality, we've been here long enough," said Reynolds, speaking to the assembled group. "By the end of today, we're to be in Aruba. Which means between now and around one o'clock, we have a lot of work to do. The mechanics started it yesterday and have identified all the repairs that are needed and the parts we should replace. And not just on the fighters but our transports as well. The list of what each needs has been drawn up so there shouldn't be any surprises. Before we start, I'd like to have all your passports again for Rafael to get stamped. Do any of you have any questions?"

"I would like to place a phone call off the base," said Van Hoff. "To my bank in Santo Domingo and I would like to make it before we begin working on the planes."

"Sure, go ahead. Only don't take too long, Claus."

The fighter pilots paired off with the mechanics, as they became available, and the transport crews climbed inside their aircraft. Panels and access hatches were opened on all the planes; at one time none of the P-40s or the C-46s had a fully cowled engine. As the repairs got under way, there was a continual stream of pilots and mechanics to the Commandoes where they picked out the spare parts their fighters needed. Oil, hydraulic fluid and engine coolant were supplied free of charge by the Dominican Army Air Corps and in reality, they were all that truly needed replacing.

By around noon, all the panels and hatches were back in place, the repairs made and the tools put away. Those who did the work were dirty and hungry. They returned to their barracks for one last time to wash up and pack their belongings. Then they went to the officers' cafeteria for lunch, where Carlos returned their passports, with all the necessary exit stamps in place. He accompanied them back to the flight line where he said good-bye to his friends, old and new.

". . . And next time, Jack, don't wait so many years to visit me again," Carlos added, embracing his oldest friend. "My wife and family would like to see you."

"Don't worry, I'll be back sooner than you'll want me," Reynolds promised. "Our little war won't last very long."

"Would you care to have some more firepower in your war? You have underwing and fuselage pylons on your fighters, I could sell you a supply of two hundred and fifty pound bombs if you wish."

"Thanks for the offer, I appreciate it but we already have another deal lined up. Don't we, Danny?"

"Yes, and my friends will deliver on time," said Green, standing on the wing of his P-40.

"I see. Then good luck with the munitions I've already given you, my friend," said Carlos. "And I will get you a proper escort for your departure."

As the P-40s and the Commandoes were preparing for takeoff, two flights of Mustangs thundered out of the base with Carlos in the lead. They provided the escort, joining up on either side of the Kittyhawk formation. Carlos stayed with his friends for almost an hour; the group was far into the Caribbean before he waggled his wings and turned back.

On their own, the P-40s broke their formation and collected around the C-46s. With no long-range navigation equipment of their own, the fighters had to rely on the lumbering transports to lead them safely across the more than four hundred miles of water between the Dominican Republic and the Dutch Antilles. And with the sky darkening and the cloud cover increasing, Reynolds decided to take no chances on someone becoming lost. In pairs the Kittyhawks sidled up to the Commandoes, like chicks running to their mother hens. Tucked in neatly on their wing tips, the group cruised on uneventfully, until they were about a hundred miles from Aruba.

"God damn it, I knew our center-of-gravity was off," the voice on the radio swore. "Reynolds-Four-Five-Victor to Hawk Lead, I've got a stowaway on board."

The transport calling in was the one Van Hoff's flight had formed around. After telling Acerrio to stay put, Reynolds jumped from his Commando to the other, edging in close enough for him to see into its flight deck. As he did so, Van Hoff moved from the C-46's right wing tip to a position abreast of Reynolds.

"Okay, who is it?" he demanded, irritated that someone would try to sneak a ride on one of his airplanes. "Have they identified themselves yet?"

"Oh, I already know who it is, Mister Reynolds and you're not going to like it. It's Marilyn, your daughter. Hank, bring her forward."

From his vantage point, Reynolds could clearly see two figures enter the flight deck, one of them had a slender frame and short, black hair.

"Jesus Christ, what the hell's going on around here!" he shouted. "Marilyn, what the hell are you doing on that plane and how on earth did you get there?"

"I was the one who put her on the plane, Jack," said Van Hoff. "There were no direct flights from Santo Domingo to Aruba so she had to come with us. I contacted her from the air base, when I was supposedly placing a call to my bank. Major Carlos and his family were able to bring her on the base itself."

"Jesus, who else is in on this? Bess Truman?" Reynolds angrily asked. "Or didn't you think to invite her? We're going to be landing in about twenty minutes and both of you had better do a lot of explaining."

In the fading light, the island of Aruba looked like a dark, elongated, patch floating on the Caribbean Sea. Along the island's southeastern shore were collections of light; the largest of which was its capital of Oranjestad. A few miles south of it lay the island's one airport, whose rotating beacon could be seen while the planes were still far out at sea.

Night had fallen by the time the group started circling over it; for the first time the aircraft had to use their landing lights. The C-46s were the first to touch down, followed by the P-40s from Reynolds's flight and then Van Hoff's. He found Marilyn and her father waiting for him at the flight line, and already embroiled in an argument.

"Young lady, I ought to take you across my knee and give you a good tanning!" Reynolds shouted, as much to be heard above the roar of Allison engines as to drive home his point. "I may not have been much of a father in the past, but I can damn well act like one now!"

"Don't punish her for this, Jack!" said Van Hoff, shouting it as he jumped out of the cockpit and climbed off the wing of his fighter. "What she's done, she has done for me. And not for some foolish, schoolgirl prank."

"Oh no, this is just what we need," said Clostermann. "A love affair. Indeed, this is a love triangle. A father versus a lover, a girl torn between being a daughter to one and a woman to the other."

"You two lied to me back in Fort Myers," Reynolds concluded. "You knew what she was doing, didn't you, Claus?"

"We didn't lie to you then and we will not lie to you now," said Van Hoff. "Marilyn is doing something very important for me. Is there some place we can talk in private?"

On an open flight line there weren't many places to hold a confidential discussion. But there were the cargo decks of the C-46s. Though crammed with spare parts of all kinds, they did offer the privacy Van Hoff wanted. Reynolds told Woods he was in charge and climbed aboard one of the transports with his daughter and Van Hoff.

"All right, suppose you tell me what Marilyn's doing for you?" Reynolds demanded, once the fuselage door had been closed. "Before I wrap a propeller blade around your head."

"I hope this doesn't degenerate into violence, Jack. There's no need for it. You have all done so much for me. Merely paying for it is not enough. Marilyn thought of a way that would be better and agreed to help me. All of our friends miss their loved ones, especially those who've been recently married. I'm arranging to bring them all to our base in Bolivia. Wives, fiancées, parents, sisters, even brothers and other relatives. You, you already have the one you love here, your daughter. But the others need their loved ones as well. Don't ruin this for them, Jack."

"Ordinarily, I wouldn't. But damn it, man you've got my daughter mixed up in this. What we're doing is dangerous and where we're going is dangerous."

"No, daddy, what you're doing is illegal," said Marilyn, glancing out one of the fuselage windows. "It would only be dangerous if someone knew about it. Like them . . ."

She pointed at the Dutch customs officials who were meeting with Woods and the other pilots outside.

". . . If you don't let me come along, I'll tell them what you're doing. All they'd have to do is open the wing panels on any of your fighters and they'd find those machine guns."

"We would have a bit of explaining to do," said Van Hoff, just before Reynolds exploded.

"Marilyn, you're blackmailing us!" he shouted. "How could you do it? I'm your father and he's the one you supposedly love."

210

"I want to be with you and I won't be treated like a little girl. If the only way I can do it is to share a prison cell, then so be it."

"You'd better hurry and decide, Jack," Van Hoff urged. "Those officials are coming to the plane. If she tells them what we have, we'll certainly be arrested and our aircraft impounded. This mission will be ruined and all our friends who are on leave will likely face court-martial."

"I know, and the Dutch will probably end up sending our planes to the East Indies. I hear they're still using P-40s out there to fight Indonesian rebels. All right, if that's what you wish then you can come along with us, Marilyn. If seems as though you have us over a barrel."

"And you won't tell the others what I'm doing here?" she asked.

"Your secret's safe with me, angel. For now we'll let them think you're here because you love Claus. That really isn't a lie, just not the complete truth."

Voices could be clearly heard just outside the aircraft. The fuselage door swung open and a uniformed official peered inside.

"Excuse please, is one of you named Jack Reynolds?"

"I'm Jack Reynolds, what would you like?"

"Could you please come out for official declaration and inspection. Your friends said you were in charge of these planes. Why are you on board this one?"

"Because the pilot thought he felt the load shift in flight," Reynolds answered, leading Van Hoff and Marilyn out of the transport. "But we checked it out and there doesn't seem to be a problem. What would you like us to do?"

First, Dutch customs wanted to inspect the planes. On the fighters they checked the cockpits and baggage compartments; on the Commandoes they checked the flight decks and their cargoes. They were little more than cursory inspections, customs never asked for the wing panels on the P-40s to be opened or for a more thorough exam of the freight on the C-46s. Afterward, they took the pilots, flight crews and mechanics to their offices where they checked their luggage and stamped their passports. They also had a message for Reynolds, a telegram the Western Union office at the airport had received.

"It's from my brother," he told his friend. "He's arrived in La Paz. Bob says he had no trouble on the flight down. He says he'll be doing PR missions soon. He sent along the name of his hotel and his room number if we need to contact him."

"Does he say anything of the political situation in Bolivia?" said Van Hoff. "I have read in newspaper accounts that it's unstable. That the leaders are weak."

"This is a telegram, Claus, not a UPI wire story. He says the city is snafu but he's getting things done. Snafu stands for situation normal, all fouled up. You can draw your own conclusions from that. We'll be out in the country, however, where things won't be so bad. If nothing goes wrong, in another two days we'll be in Bolivia ourselves. Then we'll really find out."

Dutch officials were cooperative enough to provide a bus to drive the group over to the hotel they were staying at. It wasn't far from the airport and it had a restaurant. What it didn't have was an extra room.

They had all been taken by tourists and Marilyn would have to stay with her father. She got the roll-out bed; Reynolds decided that if she wanted to endure the trip's hardships, she could start right away.

When they awoke the next morning, the group found they had become one of Aruba's tourist attractions; word of their association with a Hollywood movie had spread rapidly. At the restaurant they were given the best tables in the house and the other patrons were constantly coming up and asking for their autographs.

"I suppose if I wore a moustache they'd mistake me for Clark Gable," Reynolds grumbled, as he laid his bacon on his toast to make a sandwich. "This attention is ridiculous."

"We would've drawn attention even if we didn't have that cover story," said Woods. "We're now the most powerful military force on this island. The nearest planes the Dutch have are some navy patrol bombers on Curaçao, and they're fifty miles away. If we didn't have a cover story, no matter how ridiculous, if we didn't say anything, we would've aroused suspicion. And attention is always preferable to suspicion."

At the airfield an even bigger surprise awaited the group. A crowd of tourists and locals had formed in the terminal. They lined its windows and covered its observation deck; they had come to see the planes take off.

"Jesus Christ, this is like a damn air show," said Reynolds. "Airport security told me they had trouble keeping the people away from our planes. Let's leave the minute we can, before the crowd gets bigger and we cause more trouble."

The pilots and mechanics gave the fighters a quick, standard pre-flight check while they were being filled with gas. As usual the C-46s came to life first. They lumbered out to the runway and were lifting off by the time the P-40s were firing up their engines.

The crowd gave a loud cheer when Reynolds and Acerrio taxied out. They cheered as each pair of fighters moved from flight line to runway; then the crowd occupied the flight line to watch the formation take off.

"These people probably haven't seen anything like us since the end of the war," said Woods. "Let's do something special for them, Jack. After we're airborne."

Once aloft, the transports set course and followed the island's coastline, while the P-40s swept low over the airport, maintaining their neat flight paths. They continued on out to sea where they turned to the same course as the Commandoes. Using their speed advantage, the fighters caught up with the transports near Aruba's southeastern tip.

The planes returned to the same formation they used on the previous day. Each flight selected a C-46 and settled on its wing tips. Reynolds chose the transport in which Marilyn was riding; even in the air he wanted to keep an eye on his girl. Unlike the previous day, the formation wasn't winging across a trackless, featureless expanse of ocean but a narrow strip of Caribbean between the Lesser Antilles and the shore of Venezuela. They didn't have to do it for safety reasons, rather, it was the most comfortable formation the pilots found they could fly.

They were rarely out of sight of land. To the left lay

the ever-present shadow of the Venezuelan coast. On the right were the major islands and atolls of the Antilles chain. First was Curaçao, largest Dutch-owned island in the Caribbean, next was Bonaire and after that a series of smaller islands and coral atolls owned by Venezuela.

From Curaçao a Dutch patrol bomber appeared and climbed toward the loose formation; word of their arrival had spread far. The Lockheed Harpoon sidled up to one flight of P-40s after another, its crews talking with each of the pilots. They traded war stories, asked where the planes had been bought and where they were taking them. It went on for nearly an hour, until the group was approaching the Venezuelan island of Tortuga. The Harpoon banked away from Van Hoff's flight and flew back to Curaçao. Twenty minutes later the group was landing at Puerto la Cruz, only then did anyone talk at length about what the bomber might've really been up to.

"Do you believe they were merely doing it out of curiosity?" Van Hoff asked, the moment he met with Reynolds.

"I don't know," he admitted. "The questions seemed innocent enough. But they got an awful lot of information out of us. I just don't know if it was official sniffing at our heels or not. One thing I am glad of, by tonight we'll be in the middle of Brazil and by tomorrow, Bolivia. If the Dutch want to do anything to us, they'll have to do it now. Or else we'll be long gone."

"Jack, customs will see us," said Woods, breaking into the conversation. "And the petrol trucks will be here soon, better have your billfold ready."

"Okay, go take care of customs until we get there, Mike," said Reynolds. "Claus and I have to discuss finances. Marilyn, could we see you for a minute?"

"Yes, daddy, what would you like?" she asked, though her father waited for Woods to get out of earshot before he would answer.

"We'll be entering Brazil soon, a very remote section of it. Decent communications will be a luxury, if you want to send any more messages you'd better do it while we're still here. You won't be able to do anything until we get to La Paz."

"I have a few more telegrams to get out. I don't think I need to send anyone any more money. I'm also expecting to receive some messages. I'll go to the telegraph office as soon as we get through the customs check. Would you like me to see if Uncle Bob sent anything?"

"Yes, do that. If we don't hear from Bob at this stop, we won't until we're inside Bolivia."

For merely being an in-transit stop, the Venezuelans gave everyone in the group an unusually thorough exam. Their passports were gone over, almost page by page and the officials repeatedly asked if anyone was planning to stay in Venezuela. They even went so far as to follow Marilyn when she walked through the airport lobby to the telegraph office. Fortunately, the officials didn't do the same exacting job on the group's aircraft.

"You think that little visit by the Dutch bomber had anything to do with this?" Acerrio asked, after the customs check was finished and they were all walking back to the flight line.

"Maybe, but if that's true, why didn't they go over

our planes better?" said Reynolds. "It wouldn't have taken them more than five minutes to find the guns in the fighters or the munitions on the Commandoes."

"Probably because they didn't want a problem on their hands," said Van Hoff. "They don't want us causing any trouble in their country. And since they found that out, we can go about our business and cause trouble in someone else's country. You may find it hard to believe but it's true."

"Oh I believe it. You forget my family's done a lot of business with South American countries. Anywhere below Mexico they don't care what you're up to just so long as you don't do it in their country."

No crowd gathered to watch them depart from Puerto la Cruz. They had to mingle in with the normal traffic of local and international flights and private aircraft. Once at cruise altitude, the formation turned south by southeast for the next leg of its journey. Below the Venezuelan coast, and the mountain range guarding it, was the grassland plain of the Orinoco River. When the planes crossed the river they effectively left civilization behind. Everything south of it was remote and sparsely populated, especially the Guiana Highlands, which covered the whole lower half of Venezuela.

They looked rugged and felt remote, much more so than any other terrain the pilots had thus far flown over. There could be no doubt that beyond the next mountain or valley there would be no city, or even a village. The pilots could see no signs of civilization, no roads, no railroads, no power lines of any kind or the smoke of distant factories. It was a very hostile environment—it made the fighters hug the transports a little closer.

In spite of its intimidating remoteness, the land was also beautiful. Along their route, the planes encountered a narrow ribbon of white water plunging through the mountains. It was Angel Falls, the world's tallest waterfall, with a drop of more than thirty-two hundred feet. They circled it for a minute or so, then continued on, weaving their way through the Pacaraima Mountains of the Guiana Highlands.

Gradually, the mountains fell away; receding behind the formation as it crossed from Venezuela to Brazil. Where the foothills ended, the Amazon Basin began and with it, the web of tributaries which drained it. A few miles into the basin, the group's next refueling stop appeared. Boa Vista, on the banks of the Branco tributary.

Its airport was scarcely more than a grass strip with a collection of shacks on one side. If it weren't for the fact that Boa Vista received regular airline service, the field wouldn't have had the right grade of fuel for the P-40s and the Commandoes. What it didn't have was a restaurant or any kind of eating facilities. For that, the group would have to drive into town and there wasn't the time for it. Not if they wanted to reach Manicoré before sundown. For lunch, the group snacked on whatever the mechanics had brought along in the C-46s.

There was at least a customs desk in what passed for the airport's terminal. Unlike their Venezuelan or Dutch counterparts, the Brazilian officials showed only mild interest in the mass arrival of fighters and transports. They scarcely even inspected the planes. Just looked over the cargo manifests and other papers

Reynolds handed them. The sheets that required it were stamped and so was everyone's passport. An hour and a half after they arrived, the planes were leaving for Manicoré.

Since they wouldn't be encountering any mountains on their route, Reynolds let the planes fly at a lower altitude. It would also make it easier for them to navigate by identifying landmarks, for they were now flying deep into the Amazon Basin. Modern radio-navigation aids were nonexistent, which meant all the advanced equipment on the C-46s was next to useless. The formation huddled together, as they had when they were over the trackless ocean.

The basin looked just as threatening and forbidding as the Caribbean and the Guiana Highlands had but it was not without features. There were rivers, the vast network of tributaries that laced their way through the world's largest forest toward the world's biggest river, the Amazon. Overhanging it all were cloud-like banks of mist. Heavy and moisture-laden, the air was at saturation point; even when the fighters made normal maneuvers, they pulled contrails off their wing tips.

From Boa Vista, the formation followed the Branco River to its intersection with one of the Amazon's other major tributaries, the Negro River. It flowed to the southeast, where it would eventually join the Amazon. A broader river than the Branco, the Negro had a number of mid-stream islands which the P-40s made mock strafing runs against to pass the time. There was river traffic as well, including ocean-going ships. At least here were signs of civilization.

Where the Negro joined the Amazon stood the city of Manaus, one of the most important in Brazil. It was one of its principal ports, even though it was almost eight hundred miles from the Atlantic Ocean. Most of the Amazon's forest industry sent its products through Manaus, including the highly-prized hardwoods. Its port area was busy and it had a modern airport, which meant the navigation aids on the Commandoes were at last useful.

The airport gave them a navigation fix so they could continue on to Manicoré and the local Brazilian Air Force unit gave the formation an escort. A pair of P-47 Thunderbolts attached themselves to Reynolds's flight and said they would escort them partway to their destination. The Brazilian pilots turned out to be combat veterans and Clinton remembered their unit from his Twelfth Air Force days.

"At one time you guys and my group shared the same field," he said. "Could you tell me if Major Pedro Goulart is still in the air force and where he'd be?"

"Oh yes, Pedro's still in the air force," one of the pilots answered. "And he's a colonel now, he has command of his own squadron. It's south, at Porto Velho. Perhaps you can stop on your way and see him?"

"Maybe we can but I don't think so. The movie company wants us to arrive on time. Thanks."

The Thunderbolts departed about a half hour before Manicoré appeared. As the shadows lengthened the fighters and transports landed at the small town along the Maderia tributary. The airport was slightly better equipped than the one at Boa Vista. It had an asphalt runway and a better equipped terminal and control tower. Once they were all safely down, the group took command of Manicoré's entire fleet of taxis to drive them to their hotel. It had been a long, exhausting day and they were looking forward to a good rest. But what they got instead was a shock.

"I'm so sorry, Mister Reynolds but two days ago we had a fire," the hotel manager explained, as the group collected in the scorched, empty lobby. "No one was killed but it will be months before we reopen. I sent a telegram message to your home, warning you not to come."

"Thanks, but by then we were in the Dominican Republic," said Reynolds. "I just knew things couldn't go right forever. Well, are they any other hotels that can take on thirty-odd guests?"

"This is a small place. There are not many hotels here and those have all been filled by the guests who had to flee the fire. I'm sorry but I can't be of more help to you. You have aircraft, could you not fly to another city?"

"No, it's almost sunset and most of our planes aren't equipped for night flying. Damn, where the hell are we going to find a place to sleep tonight?"

"Hey, Colonel, how about that bordello we passed on our way here?" Acerrio leeringly suggested.

"My daughter is with us! Are you out of your fucking mind?" Reynolds thundered. "And the last thing any of us needs is a case of the clap."

"Excuse me but perhaps the airport will let you stay there?" said the hotel manager. "Often when planes do not arrive, they let passengers sleep in the lobby. I know the people who run the airport, I will call them. Again I'm sorry for the trouble I've caused you."

"All right already, you've been sorry enough in five minutes to last us a week. André, Jesse, go out and

221

stop those cabs from leaving. Before we go back, could you tell us what's the best restaurant in town?"

It was nightfall when they returned to the airport. At least the group had managed to get a meal in town and the hotel manager had cleared it with airport officials to let them sleep in the terminal. All the group had to do was provide their own sleeping gear.

On board the transports were a number of sleeping bags and blankets while the fighter pilots took their duffle bags out of the baggage compartments on their P-40s. In the terminal's main hall there were a number of wooden benches, much like the type one would find in a railroad lobby. They were hard, uncomfortable but with a sleeping bag they allowed someone to sleep, though without much real rest. Nor did the creatures of the night allow much rest either.

The Amazon jungle started at the airport perimeter and from it came the cries, screams and chatterings of everything from parrots and monkeys to the great cats and a hundred other creatures. Insects of all kinds buzzed through the night air; horned beetles, with the wing span of a small bird, would occasionally crash into the terminal's windows. It sounded as if someone were trying to throw a rock through them. All of it, plus the snoring by some members of the group, meant that no one slept soundly during the night. Nor did they sleep late. By early morning everyone was awake when a new problem awaited them.

"Weather report forecasts a storm moving into our area in the next two hours," said Reynolds. "And it looks like it's going to be a big one. Let's get the hell out of here while we can. Forget about washing up or having breakfast. Get out to the planes, Claus and I will handle the fuel trucks."

"But, daddy, do we have to rush?" Marilyn asked. "Couldn't we just wait out this storm?"

"No. You have no idea how violent or how long a storm could last in this area. We could be stuck here for a week. We can't afford that. A few days of this wet, humid weather and every piece of rubber on our planes would start to deteriorate and the fabric would rot. If we're not gone in ninety minutes we'll be in trouble, so move."

For the number of planes involved, an hour and a half didn't leave enough time for thorough pre-flight inspections. Between stowing their belongings and refueling the aircraft, the pilots and mechanics could only perform a brief ground check before the pilots climbed into the cockpits of their fighters.

A blue-gray wall of storm clouds was advancing on the airport as the last P-40s roared off its main runway. The group didn't bother to circle the field while they joined up. If they did the storm would've caught them. Instead, either alone or in pairs, the planes immediately set out for Bolivia, with the lead aircraft flying at a slower speed so the later ones could catch up.

"God, look at those nimbus thunderheads," Brandon remarked, as the formation was finally completed. "They're towering, they must top out at fifty thousand feet."

"More like sixty or seventy thousand feet," said Reynolds. "Down here in the tropics, thunderstorms can grow that high or higher. They can be very destructive, almost as bad as hurricanes. They can tear the wings off a plane, or throw it across an airport as if it were a toy. We're lucky to have gotten away when we did."

"Well, I have something that's equally towering but it isn't a storm cloud," Woods advised. "It's my oil temperature. It's rising to the red line and my oil pressure's falling like a damn barometer."

"Oh God no, not here of all places," said Reynolds, before he could catch himself.

"How bad is it, Michael?" Van Hoff asked. "How far has your temperature gone up?"

"It's at two hundred degrees and still climbing. My oil pressure's fallen from seventy-five pounds per square inch to fifty. If this doesn't stop soon, my engine's going to seize. If we don't find a place for me to land in five minutes, I'm going to crash."

Chapter Nine:
FORCED LANDING.
ARRIVAL IN BOLIVIA.

Woods's emergency galvanized everyone in the formation. His wing man, Jeffrey McCloud, slid under his aircraft to see if he could spot an oil leak and Reynolds came over to sit on his wing. Everyone else, even the transports, fanned out to search for a clearing—any kind of clearing, for him to land in.

"You have oil pouring out of your radiator shutters," said McCloud. "It's streaking across your undersides, almost to your tail. I'd say you've lost half your oil so far."

"Better throttle back," Reynolds added. "It may extend the life of your engine. Has anybody found a place for Mike to land yet? Hawk Lead to Reynolds-Four-Five-Victor, have you managed to contact anyone?"

"I got Manicoré on the line. They know what's going on but they can't help. The field's just been hit by those thunderstorms. Visibility is zero, wind direction is variable, wind speed is reaching forty-five miles an hour and they've already had an inch of rain. They can't launch any rescue planes but they've told the Brazilian Air Force about us and they say they can send a few boats down the river."

"Hey, there's an idea, Colonel," said Acerrio. "If we can't find a place for Mike to land, maybe he can set down in the river? It don't look all that deep."

"Are you kidding? He'll be eaten alive before he could get out of the cockpit," Reynolds answered. "By piranhas or caimans or maybe a jaguar. And anyway, if he dunks his plane in the river, he'll ruin it."

"He'll ruin it if he crashes in the jungle," said Van Hoff. "At least if he makes a water landing he'll stand a better chance of living through it."

"Why don't you ask me?" said Woods. "I'm the one who has to do the crash. I know what piranhas and jaguars are but what's a caiman?"

"A nasty little cousin to the alligator," said Reynolds. "They infest every river in the Amazon system."

"I think I'll try a jungle landing."

"But you'll tear the plane apart if you do," Van Hoff counseled. "And you with it."

"Then I'll land on a soft tree. I didn't fight a war for six years so I could end up being eaten by reptiles. I'll take my chances in the jungle."

"No you won't, mate. I've got a village over here," said Ward. "Eagle Four to Eagle Lead, village off your starboard wing. Distance about three miles. It's not big but it's got a couple of roads running through it. They look just wide enough for you to land on. I'm circling over the town now, can you see me?"

"Yes, I'll try to make for you," said Woods. "Locate

the longest and widest road that town has and show it to me when I reach you."

With Reynolds sitting on his left wing and McCloud sticking to his tail, Woods swung due west, heading toward the P-40 circling low over the forest canopy.

The village Ward had found was located, as usual, on the bank of a river. It had some modern, permanent buildings, most of them located along one large, dirt road that paralleled the river. Because of Ward's appearance, people were gathering in the streets, a situation he tried to change before his friend arrived.

"Ruddy damn wogs," he swore. "I almost wish I had ammo in me guns. A few good bursts over their heads would clear the street. These people are as bad as aborigines. How's it doing with you, mate?"

"My oil temperature's up to two hundred and five degrees," Woods answered. "And my pressure's down to thirty pounds. I'm going to lower my undercarriage now; if I lose my engine, I'd have to use that damn hand pump to do it. The engine's starting to run rough—I don't know how long she'll last. The moment I line up for a landing, I'll be switching her off."

"Are you sure you want to chance a dead stick landing?" said Reynolds. "That's an unnecessary risk."

"If my engine seizes, we'll have to replace it. And would you mind telling me how many weeks of river travel it'll take to ship a new one to this village? Or do you plan on tossing one out of a C-46."

"Okay, I see your point. Good-luck, Mike. Jeff and I will stay with you until you're ready to land."

Ward started buzzing the town to force the people off the road. Each time he came in lower and noisier; in his last run before Woods arrived, he was so low he was flying between the buildings.

By now Wood's P-40 trailed a thin plume of bluish smoke. As he arrived, Ward came rocketing out of the town, clearly showing him which road he should use. His landing gear already down and locked, all Woods had to do was descend and line up on the road. The moment he did so, he shut off his struggling Allison engine.

"Airspeed one-twenty, flaps down," said Woods. "Here we go, I'm committed. Say a prayer for me, lads."

"Our father who art in heaven, if you don't get off your butt and help this guy, I'll kick the shit out of the next priest I see," Acerrio quietly threatened.

Without the roar of its Allison, Woods's P-40 whistled in for its one and only attempt at a landing. He started his run about a half mile from the town, where the road was surrounded by jungle. His wing tips clipped the overhanging tree branches in the final seconds of his approach. Woods kept his tail high as he flared out and his main wheels made their initial contact with the dirt road.

The P-40 bounced back into the air, settled down, bounced again before enough speed had been killed and its main wheels were firmly planted on the road. Woods tried to keep his tail in the air for as long as possible. It allowed him to see what lay ahead of him.

There were still people on the road, even trucks and carts and few appeared to be making way for the Kittyhawk, that is until another P-40 came roaring in. It was Reynolds, he had his landing gear down and he came in just a few feet above Wood's tail. McCloud followed him through the town, as did Ward. By the time the last of them reared into a climb, the road was clear though Woods could barely see it. His airspeed had fallen off to the point where his tail had come down on its own accord and the P-40's long cowling hid most of what was in front of him.

Gingerly at first, Woods applied his brakes; he didn't know how his fighter would react to the hard-packed road surface. When buildings started to roll by on either side, he jumped on the pedals and held them down until the aircraft started to fishtail, threatening to ground loop. Its wing tips swung dangerously close to the buildings as Woods fought to control his fighter. With the rudder useless, he tapped one brake then the other, slowly straightening out the P-40's roll. Halfway through the town it had slowed sufficiently for Woods to try stopping it again.

He jumped on the pedals hard enough to lock the Kittyhawk's wheels. They scattered clouds of dirt and caused the fighter to swerve to one side. It came to a stop finally, slewed almost ninety degrees off its original course and ready to crash through what appeared to be the town bank. For several moments the town was quiet. The propeller had finished windmilling before anyone came out from under cover.

"Thank God, he's safe," said McCloud. "For a second I thought he lost it when he began swinging from side to side. Have you tried to reach him, Hawk Lead?"

"I will as soon as you let me," Reynolds brusquely replied. "Hawk One to Eagle One, do you read me? Mike, this is Jack, do you read me? Over."

"I read you, Jack, I'm safe and my ship's safe as well," Woods answered, after a long silence. "Though

I think she'll be needing a few gallons of oil. There's something of a crowd gathering here, what should I do?"

"Act friendly, and find someone who speaks English. There must be some American who's down on his luck in that town. If anyone gets nasty, just let us know."

The first people to collect around the P-40 were children and natives. Seemingly oblivious to the danger it had recently caused, they treated it as a new toy, to the extent that Woods had to shoo them off the wings. Men in uniforms and business suits were the next to arrive. They shouted at Woods in Portuguese and the men in uniforms started waving pistols at him, which made Woods grab his microphone.

"Hawk One, I'm in need of air support!" he shouted. "Make 'em understand I don't like guns pointed at me!"

Most of the airborne P-40s had by then collected above the town. They responded instantly to Woods's cry for help, forming into three-ship vees and thundering down the street as if they were strafing a target. After the third group had passed overhead, the pistols were lowered and someone came forward who spoke English.

"I regret to inform you, Mister Woods, but the police have put you under arrest," said the man who had become Woods's interpreter. "They say you threatened the safety of the town and the people. They wish to question you, they want to know about your friends and why you landed your plane here."

"And what will they do with my plane?"

"I'm afraid that the police must confiscate your

aircraft. They must do so to keep it safe. Please cooperate, Mister Woods, it will make things much easier."

"I'm sure it will. I hope they don't mind if I talk to my friends one last time." Woods reached back inside his cockpit for the microphone and started shouting that he was being arrested.

"Don't worry, Mike, we'll take care of it," said Reynolds. "Just do what they say. Ask for a lawyer and tell them you're a foreign national. Tell them you want to talk with the South African embassy in Rio. We'll find some place to land and figure a way to get you out. Let us handle it and don't get into any more trouble if you don't have to."

Together with the C-46s, the remaining P-40s made one last pass over the town and flew southwest on their original course. They had scarcely gone more than a few miles by the time Reynolds had received his tenth idea from the other pilots. They all pressed their own cases energetically, however, he had long since decided which plan they would use to free Woods.

"Jesse, you said yesterday that you had a friend in the Brazilian Air Force," he recalled. "You asked those T-Bolt pilots about him. Who is he and where is he?"

"His name is Pedro Goulart and he's now a Colonel," said Clinton. "He commands a squadron at Pôrto Velho. That's an air base near the Bolivian border. It shouldn't be far, maybe about seventy or eighty miles away."

"Okay, that's where we'll go but not all of us. I'll take one of the transports with me and some of the fighters. Reynolds-Four-Five-Victor, locate Pôrto Velho on your navigation chart and be ready to change course for it. Reynolds-One-Seven-Seven, you'll take command of the formation. Make sure it gets to San Joaquín in Bolivia. Jesse, you come with me. And Claus, you'd better come as well. The rest of you are to follow the other Commandoes to Bolivia. We'll let you know what happens."

No one but the people who Reynolds selected agreed with his orders; everyone else seemed to have a compelling reason why he shouldn't be left out.

"That's me CO we left back there, mate," said Ward. "I served under him ever since North Africa."

"He's my closest friend," added Brandon. "We flew in the same squadron during the Battle of Britain and were squadron leaders in the same wing back in North Africa."

"You can't go without me, Colonel," said Acerrio. "You'll be needing a wing man and I kinda like the guy too."

"I should go with you, Jack," said Green. "What if Mike's run into some legal trouble? Before I went to war, I was going to law school."

"All right already, I'll take along a few more," Reynolds relented. "But I can't take everyone. We all can't go barging into some air base. What if we're all impounded? That will end our mission real quick. I'm sorry, but the rest of you must go on to Bolivia. If we get stuck for some reason, you're the ones who will have to complete the mission. My friend will be waiting for you at San Joaquín. His name is Romero, Augustin Romero. Tell him what happened and to take you to his ranch. You're not to wait for us at San Joaquín, we'll catch up with you later. Dennis, you're in command until we come back. Reynolds-Four-Five-

Victor, have you located Pôrto Velho yet?"

There was a grumbling among those pilots and air crews who weren't chosen but everyone complied with Reynolds's orders. The formation split into two uneven parts. The larger half continued on toward Bolivia while the remaining five P-40s and a single C-46 changed course more to the west. Reynolds ordered the transport to increase to its maximum speed as the fighters formed a wide vee around it. After a few minutes the two groups were out of sight of each other. It took just a few more for the group Reynolds commanded to reach Pôrto Velho.

The town itself was fairly large and modern; it had both a road and a railroad which connected it with other cities to the south and west. The air base was also large and modern. It had the look of being recently built. Parked on its hangar aprons were rows of olive drab P-40s, bare metal T-6 and BT-13 trainers. Since it had a small civilian side, Reynolds's group easily received permission to land at the field.

First the fighters broke away to enter the landing pattern. As they did so, Clinton asked the tower if they could contact Colonel Goulart and inform him that a friend from his Twelfth Air Force days was arriving. Since the tower was manned by military personnel, the request was an easy one to fulfill. On roll out, the civilian fighters were instructed to taxi over to the military side, instead of the civilian side where they should have gone.

"Do you think this friend of yours will remember you?" Reynolds asked, helping Clinton climb off his fighter. "More importantly, do you think he'll help us?"

"I don't think he'll be forgetting my name or face any time soon," said Clinton. "We flew a couple of missions together and had a lot of 'experiences' off duty and while on leave. Yeah, he'll remember me though I wonder if he will help us? You'd better let me handle him."

The other three P-40s lined up beside the first two and so did the Commando. The transport's propellers were grinding to a halt when a jeep came barreling out to the flight line. It only had a driver and he wore the insignia of an officer, colonel's eagles to be exact. He waved to the pilots and called one of them by name.

"Jesse, what a wonderful surprise! It's been years!"

Clinton ran across the tarmac to greet the jeep's driver. Van Hoff and Ward moved to join him, only to be restrained by Reynolds.

"No, that's his friend," he told them. "Let's let Jesse make the first contact and do the introductions. We shouldn't dump everything on this guy all at once. We're going to have to do it in steps. Claus, go back to your plane and get that little attaché case of yours."

"Jesse, my friend, I wondered if it would be you," said Goulart, embracing Clinton. "This is wonderful, you're looking fine. Tell me, do you own the plane you have just flown in? Who are your friends and why have you come?"

It took only a minute for Van Hoff to return to his fighter, open the baggage compartment hatch and pull out the slim brief case he had carried across three continents. He got back to the group just ahead of Clinton and Goulart.

"What happens if he doesn't agree to help us and he

arrests us instead?" Van Hoff asked.

"Then we'll be up shit creek without a paddle," said Reynolds. "We could spend years in jail for smuggling armed aircraft into this country. At least half of our group will be safely inside Bolivia. They had enough equipment to continue on and carry out our mission."

"Jack, I'd like to introduce you to Colonel Pedro Goulart, of the Brazilian Air Force," Clinton announced, presenting his friend to Reynolds. "This is the man who's leading the group. And this one is Count Claus Van Hoff . . ."

"Oh yes, the Austrian," said Goulart. "No American or Australian would be called Count. And you must be Daniel Green and you must be Doug Ward. You have fine friends, Jesse, I'm pleased to meet you all. Jesse says you've had some trouble in my country and that you have some to seek my help?"

"Yes, one of our companions had engine trouble over the jungle," Reynolds explained. "He made a forced landing in a small town northeast of here. He's okay and even the plane's intact, but I think he's been arrested."

"I see, you do need my help. Come, I will take you to my office. We can talk better there."

Goulart found his jeep to be rather small for six people and there certainly wasn't any room for the passengers and crew of the C-46 when they appeared. After Reynolds ordered them to stay by their plane, Goulart floored the gas pedal and they sped away. He drove the jeep like a maniac, then, rode on the edge of a crash throughout the entire ride to his office. None of his passengers felt safe until he stopped and turned the engine off.

"My God, and I always believed that I was ruddy crazy behind the wheel," said Ward, gasping as if he had lost his breath. "You, you're positively lethal."

"He flies a P-47 the same way," Clinton added. "And with that he did prove lethal. To a lot of Germans."

Goulart's office overlooked the flight line, a curiously inactive one, Reynolds noted as he glanced at it again.

"So, you say you have a friend in trouble," said Goulart, stepping over to one of his office walls. "This is a map of western Brazil. Rondônia, Amazonas and Acre provinces. Show me the town where he made the forced landing."

That would be easy. Beyond the immediate area of the Amazon River, there were very few settlements in the Amazon Province. Almost the only town along the flight path Reynolds traced from Manicoré to Pôrto Velho was Calama. And as the map showed, there were no roads or railroads connecting it with Pôrto Velho.

"In this part of my country, the rivers are the roads," said Goulart. "The Amazon and all its tributaries. By river, it would take us about a day to rach Calama. By air, it will take us less than an hour."

"But there's no airport there," said Green.

"I know, we will do what your friend did. We will land on the road. With a light plane, it'll be much easier than with a fighter. I take it your friend was flying a P-40 like the rest of you?"

"Yes, an 'E' model like mine," Reynolds answered. "What about the local authorities? The police arrested Mike Woods. Can you handle them?"

"That is where the real trouble lies. Many officials treat their towns like they are fiefdoms, even in this, the twentieth century. I don't know how much influence I will have with them. Some of these people have even ignored orders from Rio. It is a symbol of the times. My country is in crisis. Political crisis, financial crisis, leadership crisis. Our army couldn't stop Venezuela from invading us, the navy is near mutiny and my air force is all but grounded. Have a good look at my flight line, I wondered why you did not see it before."

Reynolds and the others gathered at the office's large window to take their first real look at the lines of olive drab P-40s and bare metal trainers.

"Why, why some of your fighters don't have propellers," said Reynolds. "Or rudders or even canopies. And you have two of them propped up on saw horses. What's going on here? Many of your planes are derelicts."

"We have a critical shortage of spare parts," admitted Goulart. "Out of twenty-four fighters in my squadron, only four are in flying, combat-ready condition. Together with your friend in Calama, you have more flying combat aircraft in Rondônia Province than does the Brazilian Air Force. Out of a hundred and seventy P-40 and P-47 fighters, I would say only twenty percent are flying. That is why I have the Texans here. We took most of the T-6s from training command and armed them. Until the Rio Pact takes effect at the end of this year, they will be our most numerous combat plane."

"That's a terrible condition for anyone's air force to be in," said Clinton, a touch of sorrow in his voice. "If you help us, Pedro, I'm sure Jack will donate some spare parts you badly need. We have tons of parts."

"Yes, you did tell me you were all flying to Bolivia to make a movie. That sounds strange to me and why is it so vital that you have all your planes? Could not Holywood magic hide the fact you're missing one?"

Reynolds got ready to give his standard answer about the Flying Tigers movie when Clinton interrupted him.

"Let's not lie to him, Jack," he requested. "I've flown combat missions with Pedro. I know him like I know a brother and I say we can trust him with the truth."

"Okay, I'll trust your judgment," said Reynolds. "Claus, let's show him what we have. Jesse, if this doesn't work out, I want the top bunk when we land in jail."

In Van Hoff's attaché case were all the documents, photographs and collected intelligence he needed to prove that a Nazi coup was fomenting in Bolivia, or at least that something very odd and suspicious was happening across the border. Fifteen minutes later they had convinced Goulart it was true and he didn't feel the need to throw his friends in jail.

"What a wonderful quest you are on," he told them. "I wish I could join you, I only have one German plane to my credit. I would like to add more but my duties are here. All I can do is help you. Come, it's time we left for Calama to rescue your friend."

"How'll we go?" Clinton asked. "By boat?"

"No, we shall do it the way your friend did it. By plane. Our combat aircraft may be grounded but our transport and liaison planes can still fly. I have a Stinston L-5 here, we'll use that. I can only take three people with me. Who do you say should go, Mister Reynolds?"

Goulart's innocent remark set off a new round of compelling reasons for why one person or another shouldn't be left behind. Unlike the last time, Reynolds put his foot down. Only he, one of his mechanics and Green would go. The rest would have to stay.

"And how'll we get to the flight line?" Ward asked.

"No problem, I will drive you," said Goulart.

"What, hairpin turns with the wheels coming off the ground? No thank-you, I have no wish to end up in a Brazilian hospital. I'll walk, mate."

Green also preferred to walk but since he was one of the passengers, he had to endure another nerve-jangling drive. First Goulart stopped by Reynolds's Commando where he dropped off those who weren't passengers and picked up a Reynolds Air Service mechanic. He weaved around the line of near-derelict P-40s and armed T-6s, and screeched to a halt by one of the hangars. A ground crew pushed out onto the apron a Stinson L-5 painted silver. Of all the Brazilian Air Force planes the group had so far seen, it was the best looking one. And they were assured it could fly.

Goulart and Reynolds took the front seats; Green, the mechanic and his tool kit went in the back. Since there were no other military aircraft flying at that time and few civilian planes used the field at all; the Stinson was able to take off just minutes after starting its engine.

It followed the Madeira River's winding course to the northeast. Pôrto Velho was soon far behind the tiny aircraft, as were most other signs of civilization.

The rail line ended at the town. Anything that had to travel further into Brazil had to do so by river or by road and the road turned to the southeast just outside of Pôrto Velho; where it followed the Sierra dos Parecis Mountains.

At the Stinson's cruise speed of one hundred miles an hour, it took exactly fifty minutes for the light plane to reach the point where the Madeira was joined by the Jiparaná River before flowing north to the Amazon. Calama wasn't far from where the two rivers met; they only had to circle above the town once to see that Woods's P-40 was still intact and for Goulart to decide in which direction he would land.

"I will come down the same way your friend did," he told Reynolds. "Not much traffic appears on the road. Your friend must still be the center of attention. When we meet with the officials, let me do the talking at first, okay? We can use your lawyer later, if we need him."

The smaller Stinson was able to slide in easier between the trees than the fighter had. It rolled to a stop in less distance than the P-40 needed; in fact Goulart had to taxi the plane a few yards before he entered the town and switched off the engine. As with the last time a plane had landed in the town, a crowd gathered around it.

Goulart was the first to climb out. He immediately started to shout orders in Portuguese. The crowd responded by moving away from the plane, some ran to get the people he demanded to see while others answered his questions.

"Your friend was taken to the town's police office where he was placed in a cell," Goulart told Reynolds and the others. "They took everything off him and whatever they could take out of the fighter's cockpit. But they apparently didn't steal anything out of the fuselage baggage compartment. They probably don't know it exists."

"Who did you ask to see?" Reynolds requested.

"The local police captain, the town magistrate and someone from the bank who has acted as an interpreter for your friend. If I can't make them release Mister Woods then I shall have him placed in my custody. Until the arrival of civil aviation people, I have authority in accidents involving aircraft. That is the law."

"What about the plane? When do you think we could fly it out?"

"If you can repair it today, then it will leave today. My authority is very wide. I could order that your plane be flown to Pôrto Velho where it can receive a better inspection. Then I will write a report stating that your plane is airworthy and you can continue to Bolivia."

"I'm glad we've got someone like you on our side," said Reynolds. "Or we'd really be up shit creek without a paddle. We'd never get Mike out of this hellhole. Sorry."

"Don't apologize, my friend," said Goulart. "For I have no love for this place either. There must be parts of your country you don't like. This, I hate. It's too primitive for me. Even many of my country's cities aren't modern enough for my taste."

"Well at least they haven't been bombed into rubble or divided by conquering armies. Don't denigrate everything you have, there's a lot of things you have that many European nations would gladly trade you for."

With an arrival nearly as spectacular as that of Woods or Goulart, one of the town's few vehicles, an ancient Model A Ford, rattled to a halt next to the Stinson. Crowded into its rear seat were all the people Goulart had demanded to see. They were barely able to exchange greetings before an argument broke out. It went on for several minutes and since it was in Portuguese, none of Goulart's friends could understand what was being argued.

"Excuse me, but I could be of help to you?" said one of the men who had been in the car. "I translated for the man who landed earlier, the South African."

"No thank you," Reynolds answered, eyeing him suspiciously. "We'll wait for the Colonel to tell us what they're discussing. But since you were with Mike Woods, you can tell us where he is and how he's doing?"

"He is fine but he is being most demanding. He will be in severe trouble if he persists. He is in the police station, which is around the corner."

"Mister Reynolds, Jack, could I talk with you please?" Goulart asked, the argument suddenly over. "I'm afraid I cannot be of as much help as I wanted . . ."

"Why? What happened, what went wrong? I thought you said you had the authority?"

". . . I do but there's a saying that Jesse is fond of, if he were here he would use it. 'Those who have the guns make the rules' and the magistrate and the captain are the ones who have them. They will release your friend into my custody and they'll allow your

242

mechanic to work on the plane and that's it. They will not turn the P-40 over to my custody and they will not let it be flown out. The police captain threatened to place me in jail if I pressed this matter any further."

"Bastards, I suppose they're going to be proper little tin soldiers and go all the way to Rio de Janeiro for their orders," said Reynolds.

"No, if they were tin soldiers we would have no trouble. They would turn the plane over to me without question. These people are corrupt. They will not ask Rio for orders, they'll wait for you to offer them money."

"Well they're not going to get away with this," said Green, who had been listening in on the conversation. "Hey you, schmuck, you say you wanna translate? Well come with me, you're going to translate."

Before Reynolds could fully understand what he was doing, Green had dragged the self-appointed translator down to the magistrate and police captain. It was too late to stop him. As Green made his demands, they were changed automatically into Portuguese.

"Our friend had to make an emergency landing or else he would've crashed in the jungle. If there is any damage we will pay for it, just give us the bill. Colonel Goulart is the highest-ranking Brazilian Air Force officer present. According to your own law, he would be the officer in charge at any accident or incident involving an aircraft, pending the arrival of civil aviation officials. Interference with the performance of his duties will result in fines and penalties against you. Any unreasonable delay that you may cause will definitely result in a lawsuit filed by us against you. Now, will you continue to interfere, or will you allow Colonel Goulart to perform his duties?"

Reynolds and Goulart arrived just in time to step in between Green and the locals, who were gearing up to launch a furious diatribe of their own. While Goulart tried to soften the damage he did, Reynolds pulled Green aside and explained to him what he had done.

"You're about as useful as lead sinkers to a drowning man!" he shouted. "God damn it, I should've brought the Aussie with me. The only thing he'd start would be a fist fight. I hope you realize you may just have sunk us."

"I'm sorry, Jack. I mean, Colonel," said Green. "But I thought if I explained it to them legally, they'd see the trouble they would get in and release the plane."

"Well this is the Amazon jungle, I should've remembered what my father once said. 'You step into this place and you step back a thousand years.' The law isn't of much good here, not even in dealing with the authorities. The only things that work are money and power."

"Jack, everything is okay, for now," Goulart advised, turning briefly to his friends. "What a wonderful mess this is becoming. They wanted to throw your friend in jail but will now settle for a larger bribe. If you want to prevent this from becoming worse, keep this smartass Jew quiet. I will go with the captain to free your friend. You go and examine the plane. Take him with you, he cannot cause much trouble there."

Goulart wheeled about smartly and marched over to the officials' Model A. He climbed inside and the car sped off, leaving Reynolds and the others in the street.

"Racist son-of-a-bitch," Green swore. "When we're through I'll kick the shit out of him."

"Racist is he? You're forgetting, Daniel that the man who introduced him to us is negro," said Reynolds. "Don't be so quick to call someone like that a racist. C'mon, let's go over and see how bad the P-40 is."

With their mechanic in tow, Reynolds and Green maneuvered through the crowd and walked down the street to the Kittyhawk. It had not been moved since landing; it was still sitting almost sideways on the street, its nose pointing at the town's one bank. Underneath the nose was a pool of oil; it had leaked out from the radiator shutters and the seam lines of the cowling panels. The canopy was closed, the cockpit appeared untouched, and the access panels to the baggage compartment and wing gun bays hadn't been tampered with or opened. The mechanic took a few screwdrivers out of his tool box and, with Reynolds lending a hand, removed the lower cowling panels.

"Check the cockpit, Danny," Reynolds ordered. "Make yourself useful. Make sure nothing's been damaged or taken. If anything has, then we'll have a legitimate beef."

As the panels were opened, more oil spilled onto the ground; Reynolds nearly being drenched in the process. The engine's drum-shaped coolant radiators and oil temperature regulator were now exposed. They were covered with oil, as were all the lines and hoses associated with them. Once they had been cleaned off, it was easy for the mechanic to pinpoint where the leak had occurred.

"Here, one of the clamps on the temperature regulator feed line failed," he said, showing Reynolds a thin metal band. "I can fix this with what I have in the box. Thank God it was nothing catastrophic."

"Well we still have something catastrophic to take care of," said Reynolds. "With this kind of loss, how much oil do you think is left in the tank?"

"Not much, we'll be lucky if there's a gallon or two still left in the system. I'd better check the engine cylinders and make sure no damage has been done."

"Jack, the cockpit's okay," Green reported. "I don't think anybody actually did get inside. Nothing's been touched or stolen. I think Mike must've closed the canopy before they took him away."

"I did. I didn't want any of these buggers climbing through it, stripping off souvenirs," said Woods, walking around the wing of his plane, with Goulart at his side. "I see you really know how to wheel in the big guns when you want something done. Is the Colonel here another of your friends?"

"No, he's Jesse Clinton's friend," Reynolds answered. "I'm not the only one to have South American contacts you know. Half the group landed with me at Colonel Goulart's base in Pôrta Velho, the rest have gone on to Bolivia. They should be landing there by now."

"Have you discovered what went wrong with his plane?" Goulart asked.

"A clamp on one of the oil lines snapped. I always find it hard to believe that a twenty-nine cent part can cause a forty or fifty thousand dollar plane to crash."

"You can say it's the nature of the beast," said Woods. "You and your mechanic are looking like a regular pair of grease monkeys. Is there anything we can do to help you?"

"Get some rags and help clean off these cowling panels," Reynolds suggested. "And if you can find it, some varsol or even rubbing alcohol to clean the engine and the coolant radiators. I think all this oil may have contaminated them."

"I think I know where to obtain your varsol," said Goulart. "Like all river towns, Calama has a large waterfront. It should have its own repair shops. They will have everything. Is there anything else you need?"

"Yes, if we're to eventually fly this plane out of here, we'll need oil to replace what we lost. I suppose they'll have some at your repair shops but I wonder if it will be the right kind? Hank, what do you say?"

"I wouldn't know much about them marine oils," replied the mechanic, looking up from his work. "You'd have to find one that has the same viscosity as this stuff and won't break down under high temperatures. And whatever you get, make sure it isn't diesel oil. We'll turn this plane into a God damned fireball if it is."

Suitably informed, Goulart marched off to the waterfront while Woods, with some Brazilian centavos in hand, walked to a general supplies store. After some problems with translating his needs, he purchased a few yards of plain cotton fabric. He returned to his aircraft with the material, which was cut into several sections. They were given to Woods and Green, who started to wipe clean the detached cowling panels.

"How did they treat you when we left?" Reynolds asked, as he continued to work on cleaning the engine.

"For a criminal, not too bad," said Woods. "They didn't take my fingerprints, for instance. What they kept pestering me about was whether or not I had money or how much the group had. It made me think that, for the right price, these people might be willing to forget the whole incident."

"That's what Colonel Goulart told me. For the right bribe, they'd let us fly out in a minute."

"Is that what you're planning to do? Bribe these all too willing people to overlook my arrival?"

"No fucking way. They're not going to get a dime out of me, or Claus. As soon as we know this ship can fly, we're going to figure a way of getting it out of here. And since we're almost there, you think you can fly off this same road? At night?"

"During the day would be no trouble," said Woods. "But at night? Why at night? I'd have problems seeing those trees at the end in order to clear them."

"Night would be the best time to get you out. They wouldn't be expecting it and there would be fewer people around. We'd still have to create a diversion to cover the sound of the engine starting and warming up. I think the Colonel might help us with that, provided he can contact his base."

They had to wait until Goulart returned from his expedition to the waterfront. He came back with a gallon can of rubbing alcohol and a small tin of what he said was the best quality oil he could find.

"Well it looks about the same," the mechanic observed, rubbing some of the oil between his fingers. "And it has the same viscosity. It even smells the same. Yeah, I guess this stuff will do. But I wouldn't want to fly for too long on it. We don't know how long this will hold up under the high temperatures and pressures of an aircraft engine. If it breaks down it'll be as thin as water, and about as effective. I'd say a flight lasting longer than an hour would be pushing it."

"In a half-hour at even minimum cruise speed, Mike would reach Pôrto Velho," said Reynolds. "That's all the time he'd need and he wouldn't have to push the plane either."

"Then you believe this plane will be flying soon?" Goulart asked. "Will you pay the bribe these bastards demand?"

"Not a fucking dime. This plane'll fly if you can help us devise some kind of diversion for tonight. Is there any way you can get in touch with your base? I know the radio in the Stinson doesn't have the range, even if you were to take off and climb to its top altitude."

"At the police station, there is a shortwave radio, for government use only. I can reach the base with that and I can have complete privacy if what I am transmitting is a military secret. What would you like me to say?"

"That you want a mass formation of T-6s to fly over Calama tonight. It'll hide the sound of Woods starting up his engine. What do you think would be a good time?"

Goulart and Reynolds eventually decided on ten o'clock. It was late enough for most of the town to be turning in but not so late that the formation would have everyone waking up when it flew past. While Goulart went to the police station and demanded use of its radio, Reynolds sent Green and his mechanic to the waterfront. They returned carrying nearly a dozen gallons of the oil Goulart had found and he came back with a quiet smile on his face.

"It is all arranged," he told Reynolds and the others. "The Texans will be here and not only that, on their second pass they will drop flares so Mister Woods can see his runway. All we have to do is wait for nightfall."

Until then there was much for them to do. They had to finish cleaning the P-40's engine and engine compartment of oil, clean and reassemble everything which had been contaminated by it and persuade the local officials to move the fighter. They were eventually allowed to push it to the far end of the town, where it would be safe, more secluded and would allow for a longer take off run.

The last cowling panel was screwed into place, and the reservoir filled with oil, as the sun sank behind the jungle canopy. With the approach of night, most activity in the town came to an end. Except for its few saloons, one of which was where Reynolds and the others went for a meal and to discuss the terms of the bribe.

"Jack, what you propose is still a little too modest," Goulart said cordially, translating the police captain's response to the latest proposal. "He says it doesn't take into account the expense of clearing the street tomorrow. The public's safety must be maintained. The captain says now that your friends have retired for the evening, you can afford to be more generous without being embarrassed."

"Tell him I understand and I will try to do better," Reynolds replied then, leaning over the table a little so he could whisper to Goulart. "Are you sure this clown doesn't know any English?"

"Apparently not a word, neither he or the town magistrate. They both speak some Spanish, even French but no English. Except of course for the word, money."

"Well there's one good way to test his vocabulary. Captain? You fucking little shit, you're the load your mother should've ate." Reynolds kept his voice calm and a smile on his face. To which the captain responded by smiling and nodding in agreement. "I guess you're right, Pedro. Either that or he's the greatest actor since John Barrymore."

"I told you he does not know English. My trouble now is I must translate what you said to him. Only I dare not tell him the truth. What could I . . ."

"Make up something flowery, about how he drives a hard bargain. We don't have to keep this up too much longer. Just another five minutes or so."

"C'mon, the coast is clear," said Green, glancing up and down the darkened street. "Hank and I will take care of the wheel chocks and the pre-flight. You just take care of the cockpit check and make sure you do the night flying tests."

They sprinted across the street from their hiding place, Woods climbing up the P-40's left wing while Green and the mechanic did all the ground checks. The wooden blocks were removed from the main wheels, the control surfaces, landing gear and propeller all received exams and all tank caps were tested to make sure they were secure. Once in the cockpit, Woods strapped and locked himself into his seat before he hit the ignition switch.

That activated the plane's electrical system, allowing Woods to turn on the tiny cockpit spotlights and fluorescent lamp. Now he could do all the other checks, which included brief tests of the fuel gauge lights, running lights, landing lights and compass light. Green and the mechanic covered the landing lights with their hands when they were flicked on; otherwise their beams would've penetrated far into the town.

"Controls are free. Flaps and radiator shutters are neutral," said Woods, barely speaking above a whisper. "Have you people swung the propeller a few times?"

"Done," Green answered. "Hank's going down the road to make sure there aren't any obstacles. He'll signal with a flashlight if there are any. What time is it?"

"I have two minutes to ten. I hope these Brazilians are as punctual as the Royal Air Force."

"Do not worry, Jack, my pilots will be on time," Goulart assured. "And stop looking at your watch. I think the captain has noticed it. I told my pilots they were to arrive on 'American time.' You should know what that means."

"Yes, on this continent everyone starts arriving fifteen minutes after they're supposed to," said Reynolds. "But if you want them to come on time, you tell them they're on American time and they will."

"Listen. Do you hear? That rumble, I would know the sound of a Pratt and Whitney radial anywhere."

—

"Circuit breakers are on, all switches are on. Clear

the propeller," Woods warned, raising his voice as a familiar, flat din grew louder, loud enough to cover the sound of the P-40 starting its engine. "I've primed the motor and I'm energizing the starter coil."

The P-40 emitted a soft whine. As the first formation of twinkling lights and orange-red exhaust flames sailed through the night sky, its propeller began to tick over and brief jets of flame shot out the Allison's stacks. By the time the second formation of T-6s appeared, the Allison had come to life and the prop was a blurred disc. Woods quickly reset the throttle and mixture control to allow the engine to idle while he rushed his checks.

"I told the captain not to be alarmed," Goulart informed Reynolds. "I told him he's hearing my pilots on a night training mission. I ordered them to fly over his town so I would know they were up. How do you think it's going?"

"Mike should have his engine started," said Reynolds, rubbing his palms together to hide the fact they were sweating. "And that first flight of yours should be coming around to drop its flares. Damn it, I hate sitting here and waiting. I ought to be outside helping Mike."

"Hank's giving us the all-clear," said Green, pointing at a faint beam of light at the opposite end of the town. "There are no obstacles on the road."

"Fine, just let me do my magneto tests and I'll be away," Woods answered, glancing at the dark figure crouching beside the cockpit. He turned back to his instrument panel, where he checked his tachometer to make sure his engine was idling at twenty-three hundred r.p.m.

Woods tested the magnetos by flipping the ignition switch from 'Left' to 'Right' and watching the tachometer needle for the expected drops in r.p.m. As he did so the lead flight of Brazilian T-6s came in for their second pass. They roared in at a lower altitude than before and each of the three trainers released a single flare from their underwing racks. They all ignited the moment their parachutes deployed, becoming a trio of miniature, sputtering suns drifting toward the ground.

"Well if they don't bring out a crowd, I don't know what will," said Green. "C'mon are you ready to go?"

"Just a sec, just a sec!" Woods shouted. "I have to set my trim and all my other controls!"

"We'd better follow him, Jack," said Goulart, nodding toward the police captain. "He wants to know where the light is coming from and I think he believes we're up to something."

With a frenzied gesture from Woods, Green slid off the P-40's wing and ran for cover. The roar of its engine grew and, slowly at first, the fighter rolled forward. Soon the Allison's smooth thunder was cutting through the noisy rattle of the Texans; it echoed down the street as the aircraft entered the town.

Out on the saloon porch, where most of its patrons had gathered, the thunder was deafening. Reynolds and Goulart arrived at the same time the police captain did. He turned and shouted at them but his oaths were drowned out. He then drew his pistol and started to charge through the crowd. Reynolds was close enough to stick his foot into his path. It jammed between the police captain's legs like a monkey wrench and threw him out of balance. He sailed off the saloon porch instead of stepping from it.

Halfway into the town Woods could feel his tail lifting up. It bounced a few times before raising off the ground permanently, giving him a dramatically improved forward view. He saw the small crowds starting to form along the sides of the road, he even caught sight of the police captain's brief attempt at flight.

As he crashed, his gun bounced out of his hand and slid to a stop several feet away. The captain had barely raised his head when he had to bury it in the ground again. The P-40, tail high and riding on its main wheels, swept by him, filling his ears with thunder and covering him with a shower of dirt. The next time the captain looked up was to see his sudden windfall successfully complete its escape.

At the town's opposite end Woods felt lift returning to his wings. After another hundred yards he definitely knew his fighter wanted to fly but he held it on the ground for a few seconds more. Finally, at a hundred and forty miles an hour, Woods yanked back his control stick and the Kittyhawk eagerly leaped into the air. In the harsh, flickering light of the flares, he could see the trees lining either side of the road and their overhanging branches.

With some minimal maneuvering and wing dipping, Woods was able to avoid the larger ones. Once above the jungle canopy he breathed easier and he also raised his landing gear and flaps. At a thousand feet he temporarily rendezvoused with the Brazilian T-6s; they gave him the proper compass heading to reach Velho and the right radio frequency to contact the tower. Then he pushed the throttle forward and raised his nose slightly. The P-40 accelerated away from the trainers and climbed a little higher to the stars.

"Marilyn? Wake up," Van Hoff said softly, staying by the door of her hotel room. "Please wake up. You told me you wanted to hear any news about your father."

She turned and murmured something to herself before waking up, rising rapidly from a deep sleep.

"What? Claus, did yo say something about my father?" she asked, sitting up in bed.

"Mike Woods arrived at the air base about forty-five minutes ago. Your father managed to free him from jail. We refueled Mike's aircraft, changed its oil and sent him off to Bolivia with Douglas Ward as escort. Mike said that your father was safe and that he and the others will join us early tomorrow, in a few hours in fact."

"I'm so glad to hear that, I was worried when we didn't hear anything from him. I thought he might've been arrested like your friend."

"That is a fear we all shared. But you shouldn't worry unduly about it. This country isn't like America or Europe. Communication isn't nearly as good and simply because we didn't hear from him doesn't mean the worst has happened."

"I see, what will you do now, Claus?"

"Go back to my room, I need those few hours before your father arrives for a little extra sleep."

"You don't have to go, not if you don't want to," Marilyn replied, sliding out of her bed and walking toward the door. She wore a pair of men's pajamas and, from the way her body moved under them, nothing else. She wrapped her arms around Van Hoff's neck and embraced him tightly. After a moment's hesitation, he reciprocated. "You don't know how long I wanted to hold you like this but I couldn't. Now I can, this may be the only time we can have together. Does anyone know you're here?"

"No one, the rest of our people are asleep."

Marilyn reached behind Van Hoff and locked the door. She then slid her hand down the top half of her pajamas, undoing all the buttons. When she embraced Van Hoff again, he could feel her bare breasts pressing firmly against him.

"Marilyn, are you sure you want this?" he asked. He tried fighting his emotions but, almost without realizing it, he moved his hands under her pajama top and caressed her soft back. "Am I the man you want?"

"I've never been more sure. I know what you're like and I know you need someone, someone like me. Please don't leave me, because I do need you."

"I won't, at least for a little while," Van Hoff replied, he tugged at her pajama top and, when Marilyn lowered her arms, it glided off her back. He quickly stripped off his shirt and other clothes. Marilyn quietly stepped out of the rest of her pajamas and embraced again the man she wanted and loved. Then he gathered her up in his arms and returned her to her bed, to share it with her until dawn arrived, a few hours later.

In spite of protests by the police captain and town

magistrate, and threats of official action, Goulart and his friends left Calama early in the morning. At Pôrto Velho they found the visiting P-40s and C-46 getting ready for flight. All could have left the moment the Stinson touched down but Goulart insisted that everyone join him for breakfast in the officer's mess.

"Please, friends, I have not had enough time with you," he said. "Especially you, Jesse. It is the least I can do for you after allowing my mechanics to pick through your stocks of spare parts on your transport. Accept it as thanks from the Brazilian Air Force."

"Did they take much?" Reynolds asked, falling back to talk with Van Hoff while Goulart talked with Clinton.

"Not a great deal," said Van Hoff. "Certainly nothing major. A lot of small items, the kind no one thinks of until they fail. In sum they're a small price to pay for having one of our fighters safely back."

"Yeah, you don't know how small it was in comparison to what some people would've charged. I'll tell you later."

Breakfast took longer than anticipated, it was not until late in the morning when, with much regret, Goulart allowed his friends, both old and new, to depart.

The tiny group of four P-40s and one Commando didn't take long to form up. They did it as they climbed away from the airfield and swung over Pôrto Velho. After joining, they continued to climb, so they could clear the Sierra dos Parecis mountains on the border between Bolivia and Brazil.

Some fifty miles inside Bolivia they found San Joaquín and landed. At the customs office, where the group was getting their passports stamped, Reynolds was handed messages from both Woods and Brandon. The rest of the formation was safe and had flown on to his friend's ranch farther to the south. As soon as their planes had passed inspection and were refueled, the stragglers took off to join them. Their journey was complete and at last their mission could begin.

Chapter Ten:
REUNION.
PREPARATIONS BEGIN.

It was a little over two hundred miles from San Joaquín to the group's forward base. It had no radio or navigation aids so there couldn't be any direct communication with the base, though for Reynolds it would be easy to lead the others to it; the terrain was becoming familiar to him and there was the San Miguel River, along whose banks the airstrip was located. Following departure from San Joaquín, it took an hour for the formation to fly down the river to a point where a ranch appeared on its western bank, along with a grass field runway and a collection of very familiar aircraft.

Reynolds took the fighters down to buzz the airstrip and let everyone know they had arrived. Then they landed and taxied over to where the other P-40s were parked. The C-46 was the last to come in and, instead of joining the other two Commandoes, it swung around on the runway and killed its engines.

"Doug and I spent the night in San Joaquín," said Woods, answering Van Hoff's question. "Eric was there waiting for us and brought us here in the morning. We only arrived about three hours before you."

"Jack, my old friend, why is it that you're the last to show up?" The elderly man who greeted Reynolds wrapped his arms around him as he did so. He had pushed through all of Reynolds's other friends so he could be the first to welcome him when he climbed out of his fighter. He was, after all, Reynolds's oldest friend and the owner of the ranch, Augustin Romero.

"C'mon, Augustin, you're breaking my arms," said Reynolds. "And you're reminding me of the damn Russians. That's the way they like to greet people."

"Ah, Jack, you must expect this. It's been seven years since I last saw you. How you have changed and yet not changed. The war must've given you many adventures, I would love to hear them all."

"Soon, sometime soon. Have you heard from Bob in the last few days?"

"I hear from your brother almost every day. He flies past here on those reconnaissance missions of his. If he's up on one, he will be due soon."

"Why did you have our plane park out on the runway?" Marilyn asked, arriving at the flight line with the transport's crew. "It was so far for us to walk."

"We'll be needing it soon, angel," said Reynolds. "I want it unloaded and ready to fly within the hour. Our little escapade in Brazil has put us behind schedule but there are others who're on schedule and we have to meet with them."

"And who is this rare flower you brought along?" Romero inquired, being very suave. "She is so young and pretty. Jack, you have excellent taste in women."

"I should hope so, this one I'm responsible for. This is Marilyn, my daughter. Remember?"

Romero's eyes brightened at the revelation; he reached for Marilyn's hand and held it up to kiss it.

"You are indeed a rare flower," he said, completing the gesture. "I'm sorry for my earlier remarks. I should have recognized you but, then, the last time I saw you, my dear, you were six years old."

"Hey, Colonel, listen," said Acerrio. "There's a plane coming up the river. And it ain't no Piper Cub."

The drone they all faintly heard was smooth and deep, definitely not the puttering of a tiny, four-cylinder engine. As the drone grew it became obvious that no one engine could produce such a powerful, synchronized sound. The aircraft producing it appeared over the San Miguel River, like Acerrio had warned, and turned sharply toward the ranch. Its body glittered in the bright, mid-day sun, even its propellers shimmered. While it hung in its turn for a few moments, the aircraft's pod-shaped fuselage and twin tail booms were clearly seen. It was a P-38 Lightning and there was only one Lightning operating in all of South America, though everyone had to wait until the reconfighter was almost overhead before they could see Reynolds Air Services stenciled on its tail booms.

They could also see its pilot waving at them. Bob Reynolds stood his fighter on its tail and let it climb until he was high above the ranch. When it seemed ready to stall, he executed a slow hammerhead turn, slow in comparison to what a single-engined fighter could do, and came screaming back at the airfield. He dipped his wings as he shot by the line of P-40s and climbed away like an arrow; by the time he levelled off, Bob Reynolds had gained nearly a mile in altitude.

"At the P-38's normal cruise speed, my brother will be in La Paz in about an hour," said Reynolds. "And we're going to have to be there as well. Let's get that C-46 unloaded. I want its cargo deck to be cleared as quickly as possible and the plane ready to go."

"Jeez, Colonel, that could take hours," Acerrio complained. "You have those transports loaded to their roofs."

"Not that one. In return for helping us free Mike, we let Colonel Goulart's ground crews have some of the spares it held. She's nearly a thousand pounds lighter and should be a little easier to unload."

The Commando's cargo doors were swung open and one of Romero's ranch trucks was backed up to them. A large team led by the plane's flight crew quickly filled its load bed with all sizes and types of P-40 spare parts. While it pulled away another truck was brought in and the operation repeated. The fourth time around the truck was loaded with a pair of crated, Allison engines. The last and heaviest items to be removed from the transport. Now several tons lighter, the aircraft was ready to leave and Reynolds selected those who would go with him.

"But, Jack, wouldn't you like to see all the equipment and supplies I brought here for your movie?" asked Romero. "I have all of it in one of my barns. All but cameras, it will give truth to the lie you tell."

"We'll have to see it later, when we return. I'm sure you have more stuff than Hollywood would've thought to bring. Let's see, in addition to Green I'll take you, Claus and . . . Okay, Tony, you can come along this time."

Together with the flight crew, Reynolds also took

along the largest mechanics he had. They piled inside the awaiting transport, took all available seats in it and started the engines. The C-46, minus its heavy payload, leaped off the ground after a shorter than usual take off run. It climbed steeply, almost like a fighter, heading west.

At its highest cruise speed, the Commando took an hour and twenty minutes to reach La Paz. It had to climb throughout most of its flight, almost constantly to avoid slamming into one of the peaks of the Andes Mountains. Located in a river valley, La Paz was nonetheless some twelve thousand feet up in the Andes; making it the world's highest capital city. The C-46 landed at its airport and taxied over to the Reynolds Air Services reconnaissance P-38. The big fighter was relatively easy to spot, of all the aircraft at the field, it was the sleekest and most modern.

Bob Reynolds was standing on the Lockheed's wing, waving at them until the transport rolled to a stop beside him. He ran around to its main hatch and helped those on board deploy its ladder. The first one off the plane was his brother. They acted as if they had not seen each other for years.

"How have things gone here?" Reynolds asked, slapping his younger brother on the back.

"Oh great," he said. "Stuck here in a foreign country. With no mechanic, almost no spare parts, I don't really know the language, photo supplies are hard as hell to find. Apart from all that, things are just great."

"Well it's no easier when you have all the parts and supplies you want but a dozen aircraft to look after. Tell me, how many photo runs did you make?"

"Five, enough to cover all of Santa Cruz province.

A commercial photography store developed the batches of film. If it wasn't for Major Green's friends, they'd still be in the can. In fact, some of his friends are off getting the most recent run developed. The rest are with me, they've been waiting for you."

"Rest who?" asked Acerrio. "What kind of friends does Danny here have in this God-forsaken country?"

"Jewish agents," Green answered. "Though I think they'd prefer to be called Israelis."

"Yes, Mister Green, we would," said a man walking out from under the wing of the Commando. "Though it'll be many months before our state is actually founded . . ."

There were several other men with the first one, they all emerged from under the transport's wing and introduced themselves to Reynolds and his people.

". . . I'm from our Montevideo group, Mister Green, I'm one of Samuel Ephron's friends. We've been in Bolivia for about two weeks now. We were wondering when you'd arrive."

"Danny, are these the friends you told us about?" Reynolds asked, motioning to the man whose hand he was shaking.

"Yes, Mister Reynolds, we are," said the Israeli leader. "And we have the munitions you need. We have them in a warehouse near the airport and we'll give them to you before you leave, Jack. May I call you Jack? After all, I've grown to know your brother quite well."

"Of course you can, provided you tell me your name."

"It's Goldsmith, David Goldsmith and now if you'll come with me? I have transport and I've arranged a presentation for you. If you'll follow me?"

Transport turned out to be a weary-looking Daimler-Benz limousine. It was large, though with Reynolds, his brother and part of his group; and Goldsmith and some of his men, its interior became rather cramped.

"Christ, this reminds me of the time we were in that commie staff car," Acerrio complained, wedged in between Reynolds and Van Hoff. "Only I don't remember being this short of breath. I think my claustrophobia's getting worse."

"It isn't that, Tony," said Bob Reynolds. "You have to realize that we're more than two miles above sea level. Breathing at this altitude is rather hard for those who aren't used to it. For machines as well as man. My P-38 clicks on its superchargers almost as soon as it lifts off. And she eats up about four thousand feet of runway before she does so. You'd think you were flying a B-29."

Not long after leaving the airport, the limousine was cruising through the narrow, old world-style streets of La Paz. The car's size made maneuvering around city traffic and finding the right parking space real problems. In fact it had to park a block away from its destination; a building which had 'fotografia' somewhere in its name.

Both Goldsmith and Bob Reynolds appeared to be well known by company personnel and were met by its president, whom Reynolds introduced to his brother and friends. It was the president who took them to one of the building's photo labs and left them inside it, alone.

"Your latest run has just been developed," Goldsmith announced, turning to Bob Reynolds. "Here, these are contact prints of what you took."

Goldsmith laid out on a long table several sheets of photographic paper. Each had several images on it and some were still wet from their chemical baths. While most gathered around the table to view them, Goldsmith and one of his men went over to a locker and started dialing combinations into its padlocks.

"In reality we spotted the base the Nazis had built on my third run," said Bob Reynolds. "But we wanted to make sure we didn't overlook anything. So I completed the sweep of the province and then went back to re-photograph the base. As you can see, even in these contacts, it was rather easy to find. A paved runway and a flight line that large are difficult to hide."

"My God, how many planes are in this line?" asked Van Hoff, leaning over one of the prints, his nose almost touching it. "And those large ones, are they bombers?"

"Yes, I think they're Ju-88s. I don't know, I'm more familiar with Zekes, Tonies and Betties, Japanese aircraft, than German aircraft. If nothing's changed from my first pass there should be six bombers and at least forty fighters. We'll have to make blow-ups of these to make out any details and identify the planes."

"There aren't many facilities at this base," said the older Reynolds. He had found a magnifying glass and he didn't have to peer as closely as Van Hoff did. "Except for this, it looks like a fuel dump. And this looks like a bomb dump. Where exactly is the base located, Bob?"

"In the Sierra de San Jose Mountains," his brother

answered. "About twenty or thirty miles from a town call El Cerro. The range is a low one, only around two thousand feet. It won't give you any trouble climbing over it, even in P-40s."

"Ha, ha, very funny. Just because you have the best airplane in the country doesn't mean you have to rub it in."

"Here, you can see more on these," said Goldsmith, handing to Reynolds several envelopes filled with photographs. "They're enlargements from the first run made by your brother. The packs are all labeled. Aircraft, defenses, facilities, buildings. So you can choose what you wish."

Reynolds handed the envelopes marked defenses, facilities and buildings to Van Hoff, Acerrio and Green; he chose to keep the one marked aircraft for himself.

As the contact prints were removed, Reynolds opened the envelope and laid its contents out on the table. The enlargements went all the way down to single aircraft, they were fuzzy, a little unclear but the planes could be identified. After a minute Reynolds was able to name most of them.

"These bombers, they aren't Ju-88s," he said, holding up a photograph of the large, twin-engined machines. "They look a lot like them but they're not. You'd have to be a veteran of the European theater to know it, though. These bombers are Ju-188s. An advanced version of the 'Eighty-eight with more powerful engines, redesigned wings, tail surfaces and a streamlined forward fuselage. In level flight these planes could hit four hundred miles an hour. Apart from the Arado-234, it was the fastest bomber the

Luftwaffe ever had. Many of these fighters are Focke-Wulfs. I'd say sixteen are long-nose Doras and a dozen are 'Sturm Bird' ground-attack models. There are a dozen Messerschmitts, either '109-Ks or late-model Gs but there are two airplanes I can't identify. These, with the twin-fin tail groups."

Reynolds picked up one of the other enlargements and showed it to Van Hoff, who came around the table to get a better look at the mystery planes. To him, they did not remain a mystery for long.

"God, my God, they're Salamanders," he said. "Heinkel 162s. They're jets, see the engine pods behind the cockpits? I know this aircraft well, it was developed by Heinkel at the Vienna-Schwechat airport. It never achieved operational status, the first production fighters were just reaching Luftwaffe units when the Reich collapsed. About one hundred and twenty production aircraft and prototypes were built, I thought most had been destroyed or taken as war prizes. God, there must be some truly terrible security procedures to allow these aircraft to fall back into the hands of the Nazis."

"What's its performance like, Count?" asked Acerrio, peering over Reynolds's shoulder at the photo.

"The Heinkel 162 has a maximum speed of four hundred and ninety miles an hour at sea level and five hundred and twenty miles an hour at twenty thousand feet. Its climb rate is over four thousand feet per minute and its range is four hundred miles. It carries either two twenty millimeter or thirty millimeter cannons but no external stores. The Salamander is a rather simple aeroplane, for a jet and it was originally known as the 'Volksjäger.' The people's fighter."

"Oh this is just great. Not only do these guys have bombers that can fly faster than us, they also have jets. We'd better make sure we catch 'em on the ground and we'd better have something to make sure they stay there."

"Not to worry, Mister Acerrio, we have something for you to ensure that," said Goldsmith. "We should be leaving, Jack. If you have any questions concerning the photographs, I'm sure your brother can answer them."

"Okay, would you like the pictures back?"

"No, they are yours. Take them to the ranch for your whole squadron to see. They would be safer out there than here, in spite of our security."

"Why, are the employees trying to steal them?"

"No, the Nazis might. They know we are here, in La Paz. We've seen their agents and they know of your brother. But then it is hard to hide the plane he's flying. It's the most modern one at the airfield."

"Do you think they know about us?" Reynolds asked.

"They most likely do, though your cover story should keep them from investigating you for a time. What you thought of was very ingenious and we have some equipment to give you, in addition to the munitions. That is where we are going next. So please, hurry."

All the photographs were placed back in their envelopes and given to Reynolds. He and his brother went over the contact prints from the latest run and marked what they wanted to see enlarged. Some of Goldsmith's men stayed in the lab to do the work, the rest left with Reynolds and his group.

The limousine had been brought to the building's entrance and, the moment its passengers had climbed inside, drove off, threading its way down more narrow roads and weaving clumsily through traffic. It traveled across La Paz to an area adjoining the rail yard, stopping at a warehouse that appeared to be unused, almost derelict. There was only one other vehicle parked by it, a truck with a sullen group of local laborers milling around an otherwise empty load bay.

"Wow, this is a regular hub of activity," said Acerrio, stepping out of the car. "It reminds me of Jersey City on a Sunday, dead and dirty."

"You wouldn't want a lot of people working around what we have in here," said Goldsmith. Then, turning to the labor foreman, "I'm sorry to be late but not to worry, you'll be working soon, I promise."

Goldsmith's men opened one of the warehouse's main loading doors and stood guard while the others went inside. Goldsmith led Reynolds and his group to a corner stacked with a few neat rows of wooden crates, almost the only stock stored in the building. Half of them were about four feet high and the rest were a little over a foot and a half high.

"These are five hundred pound bombs," Goldsmith announced, patting one of the taller crates. "Twenty-four in all. They arrived here two days ago by train from Mexico. They were originally purchased for the future Israeli Air Force but it was decided they would serve a higher purpose here than in the Middle East. We hope you will use them well, Jack and we hope you'll take them off our hands now. We've been sweating over these eggs ever since they came, afraid the Nazis or the Bolivians will discover them. I know the truck outside can carry the weight, can your plane?"

"Let's see, twelve thousand pounds of ordnance," said Reynolds, making the calculations. "That's well within the load limits of the C-46. However, we're also taking off from a twelve thousand foot altitude. That is a combination most transports can't handle. Except for a C-46. We'll be able to do it, our fuel load will be reduced and the airport's main runway is long enough. Not unless you have another two tons of cargo for us to carry out?"

"Just these." Goldsmith pointed to a pair of steel boxes hiding beside a pillar. He walked over to them and pulled one out so everyone could see it clearly. Unlocking its latches, he raised the lid; revealing a movie camera with a set of lenses. "Thirty-five millimeter motion picture camera, just like the kind Hollywood uses. One of our agents bought them from a movie company in Brazil. We wanted to get you a sound recording system but they're too expensive. These don't weigh more than a hundred pounds each. Well, do you think you can take them?"

"Sure, just get it all to the plane."

The tour over, Goldsmith called in the labor crew. They brought along a couple of dollies and, with plenty of muscle power, started moving the taller, far heavier crates. It took four men to move one of the crates and two to push the dolly out to the truck. The smaller crates proved much easier to move, as were the cameras. The laborers used the better part of two hours to load the bombs, mostly because of their frequent breaks. They were well-paid, by Bolivian standards, for both their work and complaining, and were told not to speak to anyone about what they did or what they saw. With the limousine in the lead, the truck pulled away from the warehouse. Which was now even more empty and derelict than before.

"The truck will break away from us soon and go to the airport by a different route," Goldsmith informed, when he noticed Reynolds and Van Hoff looking at it. "It has to, the truck is too heavy for some of the roads we're using. We have a route all mapped for it. She'll arrive at the airport a few minutes after us."

"Those workers you hired, are you confident you can trust them not to talk about what they saw or did?" asked Van Hoff, "I worry more about them than the truck."

"I'm sure we can't trust them, Nazi agents could buy them for a few hundred pesos. Which is why I let them see those cameras of ours. Hopefully it will make the workers think they were moving film equipment. Beyond killing them, I don't know what else we could've done."

"No, Dave, you did the right thing," said Reynolds. "The last problem we need is to be linked with a pile of bodies. If anything, it should reinforce our cover story, and buy us a little more time to work with."

Barely a minute later the limousine crossed a bridge going over some railroad tracks while the truck veered away and took an alternate road. Upon their arrival at the airport, Reynolds ordered the Commando's flight crew to prepare for take off. He opened its cargo doors and started the loading operation with several small crates the Israeli agents had stowed in the limousine's trunk, the detonation fuses for the bombs.

The truck itself arrived as Goldsmith had said it would, approximately fifteen minutes later, and Reynolds had it backed up to the C-46. This time there wasn't any group of native laborers to do the heavy work, so everyone had to pitch in. Except for Reynolds and the Commando's pilot; they decided where the cargo would go so it wouldn't affect the transport's center of gravity.

"Lay the heavy crates on their sides," said Reynolds. "It'll distribute the load more evenly and we won't have to worry about any of them tipping over in flight. Let's get them in first and worry about the others afterward."

Eventually the entire floor of the C-46's cargo deck was covered with oblong wooden crates. Stacked on top of them were the smaller crates and those near the front were tied down to prevent the rest from shifting forward while the plane was in flight. Reynolds thanked his brother and David Goldsmith for everything they had done and promised he would be in touch with them in the near future.

With the late-afternoon sun rapidly fading, the C-46 rose into the thin, cool, Andean air, requiring the runway's full length for its take off roll. Its engines needed full power and the richest fuel mixture they could receive in order to climb over the twenty thousand foot peaks surrounding the La Paz river valley. Once past them, however, the power settings were eased off and the transport was retrimmed for a gentle dive. This allowed it to make the return flight at an average speed of nearly three hundred miles an hour. Reynolds and his group arrived at the ranch just in time for dinner.

"All right, this looks like as good a place as any to hold our briefing," Reynolds noted, surveying the ranch's office and library. He was the first inside the handsomely furnished room, followed by Romero, Van Hoff, Woods, all the other pilots of the group and Marilyn. He and Van Hoff carried the envelopes of photographs they had received at La Paz. "Close the door behind you, Tony. These are pictures my brother took a few days ago. They show that the Nazis are indeed in Bolivia and have established an air base in Santa Cruz province. From the look of it, they're nearly ready to begin operations."

The first envelope to be opened was the one marked 'facilities.' The photos inside showed the base and all structures associated with the base's one runway.

"As you can see, the base is rather spartan," said Van Hoff. "But it's certainly much better equipped than many of the fields we've operated from. It has no hangars, no major repair facilities though this barn is probably used to assemble the aircraft they receive. It does have a temporary fuel dump, here, and a munitions dump next to it. Both are little more than dug in revetments with camouflage nets drawn over them.

"The runway itself is paved and, while narrow, almost a mile long. Adequate for the aircraft stationed there. At one end of the runway there's a primitive control tower and along its perimeter are enough lights for night operations. There are barracks, at least one generator, a motor pool and one other dump. A junk yard where, among other items, there are five wrecked aircraft. It appears as though they've had a few accidents in their training program."

The envelope to be opened next was the one showing the base defenses. Since it was Green who examined its contents in La Pax, it was he who took over the meeting.

"The Nazis seem to be more worried about sabotage or a ground attack than an air attack. There are fences surrounding the airfield and the ranch on the hill that overlooks it. Along those fences are watch towers, probably with machine guns and searchlights. There are mortar pits surrounding the ranch and some of the vehicles in the pool are armored cars. Built in Argentina I've been told. There are precious few anti-aircraft defenses, all of them light flak guns. There are more guarding the ranch than the airfield, in fact the ranch is favored by about two to one. Which should give you an idea as to which is considered more important. There is no radar and provided we aren't spotted en route to the target, we will achieve complete surprise."

The following envelope showed all the buildings not associated with the airfield. That included the ranch house and surrounding grounds. Van Hoff described them all and then turned the meeting back over to Reynolds, who saved the best for last and for himself. He described the number and types of aircraft at the base, including the He-162s.

". . . These, are the first jet planes in South America," said Reynolds, holding up an enlargement of the Salamanders, while others were being passed around. "So far, there are only two but there could be more. Either in transit to the base or being assembled in the barn. Their presence means we have to get our mission over and done with as soon as possible. If any more appear it'll make our attack even more difficult. In regional terms this Nazi air force is powerful enough as it is. Just how powerful is it? Well, I'll let someone who's an expert tell you. Augustin, if you'll please?"

"A little over forty aircraft may not sound like an imposing force to you," said Romero, rising from his seat. "You, who have flown in air forces that had thousands of aircraft. But this is South America and the situation is completely different. Here in Bolivia, the two most powerful air forces are yours and the Nazis'. It reflects the sad state of my country. The Bolivian Air Force has exactly three flying T-6s, those are its most modern equipment. The Curtiss-Wright fighters it has have been derelict for a long time. Its only other equipment are some Stearman trainers and Ju-52s.

"Outside of Bolivia the situation isn't much better. The air forces of Uruguay, Paraguay, Peru and Chile are almost non-existent and, like Bolivia, will remain so until the end of the year when the first Rio Pact aid is due to arrive. The largest and best equipped air force in South America is Brazil's but as you all well know, it's almost completely grounded due to a lack of spare parts. Therefore, the most powerful of the South American air forces is Argentina's.

"It has almost two hundred Hawk seventy-five fighters, that's the Curtiss P-36 with fixed landing gear. They were built under license in Cordoba. The Argentines also have a hundred bombers of various types. Including Northrop attack bombers, Martin B-10s and a brand new plane, designed and built locally. It's the Ae-24 Calquin and she looks like a radial-engined, DeHavilland Mosquito. Thirty-five have so far been built and they're just entering squadron service. In spite of their numbers, the Argentine Air Force would be no match for what the Nazis have. If they wanted to oppose them, which I doubt they would.

"Politically, the Peronista government of Argentina is a close cousin to the Third Reich. It's a corrupt, repressive regime and I have no doubt that it is hiding Nazis and helping those in my country. I believe that Argentina would be the first to recognize any Nazi or Nazi-backed government that would take control of Bolivia."

"Mister Romero, if we were to fail, would there be anyone to oppose the Nazis?" asked Clostermann. "Would any units of the army or air force fight them?"

"They might, though not for long. Most air force personnel are in the United States, receiving training on P-47s and B-25s. The army is divided into four military districts, like the air force. The Santa Cruz district is the largest and is probably in collusion with the Nazis. We have a strong 'Vichy' element in Bolivia, just like your country had. The other districts are too small and too weak to resist for long. Most of the artillery and tanks are in Santa Cruz. Those who are in power have learned from the Villaroel government and moved many army units out of La Paz. That could be their doom, unless you succeed in your mission."

"When do you think the krauts will launch their attack on your country?" asked Acerrio.

"I wouldn't know but it should be soon," said Romero. "With the signing of the Rio Pact this year, our military will soon be receiving new equipment. It could be tomorrow. At any rate, I wish you would attack the Nazis tomorrow. Destroy them now so they will not cause damage to my country. Jack, when will you attack?"

"Well, I can tell you that it definitely won't be tomorrow," Reynolds admitted, collecting all the envelopes and their photographs. "But it will be in the next few days. After all, our planes have just flown five thousand miles, almost without major problems and I think they're due for an overhaul. Mike's aircraft especially; I still think we should replace your oil filters and your propeller. Augustin, do you think those craftsmen you hired could repair the dents in his wing tips?"

"Of course, they are artists. If this meeting is finished would you care to see what I've collected for you?"

Since no one else had any questions, the meeting ended and Romero took Reynolds and Van Hoff to inspect what he had collected for their fake movie project.

Short of actual cameras, sound equipment and lights, what he had rounded up was quite impressive. Romero had building materials, tools, a portable generator and paint supplies. All of it stored in one of his barns. The craftsmen he had hired came from as far away as Sucré and La Paz and he had them quartered in one of the ranch's barracks he used when he needed to hire additional hands.

"This stuff is quite good," said Reynolds, handling a large spray gun. "You even got a compressor for it. Tell me, would you use this gear to paint buildings?"

"No, this is for spray painting aircraft," said Romero. "If you are going to do a movie on the Flying

Tigers, your planes must look like Tigers. Your other friends have seen all this and appear most interested in painting their planes. The artists say they could do all of your fighters in a day, would you like them to?"

"I don't think so, it would only cause delays. We'll be busy enough as it is just repairing the planes."

"It would be of some help to us if the aircraft were numbered or painted with certain colors," Van Hoff advised, lifting a cover sheet to examine the supply of paint Romero had. "And your friend certainly has enough stock to do that. It would prevent confusion during our attack. Right now, you can scarcely tell one Kittyhawk from another."

"Okay, that I'll agree to. We'll do something simple like painting the rudders or propeller spinners," said Reynolds. "But it can't interfere with overhauling our fighters. We dare not stay here any longer than we have to. We don't know what kind of timetable the Nazis are on. They could start their take-over tomorrow, in which case we'd be sunk, or they might not begin for several weeks. We simply can't stay here for long. I'd like us to fly our mission and be out of the country as fast as possible. Sorry, Augustin."

"Oh, don't worry, I understand, my friend," said Romero. "In fact it would be to my advantage if you were to leave quickly. There are many people in my country who won't like what you are going to do. Powerful people, and if you're still here after your attack, I cannot guarantee your safety."

The inspection and overhaul procedures Reynolds demanded were nearly as complex as the ones the fighters underwent when they started their journey. In some cases they were more complex. The propeller on

Woods's P-40 was changed, as well as the engine on Acerrio's. Something on everyone's fighter needed repairing or replacing; the work started early, Reynolds had his group up with the ranch hands at dawn. They received a good breakfast from their host and then were sent down to the airstrip.

Reynolds recruited not just the fighter pilots and mechanics but the transport crews and some of Romero's men, including Romero himself. They were all eager to help the new arrivals; after all, except for what the Germans had smuggled in, the P-40s were the most modern aircraft in all Bolivia. Even Marilyn joined in, dividing her time between her father's plane and Van Hoff's. About the only one not to work constantly on the fighters turned out to be Reynolds. Around mid-morning the ranch got a phone call from La Paz and he had to leave the flight line to answer it.

"That was Bob," he said, climbing out of the truck which had driven him back to the airstrip. "Enlargements from yesterday's run are ready and he's going to try another run today. If he's successful, I think we could launch our attack tomorrow."

"Great, when do we get those pictures, Colonel?" Acerrio asked. "Are they going to be flown out to us?"

"No, I have to fly to La Paz and pick them up. I'd rather not do it in a P-40 or a C-46. Augustin, could I borrow one of the planes from your flying club?"

"Of course you can. As you can see, I still have two of the Staggerwings you and your father ferried down for me. You may have either of them," said Romero. "Do you still know how to fly one?"

"After what I went through to get them here, you bet I do," Reynolds replied.

The newly arrived fighters and transports tended to overshadow the fact that the airstrip already had some residents. Most of the planes belonged to Romero though a few were owned by other ranchers in the area. Romero's aircraft were the best and the two Beech Seventeen Staggerwings were the most modern, apart from the P-40s. The resident aircraft stood in line under a stand of trees; they occupied the permanent tiedowns while the fighters and transports were arranged along either side of the airstrip's short taxiway.

Reynolds climbed onto his fighter briefly, to retrieve his helmet and goggles from the Kittyhawk's cockpit, then walked over to the Staggerwings. After inspecting them both, he chose the one painted yellow with black trim. It appeared to be in the best shape and had the most fuel in its tanks. Though it had been more than eight years since he last flew a Staggerwing, Reynolds started the Beech without trouble and taxied it smartly past his friends.

While its engine only had one-third the horsepower of a P-40's Allison, the Staggerwing emitted a deep howl as it took off. Sounding like a muted T-6, it rattled past the airstrip, heading west and climbing as rapidly as it could. Since the Beech had no supercharger, Reynolds had to gain all the altitude he could now, before reaching the formidable bastion of Andes peaks surrounding La Paz.

"Well, what do we do while he's gone?" asked Woods, as the group stopped briefly to watch Reynolds depart. "By early afternoon we should be finished."

"Perhaps with work on our powerplant and hydraulic systems," said Van Hoff. "But we still have to check our armament systems. Because of security problems, we haven't looked at them since the Dominican Republic. If we're to go to war tomorrow, we had best make sure our weapons work."

Not only were the six machine guns on each fighter examined but their bomb shackles were as well. The caps on all the gun muzzles were removed and the barrels checked for fouling or corrosion. The access panels on the gun bays and the ammo storage bins were lifted off so they could be checked for rain seepage and the feed chutes and the main bodies of the machine guns for signs of corrosion.

Romero and his men were especially interested in and impressed by the armament the P-40s carried. To them the light, twin-gun armament of the First World War was the standard; the heavy machine guns and bomb shackles of the Curtiss fighters were from a whole new era.

". . . And I would say that even this will soon be obsolescent," Brandon observed, while Romero helped him check the guns on his plane. "In the RAF there's a great deal of talk on what future weapons will be. We now have aircraft armed with batteries of heavy cannons and in the future they may be armed with rockets, some of them guided by radio signals or radar. The day may come when aeroplanes will fight without even seeing each other."

"That would be incredible," said Romero. "But where would the honor and glory be in a fight such as that?"

"Out the window probably. But if we don't build those weapons and build the best in the world, then we will surely lose the next war. We learned that in 1940."

"Tell me, when we are done with these exams, will we arm your planes and put bombs on them?"

"No, they won't be armed or bombed up until just before we take off. Which could be tomorrow, depending on the news Jack Reynolds brings back."

Fortunately, none of the more than seventy machine guns on the group's Kittyhawks showed any signs of damage or corrosion. All their under wing and fuselage bomb racks worked, all their gunsights were operational; all the planes needed now were bombs and ammunition. All their pilots waited on was the word to begin, which they expected Reynolds would be bringing back from La Paz.

The P-40s were still being worked on when the Staggerwing droned down the river and came in for a landing. As he taxied past the fighters, Reynolds motioned for Van Hoff and some of his other friends to meet him at the tie-down spot. By the time he reached it, half the pilots were waiting for him. He swung the Staggerwing around, switched off its engine and half a dozen people were asking the same question before he had climbed out of the cockpit.

"Here are the pictures from yesterday's run," said Reynolds, handing to Van Hoff a large, stuffed envelope. "Not as many from the first one but, then, we don't need to see every detail. And to answer all of you at once, no, we won't be flying our mission tomorrow but we'll do it soon. It'll have to be soon."

"Why can't we fly it, Colonel?" Acerrio asked, beating everyone else to the punch. "The planes are all ready to go. Did something happen to your brother?"

"He couldn't make today's photo run because of

cloud cover over the target. There'll be a cold front over Santa Cruz province for most of tomorrow. That means thunderstorms and I'm not risking all our asses trying to fly through them. We could get blown into a mountain and fighting a thunderstorm will reduce our range. The weather office in La Paz said the storms will be gone in twenty-four hours. That's when we'll start our attack."

"You mentioned something about having to do it soon," said Woods. "Why? What did you find out in La Paz?"

"Bob's flight wasn't entirely unsuccessful. While at altitude over Santa Cruz, he spotted another airplane. It was flying higher than he and Bob was at forty thousand feet. Beyond his P-38, there are only two other types of aircraft in all of South America which can reach that altitude."

"The Heinkel jets," Van Hoff answered. "They can go that high but what other aircraft can?"

"Those Ju-188s," said Reynolds. "As I remember, without a bomb load they could reach forty thousand. And I've heard from Goldsmith, he has some agents in Argentina and they claim they saw a twin-engined aircraft without markings land at an Argentine Air Force base."

"Did they identify it as a Junkers 188?"

"They couldn't really tell what it was. Hell they're spies, not pilots or airmen, airplanes aren't their specialty."

"How well I know that," said Woods. "I think one of the reasons why the Nazis have come so far is no one who's a spy is an aircraft buff as well."

"How long ago was the plane spotted?" asked Van

Hoff.

"About a week, it landed at Moron Air Base outside of Buenos Aires. I'd say the Nazis were talking with the Perón government. The take-over may be ready to begin."

"And what'll we do, Colonel? We can't just sit around here," said Acerrio.

"We didn't come five thousand miles to watch the founding of a Nazi state but, for a little while we will have to sit here. Tomorrow, a few of us will go to La Paz and wait for my brother to finish his run. I'm sure the rest of you can find something to do until we return."

Of course Reynolds would be one of the pilots to go. It was his brother after all, and no one else had ever flown in Bolivia before. He finally decided to take Woods and Brandon along, because no additional work on their planes needed to be done and they had never seen La Paz. Reynolds decided to use the same Beech Staggerwing and, following lunch, took off while the other pilots continued to work on their P-40s. By this time, the only thing they could do was wash them down. To clean off the mud, grime and insects the planes had collected on their journey across South America.

"How much longer will it be before the film is processed?" Brandon asked, as he paced around the photo lab.

"The negatives should be developed," said Bob Reynolds. "The next thing they'll do is make contact prints and from them you'll decide what should be enlarged."

"I really don't see why you people need new photographs?" Goldsmith inquired, "can't you just use the ones your brother's taken already?"

"We don't like surprises," said Reynolds. "A lot could've happened at that base in the forty-eight hours since Bob made his last run. More planes may have been built, more defenses could've been added. As it is, these new photos will be eighteen hours old when we make our attack. But there isn't much we can do about that, not unless we move a processing lab to Romero's ranch."

"Or you could have let me put an agent in the province. We have all the radio gear we need and could've given you up-to-the-minute reports."

"No, I never liked relying on agents. I don't like putting people in situations they can't be rescued from, even if they do volunteer. And I don't like what my brother's offered to do. Sitting over the base tomorrow with a pair of binoculars."

"Why not? Jack, I'll be at thirty thousand feet," said Bob Reynolds. "I can see quite a bit with field glasses. Enough to let you know if they're readying for an air attack."

"I don't want you to! You'll be in an unarmed plane and we can't give you an escort!" Reynolds stormed, briefly. "But I'm not going to stop you. This isn't the army so I can't order you and I've never been able to stop you from doing anything. Short of tying you up, which I've considered. Just don't come crying to me when you're shot down."

"Here we are, Dave. Hot off the presses," said one of the Israeli agents; he came out of the darkroom carrying a handful of dripping contact prints. "Or fresh from their fixing baths I should say. Where would you like them?"

As before, the prints were laid on a table for everyone to view. Those who were to attack the base paid the closest attention to them and almost at once they discovered that there had indeed been changes.

"That's a Ju-52," said Woods, handing his magnifying glass to Reynolds. "There, on the runway. I wonder where it came from? Do you think that was smuggled in as well?"

"It's probably Bolivian," said Bob Reynolds, looking over his brother's shoulder. "Or Argentinian. Both air forces use them. It's still a rather common transport around here. I'll bet it brought in some high-level officials to talk about the coup."

"So do I," Reynolds added. "Let's get a good blowup of this and see if we can't establish its nationality."

"My God, what will we do if the plane's still at the field tomorrow?" Brandon asked, his face a little pale.

"We blast the hell out of it. I don't care if it has the chief of staff of the Argentinian Air Force on board it or Juan Perón himself. Hell, if he dies, his wife Eva can run the country. I don't care if we find a plane with U.S. markings at this base tomorrow. If it's there it's the enemy and we'll destroy it."

"You're becoming as passionate about this as Claus," said Woods. "Why should you be so fanatical?"

"I'm no fanatic, I just believe in doing my job right," said Reynolds. "It's been my experience that fanatics are sloppy and don't deliver the best performance. Besides, they tend to get in the way of things."

"I think I've found another surprise," Brandon warned, looking up from another print. "Here, by the barn. It's another one of those jets. They now have three."

"I believe it is a Heinkel Salamander," said Woods. "But at this scale it's difficult to tell."

"All right, we have enough to start making blow-ups," Reynolds advised. "Circle what you've found and we'll hand the prints back to the lab boys."

What Brandon discovered did turn out to be a third He-162. Newly built and being towed from the assembly barn to the airfield where the first two jets stood. The Ju-52 Woods spotted had Argentinian markings on its wings. While Brandon hoped it would be gone by tomorrow, Reynolds hoped the transport would still be there. He wanted to teach the Argentinians a lesson about dealing with the Nazis. Enlargements were made of the other aircraft at the field and several fighters were missing. Off on training flights most likely, it made Reynolds and Woods decide that the group would have to launch its strike as early as possible if they wanted to catch all the planes on the ground.

Enlargements were also made of an anti-aircraft guns around the base and the ranch and of the base's fuel and ammunition dumps. Reynolds and the others worked straight through the lunch hour, ignoring the lab owner's offer to take them to a restaurant, and had all the photographs they thought the group would need by early afternoon.

Goldsmith drove them back to the airport where Reynolds made one last attempt to talk his brother out of what he still considered to be a dangerous stunt.

But as he had mentioned earlier, he'd never been able to stop his brother once his mind was made up. He ended the argument by suggesting to Bob that he remove the cameras from his Lightning. In combat they would be useless and perhaps the weight savings would give him a few extra miles an hour in speed or a better climb rate. Perhaps that would be enough to get him out of trouble.

The Beech Staggerwing labored into the thin air. It needed a painfully long climbout to rise above the taller buildings in La Paz. Without a supercharger, it dared not challenge the mountains encircling Bolivia's capital. Instead it followed the La Paz river valley until the peaks were no longer so formidable and the air a good deal richer. At its top speed the Staggerwing took two hours to return to Romero's ranch. As it came in for a landing, Woods noticed there was more activity at the airstrip than what any of them had expected.

"What on earth is happening?" he asked. "Some of the Kittyhawks are missing. And look at those, they're not silver any more. They've been painted."

Woods pointed to four fighters clustered on one side of the airstrip's taxiway. One was jet black, another was olive drab and the other two wore sand and brown camouflage patterns. The sight so distracted Reynolds that he aborted his landing and did a go-around. While he realigned the Staggerwing for another attempt, they all caught sight of a fifth P-40 being towed away from the ranch. It was painted sand and brown and, on closer inspection, had British markings on its wings and fuselage.

"Those other four are also wearing insignias," said Brandon. "Two have American markings and two have RAF roundels. What in God's name is going on?"

"I don't know but we're going to find out," snapped Reynolds; unlike the others who were skeptical though curious, he was angry. He slapped the Beech onto the airstrip and, instead of taking it to its tie-down spot, he taxied the cabin biplane to the line of freshly painted fighters and parked beside them.

"Hi, Colonel, how do you like her?" asked Acerrio, pointing back at his fighter. Of the four, his was the one painted olive drab. It carried pre-war, U.S. Army Air Corps insignia and black squadron and serial numbers on its tail fin. "Now she looks just like the ship I flew at Pearl Harbor. Except that was a C-model and this is a P-40E. Say, how did things go with your brother in La Paz?"

"They went just fine. Now you tell me, who the hell is responsible for this?" Reynolds waved his hand at the whole line of camouflaged P-40s. From what he said and the tone he used, Acerrio knew he wasn't pleased.

"We all thought of it, Colonel. There wasn't much for us to do around here and those guys your friend hired can do a real fast job. Just take a look at her, she looks better than any plane I ever saw at Wheeler."

"That's because you used gloss paint on her, not flat colors. And whose plane is that next to yours? It looks like someone's idea of a damned flying hot rod."

The aircraft Reynolds referred to was the black P-40. On closer inspection he saw it sported a dark red spinner, wing tips, trim lines and tail plane. It also carried mid-war, Army Air Force markings with red borders.

"Oh that's Danny's airplane," said Acerrio. "He told me his squadron flew P-40s painted like that until they switched over to P-51s."

"Now I recognize those colors," said Brandon, gesturing at the two, almost identical Kittyhawks. "The one with the arrow on the cowling is Eric's and the one with the shark's teeth is Claus's. Michael, don't you recognize them?"

"Of course I do. Those are the markings of the aircraft we flew in North Africa. And I recognize the markings of the plane being towed here, that's Doug's ship."

A tractor was towing the Kittyhawk and Doug Ward was riding on its wing's leading edge. As it was pulled in next to the other, R.A.F.-marked fighters, he jumped to the ground and ran to meet his friends.

"Isn't she a beaut, mates!" he exclaimed to Woods and Brandon. "They put the squadron codes on right and they even put me boxing kangaroo on the cowling. Those artists your friend hired have done just a great job, Colonel."

"I know, Tony was telling me about his," said Reynolds, coolly. "Where's everyone else? Why isn't Claus down here, raving about his airplane?"

"Oh he's up at the barn. They all are. We have a couple of more ships being painted."

"Well I'm going to put a stop to this, right now! This is the damndest thing I've seen in years."

Reynolds commandeered the tractor and, with Woods and Brandon, climbed on it and sat or hung on to whatever they could find. The driver briefly protested, claiming that he had to return with another P-40, but Reynolds would hear nothing of it. He ordered

Ward to unhitch the tow bar then told the driver to take him to the barn, immediately.

A short, bumpy ride up a dirt road and the tractor was pulling alongside the barn that Romero had shown to Reynolds two days before. Outside it was still another freshly painted fighter. At first Reynolds and the others thought it was painted in Royal Air Force colors but they noticed that the blue on the undersurfaces was darker than normal, the colors in the national insignia were in the wrong order and the rudder had blue, white and red vertical stripes on it.

"Do you like her? This is what my P-40 looked like," said Clostermann, standing next to his fighter's bright red spinner. "Back in Tunisa, in 1943."

"Jesus Christ, everyone's doing it," Reynolds swore. "We'll have the most bizarre looking squadron since Von Richthofen's Flying Circus. They'll see us coming for miles."

"I have to agree with you, Jack," said Brandon. "This is ridiculous. I hope we can stop it before it's too late."

"It is already too late," said Van Hoff, stepping out of the barn as its main doors were opened. "Too many aircraft have been painted for you to stop it now."

"We'll see about that," Reynolds countered. "You couldn't have been painting for too long. Did you bother to put a primer coat on the planes?"

"No, we didn't feel it was necessary."

"Well hell, these paint jobs will start peeling off after a few days of flying."

"By then it won't matter. What we are doing is just for tomorrow," Van Hoff replied. "We want the Nazis to know who is destroying them. Please, Jack, come inside."

Reynolds, along with Woods and Brandon, followed Van Hoff into the barn. They noticed it had been cleaned out and the air was heavy with the smell of paint. They also noticed the two P-40s sitting inside it and that the first one had been painted as a Flying Tiger.

"I had the pictures of your plane you once sent me," said Marilyn, standing by her father's ship. "Augustin's men were able to copy the scheme from them. Do you like it?"

Reynolds didn't answer her; he circled slowly around his ship, looking but not touching; he was warned that the paint was still wet. The expression on his face was at first one of awe; he couldn't believe what his friends had done to his plane. After a few moments he was smiling, it was as if he were seeing an old friend again. By the time he came around to the front of the P-40, he had forgotten all about his objections to having the fighters repainted.

"My God, this is my aircraft," said Brandon, examining the other plane. "She's beautiful, when will you finish her?"

"If we're allowed to continue, all fighters will be completed by early tonight," Van Hoff answered. "Provided there are no objections. Jack, do you wish to object?"

"No. No, not if you can get them done on time," said Reynolds, still standing in front of his aircraft. He wanted so much to touch it but he knew he couldn't, just yet.

With three extra hands, the work went along much faster than Van Hoff had anticipated. They all went without dinner and, by around seven o'clock, the last P-40s, Kain's and Clinton's, were towed back to the flight line. Repainted in the colors of a Royal Australian Air Force squadron based in New Guinea and the U.S. Army Air Force in North Africa.

Romero had a late supper ready for his guests and for those who had been to La Paz, and had not eaten since the morning, it was especially welcome. During the meal, talk centered on what the newest reconnaissance photos revealed. Later, with the meal over and everyone resting in the living room, discussion turned to a more general topic. One Romero had been wanting to ask about for days—what Reynolds had experienced during the war and, rapidly, it grew to include everyone else's adventures.

". . . And this was given to me by the American Army Air Force," said Brandon, showing Romero the last of his medals. "It was for scattering some Jerries who were attacking a formation of B-26 bombers near Berlin. I shot down my last two aircraft of the war. A day later it ended."

"Yeah, but you ain't got the most unusual medal," said Acerrio. "Not even the Colonel has with all that Soviet junk. The Count has. Why don't you show us your Cross?"

Van Hoff dug through his kit and came up with a small, hinged box. It looked a little more worn than when everyone last saw it but the Iron Cross inside was still untarnished. Van Hoff lifted the medal by its ceremonial ribbon and held it out for all to see.

"This was won by my father in the First World War," he told Romero. "He gave it to me when I left home nine years ago and I've kept it with me since then. It is now mine, and always will be."

"I wonder what type of medal we'll be awarded for this action?" mused Kain, admiring Van Hoff's Iron Cross.

"If our governments ever find out what we're doing, we'll be lucky to come away with jail sentences," said Brandon. "Those of us who are still in military service will most likely be dishonorably discharged."

"Perhaps my country will give us something," Green offered. "If Israel survives what the Arabs have planned for it."

"These last few weeks have been reward enough for me," said McCloud. "For the first time in more than a year, I've felt as though I were part of something. I'm back with my brothers, I have little in the way of a family beyond you."

"My feelings exactly," said Acerrio. "Hey, if any of you guys are ever in a situation like this, just call on me. Who better to help you than a brother?"

"Brothers. Brothers," Woods repeated to himself then, speaking up. "In my country, the Afrikaaners have a secret society called the Broderbond. The Brotherhood. What we have here is a Brotherhood. An international group of pilots and airmen, one that could be far more powerful than any other organization of its kind. We wield the most powerful weapons man has ever devised. If we continue to use them as we are doing now, we could be a force for good in this world."

"I like the idea," said Reynolds. "And I'm sure my real brother would be interested in joining such a group."

"Then it's settled. If we all agree, I say we establish

a Brotherhood of combat pilots and air crew, once our mission has ended," Van Hoff announced, returning his medal to its case and rising to his feet. "Tomorrow, we may destroy the last vestiges of the Nazi threat. I will have little else to devote my fortune to, save for the establishment of such a society. Are we agreed?"

Slowly, the other men in the room rose from their seats, even the transport pilots joined in. Romero, however, bolted from his and disappeared down the cellar stairs. He was gone for a few moments, then came back with an armload of wine bottles. He recruited Reynolds to help open them and, as fast as he could, he handed out glasses filled with a dark red wine.

"Augustin, this stuff's from 1930," said Reynolds. "Are you sure you want us to use it?"

"Of course, of course. On an occasion like this, you must use the best. It is not every day that an organization is founded in my house. May I share a glass with you?"

"As our host, I would say it's an absolute necessity," Woods replied, accepting his glass from Romero. "Wouldn't you say so, Claus?"

"Yes, even if he never flew in combat, I would still say he's a brother," said Van Hoff. He waited until everyone in the room had been served and then, raising his glass above his head, he shouted. "To the Brotherhood!"

"I have reports from our agents in La Paz, he must see them at once," the man announced, as he approached two heavily armed guards. They stood watch over the last door in the hallway and came to attention as the man raised his arm in salute.

"Good, Herr Rauchman," responded one of the guards. "He's been waiting for them. But first, you know the procedure. Your ID, please, sign the log and hand over your gun."

As requested, Rauchman handed his identity card to the first guard, his Walther automatic to the second; then bent over a table by the door to write his name and the time into a book. The guards also examined the folders he had with him before opening the door. Inside, he found a short, heavily set man gazing out the window at the airfield below.

"Herr Bormann, these just arrived from La Paz," said Rauchman, holding out the folders.

Martin Bormann turned away from the window and snatched the folders out of Rauchman's hand. He took them to a desk, where he switched on a reading lamp so he could see them better.

"What do they say?" Bormann demanded, flipping nervously through the pages of the first report.

"They state that there has been little activity from those American planes since they entered the country," Rauchman answered. "Our agents can neither confirm nor deny the story that they've come here to film a war movie. The people who own them do not appear to be Jewish, though they have met with people we suspect are Jewish agents."

"They have? Which ones, which ones?"

"Those who are posing as American oil company officials. The ones who have that P-38 flying photograph sorties over the country, supposedly to find new oil fields."

"Posing, are you not sure yet?"

"If they are Jewish agents, their cover is good. The best I've seen. We have learned where those American fighters are being kept. On a ranch on the San Miguel River, in Beni Province."

"Where is that?" Bormann asked, turning his attention from the reports to a wall map over the desk.

"Here," said Rauchman, pointing at a thin, blue line on the map. "Over two hundred miles away. The fighters are what the Americans call P-40s. There's only a dozen of them and we believe our base is beyond their combat range. They could cause us trouble however, when we begin our take-over."

"Then they will be destroyed, we must let nothing interfere with our plans. They are so close, everything is almost ready. The Argentinians will leave tomorrow and, once our Army units are in position, we can start our move. From the ashes of Germany, a new Reich will appear. Our phoenix is ready to fly."

Chapter Eleven:
THE ATTACK.
THE MISSION ENDS.

At four o'clock in the morning, the first pilots were awakened by Romero. Van Hoff and Reynolds were roused from their beds, as was Marilyn. Everyone else would be allowed to sleep for a little longer; this was a private briefing.

"So far as I know, no one knows what you've been doing," Reynolds told his daughter. "They're content to think you're in love with Claus and to let it go at that. Though there was one close call. Yesterday in La Paz, I thought I saw Margaret Woods getting off an Aerolineas DC-3 while we were arriving. I think my heart would've stopped if Mike had recognized her."

"It probably was her," said Marilyn, checking her records. "Margaret Woods was one of the last people to arrive. The airlines were reluctant to let her fly because she was so pregnant. I have someone coming for each of the other pilots, including Acerrio and McCloud. I finally got in touch with Tony's girl friend and I have Jeffrey's grandfather coming from some place called Winnipeg."

"How many people in total, Marilyn?" Van Hoff

asked.

"Seventeen, if you wish to include Dennis Brandon's new daughter. His wife also brought along her mother to help her with the baby. Most of the people are either in La Paz or have been put up by Romero's friend at a nearby ranch. They'll start arriving as soon as you leave."

"How will the people in La Paz reach here?"

"Augustin's arranged for a local airline to fly them here. The flight should leave La Paz in another two hours and land here about thirty minutes before you're due back."

"Good, you've done well, Marilyn," said Reynolds. "This was a difficult job and I'm proud of how you handled it. And Augustin, thanks for helping out. I'm sure our friends will appreciate it, only I think it's going to make your house a little crowded."

"No problem, Jack," Romero assured. "I'm only sorry that you will not be able to stay for long."

"Okay, if there's nothing more to discuss, then let's go get the others," said Reynolds, rising from his chair.

The other pilots almost welcomed the wake up call. It had been more than two years since any of them had flown a combat mission and they were nervous. So nervous many didn't shave or eat a large breakfast, just as they had when they flew their first combat missions during the war.

The transport crews and mechanics were awakened as well and sent down to service the fighters. In the pre-dawn darkness it was difficult to see the planes, let alone work on them. To illuminate them, almost every vehicle on the ranch that had lights was sent to the flight line. They not only shone them on the P-40s but on one of the C-46s as well.

It was the one which held the bombs received in La Paz. First, the larger crates were broken open and their blunt, ballistic contents rolled onto awaiting trucks. Then the smaller crates were opened and the sets of guidance fins they contained were attached to the tails of the bombs. By twos and threes they arrived at the flight line where the mechanics rigged them to the underwing and fuselage racks of the P-40s. Only when the bombs were secure would the detonation fuses be inserted.

"Well my friends, this is what we've been working weeks for," said Van Hoff, as he started the briefing. "And for some of us, it has been years. What we do now is for our friends, our families, those we loved and our people. Let's hope we can end this scourge, this blight against civilization, with what we do today. Let's hope that this will be the last mission of World War Two. I've discussed our attack with both Mike Woods and Jack Reynolds and we've agreed to the following plan . . ."

Van Hoff set a map on the dining room table and tilted it so everyone in the room could see it.

". . . Here's the route we'll take to the target, our route from it and the flight path Jack's brother has planned to fly from La Paz. This circle describes the tactical radius of our fighters with external weapons. As you can see, the target is almost at the edge of our range. Which means we'll have to fly on lean mixtures until we reach it. When we do, this will be our plan of attack . . ."

The map was taken down and several photographs of the Nazi base were brought out. They had been tacked to stiff poster boards so everyone could see them.

". . . Jack's flight will hit the airfield, my flight will hit the ranch. We'll split into pairs with Jack and Tony strafing the enemy's flight line, then Daniel and Jesse following it with a bomb run. The same will happen when my flight attacks the ranch. Kain and I will strafe, Eric and André will release their bombs, all of them. Michael's flight will follow Jack's and you'll hit the airfield in the same way. The first pair strafes, the second pair bombs.

"After the primary targets have been hit, the secondary targets will be the fuel and munition dumps at the airfield and the aircraft assembly building at the ranch. If we have any bombs left after they're destroyed, the third set of targets will be the motor pool and generators at the ranch. Everything else is a target of opportunity, that includes any anti-aircraft guns, moving vehicles, or aircraft on the runway, even the Argentinian plane.

"When our attack is complete, we'll return to this base. Should, for any reason, you cannot make it here you're to divert to San Ignacio where one of our transports will be waiting for you. If your fighter is too badly damaged to make it any further it will have to be abandoned. Otherwise, you're to fly back here and then we'll all leave this country. Are there any questions?"

"What if we're shot down over the target or can't get

to this San Ignacio?" Acerrio asked, speaking up as he raised his hand.

"You're shit out of luck," said Reynolds. "You knew the job was dangerous when you took it, Tony."

"Jack, please. It's really not that bad," Van Hoff quickly added. "Though you shouldn't let yourselves be captured by the Nazis if possible. If you can't reach the emergency field then bail out and make for either San José, San Miguel or San Ignacio itself by foot. In each of these towns Mister Romero has friends and they have been warned to expect you."

"Apart from these San José Mountains, what kind of terrain do we have in this area?" Brandon asked. "And is the province heavily populated?"

"I think it best if we had a local expert explain that." Van Hoff nodded in Romero's direction as he spoke. The photographs were laid aside and the map brought back so Romero could make his description easier to understand.

"Santa Cruz province is one of the largest provinces in Bolivia," he began. "But it is also the least populated. Much of it is desolate and has little contact with civilization, especially where you are flying. In that area is the Chaco Boreal territory, a worthless tract of land my country went to war over some fifteen years ago.

"To the west of the San José Mountains is Lake Concepción, which you will fly over as you head for your target. To the north and east of the mountains is the Mato Grosso swamp that extends in from Brazil. The border between our two countries is undefined in this area, and much of it is unexplored. To the southwest is another region of swamps, the Bãnados del Izozog. And to the south is the San José Salt Lake.

"This is a place I would not want to crash in either. But should you survive and make it to any of the towns your commander listed, my friends will help you. Don't worry, they will see you before you see them."

"God, what a cheery place," said Kingston. "It sounds like Brighton on the off-season."

"Should you go down, your escape kit has been loaded with pesos and a large supply of medicines so you will not become ill," Van Hoff added. "If you have no more questions, we should move to the flight line. There's still a great deal of work left to do."

One of the few trucks not being used to service or illuminate the fighters collected the pilots and drove them to the air strip. Outside it was still dark, though in the east the sky was just beginning to lighten.

The pilots arrived to find their aircraft being fueled. Since there were no fuel storage tanks or a dump at the field, gasoline was being transferred from the Commandoes to the P-40s. Some one thousand gallons was laboriously siphoned out of the transports and carried over to the fighters in five-gallon cans. In addition, their oxygen systems and engines were getting checked and the ammunition for their guns was ready for loading.

"Of all the jobs I had to do during the war, I've never had to be a ruddy armourer," Brandon commented, watching the ammo boxes being stacked by his P-40.

"Don't worry, Dennis, you'll find it easy," said Kain. "Back in New Guinea, we had to do it all the time. Malaria and dysentery took a higher toll of our ground crews than Japanese air attacks."

More than twenty thousand rounds of fifty caliber shells were off-loaded from one of the C-46s. The access panels to the wing gun bays and ammunition stowage bins were opened on each fighter; and the long belts of bright copper shells were lifted out of their transport boxes.

The belts were drawn through the feed chutes in the stowage bins and locked into the breeches of the machine guns. Each belt was the same length, with the same number of rounds and the same mix of high-explosive and armor-piercing incendiary shells. Two hundred and eighty-one rounds were fed to each gun, a total of almost seventeen hundred rounds for each fighter.

"Remember, all of you who are flying N-model Warhawks must charge your guns now if you're to use them later," Reynolds advised, walking down the double line of fighters. "Use the manual charging assemblies on the gun bay access panels. You can't charge your guns while in flight. Your ships aren't equipped with hydraulic charging controls."

"Sure thing, Colonel," said Clinton, standing on the wing of his plane. "Who's taking care of your P-40?"

"My mechanic and my daughter are loading the guns. I'm going to get the arming fuses for the bombs."

Reynolds came back from the transports carrying two briefcase-sized boxes. Inside them were all the fuses for the five hundred pound bombs now attached to the fighters. Inserting them and removing their safety wires were the last acts in arming the P-40s. As they were completed, the access panels on the gun bays and the ammunition bins were being closed and locked.

"Claus, Augustin just told me that the first relatives have just arrived at the ranch house," said Marilyn, climbing up the wing of Van Hoff's Kittyhawk.

"Good, I hope they will all be here by the time we return," he said. "I'd like my friends to be happy."

"Make me happy and come back safe." Marilyn reached into the cockpit and put her arms around Van Hoff. "I'm so worried about you and Daddy. I don't want to lose either of you. Take care of yourself for me."

"I will and I shall watch out for your father as well. Here, could you do me a favor and take care of my kit?" Van Hoff asked, handing her a small, leather bag.

"Of course I will and I promise to take the best care of it," Marilyn replied, kissing him.

"Keep it with you, always," Van Hoff told her, then he kissed her. She eased down the wing and got off it in time to hear her father shout new orders.

"Rotate the propellers!" Reynolds commanded. "At least three or four times apiece. You can switch off those truck lights, we won't be needing them anymore."

Dawn had arrived. The first strong rays of sunlight broke over the low, eastern mountains and flooded the river valley. For the first time since they had been painted, the fighters could be clearly seen. Their glossy finishes sparkled in the early morning light.

The schemes ranged from plain olive drab to gloss black and various camouflage patterns of brown, green and desert sand. The national insignia and squadron markings made them even more colorful. The P-40s looked more like a collection of giant models than the integrated fighting unit they were.

"Okay, Colonel, prop rotation is done," Reynolds's mechanic informed. "The oil's been cleared from the engine cylinders. You wanna do the pre-start checks?"

"Yes, but I'd like to do that with my daughter," said Reynolds. "Go take care of the fire extinguishers. Marilyn, could you come up here?"

After saying good-bye to Van Hoff, Marilyn had returned to her father's plane. When she got to him, he handed her a card from the cockpit map case.

"Just read through this list for me, Angel. It'll make things easier." He told her, before shouting to the rest of the pilots to begin their own checks.

"Ignition switch?" Marilyn asked.

"Ignition switch, off," said Reynolds, placing his hand on a small, lever-like toggle.

"Gun selector switches?"

"Gun selector switches, off."

"Landing gear control handle?"

"Landing gear handle, neutral."

"Flap controls?"

"Flap handle, neutral."

"Parking brake?"

"Parking brake, on."

"Flight controls?"

"Flight controls, free." To test them, Reynolds

moved the control stick around and kicked the rudder pedals. By glancing out the cockpit, he could see the ailerons, elevators and tail fin responding to the movements.

"Turn ignition switch to battery?"

"Ignition switch on battery. And we've got power going through the electrical system."

"Fuel selector valve?"

"Fuel selector, on reserve wing tank."

"Generator line switch?"

"Generator line switch, on."

"Propeller circuit breaker switch?"

"Propeller circuit breaker, on."

"Propeller selector switch?"

"Prop selector on Automatic."

"Throttle?"

"Throttle, wide open."

"Mixture control?"

"Mixture control to Idle Cut-off."

"Carburetor air heater control?"

"Carburetor heater, cold."

"Radiator shutters?"

"Radiator shutters, open."

"Okay, is that it, Daddy?" Marilyn asked, handing the card back to her father.

"That's it, Angel. Wait, what's that in your hand?"

"It's Claus's kit. I went to him for a minute and he asked me if I would keep this for him."

"I see," said Reynolds, arching an eyebrow. "You really do love him, don't you?"

"I love both of you. Please take care of yourself and take care of Claus. I don't know what I'd do if I were to lose you. I'll be so worried until you return."

"I promise I will and you don't have to worry about me, I've come back from worse operations. Now slide off the wing, Marilyn, and go over and stand by Ted. Do everything he says, I wouldn't want to run into you. Good-bye, Angel."

Marilyn gave her father a quick peck on the cheek and climbed to the ground. Reynolds looked down the line of fighters on his right, and those on the other side of the taxiway, and noted that everyone had completed their pre-start procedures and were waiting for his signal.

"Ground crew, man your fire extinguishers!" he shouted, then he raised his hand above his head and twirled his fingers. "Pilots, start your engines!"

As the mechanics scrambled to position themselves in front of the P-40s, the quiet whine of starters being brought to speed filled the air. First the propeller on Van Hoff's fighter jerked and slowly rotated, then Reynolds, then Woods and Acerrio, then three more and inside of half a minute all twelve P-40s were coming to life. Their Allison engines rumbled with explosions and short jets of flame shot out their radiator stacks. As each engine caught and fired up, its throttle was retarded and its mixture reset to Auto-rich. Very quickly, the flight line became too noisy for shouted commands to be heard. Reynolds slipped on his radio headset and motioned for the rest to do likewise.

"Watch your oil pressures," he said. "Once you've done your magneto tests you can taxi out. We'll taxi and take off in pairs and form up at two thousand feet. Let's not waste a lot of time at this, we've got a long flight ahead of us."

The group used the same order of taxi as they had throughout their long odyssey to South America. Reynolds and Acerrio followed by Green and Clinton, then it was the aircraft in Woods's flight, followed by Van Hoff's.

The pairs of Kittyhawks swung onto the narrow taxiway and moved out to the grass strip. They waddled a bit more than usual, especially the P-40Ns, which were carrying fifteen hundred pounds of ordnance apiece, in addition to full fuel and ammunition loads. Reynolds and Acerrio aligned themselves on the strip with Acerrio set slightly behind his leader's right wing. They set their trim tabs, propeller pitch and flaps, then released their brakes and advanced their throttles.

The Flying Tiger and Army Air Corps pursuit ship rolled forward, their engines building thunder, their wings slowly gaining lift. Mid-point down the strip their tails rose in unison, a few hundred yards later their main wheels floated off the ground. By the time they reached the airstrip's boundary fence, their landing gear and flaps had been retracted. Reynolds and Acerrio had yet to swing away and complete their climb outs when the next pair of fighters moved onto the strip, Green and Clinton.

Because their P-40s carried an extra one thousand pounds of bombs, they took a little more time to become airborne. Following them were a South African Air Force Kittyhawk from North Africa and a Royal Canadian Air Force Kittyhawk from the Aleutians. When they became airborne, Reynolds's flight had already linked up and was cruising at two thousand feet. Two more North African Kittyhawks roared off the ground to join Woods and McCloud. Van Hoff's flight was last to depart. His fighter, painted in North African colors, and Kain's Royal Australian Air Force Kittyhawk lifted away with Kingston and Clostermann soon racing down the strip to join them.

The moment they climbed into their slots in Van Hoff's flight, the formation broke out of its orbit and dove toward the San Miguel River. They roared across the ranch then wheeled gently to the southeast. Marilyn watched the retreating aircraft until they disappeared; she turned away and walked back to the truck where Romero was waiting.

"I've told my housekeeper to give our new guests breakfast," he said. "And in another two hours the rest will arrive by aircraft. Your own operation has gone well, my flower. What is that you have in your hands?"

"It's Claus's kit, he told me to take care of it," said Marilyn, opening the bag. "To keep it with me always."

She dug her hand inside it and pulled out what felt to be the largest object in it. A hinged, metal box which, when she opened it, was empty.

"Sentries, attention!" shouted the watch officer, as an open topped staff car rolled to a halt beside the ranch house's main entrance. The guards standing outside it snapped into ramrod stiff postures and the watch officer marched across the walkway to greet the car's passengers.

Almost all of them wore uniforms, the only uniforms to be seen at the ranch; those who weren't so formally attired were their escorts. The watch officer raised his right hand to an oblique angle and clicked his heels together when he reached the staff car.

"Good morning, General Astiz. They are waiting for you inside," he said, the officers in the car returning more normal salutes. "Were your quarters comfortable?"

"Yes and we slept quite well," the general responded, stepping out of the car as the watch officer opened its passenger door. "But we found breakfast to be rather limited. In Argentina, many of us do not care for what you call a continental breakfast. We prefer a more substantial meal to start the day with."

"I understand. I believe they have a larger meal planned for you after the briefing. If you'll follow me."

The watch officer led the guests through the doors and the house's anteroom, to what had originally been its dining hall, now converted to a briefing room.

"Herr Bormann, it is good to see you again," said Astiz, shaking the Nazi leader's hand. "I heard some of your aircraft take off fifteen minutes ago. Including your jets. Are they off on a training flight?"

"No, for a demonstration," Bormann replied. "After our briefing is over. Come, let me show you the field."

Bormann led Astiz and the other Argentinian officers to the room's balcony. Outside the cool, early morning breezes stirred the Nazi flags flanking the balcony doors. From it, the officers were treated to a commanding view of the airfield below. On an expanded taxi strip beside the runway, stood the rows of Messerschmitts, Focke-Wulfs and Junkers bombers.

They were all painted a light gray and wore no national markings but did have fuselage numbers along with brightly colored rudders, cowlings and wing tips. The five Ju-188s stood in a single row while the fighters were parked in double rows. On the runway itself was one of the He-162 jets and another, older, Junkers product, a Ju-52 transport. Unlike the other aircraft, the Heinkel was bare metal and the Ju-52 was olive green and dark gray.

"Two of our jets are airborne, with two Me-109s as chase aircraft," said Bormann. "They are due back in twenty-five minutes. As you can see, we now have a fourth Salamander completed and ready for flying."

"Excellent, Herr Bormann," said one of the other Argentinians. "How many of the jets will you have?"

"Just four, that is all we've been able to find and smuggle out of Europe. It is very difficult to move jets, more so than to move more conventional aircraft. Several of our operatives have been caught but we've managed to have the smuggling blamed on Arabs trying to acquire aircraft to destroy the Jewish state in Palestine."

"I would not worry about numbers," said Astiz. "Since what you have are the only jet fighters in all of South America, they will be more than enough."

"I see you are servicing our transport," observed another Argentinian, who was wearing a white uniform instead of green. "Will it be ready for us when we are done?"

"Don't worry about it, Admiral," Bormann said, jovially. "Of course it will be ready. Why do you ask? Can't your fleet operate without you?"

"I'm afraid we will be spotted here. If we are, and we're tied to your take-over of Bolivia, it could make for an international incident. We just signed the Rio Pact with the United States. I hope, General Astiz, that you realize we could be thrown out of the organization if this link is discovered."

"It will not be discovered," said Bormann. "No one will even know it is us behind the coup. Not for a while at least. Not until after the Arabs have destroyed the Jewish state and the West realizes its true enemy is communism. Then we will emerge and the West shall welcome us back to rule Germany as a bulwark against the communist hordes."

"Herr Bormann? Excuse me but we are ready inside," one of the Germans informed, standing at the balcony doors.

"All right, Pritz, we will be there. Come, my friends, let me show you more of our plans."

"Hawk Lead to all flights, Lake Concepción is dead ahead," said Reynolds. "We can ease up on the formation."

The P-40s roared across the lake, spreading out to enjoy a little relaxed flying after being crammed inside the San Miguel river valley for more than an hour. Except for a small fishing village on the shore, there was nothing on the lake. No one who could identify the aircraft and no way a warning could be sent to the

Nazis.

"Eagle Four to Eagle One, me engine's starting to run rough. I knew I shouldn't have taken a Mark Four Kittyhawk. If this gets worse I'll have to abort."

"Don't worry, Doug, it's just your lean fuel mixture," said Woods. "It'll stop once we go back to Auto-rich. Which should be in the next ten minutes."

"Hey, Colonel, don't you think it's time you should try contacting your brother?" Acerrio asked.

"Roger, Hawk Two," said Reynolds. "And the next time, Tony, use my call sign. Hawk Lead to Albatross, do you read me? Hawk Lead to Albatross, report in."

"This is Albatross, I read you loud and clear, big brother. I'm over the vulture's nest and I have news for you. Iron Annie is still on the ground but some of those One-sixty-twos are gone. I can only spot one."

"Oh God, we have the worst of both worlds," said Brandon. "The Argentinians are still there and the jets are up."

"Okay, cut the chatter. Hawk Lead to all flights, arm your guns. Hawk Flight, be prepared to jettison your bombs should we see those jets. When we reach the far side of the lake, we will all go back to Auto-rich mixture settings. Albatross, can you see anything else?"

"Not much, Hawk Lead. I can't see as much with these glasses as I thought I would but I think one of those Ju-188s is missing as well."

At the opposite shore of Lake Concepción, the P-40s snuggled together again, the pilots becoming more alert and protective of each other. They also changed their mixture settings, enriching their fuel flows and ending the engine troubles some of them were suffering. In the next fifteen minutes, if they encountered no other aircraft, the squadron would be over their target.

". . . Our Ju-188s will hit military and civilian targets in the La Paz area," Bormann informed his guests, using a pointer to trace the route his planes would take. "They will go without escort. We need the fighters elsewhere and there is nothing in this country that can intercept them."

"Have you given any thought about the altitude your bombers will be operating at?" asked Astiz. "With our aircraft, we've found a significant loss of load carrying ability at high-altitude. The mountains around La Paz are in excess of twenty thousand feet, the city itself is twelve thousand."

"Yes, that is precisely why we chose the Junkers 188. It was one of our finest high-altitude, high-speed bombers during the war and the most readily available today. It does not suffer a loss of performance at altitude, the type was built for that. In fact, one of the bombers is due in soon with more members of my command staff."

"What is based here?" asked the Argentinian admiral, pointing at one of the more isolated flags on the table map. "As I remember, the Bolivians have no military base at this location. And it's not near a major city."

"There's a ranch there," said Bormann. "One of my aides can explain that target best. Herr Rauchman?"

"Some Americans are making a movie at that location," Rauchman answered, stepping up to the table. "They've imported a dozen old fighters called Curtiss P-40s and some transports to make it. The movie is apparently about the war in China against the Japanese."

"How interesting," said the admiral. "But why do you have it marked as a target?"

"Because apart from our own air force, those fighters are the most modern warplanes in Bolivia. They can't really compare to our Focke-Wulfs and Messerschmitts but they are a threat. Once we move, they'll have to be destroyed. We'll try to avoid killing the Americans."

"I hope so, you'll cause an international incident if you do. America will look into it and we can't afford that."

"Hawk Lead to all flights, we're about five minutes from target. Open your throttles and accelerate to attack speed. Falcon Flight, Eagle Flight move to your positions."

From a low cruise speed of barely a hundred and ninety miles an hour, the P-40s increased it to three hundred and changed their formation as they did so. Van Hoff's flight pulled abreast of Reynolds while Woods and his Eagles fell in behind him. They maintained their tree top altitude, even though they were entering the San José Mountains.

"Hawk Lead to Albatross, you have an update on the airfield for us?"

"The vulture's nest is still quiet, Hawk Lead. Still

no sign of those jets or the bomber."

The P-40s skirted across the low, forest-covered range, rising over its peaks and sweeping into its valleys. In between the sudden, sharp maneuvers, the pilots checked their armament systems to make sure everything would work. They followed a seemingly erratic course through the mountains, though in reality, they were being guided by Bob Reynolds.

". . . Okay, now make a forty degree turn to the west," he instructed. "That's it. All you have to do is fly around that next peak and you're there. Goodluck, you guys and give 'em hell for me."

"Wait. I hear something outside," said Astiz, interrupting Bormann's continuing lecture. "It sounds like aircraft engines, fighters. I thought your planes weren't due for some time."

"No, they aren't," said Bormann. "Perhaps one of them has had engine trouble, or some other problem and had to return. They sound near, let's go see."

With a nod from Bormann, the meeting was halted and he, members of his command staff and his guests left their spots around the table and walked to the balcony. They formed into two groups, those who were curious and went out on the balcony and those who stayed back, by the doors. In the latter group were most of the Argentinians.

"General Astiz, can you see anything?" the admiral inquired, nervously. "Is it Mr. Bormann's aircraft?"

"No, we see nothing yet. But we can definitely hear something and it's growing louder."

"Hawk Lead to all flights, split into your elements. Hawk Three and Four, get behind me."

The P-40s roared over the final summit as they were completing Reynolds's latest orders. Green and Clinton swung their fighters in behind Reynolds and Acerrio, as Kingston and Clostermann got on the tails of Van Hoff and Kain.

"My God, I think it's the Americans," said Rauchmann, as he watched a formation of oddly-colored aircraft sweep down the mountain side.

"American? I see mostly British markings on those planes," said Astiz. "Only a few are American."

"It's a trick, they are Zionists!" cried Bormann. "Air raid alert! Air raid alert!"

The fighters came roaring off the face of the mountain, with Reynolds' flight separating from Van Hoff's. Everything was laid out before them, the air base, its flight line, the ranch house and other buildings. They were drawing no anti-aircraft fire, none of any kind, they had achieved complete surprise.

Reynolds lined up on the airfield, as if he were making a final approach. Acerrio eased away from his wing in order to give himself a clear field of fire. Reynolds adjusted the range on his gunsight, aligned his aiming circle on the first Ju-188 and squeezed the trigger on his control stick.

His wing guns chattered with the same reassuring explosions he had heard for five years. Their converging streams of shells sparkled brightly and briefly all over the first Junkers, then moved on to the next one. Reynolds wanted to spray the entire flight line rather than hammer away at any one aircraft. Acerrio did likewise, raking the bombers then the second row of fighters in the flight line.

Van Hoff and Kain swept across the ranch complex, concentrating their fire on the ranch house itself. Their shells sprayed the mostly empty balcony, they even filled the briefing hall with hundreds of lethal splinters. Only those who ducked under the table survived the storm.

"We've been discovered, General!" shouted the admiral. "Those are British and American planes out there. We must leave this place. We have to escape at once!"

The admiral scrambled out from under the map table and started running for the hall's main doors.

"Someone stop that fool!" Bormann ordered. "We have an air raid shelter in this building!"

Moments after Van Hoff and Kain ended their strafing run, Kingston and Clostermann began releasing their bombs. They reached below their throttle quadrants and each pulled a handle marked 'fuselage,' jettisoning the bombs on their fuselage racks. They pulled another set of handles and salvoed the five hundred pounders under their wings. As each bomb was released, Kingston and Clostermann could feel their aircraft shake slightly, as each exploded, a bone-jarring shock wave rattled the P-40s.

The first bombs landed on the garages used to house the motor pool; destroying most of the ranch's trucks and cars. Another demolished part of a building used as guest quarters. A fourth exploded harmlessly in a garden. The fifth and sixth bombs struck the ranch house, blowing apart one of its wings and its entrance. As the admiral reached the hall's main doors, they were torn off by a fireball that sent him hurtling across the room.

At the far end of the flight line, Reynolds and Acerrio banked steeply to the left and climbed away. Almost every aircraft in the line received some sort of damage, a few were even burning by the time the second pair of P-40s started their attack. The jet black and desert sand Warhawks came in low and fast; they had used their slide down the mountain face to build up as much speed as they could. Green and Clinton repeated the procedure of releasing their fuselage bombs first, then their wing bombs.

The first bomb to land touched off a tremendous explosion, virtually disintegrating one of the Ju-188s. A giant hand slapped the attacking fighters around for an instant, Clinton and Green felt as if they might lose control of their planes. The next bomb blew the tail off another of the Junkers bombers and the remaining ordnance was scattered among the Messerschmitts and Focke-Wulfs. And since many of them had fuel on board, more violent explosions swept the crowded flight line, throwing clouds of debris through the air.

"I've been hit! Jesse, I'm getting ground fire!" Green cried. "See if I have any damage."

"That's not ground fire," said Clinton, swinging his fighter under the tail of Green's. "You've been hit by some wreckage. You got a piece of a Focke-Wulf in your fuselage. You just got one hell of a souvenir."

"Christ, look at those fireballs," said McCloud. "Mike, maybe we should break off our attack?"

"Don't worry, we've been through worse," said Woods. "Keep your speed up and we'll only have our tails singed."

Woods's flight was the last to commence its attack. As he and McCloud came roaring in, Reynolds and Acerrio came diving back, seemingly right at them.

"Hawk Lead to Eagle Lead, those watch towers on the perimeter are being manned and they have machine guns. Tony, you take the one on the right, I'll take the one on the left."

The Flying Tiger and the Air Corps pursuit ship separated and bore down on their individual targets, two watch towers on the airfield's perimeter fence. They were being manned instead of the anti-aircraft batteries, which had tarpaulins drawn over them. The crews readying their guns concentrated on the approaching British fighters, they were unaware of the American P-40s until the towers were lashed with streams of fifty caliber shells. The wooden structures were chopped apart by the heavy fire, Acerrio's collapsed soon after he was finished and broke away.

Woods and McCloud shot between the neutralized posts and lined up on the devastated flight line.

Wrapped in smoke and flame, many aircraft had already been destroyed, leaking fuel would soon destroy more. The South African and Canadian Kittyhawks dove into the cauldron, firing at the planes which still looked to be intact.

A Junkers 188 collapsed, then exploded under the weight of fire from a dozen machine guns. An Me-109 had its engine blasted off, a Focke-Wulf Dora had its fuel tanks punctured by armor-piercing incendiaries and detonated. McCloud flew through its fireball and emerged with his ailerons and tail surfaces scorched but intact. More fireballs mushroomed along the flight line, independent of the strafing run. When the two fighters emerged from the growing columns of smoke, their pilots were able to breathe a little easier and checked themselves for damage.

"God, that was close," said Woods. "A bit lower and we'd have been cooked. Eagle Lead to Eagles Three and Four, don't go in too low or you might not make it out, lads."

On the road leading from the assembly barn to the airfield was a tractor towing a newly completed He-162 Salamander. Though it was not yet time to go after targets of opportunity, for Van Hoff it was too choice to pass up. He and Kain turned away from the ranch and dove on it. The tow crew abandoned the vehicle long before they opened fire, though the tractor continued to blindly pull the Heinkel along. Since it had no fuel in its tanks or ammunition in its guns, the jet didn't explode when the Kittyhawks hammered it with half-inch shells. The incendiaries sparkled all-over the Heinkel and the high-explosive slugs tore open its outer skin. It crumpled and sagged to the ground and the driverless tractor pulled it to the side of the road where it rolled into a shallow drainage ditch.

"Look, Claus shot up a jet," said Kingston, glancing out his cockpit to see what the rest were doing.

"You'd better worry if someone will shoot us up," warned Clostermann. "The flak guns at the ranch are being manned."

Brandon and Ward streaked over the perimeter fence, the only ones still loaded to the hilt with bombs. By now their target was a true inferno, fires ranged from end to end of the crowded flight line. Its aircraft were either burning or hidden by the thick pall of smoke. It scarcely seemed necessary to drop more bombs on the line but the two fighters continued on, climbing a hundred feet before disappearing inside the pall.

Though it was almost impossible for them to see their targets, Brandon and Ward started releasing their bombs a few moments before crossing the taxi strip's perimeter. They had to in order to compensate for the slightly longer trajectories of the bombs. They were virtually bombing blind, they could only catch occasional glimpses of the aircraft below, but their attack did have an effect on the inferno, their bombs did find some targets. Part way down the flight line, someone's bomb triggered a sharp, jarring explosion and out of the flames hurled a disintegrating Focke-Wulf.

The only aircraft on the flight line to become airborne, it was coming apart in mid-air. The long-nosed

'190 sailed about seventy feet before crashing onto the runway, where it snapped its main landing gear struts. Cowling panels and tail surfaces were jarred off as it skidded across the runway and came to a halt on its far side. The last bombs Brandon and Ward dropped scattered some more airplane parts and then it was over. What had taken months and a fortune to smuggle out of Europe had been reduced to twisted scrap in only a few minutes. Now the Eagles had to complete the annihilation of the base.

"Falcon Four, take the batteries on the right," Kingston ordered. "The rest are all mine."

The anti-aircraft guns at the ranch were being manned faster than the ones at the airfield. Their crews had just loaded them with ammunition when Kingston and Clostermann walked their fire through the gun pits, killing everyone who'd been foolish enough to be caught in them.

"All right, let's take care of our primary objectives, Tony," said Reynolds, as they swung their aircraft around for another run. "You hit the ammo dump, I'll hit the fuel dump."

Reynolds and Acerrio separated again, this time by several hundred feet so they could attack their targets simultaneously. Between the ranch and the airfield were gasoline and munition dumps, partly dug into the hillside. The two P-40s pounced on them like dive bombers, with the Flying Tiger slightly ahead of the Air Corps fighter. Reynolds pulled his bomb release handle and yanked his control stick back at the same time, allowing him to jettison his bomb without worrying about it hitting his propeller disc. Acerrio salvoed his an instant later and climbed away to the right.

The first bomb plunged into the huge revetment, spawning a giant pillar of flame that erupted through the camouflage netting. It spread out as it rose, becoming a boiling fireball which rapidly consumed everything in and around the revetment, including vehicles and anti-aircraft guns. The second bomb touched off a thunderous explosion. It created a momentary flash that rivalled the neighboring fireball and sent out a shock wave that hit each of the P-40s like a giant hand. It rippled through the columns of dark smoke, temporarily roiling them. The sound of the explosion stung the ears of everyone in the vicinity, even those who were wearing leather flying helmets.

"Shit, any closer and my eardrums would've ruptured," said Green. "Will you two watch what you're doing the next time you set off fireworks."

"Albatross to Hawk Leader, Albatross to all aircraft! Enemy fighters are returning! Jack, they're in your area. They'll be coming out of the east."

Bob Reynolds's warning made everyone's heart skip a beat. Those who were preparing to make another pass broke off; the rest wheeled around to meet the enemy and, more importantly, to be the first to spot them.

Out of the early morning sun they came, just like the P-40s had a few minutes earlier. Two silver He-162s, each with a red and light gray Messerschmitt as an escort. They dove on the ranch rather than the airfield, as if they were doing a demonstration pass and had no idea that an air attack was under way. They didn't fire at any of the P-40s, even when some passed in front of them. Like their base, they'd been taken completely by surprise.

"Get those jets!" Reynolds shouted. If we don't get 'em now, we never will. Don't be fancy, just blast them."

Green and Clinton, who had been prepared to strafe the last intact aircraft on the runway, swung away and selected one of the '109 - '162 pairs. Their angle of interception was almost perpendicular to the German fighters, they would have only a second or two to knock them down.

"The jet's mine, Jesse," said Green. "I never had a chance at one and you got yours in the last war."

The black and red Warhawk pulled a tighter turn than its desert camouflaged wing man, so it could line up the He-162. Green allowed his gunsight's aiming circle to drift, then correct and lock onto the Salamander. He opened fire the instant it did so, with hits sparkling all over the cockpit area and the engine pod mounted atop the fuselage. The Heinkel jet banked desperately to avoid Green's fire, only to expose its undersides to it and nearly collide with the Messerschmitt as well.

The Salamander's engine emitted a thin plume of dark smoke, then a tongue of flame that reached back to its twin tail fins. Its slender fuselage was peppered with hits and the access panel to one of its cannon bays blew off as the cannon shells inside started exploding. Crippled and losing power, the Heinkel rolled on its back and plunged into the ground just beyond the base's perimeter fence. Its Messerschmitt escort fared better. In avoiding collision with the '162, the Me-109 was able to throw off Clinton's aim and escape, climbing away while the other pair of German fighters passed through the valley and continued to head west. For a time.

"They're joining forces," Reynolds warned. "They'll be back. All aircraft that still have bombs, don't jettison them. We still have targets to hit. Don't let 'em go unless you get in trouble. Eagle Lead, complete your attack, we'll do our best to protect you."

Woods and McCloud resumed their run on the aircraft assembly building. They banked tightly and came roaring over the ranch, descending as they closed on the barn. In spite of what Reynolds promised, neither of them could stop glancing back at the gathering trio of fighters. Dividing their attention had an effect on their accuracy. Woods's bomb dropped through the barn's roof and demolished almost half of it but McCloud's overshot and only managed to blast out a twenty foot crater beside it.

"This is Hawk Lead. Look out, here they come!"

Using its superior speed, the Salamander came streaking in ahead of the Me-109s and unleashed a stream of tracers on Van Hoff and Kain. Theirs were the only aircraft to still carry bombs and, in spite of the danger, hung onto them as they clawed through a turn; the tracers fell wide of their mark. The Heinkel tried to follow the P-40s but its one hundred mile an hour edge in speed became a disadvantage. It nearly rammed one of the valley walls in an effort to stay with them; though its speed edge did allow the jet to escape interception.

It was different for the Messerschmitts. At low-altitude, their top speed wasn't all that better than the P-40s and Kingston and Clostermann had the time to position themselves in front of the approaching '109s. The two sets of fighters flashed toward each other at more than six hundred miles an hour. Such a closure rate didn't allow either side enough time to get a precise fix on each other; they started firing as soon as they were within range. For a few seconds the wing guns and nose cannons blazed away furiously but without effect. The Messerschmitts broke off the duel by splitting their formation and banking away. Kingston and Clostermann hung together and maintained their course. They hoped to trap one of the Messerschmitts as it came out of its turn, only to find they were the ones being trapped.

The Me-109s easily outturned the P-40s and were just latching onto their tails when Kingston finally noticed them and ordered Clostermann to break away. They both managed to swing back toward the airfield and started calling for help from the other flights.

"This is Eagle Lead, I'm in front of you, Eric. Standby to cockscrew," Woods ordered. "Hang back, Jeffrey, I'm going to need room. Ready Eric? Two, one . . . Corkscrew port!"

McCloud retarded his throttle, losing some fifty miles an hour in airspeed and falling far behind

Woods as he rolled his aircraft to the left. Kingston did likewise, barrel rolling to the left, though because they were approaching each other, they were rotating in opposite directions. As each completed a revolution they called it out.

"Roll two!" Woods shouted. "Keep your nose level, Eric, keep your nose level! Another three should do it."

The two sand and brown Kittyhawks spiralled toward each other, seemingly out of control and heading for a disastrous collision. The spectacle held everyone in awe, even the Messerchmitt pilot behind Kingston. Why waste cannon shells on someone who was going to crash anyway? Reynolds wanted to order Woods and Kingston to stop and disengage but he couldn't find the voice to. And at any rate, Woods and Kingston were filling the air with chatter in the final moments before their collision.

"Increase your roll rate, we're not matching!" Kingston warned.

"Matching you now," said Woods. "Standby to stop. Three . . . Two . . . One . . . Now!"

The two P-40s froze with their wings almost perpendicular to the ground. They had only a second to adjust their altitudes, perfect them, and then they flashed past each other, their propellers and their bellies almost touching. Woods immediately righted his ship, and without bothering to use his gunsight, opened fire on the startled Messerschmitt.

He kicked the rudder on his fighter, causing his streams of shells to fill the airspace around the Me-109, hosing it down, until hits started sparkling on it.

They were enough to make it break away, trailing a thin plume of white smoke from its cowling. By then Woods's gunsight had recovered from the wild maneuver and showed him the correct lead on the '109. He placed the aiming circle on the Messerschmitt's briefly exposed belly. It took hardly more than a second of pounding from the P-40's six wings guns to put a few armor-piercing incendiaries through its fuselage fuel tank. The Messerschmitt flowered into a fireball and fell like a sputtering meteor on the valley's northern side.

The '109 chasing Clostermann was bounced by Brandon and Ward. A dozen machine guns roared in unison, their long, accurately placed burst chopped the German fighter apart. It exploded and crashed near the valley's western end, another few seconds and it wouldn've been Clostermann who would have gone down.

"If you want to fuck around with Eagles, you'd better learn how to fly first," said Acerrio, admiring the two kills.

"Mike, what kind of crazy damn stunt did you pull?" Reynolds demanded, considerably less impressed.

"An old trick from our North African days," said Woods. "Dennis and Doug and Claus know it. Sure it's dangerous but when you have an ME on your tail it's the only maneuver that works. It has every time."

"Okay, just don't go around pulling it any more."

"They won't have to, Colonel," said Acerrio. "All we have to worry about is one jet and here he comes."

"Coming from where?" Kain asked. "Falcon Two

to Hawk Leader, what's your wing man talking about? I've got the Heinkel spotted and he's circling above us."

"Oh shit, that means there's another plane," said Reynolds. "Tony, where is he? What direction is he coming from?"

"Out of the west, Colonel. Eight o'clock high."

Visible just above the funeral pyre of the last Messerschmitt was a rapidly growing speck. Reynolds and Acerrio turned to face the unknown and soon one was able to identify it.

"It's twin-engined," said Reynolds. "And it's too large to be a fighter. Jesus Christ, it's a bomber! It's a Ju-188!"

The Junkers had its flaps and landing gear lowered, as if it were getting ready to land. It was slowly descending when suddenly its bulbous nose pointed back into the air and its landing gear began retracting back inside the engine nacelles. Thin curls of smoke shot out of its exhaust stacks and its flaps pulled flush against the trailing edge of the wings. In a few seconds the Ju-188 had cleaned itself up. Its engines were howling at full throttle and the bomber stood on its tail, clawing to get out of the valley. By the time Reynolds and Acerrio had reached its position, the Junkers was gaining altitude rapidly, climbing the way at one time only a fighter could.

"This one's mine!" Reynolds shouted. "Hawk Lead to all planes, continue blasting that base. I'll be back as soon as I catch this bastard."

Reynolds banked his fighter steeply and reared it up on its tail. Acerrio fell back to watch over his leader but kept his position by his side. The two P-40s raced after the escaping bomber, which was still accelerating, still increasing power. If it wasn't stopped it would soon be in the stratosphere.

"Keep an eye on that jet, Tony," said Reynolds. "He may come after us if he sees who we're chasing."

The remaining P-40s turned back to hitting the base. Van Hoff and Kain dove on the partially destroyed aircraft assembly building. Van Hoff didn't release his bomb: instead he strafed the anti-aircraft guns around the barn that had been manned, which allowed Kain an unhindered run and he easily planted his bomb on what remained of the target. The initial explosion was quickly followed by a fireball. It boiled out of the storm of barn debris and rose into the sky. The Heinkel jet, which had been ready to roar off in pursuit of Reynolds and Acerrio, swung around and dove on the base.

"Watch it, here he comes," Green warned. "Claus, he's after you! Six o'clock high and closing. Get rid of your bomb!"

Van Hoff's Kittyhawk was the last fighter to still be carrying its external ordnance. It made him an obvious target and the He-162 came whistling in, trying once again to walk a line of tracers through his plane.

"Eagle Three to Falcon Leader, jinx to the left, now!"

Responding to Brandon's command, Van Hoff racked his aircraft through a steep left turn. While still in the maneuver, he saw two Kittyhawks shoot over him, Brandon and Ward. They closed on the Salamander, their wing guns snapping back at its cannons. Brandon walked his fire into the '162's engine pod; all it took was a few shells to disintegrate its turbine blades. They came tearing through the sides of the pod, followed by thick plumes of black smoke.

Crippled, the jet turned desperately to escape, only to fly through a hail of shells from Ward. Hits sparkled across its left wing, which suddenly separated at the root. The Salamander spiraled out of the sky and crashed next to the ranch, its fuel creating a brief fireball. The last airborne enemy fighter had been eliminated, now the squadron could focus its full attention on the ranch and airfield.

"Claus, why didn't you drop your bomb when you had the chance?" Kain asked, sliding back on his leader's right wing.

"Because I want this one for a special target. Come, it's time to use it."

"Hey, Colonel, I think someone scratched that second jet."

"Good, then I won't need you to protect my tail," said Reynolds. "Get back there, Tony and finish off that base."

"But, but Colonel, you can't mean that. You always told me a wing man should stay with his leader."

"Not this time, we need every available ship to work over the target until it's gone. Now head on back."

"But who's gonna help you shoot this guy down?"

"My brother will. This bomber might be able to outclimb me but it won't get past him. Now move." Reynolds was adamant and Acerrio knew it; after a moment's hesitation he dipped his wing and banked away. Reynolds watched him depart, then turned to contacting his brother. "Hawk Lead to Albatross. I'm at angels nine and in pursuit of a one-eighty-eight. Do you read me, over?"

"This is Albatross, I read you, Jack. Looks like you found the one I couldn't see. What's up?"

"You are, you're the only one who has an altitude advantage over this guy and I need you to run interference."

"Let's take those planes on the runway," said Green. "Hawk Four, you can have the jet. That trimotor is all mine."

Green and Clinton dove on the smoke obscured runway, lining up on the last two intact aircraft on the base. The Ju-52 was fueled and ready to fly; the He-162, tucked in next to it, had its canopy and service panels open, as if it were waiting for an official inspection. The P-40s roared low across the base's perimeter fence, finally drawing some tracer fire from the ground. Green and Clinton opened up on their targets simultaneously; the storm of shells sparkled all over the aircraft and raised small puffs of dust when they hit the runway's concrete surface.

The Junkers took just a few seconds of such a beating before its fuel tanks were pierced and exploded. Its low set, angular wings were open by a series of fireballs. They bent and split the main spars, causing the transport's box-like fuselage to sag to the ground, where it was enveloped by flames. The Heinkel jet did not explode. It wasn't filled with fuel and ammunition and Clinton could only hose it down with streams of half-inch diameter slugs, leaving it a sieve.

"Okay, Jack, I got that bomber of yours," said Bob Reynolds, "Christ, is he climbing fast. You're just barely staying with him. I've never seen a bomber do that before."

"The Japs never had a plane like the one-eighty-eight. At high altitude, when its superchargers cut in, it'll just walk away from me. I need you to 'interfere' with his escape so I can overtake and destroy him."

"And how do I go about doing that? Remember, my ship doesn't have any guns."

"How would they know? Just dive at them."

"All right, here we go, I hope they aren't armed."

Bob Reynolds stowed his binoculars and grabbed hold of his plane's twin throttles. He stood his huge fighter on one of its wing tips and allowed it to fall on its back. The Lightning immediately began to pick up speed, in less than a minute it was hurtling to earth at more than four hundred and fifty miles an hour. Fast enough for it to be buffeted by compressibility waves and for its dive recovery flaps to extend.

It wasn't long before Bob Reynolds could see the Ju-188 and his brother's P-40, far behind it. He aimed his P-38 at the bomber, closing on it as if he were making a head-on pass. At first, they didn't notice him. He was beginning to wish he did have some guns on his ship when suddenly the Junkers broke to the left. It levelled off and started to head east, while the

P-38 roared by.

Because of his high speed, Bob Reynolds couldn't end his dive as easily as the bomber had stopped its climb. He was filling his brother's windshield by the time he got the Lightning to bottom out and rear onto its twin-boom tail. It zoomed past the altitude the Junkers was travelling at before it could level out.

"That's it, Bob, we got 'em now!" Reynolds shouted. "Just keep him busy until I get there."

"Claus, you'd better watch it. The flak guns around the ranch are rather active," said Brandon.

"I know, that's why I'm letting Kain go in first."

This time, the wing man would lead the way. Since Kain had no bomb, he could concentrate on silencing the guns while Claus concentrated on destroying the ranch.

Some of the batteries strafed by Kingston and Clostermann had since been remanned. Tracer fire came from several points on the ranch grounds, Kain couldn't possibly deal with them all; he could only take care of those in front of him. He snapped out short bursts at each of the gun pits as he made his approach. If they didn't kill the battery crews, at least the bursts would keep their heads down.

Van Hoff came in right behind him. He kept his course straight and his wings level. There would be no jinxing or wild maneuvers, he wanted to make sure his bomb would find its intended target. As he pointed the nose of his Kittyhawk at the remaining intact section of the ranch, a line of tracers caught up to him and walked their way through the fighter's fuselage.

"I'm hit!" Van Hoff cried, pulling his ship into a steep climb. "Someone come and look me over!"

After levelling out above the Ju-188, Bob Reynolds slid his Lightning in behind it and dove to get on its tail. The Junker's crew responded by racking the bomber through a tight turn. Since the two aircraft were roughly the same size, Bob had some trouble staying with the '188 but at least he got it to turn back toward his brother.

"You're doing it," said Jack Reynolds, his fighter already encountering trouble in the thin air. "I've got him in my sights! Break away, Bob, I don't want you getting hit by any stray shells."

At eighteen thousand feet, the P-40 maneuvered sluggishly. To Reynolds, it took an eternity for his aircraft to level off and turn in the direction of the oncoming bomber. Behind it, the silver and red trimmed P-38 broke to the right, climbing steeply as it left. By now the Junkers crew realized they had been boxed into a trap and tried to escape it. The bomber swung to the left but Reynolds managed to keep his gunsight's aiming circle of orange diamonds centered on it and waited the few moments for the '188 to enter his maximum range.

"Damage looks bad aft of the cockpit," Woods reported, edging his Kittyhawk in next to Van Hoff's. "I'd say it was twenty millimeter. Jeffrey, go check his port side."

"I'd say it was twenty millimeter shells as well," said Van Hoff, struggling to get his words out. "One of them exploded inside the cockpit, Michael."

"Oh God, no. Claus, jettison your bomb and leave. I'll escort you to the emergency field.

"No, I must do what I've come here to do! This will not take long, I promise you."

The Ju-188 just barely filled the gunsight's aiming circle when Reynolds opened fire. Because it was done at extreme range, it took several seconds for the streams of shells to travel the distance from the P-40 to the Junkers. Reynolds could barely see his hits registering on the aircraft, though his brother filled him in as best he could.

"You got him, Jack, you got 'im! He's taking it in the left engine and the forward fuselage. That bug-eye canopy is just getting smashed. You're really blasting him!"

The bomber slowed dramatically as it lost one of its engines. A thick plume of smoke trailed out its left nacelle and the propeller ground to a halt. Reynolds kept firing as he closed on the Ju-188, expending most of his remaining ammunition. One by one he could feel his machine guns cut out, their supply of fifty caliber shells gone, until he had only two guns left when the battered Junkers exploded.

Its left wing collapsed against the fuselage side, then tore away. The bomber started to roll uncontrollably, the wild gyrations prevented anyone from bailing out, if there was anyone on board still alive, and caused the rudder to tear off as well. Fire spread along the length of the fuselage, converting what was left of the aircraft into an orange-red comet. Slowly the Ju-188 nosed over and began a long, four-mile plunge to the forest below. Reynolds felt it was a fitting end to the operation and cheered the bomber's demise, until he heard Acerrio shouting for him on the radio.

"Colonel! Colonel, you'd better get down here right away! Claus got hit and I don't like the way he's acting. He's wounded and he doesn't want to leave."

"I read you, Tony. Hold on, I'm coming."

Reynolds flipped his P-40 on its back and dove, followed a few seconds later by his brother. Far below they could just barely make out the other P-40s, swarming over what appeared to be the ranch.

Those who hadn't gone to Van Hoff's aid went out for vengeance instead. More than half a dozen P-40s screamed across the ranch, firing at any gun pit they saw, at anything that moved. In their desire for blood, some of the fighters nearly collided with each other, but they quickly and permanently silenced the ranch defenses.

Van Hoff circled the area slowly, with Woods and McCloud on either side of him; Kain, his own wing man, had joined forces with Acerrio to attack the ranch. As the others came off their last runs, they sidled up to the tiny vee of aircraft to see if they could help.

"No, I'm afraid I will not make it, Michael. I'll be

dead by the time I could reach San Ignacio," said Van Hoff.

"Don't say that," Woods pleaded, even though he could see Van Hoff bent forward and holding his side. "There were times in the past you didn't think you'd make it but you did. Please, you have to try."

"Claus, this is Jack," Reynolds interrupted. "If you can't make it, just get out of the valley and hit the silk. I'll crash land next to you and together we'll both get out of here. I promised Marilyn I'd take care of you."

"And I promised Marilyn I would take care of you. No, I won't allow you to take that risk. If there's one thing Marilyn needs now, it's her father. Tell her that I love her, Jack. That I always will love her."

"Claus, please damn it, please," Woods begged, he could feel his eyes start to burn and tears roll down his cheeks. "You can't let it end this way. You can't."

"Perhaps it's best that it does. Don't feel sad for me, my friend. My brothers. I shall be with those I love as I destroy those who killed them. Can you see this, Michael?" Van Hoff reached into his vest and held out a small, black medal at the end of a ribbon. Even from his distance, Woods could identify it as an Iron Cross. "Perhaps I will at last be able to give it to him. Good-bye, my friend."

Van Hoff pushed the medal back in his vest and reached for his throttle; shoving it to the gate stops. The resulting surge in speed carried him away from Woods, McCloud and the others gathering around him. He dipped his right wing and turned back toward what was left of the ranch.

"Someone stop him, God damn it!" Reynolds demanded. "Mike, do something! For Christ's sake, don't let him . . ."

"What can I do?" Woods asked, his voice breaking. "This is the way he wants it."

Van Hoff appeared to have some trouble bringing his Kittyhawk out of its turn. For a time it was flying lopsided, then the wings levelled out and its nose dipped below the horizon line. With its engine howling at full power, the sand and brown P-40 dove on the ranch like an arrow. It aimed for the balcony where the tattered Nazi flags were still flying. It virtually crashed through the balcony doors. Van Hoff's fighter plunged deep into the ranch, reaching its foundations before the bomb it was carrying exploded; followed by the gasoline left in its fuel tanks. The resulting blast and fireball demolished and consumed what was left of the ranch. The debris that wasn't blown into the air collapsed in on the building's foundations. Those who hadn't died were trapped and there would be no one to rescue them.

Reynolds and his brother arrived as the fireball that erupted out of the ranch burned itself out, leaving behind a black curl of smoke. There was nothing they could do, there was nothing anyone could do. The P-40s and the lone P-38 wheeled above the demolished target. The only activity below were the fires raging across the base. Nothing moved, there was nothing left to move. The last mission of World War Two was over and the only thing left for the victors to do was to return home.

"I have had no telephone reports from San Ignacio," said Romero, arriving at the runway perimeter line, where Marilyn had gathered all the relatives together. "I left one of my men by the phone, he will send us a word the minute he receives a call."

"I hope it's more than one word," said Marilyn. "Oh God, this waiting is terrible. At least no report from the emergency field means none of them had any serious trouble."

"But it doesn't mean that one or more of them might not have been shot down," added Margaret Woods, sitting back in the chair she'd been given. "I know how you feel, Miss Reynolds. Two years ago I thought I'd never have to worry like this again. Dear Lord, how could Michael do this to me . . . To us."

Margaret placed her hands around her greatly expanded waist and gently held her unborn child.

"It was something your husband felt he had to do, Mrs. Woods," Clinton's father offered, placing his hand on her shoulder. "The last letter our son sent us, told us about him. He said he was a good man, with strong ideals. I pray they all come back safe. My wife and I hope this mission will end our boy's hunt for his brother's killers. He's the only son we have left."

"I think if my grandson were to die today, he'd be happy," McCloud's grandfather admitted. "He always told me he felt at home in a fight. These last few weeks must've made him feel very happy."

"You mustn't say that," said Margaret Brandon. "At times I think Dennis must feel the same way. I grow so worried when someone says that."

"Look, a horse is coming from the ranch," said

Romero, pointing at his home. "He's coming this way. I think the rider is the man I left by the phone, Manuel. I wonder why the horse? I thought I left him a truck to use?"

Only Romero really cared to know the answer to that question. Everyone else wanted to know the answer to another and waited with growing anxiety as the chestnut brown horse was reined to a halt and its rider talked with Romero.

"It is good news," he said. "One of my friends down river has just called to say a large formation of planes just flew by his house. He says it was the same ones that flew past a few hours ago."

An audible sigh broke the group's tension, though it had hardly died away when another warning caught everyone's attention.

"I think I can hear them," said Margaret Brandon, turning toward the river. "I know the sound of fighter engines anywhere. It's them, I tell you, it's them."

Everyone turned toward the river. Those who were sitting rose to their feet; even Margaret Woods was helped up. The low throb at first barely registered. Quickly however, it grew until those who were used to the noise could almost count the number of engines making it. The roar was filling the valley when the P-40s began to appear.

A Flying Tiger and an Air Corps pursuit ship were the first to break formation and sweep across the airstrip, followed by jet black and desert camouflaged Warhawks. Marilyn started to cry at the appearance of her father's plane; the same happened to Acerrio's girl friend and Green's and Clinton's parents when the other fighters shot by. Wood's flight appeared next and thundered overhead as Reynolds and Acerrio came in for a landing.

Marilyn grabbed Van Hoff's kit off the truck she stood beside and ran after her father's plane. The rest of the group either climbed inside the truck or accepted a seat in Romero's jeep. In spite of the advantage the vehicles offered in speed, Marilyn beat them out to the flight line. She cut across the taxiway, running behind Acerrio's P-40, and reached her father's ship as the propeller ground to a halt and the canopy slid back.

Reynolds eased himself over the side of his fighter and walked down its wing to be greeted by his daughter. Initially, she was joyously happy; but then she realized something was wrong because of her father's subdued response.

"Daddy, what's the matter?" she asked, apprehensively. "Did something go wrong with the mission?"

"Yes. Yes, something did," Reynolds answered, putting his arms around her. As he went on, his voice started to break. "It's Claus. I'm sorry, Angel. Oh God, I'm sorry. We all tried to stop him but he isn't coming back."

"No!" Marilyn cried, repeatedly. "No, it can't be. No, he promised he'd come back. He loves me!"

"I know. I know he did but he isn't coming back. See, there's his flight now."

Marilyn looked up to see a trio of P-40s circling the field, waiting for the others to land. None of them wore the markings of Van Hoff's ship, a red spinner with a shark's mouth on the engine cowling. Marilyn dug through Van Hoff's kit and came up with the empty box which she opened for her father.

"Mike told me he had the medal with him. I guess it will belong to him forever." Reynolds ran his hand over the box's velvet lining. He could barely control his voice and tears flowed down his face without a stop. "I know I promised I'd take care of him, Angel. But I'm sorry. I tried. We all tried but nothing worked. He was hit and he dove his plane into the ranch."

Reynolds couldn't find the strength to say anything more. He hugged his daughter again and cried with her.

The remaining aircraft of the squadron taxied to their points along the flight line, swung in, and shut down. As their pilots climbed wearily, sadly, from their cockpits, each found there was someone special waiting for him.

"Margaret, my God is it really you?" said Woods, reaching out hesitantly for his wife.

"It's me, Michael," she said, easing into his arms. "Your friend wanted me to be here for you. Where's Claus? I want to see him and thank him."

"Dad? Mother?" Clinton asked, not quite believing his eyes. His parents rushed forward and put their arms around him. His mother started kissing him, his father slapped him on the back.

"Your friend sent for us," said Clinton's father, answering the most obvious question. "Claus Van Hoff. I'd like to meet him, where is he?"

The story was repeated, a dozen times and more, to all those who asked where the missing plane and pilot was. It didn't get any easier for anyone to retell it but the process did have a helpful, almost cathartic, effect. It washed away some of the sorrow over losing a friend. Those who could not cry over his death cried along with their loved ones; it seemed to help ease the burden. Slowly, everyone gathered by Reynold's fighter. For it was here they knew they would find someone who lost more than a friend, but a lover as well.

"Maybe he knew he wouldn't come back," said Woods, looking at the empty box. "If I had seen this before we left, I would've known something was up."

"We all would've, mate," Ward added, standing alongside his sister. "Those of us who flew with him at least. Marilyn, is there anything else in his kit?"

"A letter addressed to my father," she said. "I thought he might want to read it later. But I guess it would be okay to do so now. Would it, Daddy?"

"I don't see why not," said Reynolds, accepting the envelope Marilyn offered him. When he opened it, he found the letter was addressed to a larger audience than him.

To my brothers,

This is to be read in the event I do not return with you, I have made changes in my will to reward all of you for your actions. Michael and Douglas will be able to obtain the aircraft they want. Please don't let this operation be the end of our relationships and ties with each other. The balance of my estate will go to the establishment of a society for our kind. For the sake of those who flew with us and died for our countries, may you all remain brothers.

> Your Friend As Always
> Count Claus Van Hoff

"What does it say, Jack?" Woods inquired.

"That we are brothers," said Reynolds, the tears starting to roll down his face again. "And that our friend's last request is that we always will be."

TOP-FLIGHT AERIAL ADVENTURE
FROM ZEBRA BOOKS!

WINGMAN (2015, $3.95)
by Mack Maloney
From the radioactive ruins of a nuclear-devastated U.S. emerges a hero for the ages. A brilliant ace fighter pilot, he takes to the skies to help free his once-great homeland from the brutal heel of the evil Soviet warlords. He is the last hope of a ravaged land. He is Hawk Hunter . . . Wingman!

WINGMAN #2: THE CIRCLE WAR (2120, $3.95)
by Mack Maloney
A second explosive showdown with the Russian overlords and their armies of destruction is in the wind. Only the deadly aerial ace Hawk Hunter can rally the forces of freedom and strike one last blow for a forgotten dream called "America"!

WINGMAN #3: THE LUCIFER CRUSADE (2232, $3.95)
by Mack Maloney
Viktor, the depraved international terrorist who orchestrated the bloody war for America's West, has escaped. Ace pilot Hawk Hunter takes off for a deadly confrontation in the skies above the Middle East, determined to bring the maniac to justice or die in the attempt!

GHOST PILOT (2207, $3.95)
by Anton Emmerton
Flyer Ian Lamont is driven by bizarre unseen forces to relive the last days in the life of his late father, an RAF pilot killed during World War II. But history is about to repeat itself as a sinister secret from beyond the grave transforms Lamont's worst nightmares of fiery aerial death into terrifying reality!

Available wherever paperbacks are sold, or order direct from the Publisher. Send cover price plus 50¢ per copy for mailing and handling to Zebra Books, Dept. 2487, 475 Park Avenue South, New York, N.Y. 10016. Residents of New York, New Jersey and Pennsylvania must include sales tax. DO NOT SEND CASH.

TURN TO RICHARD P. HENRICK
FOR THE BEST IN UNDERSEA ACTION!

SILENT WARRIORS (1675, $3.95)

The RED STAR, Russia's newest, most technically advanced submarine, has been dispatched to spearhead a massive nuclear first strike against the U.S. Cut off from all radio contact, the crew of an American attack sub must engage the deadly enemy alone, or witness the explosive end of the world above!

THE PHOENIX ODYSSEY (1789, $3.95)

During a routine War Alert drill, all communications to the U.S.S. PHOENIX suddenly and mysteriously vanish. Deaf to orders cancelling the exercise, in six short hours the PHOENIX will unleash its nuclear arsenal against the Russian mainland!

COUNTERFORCE (2013, $3.95)

In an era of U.S.-Soviet cooperation, a deadly trio of Kremlin war mongers unleashes their ultimate secret weapon: a lone Russian submarine armed with enough nuclear firepower to obliterate the entire U.S. defensive system. As an unsuspecting world races towards the apocalypse, the U.S.S. TRITON must seek out and destroy the undersea killer!

FLIGHT OF THE CONDOR (2139, $3.95)

America's most advanced defensive surveillance satelllite is abandoning its orbit, leaving the U.S. blind and defenseless to a Soviet missile attack. From the depths of the ocean to the threshold of outer space, the stage is set for mankind's ultimate confrontation with nuclear doom!

WHEN DUTY CALLS (2256, $3.95)

An awesome new laser defense system will render the U.S.S.R. untouchable in the event of nuclear attack. Faced with total devastation, America's last hope lies onboard a captured Soviet submarine, as U.S. SEAL team Alpha prepares for a daring assault on Russian soil!

Available wherever paperbacks are sold, or order direct from the Publisher. Send cover price plus 50¢ per copy for mailing and handling to Zebra Books, Dept. 2487, 475 Park Avenue South, New York, N.Y. 10016. Residents of New York, New Jersey and Pennsylvania must include sales tax. DO NOT SEND CASH.

ASHES
by William W. Johnstone

OUT OF THE ASHES (1137, $3.50)
Ben Raines hadn't looked forward to the War, but he knew it was coming. After the balloons went up, Ben was one of the survivors, fighting his way across the country, searching for his family, and leading a band of new pioneers attempting to bring American OUT OF THE ASHES.

FIRE IN THE ASHES (1310, $3.50)
It's 1999 and the world as we know it no longer exists. Ben Raines, leader of the Resistance, must regroup his rebels and prep them for bloody guerrilla war. But are they ready to face an even fiercer foe—the human mutants threatening to overpower the world!

ANARCHY IN THE ASHES (2592, $3.95)
Out of the smoldering nuclear wreckage of World War III, Ben Raines has emerged as the strong leader the Resistance needs. When Sam Hartline, the mercenary, joins forces with an invading army of Russians, Ben and his people raise a bloody banner of defiance to defend earth's last bastion of freedom.

SMOKE FROM THE ASHES (2191, $3.50)
Swarming across America's Southern tier march the avenging soldiers of Libyan blood terrorist Khamsin. Lurking in the blackened ruins of once-great cities are the mutant Night People, crazed killers of all who dare enter their domain. Only Ben Raines, his son Buddy, and a handful of Ben's Rebel Army remain to strike a blow for the survival of America and the future of the free world!

ALONE IN THE ASHES (2591, $3.95)
In this hellish new world there are human animals and Ben Raines—famed soldier and survival expert—soon becomes their hunted prey. He desperately tries to stay one step ahead of death, but no one can survive ALONE IN THE ASHES.

Available wherever paperbacks are sold, or order direct from the Publisher. Send cover price plus 50¢ per copy for mailing and handling to Zebra Books, Dept. 2487, 475 Park Avenue South, New York, N.Y. 10016. Residents of New York, New Jersey and Pennsylvania must include sales tax. DO NOT SEND CASH.